I 50

☑ W9-DDK-156

SWORD OF THE CONQUEROR

The Master Sage Reovalis turned to the table and lifted the heavy box which had been lying there. With some effort, he carried it to Palamon. "I bid you open this."

Palamon flipped the bronze catch, revealing an interior of soft velvet on which rested a great, two-handed sword.

"The sword of ancient Parthenon," Reovalis told him. "With this, he conquered all the lands and formed an empire. The name's inscribed beside the pommel."

The inscription was in the tongue of the Great Empire. Softly, Palamon mouthed the two words thus formed. *"Spada Korrigaine."*

No one saw the weapon move, but the handle was suddenly in Palamon's hands and the blade was raised, ready for battle.

"The sword has chosen," Reovalis said. "It is yours to keep."

FLIGHT TO THLASSA MEY

Dennis McCarty

A Del Rey Book

BALLANTINE BOOKS • NEW YORK

Library of Congress Catalog Card Number: 85-91206

ISBN 0-345-32653-9

Manufactured in the United States of America

First Edition: March 1986

Cover Art by Darrell K. Sweet

THE AUTHOR WOULD LIKE TO DEDICATE THIS
VOLUME TO JACK HALE ADAMSON, WHO PILOTED
A YOUNG MARINER TOWARD THE PILLARS OF
HERCULES; WHO LEFT HIS YOUTHFUL CHARGE
SAILING ORDERS AND PRICELESS INSTRUMENTS:
COMPASS, ALIDADE, SEXTANT, OF FINELY
WROUGHT AND POLISHED BRASS, INLAID WITH
(OF ALL THINGS) STEEL; WHO BOARDED THE PILOT
BOAT UNWILLINGLY AND NEVER LEARNED THE
ULTIMATE FATE OF VOYAGER AND CRAFT—
WHETHER THEY WERE LOST ON ROCKY, FOG-
BOUND SHORES, OR REACHED THAT MIGHTY,
GATEWAY AND THE OPEN SEAS WHICH LAY BE-
YOND.

A knight there was, and that a worthy man,
That fro the tyme that he first began
To riden out, he loved chivalrie,
Trouthe and honour, fredom and courtesie.
—Chaucer, *The Canterbury Tales*

Chapter One:
Lady Aelia

THE ANCIENT CITY of Buerdaunt slept restlessly; stone towers loomed against the moonlit sky above an eastern bay of the inland sea called the Thlassa Mey. She was the capital of a great feudal land, this Buerdaunt, and home to many a mysterious sight.

All manner of folk filled her streets and buildings, living, breeding, and dying like maggots on a piece of meat. Near the docks, in the oldest section of the city, the streets were narrow and unlit. It was night; the sun would not rise for awhile and, even when it did, its light would barely penetrate these tangled alleys with their overhanging buildings. Here, a catcall uphill from the wharves, dwelt denizens from every corner of creation. The streets were infested with beggars, cutthroats, pickpockets, usurers; every form of human scum was known to lurk here.

To this place came outcasts from every shore of the Thlassa Mey. If a man's debts were relieved by the sudden death of one of his creditors, that man might be found here. If a village maid produced a fatherless child, the scoundrel responsible was likely to find his way to these streets.

In the center of this pustule of humanity stood a tavern. There were no letters upon the signboard before the place, only a faded painting of a knight sitting astride his horse. So faded were the figures that there was hardly any color left to them; they were ghosts against the exposed wood of their background.

In a garret chamber above the tavern itself, in a rough cot hardly long enough to bear him, lay a man. He was only one of many brought to Buerdaunt by the endless tossing and whirling of the fates that propel all mortals. On this night, his sleep was fitful.

It was dark. But had there been enough light in this chamber, an observer would have noted that the sleeper's face was handsome enough, although it was creased by the turmoils of his life. He was about forty years old. His dark brown hair had faded to gray at the temples and there was a broad moustache which also contained much of that neutral color. The nose was long and straight, the mouth well formed below its boundary of mustache, the jaw angular.

The man slept without resting. He writhed upon the cot, throwing back the blanket, kicking it away with long legs. He groaned. Broad arms shielded the face, as if from blows or some other form of abuse. Sweat crawled across his features. He was having a nightmare.

With a cry, he bolted upright, blue eyes staring into the darkness. His breath came in gasps. He sat for a moment with his hands clutching his face, breathed deeply, then swung his legs over the edge of the cot. Rising unsteadily, he staggered to the room's single window and leaned against the casing, gazing out at the predawn lights of Buerdaunt.

He smiled. It was a bitter smile, this smile of his, full of anguish and woe. As he peered out through the narrow opening, he spoke a weary speech to no one but himself: "The dead humiliation of my past still pierces me with memory's sharp lance. A wicked jest it is: relentless Time rolls on. He cycles forward, searing me with flames and stale regrets at every turn." He paused to heave a great sigh. "O Pallas! O thou Maiden whom I wronged. Oh, would that I could once reverse the wheel, undo the deed that makes such racking nights as these."

He turned from the window and began to dress for the day, still speaking to himself. "Ah, well, the past won't be erased by longing. Were that so, I'd laugh all day. There'll be no sleep till eventide comes 'round so best that I bestir myself. The past that ne'er may be forgot might still be worked to death. Stout labor is my faithful friend."

It was a puzzling scene. But while this early riser dressed, the rest of the city of Buerdaunt also awakened. In the gaining light of the new day, the streets filled and came to life. Great towers gleamed in the rising sun and pennants above the high walls crackled and snapped in the morning breeze.

The great marketplace was one of the first districts to come to life. It was a busy place on this day, as it was on all days. Fat merchant ships from all the lands washed by the Thlassa Mey lay in the harbor, as well as craft from beyond the Narrow Strait, far to the northwest. Only in the last two years had the Strait been opened by the diplomacy of Buerdaunt's ruler, King Lothar. Now ships of every flag passed there, all bearing wealth for this city. For this, Lothar was honored as well as feared by his subjects; they knew him to be a great man, although it was for his manner as well as his appearance that he was called Lothar the Pale.

The marketplace was colored by a blinding variety of trade goods. So jammed was it with blankets, booths, tables, stalls, and flimsy portable shops that a person could not pass from one end of it to the other without bumping into milling folk and being often jostled in return. This made it a rich hunting ground for pickpockets. Those who wished to keep their finances from being surreptitiously altered kept their purses covered and tightly tied.

And there were many reasons to open those purses. Merchants in dyed linen robes bartered the gold, copper, and timber from the hills above Buerdaunt for the silks, jewels, spices, and slaves from far lands. Musical instruments filled the air with their pipings and strummings, dancers whirled, and gamblers and gamesters plied their noisy trades.

From one of the streets that emptied into this great square appeared an attractive, middle-aged woman. She was richly dressed. Her bearing was regal and she was followed by two attendants, although her robes were actually not those of a noble. She wore on a chain about her neck a silver replica of the heavy iron collar of a slave. She was Lady Aelia. She had been sent there to do the weekly trading and other business of her mistress, Princess Berengeria of far Carea.

Aelia was tall, as tall as her male attendants, and her eyes surveyed the turmoil of trade within the square with an air of detached mastery; she was like a general watching a battle from a hilltop. She measured the activity before her, but she was not moved by it; it was something she would deal with as she wished, but only if she so wished. She was that general saying, "Yes, it happens the way I knew it would. I can strike here toward this goal or I can strike there toward that goal, but I choose to do neither of those things at this moment."

She stood for some time. But, though her eyes flashed across the marketplace, she was not trading on this day. She was waiting. The corners of her mouth curled, making the fine lines in her face jump and dance. Her foot, its five athletic toes encased in a light sandal, began to tap in the dust. She was becoming impatient.

After a bit, her face brightened as she saw a man crossing the square. As he hurried up to her, she grasped him by his chiton—his knee length tunic. Her voice was urgent. "Well? Have you found the place? And is he there?"

The man was a slave and he wore an iron collar—a real collar rather than the replica she wore. He nodded, still out of breath. "It was a hard search, Lady, but I was able to find an inn where a man works who fits your description. He dresses as a commoner, although he keeps himself trim and well groomed. He's tall and of middling age. And though he's only a workman, he speaks with noble patterns."

She studied the slave, trying to find in his face something to fill out his brief description of her quarry. Then she turned to the other attendants. "Then we must go and see. We hurry now, we have but little time."

But something caught her eye and she hesitated. There was a familiar face among the ocean of faces jamming the square; it was the face of Gymon, the King's palace steward. "But wait." She rested her fingers lightly on the shoulder of one of her attendants, then turned and pretended to examine the goods at the nearest stall.

Although she appeared engrossed by the items before her, she observed everything that happened in the square. She watched the face of the stallkeeper. She watched several soldiers who stood about the square, all wearing the purple-and-gold tunics which marked them as warriors of King Lothar. The tunics fit badly; she knew that was because they concealed shirts of heavy chain mail. And she knew the soldiers patrolled this square regularly, keeping order by their presence. They did not interest her.

But the presence of the palace steward did interest her; she watched him most of all. Out of the corner of one eye, she saw him glance at her, then turn away. He stopped at a gaming table and pretended to watch what happened there but his eyes returned to her more than once.

Was the King having her followed? That would have been no surprise. Lothar the Pale trusted no one, least of all a person as important to his plans as Aelia, Princess Berengeria's guardian. Still, he could employ more cunning agents than this clumsy stalker. Most likely, the steward followed her for his own reasons—curiosity, hope of blackmail, hope of advancement.

None of those reasons mattered. What mattered was that he was in the marketplace; she could not do her business beneath his eyes. She knew her attendants could be trusted, as could the slave, who owed no loyalty to Buerdaunt's rulers. But this interloper had to be dealt with.

Her eyes moved without pausing, absorbing all that happened about her, missing nothing. The game the steward was watching was rigged; she could tell that by the motions of the operator as he cast the spinning ball. A pair of the soldiers in the square were drunk. And a few paces away, a pickpocket was liberating the purse of a merchant. The thief's movements were lithe and fluid as he slid the money pouch from its belt and hurried away from his victim, moving quickly without running or attracting attention. He would pass near the place where she was standing.

But the merchant discovered his loss. His voice filled the air. "Robbery, robbery! Harrow and alas."

The pickpocket paid no attention to the shouting; he walked at a steady pace. Then Aelia flicked her foot forward as he brushed by. He pitched onto the cobblestones as their shins met, the purse flew from his fist, and coins scattered across the paving.

The square erupted into chaos. Children scrambled for the money; soldiers drew swords and shoved themselves into the crowd. The thief leaped to his feet, but a pair of citizens caught at him, turning him about. His fist crashed into the mouth of one and he wriggled free. Again he bolted away but several men leaped after him; there were shouts and screams, a stand collapsed, and a dog ran yelping through the mob.

More soldiers shouldered their way through the packed bodies, rushing toward the mêlée. The square filled with surging humanity. The commotion was enough to conceal Aelia as she departed. She started out of the square, moving at a hurried pace that made it hard for her attendants to keep up with her and to form a protective wedge about her which shoved aside onlookers who failed to step out of the way quickly enough. She placed her hand upon the slave's shoulder. "Now show the way. We must begone from here."

They escaped the tumult of the marketplace and hurried along an ancient street, to turn into another street, a narrow, cobblestoned way which was little more than an alley leading toward the docks. She looked back. The steward was not behind them. Had they eluded him?

Their footfalls echoed off the smoke-and-oil-stained buildings that loomed two and three storeys above them. Many of these buildings showed broken shutters and there was refuse everywhere. The oppressive air of the district affected the attendants; they glanced about and fingered the hilts of the long daggers they wore at their sides.

They met few people. Those they did encounter eyed the weapons of the two escorts and slunk away or stood silently, watching them with listless eyes as they passed. Finally their guide stopped. He pointed to the place they had reached, an inn where ale and wine were sold. If nothing else, it was a bit cleaner than the surrounding buildings and the signboard that hung out over the street bore the likeness of an armored warrior sitting astride a horse, the color of which might once have been white. There were no letters on the signboard. None were needed; few of the denizens of these streets could read.

The slave gestured up at the weathered piece of artwork. "Lady, you told me to find an inn called the 'Silver Knight' or the 'White Knight.' You said you had heard both names. This is the place I found. It hasn't got a real name; there's only that likeness there, but a man works here and he is much like the one you seek."

She glanced up at the signboard. Her agitation showed in the way she played with the end of the colored sash about her waist. "Then I will speak with him." She turned to her attendants. "Please wait for me. This must not take me long."

One of the attendants caught at her wrist. "Lady, it's a bad section of the city, and we might be followed. Perhaps one of us should go with you."

"This man will be with me." She gestured back toward the slave. "And if the man I seek be found within, I doubt there's any danger to be feared."

Quickly, she stepped through the tavern door and found herself inside a large, low chamber. The place was full of the sour smell of ale. That pungent odor was an improvement, however, over the smell of sea water, rotting fish, and garbage which filled the street outside.

There was an innkeeper, or at least a man who looked like one, wiping the top of the long counter that lined the far side of the room. This host looked up as they entered. He was impressed by the wealthy fashion of her robes; Aelia could tell that. She looked at the slave. "Is this the man? He doesn't look the part."

The slave shook his head. "The one you seek is only a worker here, a chucker-out. He keeps the peace on busy nights, repairs the furniture, and helps keep the place in order."

She nodded and stepped forward. "Good innkeeper, I seek the one who labors here. Four decades old, or near, should be his age; he should be tall, broad shouldered, wearing several scars along his arms."

The host looked at her warily. "You're the second one to come here and ask that question." He nodded at the slave. "There's the other. Why should my hired help interest you?"

"Because he does." Her voice had become soft and persuasive but there was no softness in her eyes. "Now do you know this seal?" She extended her right hand, where she wore the ring marking her as Princess Berengeria's personal attendant.

The host was a poor man of humble birth. He did not recognize the ring, nor did he have any concept of the office it represented. But he noted the rich garb of the woman he faced and he could see her attendants watching through the outer doorway; he saw the ring, which was large and of great value. So he realized the ring must have meant *something*. "Yes, of course, my Lady."

"Then answer me at once." Her voice was still gentle. It cushioned the harshness of her words.

"That description fits the man who works for me, yes." There was an interruption just then; a noise from a shadowy corner of the chamber turned the host's head and a gravelly voice called for wine. "One moment, Lady." The host grasped a worn pitcher and dipped into the open amphora below the counter. He hurried to the table where

the men were calling; they were a scruffy pair of vaga-
bonds if ever Aelia had seen such. He poured the wine
into their clay bowls and accepted a coin from each man,
all the while watching his stately visitor over one shoulder.
But instead of returning to the counter, he vanished through
a doorway on the far side of the room.

Nothing happened for a moment. Aelia waited with the
slave, the two men at the table conversed in low voices,
and the attendants peered in through the street door. Then
the host came back into the chamber, this time with another
man.

Aelia looked at the newcomer. His appearance did fit
the stories she had heard about an imposing figure working in one of Buerdaunt's waterfront taverns, a man whose
bearing, speech, and prowess revealed some greater past
than the life of a handyman. He was feared and respected
by the denizens of these dingy streets. His hair was laced
with the first tracings of gray, as was his mustache. His
eyes were blue, his nose long and straight, his jaw angular.
He showed no sign of the restless night he had spent.

There were questions in those blue eyes. She noted
that. But she could see more than simple curiosity in his
expression; she also sensed a certain ill-concealed knowledge of the reason for her interest in him. She displayed
the ring that had so impressed the host. "I show you this,
my ring, sir. Know you what it means, or do you not?"

His eyes flickered toward the ring, then back to her
face. "It is a ring of office, I know that. The house of
Berevald, Carea's royal house, displays such rings." He
shrugged. "I know no more than that. Such rings of office
are not needed here. A coin or two of bronze will purchase
the respect of anyone that serves within these walls." A
bitter smile peeked from beneath his mustache as he spoke.

He interested her. There was dry wit to his words and
an air of equality with her she would not have expected
from any man she might have found in this section of the
city. "Where have you come from?" she asked. "What
might be your name?"

He did not answer her directly. Instead, he glanced
over his shoulder at the two men drinking wine in the far

corner of the tavern; an argument had sprung up between them. Their voices grew loud. "My name is Palamon. I came in from the street that lies outside."

Without waiting for her response, he crossed the room, moving toward the two fellows with a quickness that belied his height and age. He leaned over the two and said something in a low voice. They looked up at him. Then they stopped speaking and watched him as he returned to face Aelia.

"What was it that you said?"

"I bade them both observe your beauteous self, with what fine, regal grace you move, and how your features brighten up this room. I think they were so stunned at what they saw, their voices died away—or faded, rather, as would fog, come morn." He smiled at her again, a bland smile this time. His face was like a mask.

Aelia needed to make a decision. She knew little about this man; she had heard odd rumors of his prowess and unknown origins but she could neither confirm nor deny what she had heard. She could guess by his attitude that he would not add to her knowledge. She and her Princess, the lovely hostage Berengeria, would require a staunch warrior to help them pass through the ordeal they were facing. But they needed to find one who had no connection to the court of Lothar the Pale, and who was unknown to the armies of Buerdaunt.

She angled for a clue. "If I could set a sword into your hands, then could you wield it fiercely and with strength?" The question meant much to her. "If I could promise riches, honor, fame, then would you serve me faithfully and well? Or would you fly when danger first appeared?"

She studied his reaction. A wary, weary look crawled across his features; he was reluctant to enter into the game she was playing. But the game did seem familiar to him. "I keep the order here within these walls, expelling those who come to break the peace, replacing legs on chairs, discarding slops. The challenge that you issue fits me not; 'tis like a heavy sword in pander's hands."

"But would you take it up for riches, sir?"

He shrugged. "If riches were my goal, would I be here?"

She looked him over again. He had been a warrior, there was no doubt about that. He was no longer young; he approached two score years in age—her age or a bit more. Still, his body was trim. She looked at his arms and legs; they were knotted with muscle. His chiton hung loosely across his lean midriff. She could count several scars: one great, pale slash on one calf, another on the right arm above the wrist, a couple of smaller marks on his left forearm—his shield arm. Yes, he had been a warrior. But what sort of warrior? Had he been a mercenary, killing for whatever patron would pay the most, or had he been a common soldier? Why did he hide himself in this tavern in this cesspool district of the city? "You do speak well and also with some wit. Then might you even be of noble birth?"

"I cannot say of what birth I might be."

More half answers. Was he toying with her? Perhaps he was a fugitive; she would have preferred a man of honor. Still, a fugitive could be made to suit her purpose; she could offer wealth and security, although at the price of some risk-taking. Be he renegade knave or honorable warrior, the offer she could make would be attractive. But did he have valor? That was cardinal and she would never find out in the public room of a tavern.

She glanced at the host. He had retired behind the counter but still watched her with suspicious eyes. She leaned her head close to Palamon and spoke softly so only he could hear. "I do not know you, sir, but I've heard talk. You do not give me facts to help my choice but still I have these words to say to you: you seem to recognize my ring; the house I serve is that of Berevald. Then you must know that Berengeria is long held hostage. That is why I come out from behind the heavy walls of Lothar's Pomfract Castle. Just one time each seven days, I may come forth to do my Lady's shopping in the town.

"Arrangements have been made for our escape, attendants bribed, some secret corridors made open by my keys. In five nights, there will be no moon above. Then with my dear Princess, my Berengeria, I shall emerge outside the castle walls. For we must flee pale Lothar's custody and make our way around the Thlassa Mey and to her father, grieving Berevald."

His expression wavered. It was only a matter of a degree or so, a hair's breadth movement at the corner of his mouth. But she noticed it all the same. The burden of uncertainty upon her eased a bit; she would choose this man to help her and her Princess in their flight. "You are not wise to tell me of your plan," he said. "You know me not. I might pass on this tale for one small handful of pale Lothar's gold."

She shook her head. "No, you will not. Deceit's not in your face."

He ignored the remark. "To journey all the way to Carea is rashness born of desperation. Two women, both of high condition such as yourself and Berengeria, will not fare well, for many dangers lurk in any transit of the Thlassa Mey."

"Then will you help us? Riches shall be yours; high honor, glory, all a man might wish will be your lot when we reach Carea."

He sighed; that sigh meant much to her. She knew she had read him correctly. He had taken part in such adventures before. There was no fear in the sigh, nor was there the gleaming eye of one who took up a challenge without knowing the dangers to be faced. It was the sigh of a man who had faced danger, who had overcome that danger, and who was weighing many factors before he consented to face it again. He gazed back at her, his expression shifting with the thoughts that boiled behind his face. "It is a hard thing that you wish of me. You wish me now to reembark upon a life I cast away some years ago." He paused, his eyes shifting about the room. "'Perhaps' is all I say." He looked at her for a moment, then turned and strode toward the doorway.

Her eyes followed the swaying shoulders. He had not given her much of an answer. But she prided herself on one thing; all her life, she had read volumes in words or gestures that had meant nothing to others, though they might have observed as keenly as she. He had been moved by her words. "Wait," she said.

He turned to look at her once more. She glanced at the host, then back at the tall warrior. "Have you ever seen the starlight dance its way across the river's crests outside the gates of this Buerdaunt? I say to you the nearest grove unto the gate is most majestic just at sunset time. I often go there; I have watched that sight as many times as there are fingers on my hand."

He stared at her for a moment. His face was a mask once more. "No, I have not been there." Then he turned again and disappeared.

She did not wait to be approached by the host; she gathered her attendants and departed, hurrying to reach Pomfract Castle, the King's stronghold, in time to avoid casting suspicion upon herself. After all, she did not know for sure what the palace steward had seen and reported.

But she had risen from humble status as a lowly sub-priestess dedicated to the deity Hestia, to her post as guardian to Princess Berengeria. She had been able to do this because of her insight into human nature. She had no choice but to trust her judgment, now.

As for Palamon, he did not return to what he had been doing before, scrubbing out the great amphorae in which wine and ale were carried to the tavern. Instead, he climbed the rickety stairs that led to his garret chamber. He returned to his tiny room with its single window which now admitted sunlight and the noise and stink rising from the street below. There was nothing here but the cot, a large wooden chest, and a heavy mourning cloak hanging in a corner.

He sat heavily upon the cot and stared at the blank wall facing him. Then, drawing forth a key from about his neck, he unlocked the chest, lifting the heavy lid with the air of a man about to release a viper.

He removed odds and ends from the chest—clothes, parchments, other articles. At last, near the bottom, his hand rested upon what appeared to be a pile of light chain. He moved it with the tip of one finger and there was a low, metallic rustling. He lifted the object, withdrawing a hauberk, a long shirt of the finest chain mail, an object of cunning craftsmanship not often found along the shores of the Thlassa Mey. It gleamed softly, greenish gold in the sunlight.

There was another object left in the box besides the suit of chain mail. That he also reached in and removed. It was a large sword. The blade had several knicks in it, but the double edge still gleamed where it had been last touched by the stone. The haft, which was long enough to accommodate both of his broad hands, was finely wrought but was worn nearly smooth with age and use.

The sword's pommel was unusual; in fact, it was not a pommel at all. It was the end of a finely carved cylinder of horn roughly the diameter of a large coin, polished and painted crimson, although much of the enamel had been worn away. Enscribed into it was a single word: BLOOD. He passed his finger along the word several times. "Blood is the word which links me to my past, and would that I could know its meaning. Ah, my noble blade, should I take you on one more quest? But then, how can I take you up again and open up the portals which defend me from my shame, the anguish of that awful, bygone day?"

With a groan, he cast the two objects back into the box. He sat once more upon the cot and rested his face in the palm of one hand. Were there tears? With his face shielded by his fingers, it was difficult to tell. And there was no one there to see.

Chapter Two:
A Dangerous Meeting

THE ANCIENT CITY wall stretched into the distance like a sinuous, upright shadow. The towering inland gate loomed overhead, its cavernous archway full of darkness. The men of the evening guard loitered casually, leaning against the massive stones that formed the gate itself, trading lies and jokes around a bonfire built beside the road leading southeast from the gate.

Beside the road rolled the river Priscus, dark and dank smelling, through a huge, barred aperture a few cubits from the gate. Its gurgling accented the low voices of the guardsmen.

To this gate came a tall figure dressed in a mourning cloak that hid everything but his face, hands, and feet. It was Palamon. He had come, as Aelia had known he would. The guardsmen glanced idly at him as he strolled past them, then one finally stepped in front of him to ask his business. They talked for a moment, Palamon gave an excuse, and the guardsman stood aside and watched the dark form until it passed out of the firelight and disappeared. Then the guardsman turned and spoke to another, who mounted a horse and rode into the city.

Palamon walked steadily, his sure step on the dark roadway showing that he was no stranger to travel, even on the blackest nights. He gauged his step by the sound of the river, by the feel of the road's surface, and by the calls of the animals out of the darkness. He made surprisingly good time. He walked until he could hear the wind playing turnabout with the leaves of many trees. This was the first grove that stood along the road leading southwest from the inland gate. If he had rightly followed Aelia's statements in the tavern, this was where he was to await the fleeing hostages. For it was the fifth night and there was no moon.

He stopped. There was no sound but the wind, insects, and small animals. Either he was mistaken or Aelia and her Princess Berengeria had not yet made good their escape from the city. Perhaps they would not come.

He stepped to the roadside, then took a few paces more, his feet rustling through the spring grass. He felt the trunk of an oak before him and leaned against it, gazing back into the darkness where the road lay.

Palamon knew about this Princess Berengeria and her imprisonment. More than two years ago, she had been taken hostage by Lothar the Pale, although no one who spoke of it ever knew how. But her presence in King Lothar's keep was the keystone of his diplomacy and the reason for the sudden upsurge in Buerdaunt's fortunes.

It was common knowledge. The kingdom of Carea controlled the strait between the Thlassa Mey and the ocean. But Princess Berengeria was the only surviving child of Carea's King Berevald and his Queen, Goswinth; her life had to be preserved to maintain the integrity of that land's royal line. For that reason, to prevent her execution, Berevald had opened without duty the Narrow Strait, granting passage to Buerdaunt's fat merchant ships. The wealth of the lands beyond the Strait had poured into Buerdaunt since then, making her the Queen City of the Thlassa Mey while the fortunes of Carea had ebbed in proportion.

So Princess Berengeria had made her choice, it seemed.

She had to escape and make her way back to her homeland or she had to perish in the attempt. In either event, Carea's sway over the Narrow Strait would be restored and the land's fortunes would recover, though the line of Princess Berengeria's fathers could be wiped out in the bargain.

Palamon stared into the darkness. A familiar sigh escaped his lips. He had fought along the shores of the Thlassa Mey for many years and he had little stomach for further danger, further carnage, further pain. What interest could he have in the fates of nations?

But a courageous lady faced danger. Her mission was a noble one—to return to the arms of her father and to restore the fortunes of her land. Her body was not her own in this; she was forced to risk herself because the gods, in their wisdom, had given her the responsibility of a royal title. And if need be, she would sacrifice herself for the good of her homeland. What sort of knight would have been craven enough to refuse aid to a maiden in such a position? So Palamon waited beside the road, even though his heart was not in the adventure. Aelia had read him correctly.

After a time, he heard horses coming along the road from the city gate. There was no mistaking the tread of their hooves in the dirt roadway or the *whuff-whuff* of their breathing. They approached, then stopped, and someone dismounted. Palamon heard the scrape of the shutter being raised on a hooded lantern. A sickly ray of light appeared and played along the tree trunks around him.

The light finally came to rest on Palamon. It was too feeble to blind him and he began to walk toward it. A man's voice came from behind the lantern. "Who are you?"

"I came to watch the starlight dancing softly on the river's crests beside this grove." Palamon's agitation was not revealed by his voice.

"Then it is he." This was a woman's voice; it belonged to Aelia. "Please hurry, let us down."

The hood was lifted from the lantern, revealing a party of four men on horseback, or so it appeared. The three men who were still mounted, all dressed in the livery of court attendants, climbed off their glistening steeds. The long silks and bardings that hung far down the sides of two of the horses were lifted. Palamon smiled. Strapped by broad thongs to the bellies of two of the animals were two females, Aelia and a young woman, doubtless Princess Berengeria herself. It was as good a way to pass the sentry as any.

The attendants freed their passengers, who stood stiffly, rubbing themselves and straightening their robes in a most unroyal way. Princess Berengeria was a tall beauty, full bosomed and hearty, though much of her form was hidden by her traveling robe. Enough of her was visible to capture Palamon's gaze—he could not tear his eyes from her. She did not look familiar to him as such; he had no doubt he had never seen her before in his life. Still, there was something about her features which *spoke* to him, which played chords upon the nerve endings at the back of his mind.

The lantern gave her amber hair a sparkle as she smoothed it over her shoulder. "Now, by my faith, these horses' bellies make a tiresome, tedious ride. But freedom's gained. The balance of our journey will be play until we look upon the walls of Carea."

She was speaking amiss, of course. The trek to Carea would be full of dangers, especially once Lothar the Pale learned of her escape. She knew this. The attendants knew it. Doubtless, even the horses knew it. There was little conviction in her voice and the smile was quickly gone, replaced by a look of stress and fatigue. The smile did not return.

Aelia stood and stretched, then nodded to Palamon. "'Tis good you've come, mysterious warrior. There are but three of us, as you can see: myself, our good Princess, and young Ursid, who holds the lantern forth. The others are attendants who will all go back tonight." She gestured toward the three men who busied themselves removing the silks of the horses, revealing sturdy travel packs and longbows secured beneath.

"Four mounts, four horsemen, rode out from the town. Three men will now walk back while we ride on, two

horsemen and their ladies, riding south." Aelia turned to
the young man who held the lantern. "Ursid, this man
will mount and ride with us. His broad experience will
serve us well."

Ursid was young; he wore the uniform and insignia
which marked him as an officer of the King's light cavalry.
His features were round and indistinct in the lantern light
and no moustache or beard decorated his face. He was a
well built fellow; he stood taller than most men, though
he was still a hand's breadth shorter than Palamon. All
in all, he was a strapping youth and well bred; his face
would show considerable character once it had had time
to develop. He nodded at the tall warrior. "Whence came
you, stranger?"

Again Palamon smiled. "Along that selfsame road you
traveled on."

"An answer I like not." The young knight looked at
Aelia. "My Lady, how well do you know this man? How
can you know he'll not betray us all? When comes the
time to stand and fight our foe, how can you know he'll
not turn tail and fly?"

"I trust my judgment," was Aelia's only reply.

Princes Berengeria spoke. "Ursid, you must not let
your caution strip you of your trust in Lady Aelia's choice.
Her insight fails her seldom—never, by my faith, in times
when her decision bears such great import as does the
choosing of this warrior. And now we must away. Time
passes on, and with it comes discovery of our flight."

Suddenly she paused, her gaze fastened to the tall warrior's face. All the life had drained from it; he was a stone
likeness of his former self. She looked at him in dismay.
"Sir, what may be the matter?"

Palamon resumed his former expression. "Not a thing.
And I must note the wisdom of your words. We must
move on. To tarry breeds attack. We shall be taken, having
done no more than made acquaintance, one with all the
rest, assuring one another as we march unto King Lothar's
donjon that we were a company most fit to make this
flight." He stood gazing at them thoughtfully. "Prepare
the horses. I must step aside."

With that, he walked from the circle of light cast by Ursid's lantern, leaving the three nobles to gaze at one another. Aelia looked after him for a moment. Then she turned to the attendants to complete her orders for the horses' preparation. That done, she spoke with each one of the servants quietly and sent them away.

Ursid turned to her. "This warrior of yours is strange. Though he suggested haste, his absence breeds delay."

But Ursid's criticism was cut short by a cry which rang out of the darkness. Not far off, in the brush along the road, there was the sound of a furious struggle. An oath split the air. His lantern swaying, Ursid dashed toward the commotion; the light revealed two men rolling over and over as they struggled on the ground. One of them was Palamon. The man he grappled with was unknown to any of them. But the stranger fought desperately, almost slipping from the tall warrior's grasp. Still, Palamon gained mastery even as the others arrived; he gained control of the other man, dragged him to his feet, and slammed him against the trunk of a beech tree.

"Who are you?" Palamon's voice was a savage growl. "You are quite a clumsy spy. Who set you to surveillance of our talks?"

The man stopped struggling. He stood limply in the tall warrior's grasp but did not respond to the interrogation. His breathing was harsh and erratic.

Ursid drew his longsword. "Let's slay this fellow, then be on our way."

Palamon looked narrowly over his shoulder at the young knight. "The sword is yours. You do it."

"Wait a bit." Aelia approached the captive and looked at him closely. "Do you know Gymon, Steward to the King?"

The captive nodded.

"Why were you sent to spy on our escape?"

"I know not."

She reached past Palamon and grasped the captive by his rough beard. "What's the game the Steward plays? Is he directed by some higher post or does he act upon his own? Speak out."

The captive could only shake his head. He was sweating freely. "Word came from a guard in the Steward's hire that this fellow had left the town." He jerked his head toward Palamon. "My orders were to follow him and mark what transpired."

"And while you did, your master took his tale unto the King. That much I'll wager." She turned away from the man, giving orders to Ursid over her shoulder as she walked away. "Bind him. Get some rope. These meddlers slash the web of my intrigue. We must away, to ride as fast as may be dared in darkness, ere the cavalry comes down about our ears. Our hope's in speed." She stamped her foot on the rough forest floor. "One night, at least, I'd hoped to gain. Foul chance."

They bound and gagged the spy, then leaped onto their steeds and turned the animals' heads away from Buerdaunt. Ursid's lantern was again shaded until a feeble beam of light showed the road in front of them. Ursid himself rode beside Palamon, looking at him often. There was no speech. Still, the four of them had to be thinking along the same lines. There would be no sleep through this night; they would ride the darkness out if they were to have hope of outdistancing the King's pursuit. So the night would be a long one; still, there was fear it would not be long enough.

Chapter Three:
A Skirmish

THE HOURS OF the night crawled away as the four fugitives rode their horses through the darkness. The pace was tedious; they could only hope the King's mounted soldiers could move no faster than they themselves were moving.

Dawn came at last. The hills about them became silhouettes against a gray sky and stands of forest began to appear as dark patches against a paler background of meadow grass. Palamon found himself looking back for signs of pursuit, but the road behind them remained empty.

As they reached the crest of a hill, Ursid raised his hand. The details of the member, the smooth knuckles and the shining fingernails, were already visible in the light of the new day.

"But hold." The young man's voice was a murmur in the chilly air. "I see his Majesty's patrol." He pointed. The road ahead of them dropped along the hillside, crossing a dew-glazed meadow until it was interrupted by a stream a dozen cubits in width. There, four horsemen in the long cloaks of Lothar's cavalry were watering their steeds. "However did they pass us in the night?"

Berengeria caught her breath. "The trees. We must ride for the trees, our only hope."

"No, wait." Palamon's voice was low and calm. "There is no doubt that we are seen. We stand against the telltale skyline now; for us to ride away will bring pursuit."

"What shall we do?"

Palamon paused, then a smile brightened his features. "Ride down and greet them. No alarm could lie among these men of Lothar's at this time. The word cannot have passed us as you think."

Ursid's voice was uneven. "But they shall carry news that we were here."

Palamon shook his head. "They cannot give that word till they report. And by that time, some hours will have passed to give our trail a chance to cool and dry. They've seen us, don't you see? To flee them now excites their interest and builds cause for quick pursuit where it might be delayed. Besides, we can't return along this road."

Aelia entered the conference. "These words are wise. As we ride on, Ursid, construct a tale which, told from out behind your uniform, will make them let us pass."

"As you request." Ursid's gaze turned toward the soldiers who sat astride their horses, watching the fugitives. There was no hesitation in Ursid's movements but Palamon noted the strain reflected in the young officer's smooth features.

As the four riders approached them, the cavalrymen rode up onto the near bank, the water splashing from their horses' hooves. One of them rode ahead of his mates to greet the foursome. Palamon was relieved to note that he wore only the insignia of a horse sergeant; as an officer, Ursid had a good chance of bringing off the encounter with success.

"Good morrow, sir. And you, too, ladies." The sergeant saluted them crisply with a gloved hand. "What brings you through this district at this early hour?"

"The business of the court," Ursid replied sternly. "But what of you? The selfsame question could be asked of you and your companions at this hour." Palamon watched with concern; although he appeared relaxed enough, every muscle was tensed for action. Ursid faced entrapment by his own nerves. Turning the question back upon the questioner was a good enough tactic, but it was overdone in this case. And the young officer's fingers played nervously with his reins.

The other three soldiers rode slowly forward and now waited behind their sergeant. Having answered Ursid's retort only with a smile, that man spoke again. "Which way do you ride?"

"North, toward the Greenlands city of Lacourd. Your probes delay our journey, so relent." Though Palamon gazed off at a distant herd of sheep, the conversation remained in the center of his consciousness. The situation was deteriorating. Ursid was getting more anxious by the moment.

The sergeant showed he was an old hand at picket duty; doubtless, he had been in uniform long enough to enjoy his authority. He was uncowed by the young officer. Walking his horse forward a few steps, he gazed past Ursid at the two women; his eyes fastened upon Berengeria's face. "My pardon, Lady. Now it almost seems that I have seen you somewhere else before, although I cannot place you at this time."

He had no chance to ponder further. With a lightning motion, Ursid drew his longsword and there was a sickening thump as the blade ended its vertical arc in the sergeant's neckbone. The victim's hands slid off his pommel as he fell beneath the stroke. "Now ladies, flee." The words rose from Ursid's throat in a harsh cry as he wheeled to meet the other three soldiers.

Many things happened at once; the two women spurred their mounts and galloped toward the stream, Ursid charged the soldier who lunged after them, and Palamon straightened in his saddle to confront the other two. With both hands, Palamon reached behind his neck and brought his heavy sword hissing from its concealed hanger, the sword he had pondered in his chamber after his first conference with Aelia. The carved horn pommel ornament was nearly hidden by his broad hands.

The battle was a short one. Palamon's weapon sent one horseman's sword shivering from his grasp and a second stroke cleaved the man from his saddle. The other adversary had no stomach for fighting; he spurred his mount so heartily it reared, then fled at a gallop along the road that led back to Buerdaunt.

Palamon did not pursue the man because a glance showed he was well mounted and would be run down only after a long chase, if at all. Palamon watched him for half an instant, shrugged, then turned toward the stream bank.

Ursid was locked in a vicious duel with the last horseman. But before Palamon could reach them, Aelia plunged her dagger into the man's thigh, distracting him. This was all that was needed to enable Ursid to land a fatal blow.

Aelia turned upon Ursid, lecturing him in harsh tones, her voice searing the cool air. "Your thoughtless act lays bare our very lives. Have you no better brain than what you show—to make yourself a fugitive before the man has fully challenged you?"

"He knew us, madam. That was in his eyes."

"The man knew nothing. All he did was wear the attitude that makes a guilty heart reveal itself, a method doubtless learned through many years of duty. And you cracked. You fool. And now our path of flight is known. No secrets can we keep; our foes learn all." Her lips drawn into a tight line, she turned from him. "So tell me, Palamon, how little time remains before this infant's thoughtless deed brings all Buerdaunt's horse soldiery about our heads?"

Palamon's answer was lightly delivered. "A trifling question, for the act is done. These three will never tell a soul with speech." He gestured about him toward the three fallen cavalrymen. "There may be powers evil and occult to pry the story from their lifeless lips, but, for the moment, we may rest assured that they will never speak in tones which soldiers hear. As for the other..." He paused, twisting in his saddle to look at the hilltop over which the last soldier had disappeared. "As for the last, he'll not appear before a rigid officer, at least until his undergarment's changed. So greatly did we fright him that I fear his late digested supper shares his seat. He fairly reeked in bidding us farewell."

So glibly was this last statement uttered that it brought half a snicker, even from Aelia's lips. But the moment passed quickly and she was serious once more. "Your humor blunts the edge of anger, sir. But still we must ride on."

"That's true," Ursid said. "But which way shall we ride? I told the sergeant we were riding north, a word his cohorts surely overheard. If so, then that way's closed to us." His head sank down upon his chest. "Oh, curse me for my youthful lack of guile."

"Yes, that way's surely closed if our man heard." Palamon's eyes searched the thick woods nearby as he spoke. The trees were tall and spreading and they enclosed the stream where it frolicked out of the meadow. "But then our route about the Thlassa Mey will form a circle, either way we go. 'Tis true the northern way is easier. The northern lands about the Thlassa Mey are known, well covered by small settlements. The southern route will cross more rugged lands, and unexplored to boot. But then, if it seems rough to us, 'tis so for them as well."

"And strange to Lothar's soldiers, same as us." Aelia nodded. "A point that's worth considering."

"Indeed. In point of fact, there's little difference, as like as not. For Lothar's soldiery will start from here and fan out north and south. The forest's thick within its darkened groves, but thickest to the south. So let's ride there."

He turned his mount toward the south, assuming a role as leader which the others wordlessly accepted, so easily did he take it up. He led them at a smart pace along the wandering stream, sometimes following its bank, sometimes riding at a distance. Later, the trail led them away, along the side of a deep, grass-covered valley. They followed it, always staying within the shelter of the trees that lined the rim.

As they rode, they ate prepared meals from the horses'

packs. Ursid was riding alongside Palamon again. The miles fell away; Palamon watched the trees about them so intently he hardly even noticed the younger knight's presence. Then it occurred to him that Ursid was staring at him.

Palamon turned his head, and a slight smile lifted the corners of his mouth. "You wish to speak?"

Ursid took a long time to reply. "I had suspicions of you at the start. I think that I was wrong."

"It's to be hoped."

"Your life is forfeit now, back in Buerdaunt. You laid a guardsman low. I've noble blood, which does protect me some. These ladies here are valued hostages; they'll not be killed. So Lothar's wrath will therefore fall on you."

"The wrath of kings, an honor to be prized." Palamon's smile did not change.

"His vengeance will, without doubt, cost your life."

"All life must end."

Palamon's response made Ursid pause. "It means so little, then?"

"The value of a life is nothing more than how it's prized by him who yields it up. I have seen dogs with which 'twas greater sin to snuff them out than it would be with me."

"You cannot mean that."

"That is very true." Palamon looked at Ursid, still smiling.

Perplexed, the younger knight finally shook his head. "You do not seem to care. A trifle, then, is all life's worth to you." He was silent for a long time. Finally he spoke again. "I owe you thanks for turning Aelia's wrath."

Palamon's eye flicked toward Ursid again and he noted that the younger knight glanced over his shoulder at the two women as he spoke. Palamon did not bother to stifle a laugh. "She's quite redoubtable. I think her wrath is much more to be feared than that of kings." He paused. "A noble lady—noble, all the same."

Ursid gazed back at Palamon. "I thank you from my

heart. I do not know if such things count with you, but
if they do, you have my thanks and also my respect."

Palamon did not reply.

Ursid continued. "One question more. When we first
met with you in darkness, east of Buerdaunt's river gate,
I looked at you and thought you went unarmed. Your
cloak concealed no weapon greater than a dagger's blade.
But now I see you wield a mighty sword, and with a
warrior's touch."

The smile Palamon had been wearing until now wrinkled into a different expression. "The art of killing's not
so hard to learn."

Ursid reached out and laid a hand upon Palamon's
shoulder but the tall warrior flinched at the touch. "And
then I find, beneath your cloak and hood, you wear this
gleaming chain mail, finely wrought, constructed with a
craft I've rarely seen."

"Beware, young man." Palamon drew away from the
young knight. He had not noticed the tear in his cloak
until now. It was actually a cut, rather than a tear, put
there by the sword of the horseman he had killed. But
the blade had glanced off his hauberk so harmlessly Palamon had never even noticed the blow.

A few days ago, when Palamon had pondered his sword
and this hauberk in the uneven light of his chamber, he
had been overwhelmed by the rank mustiness of the
thoughts stored in the vaults of his mind. But now he
wore the finely crafted armor beneath his cloak, its links
gleaming even in the shade of the overhanging trees. His
smile returned as though rushed into place. "Beware,
young man. You do not know from whom I stole this
shirt. You cannot know what knight, in drunken stupor,
gambled it away or sold it for the price of Buerdaunt ale
or lost it, lying in an alleyway."

Once more Ursid was surprised by Palamon's reaction.
His questions became confused, erratic. "You've fought
before. What places have you been? What is your history?
Whence came your hauberk? You have filled me up with
questions but you answer none of them. Whence came

this shirt?" His voice faltered. "But do not answer if you'd rather not."

Palamon laughed once more at the young knight's uncertainty. "Indeed, I'd rather not." He nudged the flanks of his horse with his heels and cantered ahead between the trees, still chuckling.

But as he neared the crest of the next hill, he reined in his mount and looked back at the two women and Ursid, waiting for them to catch up. He thought better of his cavalier attitude toward the young knight as he watched their approach; the passion of the fight with Lothar's cavalrymen had passed away, leaving them all sagging like empty wine skins. They were in danger at all times; he wished to do nothing to break down the unity of this tiny party. Most of all, at this time of fatigue, they needed to remain alert.

Something had to be done to keep them from being overcome by drowsiness; besides, Palamon really was tired of Ursid's questions. So he looked at Berengeria as she came near. "Princess, strange fortune was the force required to sweep the two of you to Lothar's hands. Methinks it might help pass the hours away if you could tell me this odd tale. Tell how you came to be his hostages, and by what fortune did you find escape."

Aelia interrupted. "We have no time for tales. When we are safe and free from all pursuit in Carea, then that will be the time to tell a tale."

"Perhaps. But if I fall this afternoon in bloody combat, aiding in this flight, I should be three times saddened by my fall, not knowing the beginnings of the tale."

Berengeria herself responded to his words. "Perhaps that would be well. I need to speak. So many thoughts make war within my soul, reflections both of hope and also fear, that speaking might unburden me a bit."

As he listened to her, Palamon felt himself lanced once again by a pang of sympathy for Berengeria in her plight. His softness for young women in distress had cost him dearly in the past; still, it was a part of his nature. He could not overcome it. "Then tell your tale, Princess. And tell it well. Then, though I face a hundred cruel deaths in coming weeks. I never shall complain. The very gods will gaze down at my corpse and envy me for dying well informed."

"You make a joke of death. But that is well." Berengeria's tone had become lighter. That was good; perhaps she was even smiling. "You've earned your tale, then, mystery warrior—a strange one to relate, by Hestia's veil. I'll tell it all; I'll tell how Berevald, Carea's King, had all his lovely children torn away. A sad tale it will be and strange besides; a tale of magic, vengeance, enmity. I still must marvel at it all, myself."

Chapter Four:
Berevald and His Children

THE PARTY RODE on into the afternoon, urging their mounts forward at the quickest pace that could be set without jading and galling the animals. Berengeria took a deep breath. "My tale is rooted in the mists of time, and to recount its origins will take some thought. But be that as it may, I'll do my best.

"I shall begin the telling of my tale and speak of such a time, long years ago, when Berevald, my father, was a youth."

Palamon listened carefully as the maiden began her story. His eyes scanned the hillsides about them, but all the while he listened to the rise and fall of Berengeria's voice. In the telling of this tale could lie some clue to the dangers they all might face later.

Berengeria had not been born at the beginning. King Berevald had barely assumed the throne of Carea and was still seeking a wife. The newly crowned King was already a noted warrior and was a fine match; his name was spoken often in the courts about the Thlassa Mey.

But a match had been made for him. Before his death, Bereyald's father had arranged for the Prince to wed Goswinth, a Princess of the Outer Island kingdom of Artos. After much consideration, it was Bereyald's decision to honor this betrothal. Therefore, a deputation was selected and a fleet was levied to be sent to Artos to fetch the new Queen.

The leadership of the deputation fell to a man called Alyubol, an advisor to King Bereyald as well as a longtime friend. This Alyubol was an interesting, unpredictable fellow. He had met Bereyald as a boy because he had been the son of Bereyald's history tutor. They had played together. Later, they had campaigned together.

But Alyubol had never been a typical warrior. Never had he made bones about his distaste for battle itself; still, he had become a cunning strategist. His tactical advice was seldom proven wrong, whether in war or politics; he was constantly studying the volumes and memoirs of past kings, soldiers, statesmen, and sages. He searched endlessly for stratagems, facts, and policies. Any means of achieving an end without direct risk to himself or his position was policy for Alyubol.

He had proven to be a valuable friend, a crafty negotiator, a canny advisor. And so it was that as Bereyald had risen, Alyubol had risen by his side. And Alyubol was made leader of the delegation to Artos.

Once in Artos, however, Alyubol did something held by his friends and foes alike to be impossible. He fell in love. From his first sight of Princess Goswinth, he was possessed by a ravening desire for her which was only intensified by any amount of modesty she might display, any devotion to Bereyald she might proclaim, any distaste for Alyubol himself she might reveal. He wanted her. He determined to have her.

Because of this, the negotiations over Goswinth's dowery went badly from the start and her voyage to Carea was postponed time and again. And while Alyubol haggled over the smallest details of the affair by day, he attempted to gain access to Goswinth by night. At last her father, learning of these advances, sent a secret protest to King

Berevald himself. Alyubol was recalled to Carea, much to his chagrin.

There followed an awful scene between the two friends. There was arguing, shouting, and, on the part of Alyubol, even threats and weeping. The two men parted company forever. When the royal wedding at last took place, Alyubol watched, seething, from a place reserved for the lesser nobles before Carea's Temple of Hestia.

So the friendship was ended. After the nuptials, the royal couple received a large package from the frustrated courtier. When opened, it revealed a large urn which burst asunder before it could be approached by Berevald or Goswinth, filling the room with flying shards, smoke, serpents, and poisonous fumes. Unhurt but aghast, the couple stared at the shambles which had been King Berevald's presence chamber. There could be no doubt: Alyubol had included some forbidden lore in his voluminous readings.

His arrest was ordered, but he had disappeared. And the matter did not end there. For several more weeks, urns of greater or lesser size appeared in the streets of the twin cities of Carea, each one bursting and releasing smoke, gas, birds, vipers, or even rats and swine. Many citizens were hurt, and some were killed. Then Alyubol's new hatred of the King took another, more sinister, turn. The last word from him was contained in a short letter, a missive left on the steps of the palace. It warned Berevald that all the children produced by his union with Goswinth would be Alyubol's, to do with as he wished. After that no more was heard of or from the strange man.

But at least no more urns were found and no more letters appeared. Alyubol was proclaimed an enemy of the court for treason, attempts upon the lives of the King and Queen, and the practice of wizardry. But he was never found.

The months passed and he was forgotten. After a year, the royal couple's first child was born, to be named Beredoric. There was rejoicing at the birth of the heir. A great tournament was held in his honor. From all the lands that ringed the Thlassa Mey came knights and spectators, from Oron, Buerdaunt, and Gesvon. From the Fastness of Pallas they came, from the Outer Islands and Artos, and of course, from the twin cities of Upper and Lower Carea. King Berevald himself competed in these games, for he was still a young and robust man.

All the court turned out to see the jousting and the swordplay. And since the listing grounds had been set up in a nearby village, Upper Carea was left nearly deserted; no one of account was in the capital save the infant in whose honor the tournament was being held, the ladies who were to attend him, and the palace guard.

At the end of the first day's gaming, Berevald and Goswinth returned to their castle to find a scene of mystery spread before them. The guards at the great gate were asleep. In the private quarters of the royal couple, the attendants were asleep. Fearing the worst, Goswinth and her husband rushed to the nursery where their fears were confirmed: the nurses were also asleep and the infant Beredoric was gone.

Once revived, all told the same story. The day had gone peacefully enough until sunset. At that time, a soft, yellow vapor had risen up from several potted ferns kept about Castle Conforth's grounds. No one had marked it much. But within moments, the mist had thickened and had begun to roll across the tiled floors, along corridors, and up staircases. The plants in the palace gardens had begun to exude the same mist. All who had watched them—maid, nurse, and guardsman alike—had grown drowsy so quickly no alarm had been sounded. The townsfolk had noticed the wicked-looking mist rising up within the walls of the castle but none had questioned it. All had thought it a part of the great celebration.

The court was thrown into chaos. Ignoring the loss of prestige it caused him, the King canceled the remaining events of the tournament. The army of Carea was turned forth to scour the kingdom in search of the missing heir. Weeks passed. In spite of all the efforts of King and commoner alike, the child was never seen again. Ships dragged the bottom of the Narrow Strait, parties searched the rocky cliffs above the city. The bodies of all infants reported dead during the next fortnight were examined by the King personally, as well as all those that were living and were below the age of one year. The results were all the same. Beredoric was gone forever.

Time passed. It did not remove the pain caused by the loss of the infant Prince but it did bring another baby boy to replace him. This time precautions were taken that Berethar, as he was named, be protected against accident or the intrigues of Alyubol. He was surrounded by armed guards at all times. He never set foot outside Castle Conforth except under armed escort. Whatever area of the castle he entered, whatever tower chamber, whatever yard, was locked and barred against any intruder except the King and Queen and those in their presence. The passage of any member of the royal family was now marked by the sliding and crashing of bars, the snapping of locks, and the scuffling of feet.

These measures had good effect; the child passed his first birthday without mishap. Then his second year came and went. A third year passed and after it, a fourth. That year brought more joy to Berevald and Goswinth for the Queen gave birth to another child, this one a girl who was named Godigisel.

The precautions that had served Berethar so well were adopted for Godigisel, and with the same results. The private lives of the royal family ran undisturbed for some months. But before the year was out, Godigisel became ill. She wasted away day by day, while the parents grieved, not knowing whether she suffered from some sickness or from the baneful influences of Alyubol. For fear that Berethar would be affected by the malady, he was sent under guard to Lower Carea, a few leagues away. Shortly thereafter, Godigisel died.

But that was not all. On the same night the infant girl passed away, a great fire erupted in the dockyards of Lower Carea, spreading through the port city in astonishing time. All things were thrown into chaos by it. Members of the young Prince's guard rushed about, moving him often to keep him from the crawling flames. Many went to fight the fire themselves. In the confusion, he was passed from the arms of one guardsman to the arms of

another; by the time the rising sun looked down upon the
smoldering ruins of the flame-shattered city, Berethar had
passed into unknown realms, never to be seen again.

If the loss of the infant Beredoric had been a tragedy
for his parents, the losses of Berethar and Godigisel, coming as they did on the same night, were a catastrophe.
The Queen took to her bed and would not speak while
the King wandered through his chambers far into each
night. He would brood, staring vacantly, hearing nothing
said to him until it had been repeated several times. Sometimes he would gnash his teeth and snarl the name of
Alyubol.

As they had before, the royal couple recovered, but
their great losses left scars, both without and within. They
seemed to age and shrink within their own bodies. They
grew sullen and suspicious, speaking to few and trusting
no one, not even one another.

Four years later, when a fourth child, Veranus, was
born, the event was greeted with more fear and whispering
than joy. Neither his mother nor his father could look
upon the babe without turning away to avoid a display of
tears. Perhaps it was this absence of any happy emotion
in his tiny world that spelled the end for little Veranus.
At any rate, he died before his first birthday.

The King and Queen accepted this loss, each with the
air of one whose lack of hope serves as guardian against
more pain. They slept apart now, and the King's footsteps
never sounded in the Queen's chambers. He administered
his realm from rooms within his own wing of the palace
while the Queen performed her functions in hers. The
great hall at Castle Conforth stood empty. The royal couple rarely met and never spoke more than a word or two
to each other; they became strangers separated by their
fear of more grief.

They lived that way for years. Then, in the eighteenth
year of their marriage, something happened. Each year
it had been the custom of the royal couple to go to the
Temple of Hestia in Upper Carea to preside over the festival dedicated to the divine patroness of hearth and home.
In this year, the opening prayer of the festival was given

by a new acolyte, a subpriestess of few years, newly ordained and very courageous.

In her prayer, this maiden asked for the blessing of the goddess upon Carea and upon the rites taking place in her holy temple. Then she turned her youthful face toward the King and Queen, who were sitting in their pavilion, each surrounded by a different troupe of courtiers. "We ask thy blessing, Hestia, on these two," ran this portion of the maiden's prayer. "Forgive them; they forsake the marriage bed. Through fear of earthly pain, they do thee wrong. Bring them together, Goddess, in thy name; 'tis for the sake of our most blessed homeland that we pray."

In the years following the death of the fourth child, the fate of a kingdom without an heir had been a common topic for discussion in the closets and empty corridors of the palace. But it had never been broached in the presence of the King or Queen. For this reason, this prayer by this unknown acolyte caused a sensation.

The Queen burst into tears and fled from the temple while the King simply sat in stunned silence. The subpriestess who had uttered the prayer, she who had shown the effrontry to upbraid the royal couple before the populace, was arrested.

After the premature ending of the festival, the offending maiden was brought before the King. She was very young and Berevald towered over her. Still, she refused to acknowledge any wrongdoing and refused to withdraw the prayer from the temple's chronicles, however her life or position might have been imperiled. She remained adamant against both threats and pleas. She spoke tearfully of the duty of King and Queen to produce an heir, regardless of their own misery. She was then taken before the Queen and later was imprisoned.

But that evening Berevald visited the chambers of Goswinth for the first time in eight years. The result of this union was Berengeria herself.

But the birth of this daughter renewed the old fears that lay across the royal marriage. She had to be protected. But how? Carea's entire army had not prevented the losses of the other four children. It was decided to

send little Berengeria away to Artos, the land of her
mother; perhaps there she would be beyond the reach of
Alyubol.

The subpriestess from the Temple of Hestia, whose
name was Aelia, was brought forth from prison. In spite
of her tender years, she had shown courage and integrity;
she was taken into the royal service and the baby was
placed in her charge. She was given the role of a young
mother with no husband; together, maiden and baby took
ship for the Hestian refuge on the island of Artos. A
common foundling took the place of royal Berengeria.

Thus was it that Berengeria was separated from her
parents and taken to spend the first eighteen years of her
life in a little chapel that stood alone in the northern forests
of Artos. The foundling survived to the age of six years.
Then she died like the other children before her, bringing
more grief to the King and Queen, who had come to look
upon her as their own child. But this time their real daughter still lived.

Still, the story was not ended. For those eighteen years,
Aelia fulfilled her duties faithfully. She instructed the young
Princess, was mother and father to her, guided her in the
ways both of a virgin dedicated to Hestia and of a future
Queen. At last the time came to take ship again, this time
for the voyage back to Carea.

But the vessel upon which they sailed had barely lost
sight of land when it was overtaken by a gleaming black
warship, a many-oared craft that bore down upon its victim and seized Berengeria and her guardian with hardly
a battle. They would never see her homeland. Instead,
they were kept bound and gagged as they were smuggled
overland to the Thlassa Mey and then to Buerdaunt, where
Berengeria became the hostage of Lothar the Pale.

How did it happen? How did King Lothar obtain the
information that allowed him to scoop up this crucial hostage? No one knew. Lothar himself did not care to discuss
the matter, even with his closest advisors. But he had
obtained the priceless person of Berengeria. His note to
Berevald, who had never been an ally of his, arrived with
the impact of one of Alyubol's bursting urns from earlier

years. The court in Carea was devastated. Not only was Berengeria's existence known to other nations but her transport home had been intercepted and she was as lost to her parents as ever she had been.

Only then did the fortunes of Carea begin to decline. Through all the years of grief and frustration, King Berevald had carried on his royal duties despite the tragedies that had pursued him and his family. But now King Lothar demanded free passage for his merchant vessels and warships through the Narrow Strait, of which Berevald was the master, in return for sparing the life of Carea's heir. Faced with the loss of his remaining child, Berevald consented.

So the riches of the Outer Islands, as well as the products of other lands beyond the Narrow Strait, found their way to Buerdaunt. And the fortunes of Carea declined in like measure. King Lothar had his key to domination of the region and he was unlikely ever to let her go. The number of vessels in the harbor at Lower Carea dwindled, the royal coffers emptied, the army shrank, and the people grew restive. But King Berevald remained paralyzed.

Military action was out of the question. So it remained for Berengeria herself and her able mentor, Aelia, to seek a solution of their own. After two years, that solution presented itself in the person of Ursid, a nephew of Lothar the Pale and a newly commissioned officer in Lothar's light cavalry.

It was Ursid who resented the politics of his uncle enough to steal away the keystone of Lothar's foreign policy. And though it was not to be said, it was Ursid who, from the beginning, was infatuated enough with Princess Berengeria to risk his uncle's wrath to free her. But this fact was not presented by Berengeria as she told her tale.

Chapter Five:
A Night in the Wilderness

PALAMON WATCHED BERENGERIA as she spoke the last words of her story, her voice trailing away. When the tale was done, she became silent and sad. She had not spoken a word about how Palamon had been selected for the journey, although he guessed that was a question Aelia could have answered best.

Palamon had known parts of the history, though not in the detail given by Berengeria. He had heard of the tragic marriage of Berevald and Goswinth, though he had never before heard the name of Alyubol. And like the rest of the world's onlookers, he had known of Berengeria's existence only since Lothar's triumph over Carea's King.

"It is a wondrous tale," he said. "I thank you that you thus inform a man you do not know."

"A trifle," Aelia said. "When it seems those secrets held most tightly in one's bosom find their ways to all one's enemies, then it's no sin to tell one's allies, too."

They rode on into the evening and the air became chilly as the sun sank over the verdant hills to their right. The gathering darkness slowed them greatly. The trail climbed into a granite-rimmed ravine and the way became rocky and difficult. The tired horses picked their weary way among the rocks, occasionally stumbling.

At last the weak beam of Ursid's lantern showed a slight widening of the trail they were following and Palamon called a halt. "Fatigue now slows our progress more than stony obstacles," he said. "We now should stop and rest."

Berengeria yawned as Palamon helped her from her horse. Her form was full within her robe, her supple body was a pleasant weight as he helped her to the ground. He could not keep from noticing the sublimity of the curved shape within his grasp but he blocked the thought from his mind. She was not for him.

Although she was plainly tired, Berengeria's fatigue was warring with her resolve. "We've come a way indeed. But Lothar's men pursue us still. This pause might well afford to them the chance to gain much ground on us."

Palamon smiled at her. "Indeed, that's possible."

"Then any flight should be preferred to sleeping while our hot pursuers ride us down."

Palamon and Aelia both looked at the young woman, then at each other. Berengeria's face was a weary mask. But still she was driven, kept upright by the desire to reach her homeland.

Palamon laughed a short laugh. "Then you go on. But I'll sleep here tonight."

"Now, mystery knight, whoever you might be and whatsoever you have done for us, this mirth before this good Princess reflects most poorly on you, sir." Aelia's voice was full of anger.

Palamon looked at her, his smile never wavering. "Forgive me, then. But this great world in which we pass our days will not revolve the less nor cease to team with life if we should rest. The sun will drive his chariot across the heavens on the morrow, I am sure. Whatever is our fate, my Lady, rest assured our horses still shall chew the budding grass, these leaves we hear shall rustle through the night. The gods will watch a hundred years from now and entertainment they derive from this, our crucial flight, will long have left their blessed consciousness. So let us sleep. The gods will not bar sleep."

"The fate of kingdoms matters not to you?"

"If my old body fails to get its rest, it matters not what matters not to me."

But the dialogue was interrupted. Stress and fatigue had overcome Berengeria; her knees buckled, she touched her forehead, and a weak gasp escaped her lips. Together, Palamon and Ursid caught her and lowered her gently to the ground. "Our flight must wait till dawn," Palamon said. "The maid needs rest."

Aelia fetched a blanket from one of the horses; Berengeria was placed upon it and it was wrapped about her. Her eyes fluttered open with the disturbance. "Fly now. Fly we must."

"Her courage far outweighs her body's strength." Aelia's face was drawn with concern. "We must allow her rest." The discussion with Palamon was ended but Aelia's displeasure still showed in her last glance at him.

There was a pause while Berengeria was tucked away on a level bit of ground. Then Palamon turned to speak to Ursid. "One man at least must watch for danger, now. I've seen such times as these before; therefore 'tis I who first should man the sentry post."

"Nay," Ursid countered. "I'm the younger man. These hours rest but lightly on my neck. I'll take the watch."

Palamon shrugged and then unstrapped his sleeping roll from his horse. "It's as you wish." He gazed at Ursid with a smile, the same slight smile he had worn many times during the night and day they had spent together. It made Ursid uncomfortable. Was Palamon mocking him? "It's as you wish, young knight," the tall knight said. "But wake me in awhile, two hours or three."

"I'll wake you and we'll take turns through the night."

"I'll stand watch, too." Aelia had finished pulling a second blanket over Berengeria's full body; now she stood and looked at the two men. "You warriors need rest as much as I, I'll wager that."

"You'll stand the watch and wake us if there's need?"

"I will."

"So be it, then." Palamon unrolled his own blanket and stretched out upon it. "The roster's set and since that's so well done, I'll go to sleep." With this, he flipped the edges of the rough cloth over his chest with a flourish, rolled up one end of it for a bolster, and closed his eyes.

"And that is that?" Aelia looked down at him without expression.

"An odd man, though he seems quite capable." Ursid seated himself upon a large stone and blew out the flame in his lantern. The other members of the party became invisible in the sudden darkness. "How was it that you chose him for this trek?"

"I wind into my knitting gossip's threads," Aelia said. "I heed those whom few others stop to hear, committing into memory's counterpane all things that pass into my weaver's grasp. But still and all, there's much I do not know about this man." She yawned, then spoke again. "I'll know it in a month, I warrant that."

The travelers gradually became silent. Finally, Ursid could hear only the whirrings and gruntings of insects and toads and the occasional howl of a wolf away, away down the canyon below him. He had to stand his watch with his ears; darkness had devoured everything. The only light left in his world was the star-speckled ribbon of night sky that wound between the looming granite walls of the ravine itself.

Time passed. It seemed as if it had been eons, but a glance at the movement of the stars between the cliffs showed it had been hardly any time at all. Ursid yawned. He drew his longsword and placed it across his lap, the cool weight of the blade comforting him in this wilderness. The night sounds made their own music by which to stand his watch. He yawned again; time crawled by.

The youthful watchman deserved sympathy. He had ridden for a night and a day and the nervous excitement which had kept him alert had deserted him at last. Now he was weary. He was weary beyond measure and the hours that separated him from the end of his watch were guileful enemies.

Then Ursid opened his eyes and started as he saw the first gray, predawn glow filtering between the cliffs above him. He was mortified. He had slept. He had committed an unforgivable sin and when the others awoke, he would be chastised for his blunder. It was his second in as many days.

He scrambled to his feet, picking up his sword from where it lay in the grass. Sliding it back into its scabbard, he cast a nervous glance about the clearing.

"Are you well?"

Leaping, Ursid turned to look for the speaker of those words. It was Palamon. The tall knight sat like a death-watch, his back propped against the base of a tree and his mourning cloak wrapped about his shoulders. It was still too dark to see whether he wore his enigmatic smile.

Ursid stared down at him. "How long have you been there?"

Palamon gazed back, his face shadowed by the hood of his cloak. "I've been here since I started from my sleep, awakened by the sigh of steel on stone, a young man's longsword slipping from his grasp as slumber slowly dragged him from his post."

Ursid fumbled for words. But there was nothing he could say. He could feel his face growing warm as the blood flooded up into it and he hoped the dark form before him did not notice that in the dim light. "Forgive me."

"Ah. Sleep's an ancient friend—and enemy. He comes quite uninvited many times and some have neither weapons nor the skill to drive him off when he arrives uncalled. I know him well. I've learned to stave him off when that's my wish and call him in a trice when I desire. I recommend this skill to all young men."

Ursid sank down onto one knee in the moist grass, his head drooping. "And I have shamed myself."

"No, not at all. A single honest error brings no shame— or should bring none, if men were equal to the high ideals they oft proclaim. No harm's been done, for I have stood your watch."

There was no condemnation in the tall knight's voice. In fact, in this moment of forgiving Ursid his error, he seemed more human and approachable than at any time during the journey so far. Still, the matter cut Ursid deeply. Palamon had done him a favor, and, being an honorable young knight, Ursid appreciated it. But it was time to speak of something else. "I ache. I feel as stiff as if I were a corpse."

"You slept without a blanket in the dew. Ah, well. To feel as stiff as if you were a corpse is no great thing if you can say 'tis so. If stiffness welds the joints of all your frame and yet you cannot say that is the case, it's sure you're dead in truth, a state more serious." Palamon stood. The slice in the woolen fabric of his cape allowed his hauberk to shine through; the chain mail gleamed dully, even in the half light. "A stream's downhill from us. I'm going to wash."

Ursid watched him as he swept through the brush that surrounded them, quickly moving downhill and out of sight. He did not return immediately. After awhile, there was a stirring in one of the remaining blankets; Aelia sat up and looked at Ursid. She yawned and stretched. "You did not wake me. It's not in my heart to censure you and yet I should protest. We all need sleep and I should share the watch."

Ursid did not answer and hoped she did not notice as he blushed once more.

Aelia glanced about. "And where is Palamon?"

"He left some moments past to go and bathe."

There was a sound in the brush and Palamon reappeared. Aelia looked at him. "Bathing, were you? Yet my feeble eyes can see no moisture. You have dried off well."

"Your eyes are keen. No, I have not been wet. Yet sometimes one must walk into the brush."

She gazed at him steadily. "Yes, that is so. I also will have to take a little walk and all of us may have to do the same before we ride. Awake her Highness gently, but with haste."

As Aelia made her own way from the clearing, Palamon knelt by the side of the sleeping maiden. She looked like a vision transmuted into flesh as she lay before him; her cheeks were pink with the bursting life of her youth and her lips had parted slightly to reveal the even pearls of her teeth. Palamon found himself staring at her. There was something different about her, something striking. Palamon could sense the stink of fate about her. Did that fate, that sense of fate which lay before him so palpably bode well or ill? Did it lie between them or did it draw them closer together? He could not tell and it did not matter.

He turned away from her and summoned Ursid. "The task is yours to wake her," he said. "She is young; her sleep is deep. For her to be so shocked out from her sweet repose by such a sight as I . . ." He paused. "She knows me not. We've only kept short company. 'Tis better, far, that she should see your face, its youthful down so well reflecting her own youth, than that she should be shocked into the day by looking at my weathered, dried-out form."

He stood and watched as Ursid knelt where he had knelt, tugging gently at the blanket Berengeria clasped tightly about herself. Ursid was earnest about this task; there was no doubt he would use the prescribed amount of gentleness. Palamon turned and began to saddle the horses.

Chapter Six:
A Knight of Pallas

AFTER THE HORSES had been saddled, goatskins were filled and each member of the party took a long drink from the stream that danced merrily along the floor of the ravine. Then they started on their way, munching hardtack wafers and dried strips of mutton from their packs.

The ravine was spectacular as they rode upward toward the stream's source in the rolling mountains to the south. It reminded Palamon of the way a great log would have split when the splitting wedges had first been driven into it: the narrow, rough gash that would have been produced just before the two sections would have groaned, cracked, and broken apart. This ravine was like that, carved into dark granite, covered with brush and lush undergrowth until the stone itself could be seen only in occasional bare spots which offered no foothold, even for the most tenacious plants. The four of them followed the trail scratched along the bottom of this cleft. Nothing could be seen except the verdure-covered walls towering a hundred cubits over their heads; even those were visible only through breaks in the brush that covered the rocks above them.

But there was no shortage of sound. The brush-cracking steps of the horses blended with the chattering of the stream, the squalling of birds, and the crooning of breezes that blew up the ravine past them, until the sense of hearing was rendered as useless by surfeit of stimulation as the sense of sight was crippled by the blinding screen of vegetation. But if they could not see out, neither could others see in. And they would reach the top of the canyon sometime.

"You are a native of Buerdaunt, Ursid," Aelia said. "So tell us of this country to the south, and what lands we may find by traveling on."

"I do not know a lot," Ursid said. "The country's rough, unmapped, and harsh. Few travel here, or none. Most trading's done by coastal ships because all travel is so difficult by land."

"That suits our purpose well, as I had hoped." Aelia's voice was a murmur, addressed more to herself than to the others. "Our route will take us in a sweeping arc, first west, then northward, casting off pursuit. At last, when many miles lie at our backs, we'll make our way unto the Thlassa Mey and there we'll find conveyance to our home."

"A noble plan, my Lady," Palamon said, giving Aelia a sidelong glance. "I misdoubt, however, that you first conceived it here. Methinks your mind to be a fertile womb, but not of sudden plans. You've thought this out."

"I do keep one or two schemes as alternatives, fermented over years' captivity. A simple mind it is that has but one."

"Ah, bravo, then. Your plan is nobler still for having won a competition with, doubtless, many others, all with facets recommending them to us, so I am sure. May all the gods look down upon our flight and grant success, for I am told the gods will always favor thoughtful men— and women, too. So may they favor you."

"I thank you for your benediction." Aelia smiled through her reply. "Though mockery is also in your tone. Beware, mysterious knight. Tease only me. Do not aim disrespect at mighty gods."

"Ah, never fear for me, my Lady. For the gods can peer into a warrior's heart as easily as you into a glass. Almighty Maiden Pallas, with gray eyes, and dear Hestia, who presides o'er hearth and home, cannot find disrespect in what I say. My words contain unbounded fear and awe, respect and adoration without end, inspired in me by them—as well as you." It was pleasant banter, this sophist's trick that Palamon had played on her. By placing her on a level with the gods in his estimation, he made the crime of disrespect hers as well as his, even though only in jest. Aelia smiled again, in spite of herself.

They rode onward, climbing toward the source of the stream they were following. Midmorning came and the sun climbed into the heavens until they could see the edge of his brightness peeking over the cliff on their right.

By afternoon, they were following a trail that wound steeply upward, switchbacking to and fro as it took them over a lofty divide between two ravines. At the summit, they paused to look down on the way they had come. The lands they had crossed stretched away below them, rolling off into the distance.

Suddenly, Ursid became tense. "Look there," he said, pointing. "Can those be men?"

Palamon followed the extended finger. Off, far off in the distance, a cluster of dark dots crossed a hilltop not far from the way they themselves had passed.

Berengeria also stared at the tiny figures. There could be no doubt they were horsemen. "Do they see us?"

"That's hard to ascertain," Aelia said. "But still their way's not far from ours."

"Indeed. And we have skyline at our backs." Palamon spurred his horse over the top of the pass. "Ride onward, for we must assume we're seen."

They dropped down the other side of the divide, setting a smart pace along the steep trail. Still, there was no way of knowing how quickly King Lothar's cavalry would gain upon them. They could not even be sure the horsemen behind them had come from Buerdaunt. But they had no choice but to assume the worst in both cases.

Evening came. They camped without a fire for fear of discovery and slept restlessly with one of their number always on watch. When dawn arrived, the gray light made the waving tops of the trees stand out against the sky like shadows thrown by writhing fingers onto a draped sheet. Aelia looked up at the tree-guarded sky, then back down upon her sleeping companions.

There had been no disturbance through the night. Now she had the watch and she stood silently, leaning against a tree while she pondered whether she should continue with her earlier strategy. Should she still seek a seaborne route back to Carea or was it more advisable to stay inland, away from cities and towns? Unexpected events made planning difficult. The sight of the King's horsemen had removed hope of eluding pursuit, and with it, hope that they could reach a seaport which had not been warned against their coming.

So she pondered. And as she leaned against her stout tree trunk thinking, she saw one of the party stir, then sit up. It was Palamon, the knight of unknown origin. He did not sit looking about as she would have expected of a man newly awakened, but stood quickly and walked toward the trees.

"And whither go you, gentle Palamon?" she asked of his departing back.

He stopped, then turned, looking back at her. "I'll walk a bit to stretch the muscles out."

"The body's movements call you as before?" The question was a mildly barbed one; Aelia remembered Palamon's jaunt of yesterday and his excuse for it.

"Perhaps." He disappeared into the trees, the dark mass of his mourning cloak fading quickly from view.

This was all a bit odd. With her eye for the niceties of human nature, Aelia was concerned about the tall knight's absence two mornings in a row. He had been gone the day before and the King's horsemen had appeared, even though only at a distance. She was suspicious. She knew too little about this man. With a departing glance at the sleeping forms of Ursid and Berengeria, she followed Palamon into the forest.

He could not have gotten far ahead of her, yet he was hard to find. His pace had been a quick one. She saw no sign of other humans in this forest and that was important; her throat became dry even at the thought of finding Palamon in the act of leaving a secret cipher at the foot of some marked tree. But he was not to be found at all. She shook her head. Certainly he was a master at concealing the act of relieving himself, if that was actually what he was doing.

As she turned back, her eyes swept the crowding trees one more time. There! She saw it—a glint—the play of light upon metal in the shadowy distance.

Her suspicions revived, she crept toward the spot, moving silently, using skills she had not used since she had been young, playing hide-and-seek on forested Artos. Her feet left hardly a mark on the leafy ground.

And then he was there. Before her was Palamon, a Palamon she had never seen before. The mourning cloak had been thrown down along with the worn leggings. He was resplendent in a full suit of chain mail which captured the brilliance of the rising sun and set it bounding, dazzling the eye. Seen in full, the greenish gold mail was stuff of wonderous workmanship and it enclosed his kneeling body like a second skin, accenting the breadth of his shoulders, the tapering muscles of his back, the fullness of his hips and thighs. She had seen such a hauberk before.

He was kneeling. His back was toward her. The big sword rested pommel upward, against a tree; he knelt before it in supplication as if the sword itself represented the great power to which he was praying.

His words floated softly through the morning air. She could barely make them out and she was not sure she wanted to. Her fear that he might have betrayed her Princess had led her to intrude upon some private moment; she was lanced by the feeling that she had betrayed him, instead.

He stretched his scarred arms out toward the sword as he spoke with a reverent intonation. "O mighty Pallas, gray-eyed Maiden dear, give audience to one who calls thy name. Thy humble servant seeks not wealth or fame, but only that his prayers thou shalt hear. O blessed patron, grant surcease from fear and let they power guide my arm and aim. I am a simple warrior without claim but that thy aegis be forever near."

Aelia's hand crept to her lips; she knew why Palamon was wearing the lustrous chain mail. She knew his secret even before he had finished the prayer.

"Oh, guide me in my quest to do thy will; bring succor to all those who cannot speak to thee themselves. With power this sword fill, that it might bring protection to the weak. Through this imperfect world I seek thee still. Oh, grant that I might find the things I seek."

The head bowed and the arms relaxed a bit. Unintentionally, Aelia relaxed, too, and a sound escaped her throat. It was a small sound but Palamon heard it.

He whirled about, the hilt of his deadly sword clenched between his powerful hands. But he dropped it when he saw her. He fell sideways as he scrambled to retrieve his cloak and pull the dark wool over himself like a maiden surprised during a bath.

His eyes flashed as he looked up at her. She had seen many things during her life; she had traveled the length of the Thlassa Mey. But the resentment and anger that flashed in those dark eyes shocked her to the point that her stomach tried to wrench itself free of her control. She nearly gagged. "Forgive me, sir. I swear I did not know."

"You seem to think you must know everything." All the condemnation that could be produced by one body was hurled forth in those words as the man before her flung his cloak about his shoulders.

"To be a Knight of Pallas is no shame; 'tis honor greater than most men can know. What forces you to hide your state from us?" The question was an honest one. The Knights of Pallas was an order bearing immense prestige. Why had Palamon chosen to hide such an honor from his companions?

"Do not believe all things your eyes may see. A man may wear a title he's not earned and words mean nothing;

words are nought but air." These phrases were little more than grunts, uttered hurriedly as Palamon laced up his leggings.

But Aelia had recovered from her shock. There was more here than met the eye and she leaped onto the scent of this mystery with all the intensity of the true huntress. Why did Palamon wish to hide what he was? "A stout façade you throw up, but for what? You feign the mind of one who does not care, of one who makes a joke of everything. And yet, in that one sonnet—that short prayer—I heard more true devotion than some men may show in years spent in a temple's halls. I ask again, mysterious Palamon, why do you hide the honor that you bear?"

"I make a joke of things? Indeed I do. Does living have more purpose than a prank?" It was back in place now, the façade Aelia had spoken of. There was nothing in Palamon's eyes now but empty mirth. His lips curled at the corners and there was no sign on his face of the emotions that had been stamped upon it a moment ago.

Aelia also noticed the deft way in which he had turned her question. "I'll not be led astray," she said. "I've watched you well. In old Buerdaunt, I heard some tales that did not rhyme, of one who seemed much larger than his place, and so I asked him to accompany us. With every move, you show my judgment's good. And now I see from where you take your skills, your leadership, sound judgment, and strong arm. Gray Pallas' Knights, an ancient order, sir, a holy order of the noblest men. Without stain are these men and without blot, all chaste and modest; never woman's bed, nor heavy drink, nor riches do they know. And yet you carry modesty too far, denying membership in any sense. To hide your membership in those exalted ranks—oh, Palamon! Is not that, too, a sin?"

The strength ebbed from the man before her. He sagged against the tree behind him, the lines of his face making him look ancient, far older than his four decades. "I'll not deny what you have said to me. And yet you question things too near to me by far. My past does not need be discussed for me to carry out my duties here. This subject must be closed, I ask of you."

"But I will still inform my own Princess. For I will have no secrets standing 'twixt her and all truths."

"That's as you wish. But mention it no more to me, though you may shout it to the world." Palamon's voice dripped with bitterness.

It was all very strange to her. The Knights of Pallas was the most rigorous of the orders of knighthood to be attained on the shores of the Thlassa Mey. They lived out a monklike existence within their great, vaulted fastness on the northern cliffs, riding out to give aid where it was needed most. Noble youths from across all lands aspired to those ranks, but few were the ones who attained that goal. And yet Palamon concealed his honor—did not even seem willing to discuss it. Aelia did not press the matter further, but she resolved not to forget what she had seen.

They were suddenly interrupted. There was a sound in the trees above them, a thrashing of branches as if a large bird or a tree cat might have been disturbing the boughs. Palamon looked up. "Did you hear that?"

"I heard it." Aelia also looked into the branches that supported a lush green canopy above their heads. She saw nothing but the leaves that filtered the growing daylight. Even the usual morning birds were not to be heard. "I cannot see the source. All's quiet now; perhaps 'twas just a branch which, cracked with age and early springtime's rains, has fallen down and drawn our ears to it."

"Perhaps." Palamon's eyes continued to search through the endless leaves, which became even greener in the increasing daylight. He stood, still holding his sword in his right hand. "I do not like this."

"The fact may be that, in your warrior's way, your nerves assign a life to every sound and seek a hairy owner for each branch which, with the wind's caressing, rubs its mate. That may be so—indeed, 'tis likely so. And yet as I behold your two blue eyes a'darting to and fro as though to sift the very leaves themselves, I think that we should do whate'er you will."

"We must return and find the others, then." Palamon

started at a trot up the tree-studded hillside and Aelia followed him. But they had gone only a short way when a throttled cry assailed their ears. Aelia felt the color wash from her cheeks like cheap dye from a coarse garment as Palamon sprinted ahead of her, his cloak opening out behind him like woolen wings. Were King Lothar's cavalrymen upon them? She drew her dagger and followed. Her breath became heavy with the effort of her dash but was almost forced from her body by the sight which confronted her.

Their four fine horses had been driven off; the animals thundered away, showing only their tails and their broad backsides as they galloped through the trees. But there was worse. Berengeria and Ursid had been dragged from their blankets and now were struggling against two hooded, white-robed assailants. These strange figures were not marked by the uniforms of King Lothar's men but their intent was no less deadly. Already, one of them had thrown struggling Berengeria onto his jet stallion and was swinging up into the saddle behind her. Turning, he saw Palamon. With his free hand, he drew his sword and aimed a blow at the neck of the Knight of Pallas.

Chapter Seven:
Riders in White

PALAMON WAS READY for the blow from the pale-robed rider. He pivoted to let the sword's blade glance off his mail-bound shoulder; the weapon sliced a great strip from his cloak as it traveled the length of his back. But as he returned the blow with his own sword, the remnants of the cloak bunched about his arms and he had to pause long enough to shrug himself free of its folds.

The rider's hooded eyes froze upon Palamon's lustrous chain mail; the man hesitated as he stared at it. "A tall Knight of Pallas, Navron. Why did Alyubol never make mention of this?"

Many things happened during this pause; Berengeria took advantage of her captor's distraction and struggled from his grasp, dropping heavily to the ground minus a handful of amber hair. Palamon writhed free of his own cloak and aimed a mighty blow at the chest of his adversary. And in leaning to escape the blow, the hooded man lost his balance and fell screaming from the saddle, with one foot still tangled in a stirrup.

By this time, Aelia had reached the scene of the struggle; in fact Palamon's opponent hung directly before her. There was no time for thought. With a gasp, she buried the blade of her drawn dagger in his chest.

She was half-sickened by the blood that fountained forth. The thin lips of her victim drew back in a grimace and there was a rattling from the throat; he was finished. The horse trotted away a few steps and stood, its rider still dangling from the stirrup.

Aelia looked up to see that the fight about her was over. The other rider was in flight, his horse's hooves thudding dully between the trunks of the trees. Ursid was struggling to his feet, nursing a place on his forehead which was already beginning to swell. "Now by the gods, what manner of men were those?"

Berengeria was also standing now, blood trickling from her scalp where the hair had been torn out. She touched the wound with one hand, wrinkling her face at the pain. "I fear the worst. My Lady, did you hear?" Her voice was little more than a whisper.

"The name, you mean? The name of Alyubol?" Aelia nodded quietly. Her stomach was still twisting inside her, both from the sight of the man she had killed and from her knowledge of that other player who had joined the game. "And 'twas his henchman Navron who decamped."

Palamon gazed in the direction taken by their four horses. "They may have failed to snatch our good Princess but still they've done much harm, these men of Alyubol. We now must go afoot; our horses flee."

"Can they be caught?" Ursid ran a little way into the trees but quickly returned, his face downcast. "There is no hope. Their panic takes them far."

Palamon walked toward the black horse which stood a few cubits away with the fallen rider still hanging from his stirrup. Reaching the animal, he used the tip of his sword to pry free the entangled foot; the body dropped to the dark earth with a thud, the air sighing from the dead lungs.

"Two pale-robed emissaries riding here, directed by the will of Alyubol. The selfsame Alyubol you spoke of once, the one who was your father's enemy?" Palamon knelt beside the body but his words were directed toward Berengeria.

Berengeria nodded grimly. Her face drooped. She still held her slender fingers to her torn scalp.

Palamon paused to look up at her, then his face grew long and he rose as he noted her wound. "You have been hurt. I had not noticed that." He approached her, removed her hand from the crown of her head. It was an ugly mark and the blood flowed freely, irrigating the silky locks that surrounded it.

"A small wound, by my troth," she said. "Far better than the fate that was ordained when I was taken up by *his* foul hands." She jerked her head at the fallen rider and winced as Palamon examined her, picking bits of dirt out of her scalp.

He patted her on the shoulder and stepped back. "A tearing such as that may well cause strife, although the damage done at first is small. But thickly wooded forests such as this can often give us remedies for such infectious hurts." He rubbed his chin as he gazed between the knotted tree trunks. "One moment's all I'll need until we know." Walking away from the others, he reached a particularly shady place, bent, and plucked something from the lush undergrowth. While his companions watched, he returned with several broad leaves, dull green, thick, and fan shaped.

Aelia and Berengeria both looked at them. "And those will help?" Aelia asked doubtfully.

"Perhaps they will." He returned to Berengeria's side, folding one of the leaves and squeezing the juice into the wound. "These akos leaves, 'tis said, can help protect such rough, raw, open wounds."

Palamon could tell the fluids he was squeezing into the wound were bringing pain; he could feel Berengeria's breath on his throat as she gasped quietly. He regretted that. In a moment, having done with one leaf, he placed a second in his mouth, chewing it to make a poultice. "Now I must place this paste out of my mouth onto the open flesh, but do not fear. It does not smart, as does the sap itself." He glanced at Aelia, who was watching without comment. Then he smiled a wry smile. "But do not think me too impertinent. They say the spittle of the lowly dog can help to heal the very deepest cuts. No dogs have we, so I must fill that role."

Berengeria seemed reassured by Palamon's banter. Ursid also watched, fascinated. "Where did you learn these healing arts?"

"It does not matter." Palamon kneaded the chewed mass into place.

Ursid said no more but he still watched Palamon silently as the tall knight completed the ministration.

"Now, does it still hurt?" Palamon gave the poultice a final pat, then stepped back. Touching Berengeria had produced an inner tension which decreased some as he moved away from her buxom form. As he had noticed before, there was something about her he could not fully comprehend. When he had been touching her, he had again felt fate tugging at her, as if those forces were forming a field between the two of them. Fate and young women did not bode well; he knew that. It was all very disconcerting.

Berengeria looked up at him with a bemused smile. "It feels much better. Thank you, Palamon."

Abruptly, Palamon turned from her. "Now back to business." He handed the remaining leaves to Aelia. Walking back to Alyubol's slain minion, he grasped the handle of Aelia's dagger, which still protruded from the robes of the fallen rider. With a little effort, he wrenched it from the wound. There was a last blurting of gore from the man's chest and Palamon's mouth twisted in disgust as he wiped the blade clean on the coarsely woven white cloth. He handed the weapon up to its owner. "Then Alyubol is our opponent now, perhaps more so than Lothar and his men."

"How could he find us here?" Berengeria asked.

"Would that we knew." Palamon shifted to the fallen man's head and drew away the hood. The face beneath was sinister; the lips were thin, the nose was pinched and hooked, and the fine line of a closely trimmed black moustache accented the narrow upper lip. The skin was white

as a midnight moon. It was paler than ever, now that the
body encased within was dead; it was as pale as a fish
floating in a slough. It caused Palamon himself to blanch.
He looked up at the others. "One thing is sure: we must
be on our way." He rose, then gazed at the dead man's
mount. "We must attempt to minimize our loss. Perhaps
this horse should help to bear the load. Some goods and
one light rider it could bear, to speed us on our journey
by that much."

"'Tis said, 'tis done, O Pallas' noble Knight." Ursid
leaped forward to catch the animal by its reins and began
rearranging its saddle and pack. He stopped when he saw
the glare in Palamon's eyes. "What did I, Lord? I said
just what I heard and what's already shown by your own
armor, not to mention all your skill in nature's healing
balms."

Palamon looked down at himself. Only now did he
seem to notice that he had thrown off his gray cloak in
the heat of the fight against Alyubol's men. He looked at
the other members of the party. All of them were gazing
at him with expectant eyes; each face showed a different
emotion. Aelia appeared to be observing, waiting; Ursid
bore the look of a scolded schoolboy; Berengeria simply
watched the exchange, her fingertips touching the packing
Palamon had applied to her scalp a moment ago. Palamon
looked back at them one by one; then a wry expression
again crawled across his features.

A noise in the branches above them interrupted. As
one, they looked up to see a dark green shape flash from
view. "What was that?" Berengeria asked.

Palamon stared upward as he spoke. "It makes no difference what thing it might be. We must be on our guard
in any case, though it be Alyubol's foul thing or Lothar's
creature or a fiend that owes its loyalty to both or neither
one. But though it's just a bird or our next foe, I'll keep
my sword upraised where e'er I go." He touched the
pommel of his weapon, the molded section with the strange
piece of horn set into it, then leaned down to retrieve his
cloak. "And this is good material, withal. I'll wear it though

it's slashed along the back and mend it when the time and place allow."

Once again he wrapped himself in the cloak, though the links of his hauberk still glinted through the huge tear in the back. No one said a word until he himself broke the silence once more, to speak to Ursid. "Remember this, my youthful champion: a robe of lion skin fits quite as well about the shoulders of a craven cad as any noble warrior's stout form. When every man is judged just by his clothes, then kings and warriors alike will fall while low apprentice tailors conquer all." He walked to the bedrolls and packs and drew their longbows forth. "We may have cause to use these as we go."

Though they rushed through the process of burying the stranger and packing their gear onto the horse, much time passed before Aelia escorted Berengeria to the animal and watched as the young women placed one foot in the stirrup.

But to Aelia's surprise, Palamon stopped them. "My Lady, though it goes against the norm, 'tis best you ride upon this borrowed steed and let the good Princess remain aground with us."

Aelia was displeased. "What right have you, Sir Knight, to alter rank; to make princesses walk while servants ride?"

Palamon smiled. In fact his expression was more of a smirk than a smile, as if he were enjoying some private joke. "The right that's given by necessity. The fair Princess is young, a tall, strong maid, and she can cover ground much faster than your aged, though still comely, ankles can." He winked at her.

Aelia began to respond to the barbed refusal but Berengeria interrupted her. "And methinks there is wisdom in these words. Now, Aelia, come, climb up onto this steed and if your conscience frets you, bear in mind this animal belonged to Alyubol. Perhaps your riding it instead of me protects my royal body from some harm."

Aelia said no more. She allowed Ursid to help her into the saddle, where she sat uncomfortably, her mouth turned in distaste. With their eyes directed into the leafy canopy over their heads, the fugitives began their journey once more.

Although it was not without beauty, this forest had become exceedingly dense; the leafy branches of the trees spread above them without opening or end. But the verdant covering should have echoed with the chattering of birds and small animals. They heard nothing. Nor did they see any more of the dark shape they had seen in the morning. Palamon remained ready, holding his longbow with a keen arrow ready to nock at any sign of danger. The creature they had seen was large; there was no doubt of that. And since they were almost without horses, anything larger than a squirrel was a threat now.

Still, the day passed without event. In the afternoon, Ursid proved his prowess with his longbow, slaying with one shot a dwarf deer which sprang up at their approach. It was an animal of singular beauty. Its antlers had only begun to sprout tines for the new season; its skin was soft and smoothly covered instead of bristly in the manner of most deer hides.

They stopped while it was still light and cooked Ursid's kill. But as dusk came, Palamon bid them douse the blaze. "There's something in this forest we know not. A fire will dull the senses, blind the eyes, and make the task of watching through the night most difficult for us—but not for those who watch us, if there be such in these woods. Now we have supped till full, so kill this flame and let us post a double watch tonight."

Berengeria looked up at him. "A double watch? You fear the worst, I see."

"These woods seem full of visitors, Princess. If one should come to call on us unsought, it would not do to have that courtesy go unobserved by all of us save one."

"Then you still fear the work of Alyubol?"

Palamon shrugged. "I know of Alyubol by name, no more. But I know this: we fought two men this morn. We saw King Lothar's soldiers yesterday. We knew the hounds bayed hot upon our heels, but knew not till today there were two packs."

"I must agree," Aelia said. "But how do they pursue

so closely? If some great, all-seeing eye spied down on us, relaying all our acts to Lothar's ear, his men could not more quickly have appeared or trailed us with more ease than they have done."

"I don't agree." Palamon's face became serious for the moment. "Though Lothar's men came close, they did not seem to have the scent itself. We met a troop of pallid Lothar's guards beside the ford—the river crossing. That's their post. We watched another unit of the Buerdic guard go riding on a hillside, far, far off."

Palamon looked at Aelia and Berengeria. Their eyes showed agreement even before he had finished his analysis. "But those two riders who named Alyubol came down upon us at the break of dawn, set free our horses, drove them all away, and came close to capturing our fair Princess. By my eyes, these are foemen to be feared."

"Therefore, you see the hand of Alyubol." Berengeria nodded her head, her amber locks falling across the mantle of her robe. "My mind proceeds along your lines, Sir Knight."

"But if he traces out our path of flight, his powers must be mystical indeed." Aelia's face was covered with concern, even more than Palamon had already seen there.

"Then tell me, fair Princess," Palamon said, "Walk down the hallways of your memory. Do you remember anything of him, this Alyubol, some facts or recollections which might help us understand our foe and turn his strategies?

"Perhaps my memory would better serve," Aelia said. "This maid was just a tiny babe, no more, when she was sent from fair Carea's court to spend her childhood days in Artos' woods."

"Then spill your wisdom forth and let me lap it up, as would some scullery's gaunt cat if he could, with great fortune, come upon a broken milkmaid's bucket all alone."

Aelia glanced at Palamon without smiling, then began her story. "When I was just a girl, I met a priest who once had known this wicked Alyubol. It was long years ago, before the rise of good King Berevald, the father of our dear Princess.

"This priest, my friend, had studied in the halls of Upper Carea's great library and long had come to recognize this man who stood so high in Berevald's esteem. He was a young man then. His coal black hair and closeset, blazing eyes had such effect this priest could ne'er forget them all his life. He noticed, on occasion, Alyubol would search the building's archives for some scroll as some possessed, two-legged terrier would dig ground for a rat or for a mole.

"And once his prize was found, though it would be all caked in dust or writ in unknown tongues, this Alyubol would tuck it in his robe and hurry fast away. Sometimes he brought the borrowed document back to the great library, sometimes not. He was not disciplined. He had, you see, the favor of the Prince.

"This happened, as I said, long years ago, before the falling out of Alyubol with Berevald and all the children's loss. But though his memories preceded all these things, this priest declared their coming shocked him not. For he had seen the madness. Long it lurked behind the flashing eyes of Alyubol before it brought such sorrow to the land. It was miscalculation without end for Berevald to place the slightest trust in such an unsound man, however deft he was in unknown sciences and crafts." Her eyes flicked toward Berengeria. "My dear Princess, I mean no disrespect. I just repeat the story I was told."

Berengeria's voice was subdued. "My father is a good man, I know that. It was an error, as you say it was, to place his slightest trust in Alyubol, to raise him up in rank and give him place. To make of him an influential lord was folly in the most extreme degree. It also granted Alyubol e'en more—the opportunity to gather up the information and material, as well as cohorts and accomplices, to do that host of deeds most terrible for which he has been blamed. Be that the case, my father paid for his misplaced regard. He paid with all his slaughtered progeny, as well as with a land that groans beneath the blight of Alyubol. Methinks it price enough."

There was silence. Ursid placed his hand upon Berengeria's shoulder; his eyes were full of sympathy. It was plain to see the discussion had distressed her. Although she continued to smile with her mouth, that humor was not reflected in her manner. She placed her hand over Ursid's, but she seemed to derive little comfort from his gesture. "I stand alone," she said. "I am my father's sole remaining heir. I shall return to storm-bound Carea and help her raise herself from her nadir; this thing I vow, though it be on my life."

Again Palamon was struck by the resolve within the maiden. "Oh, my Princess, I have not mystic eyes to scry the riddles that your future holds, but methinks you will do the things you say. If Alyubol and Lothar are as awed as I am by your royal countenance and bearing, they will not dare say you nay."

"This vow made by our good Princess is brave," Ursid said. "It shows a soul as good and heart as strong as any knight's. To ridicule her words as you do now, brave Palamon, belittles both those words and you, as well."

For the merest fraction of an instant, Palamon appeared surprised at the severity of Ursid's words. Then he smiled and replied. "You must mistake my meaning. My respect for all who form this party knows no bounds, the most of all for this, our young Princess. But we need sleep. The stoutest heart will fail in its resolve without the body's aid. And I, not of stout heart, must still maintain that sleep comes best if we post double guard."

And so it was done. The four fugitives allowed the fire to burn down and the darkness gathered in on them as they sat. Eyelids soon grew heavy. Berengeria herself asked to stand the first watch; she felt no desire for sleep; her mind had not yet digested the portents of the day's events.

Palamon also watched. He sat comfortable, his back resting against a boulder as he stared into the darkness. Berengeria found herself watching him as he sat that way in the dim light of the dying blaze. He maintained his watch like a statue; his face was impassive, his breath came in a series of steady draughts, and his head hardly moved as his eyes bored into the night. Only occasionally did he turn his head to look in a different direction. But he never met her gaze.

Time crept by. The darkness became nearly complete. Still, they sat silently opposite one another, waiting for the movement of the stars to mark the time when they could wake their companions.

After a long while, Berengeria spoke. "You make a steadfast sentry, Palamon," she said. "How many nights, I wonder, have you passed encamped with Knights of Pallas on some quest?"

His eyes flicked toward her as she spoke, then he looked away once more. "So many nights lie in my past, Princess, that I could hardly concentrate on one."

"Or will not." She watched him the way she had seen Aelia watch people. He was hard to see in the darkness.

He smiled but he did not reply.

"I've noticed how you donjon up your past," she said. "My curiosity cannot but be aroused by all the things of which you will not speak."

"My past is mine," he replied. "It is of no import. Therefore, I do not choose to spew it up."

"It makes you all you are."

"And is that good?"

"I do not know." She was somewhat taken aback by his quick replies. "You taunt me, Palamon."

"You taunt yourself, Princess," he said. "I did not choose the subject of this conversation."

"Yes, that is so." She frowned. This tall knight did, after all, have the right to the privacy of his own past. But what was there about his past that required privacy? It would have pleased her to know more of the forge in which he had been produced. He was no ordinary warrior, whatever his past might have been. "You are a far cry from our own Ursid, who helped us to escape from Lothar's keep."

"I wish I had his youth."

"You wear age well."

"I would that there were less of it to wear."

His response made her smile. There was a pause as she looked in his direction in the darkness. She wished she could see him better—beneath this star-speckled sky, he was little more than a shapeless shadow in front of her.

"You are aware," he said, "this gallant young Ursid loves you quite deeply?"

Unlike his last statement, this one did not cause her to smile. This time it was she who glanced away into the darkness. "Yes."

"And he has cast himself from favor, aiding your escape?"

"Yes." She formed the word with difficulty.

"Do you, in any part, reciprocate this love he bears for you?" Palamon spoke with the tone of one who was making the simplest query in the world. The same tone of voice could have been used to inquire about the weather or some masque held the week before.

A long pause followed that question. No answer came until Berengeria said, "I like him very much. His heart is good." There was a kind of reluctant tone to her words; it was obviously not easy for her to frame even this enigmatic answer.

"Some subjects lie too near the heart by far to be bled out by idle chatter," Palamon said. "Please forgive me, good Princess. I'll ask no more."

Berengeria gazed at the dark, damp ground at her feet. "I see your meaning."

"Then shall we declare a truce?"

She nodded, though she doubted he could see the gesture in the darkness left by the extinguished fire. Then she sighed. "Ursid does make a fair, courageous knight. I like him well—but sometimes what we do is forced upon us by necessity."

"Indeed," he said. "The altar of necessity is quite a brutal one. Each one of us must sacrifice upon it, now and then. But still, Ursid's conditions for my own I would exchange."

Berengeria looked up at the tall knight, almost hidden from her by the darkness. There was a real note of longing in his words. "I doubt you mean that."

"You're quite correct. I mean it not at all." His tone

was light again, somewhat flippant. The wistful note she had detected for that instant was gone." Trust not the words of knights, my good Princess. Too many maidens learn, to their dismay, some knights ride more by darkness than by day."

Chapter Eight:
Green as Caterpillars

IT WAS MORNING in the forest. The adventurers sat huddled together in the predawn chill, finishing off the deer killed by Ursid the day before. There was little speech. Hardly a sound of any kind was to be heard, in fact.

There was dew everywhere. It dripped from the silent trees and their only horse shook showers of it from the tussocks of grass he was ripping up. His hearty breathing and the sound of each mouthful of turf he tore from the floor of the clearing were all they could hear.

When they started out again, Palamon held his longbow ready, searching the branches with each step. There! There in the fog twenty cubits ahead of them. "What was that?" Palamon's eyes attempted to burn holes through the thick vapors.

"My eyes find nothing in this cursed fog. What was it that you saw, O Palamon?" Ursid also stopped.

"The eyes are clumsy servants, that is true. But I still think I spied a small, two-legged form. It's gone, now."

"Which way should we pursue? Perhaps a lucky shot

might bring it down." Ursid's voice became urgent in the damp air.

"It's folly to go hunting at my words. Perhaps I see things just to lead you on." Palamon gave Ursid a wry smile as he spoke. "My vision is not error free, Ursid. I make mistakes. Still, we must keep a watch."

Ursid gazed at the older knight a moment, then began walking once more. They did not see anything more of the little figure Palamon saw, or thought he saw. By noon, the sun had burned the fog away. They paused to drink at a watercourse that tumbled toward the southwest, then turned and followed it, for the terrain was rough and hilly.

More than once, Palamon noticed the furtive glances directed at him by Ursid. They made him feel ill-at-ease, then uncomfortable; finally he spoke to the younger man about it. "You might be wiser to direct your eyes at dangers to your own Princess, my lad. You cannot spy them gazing just at me."

Ursid bridled at being chided this way; his manner was defensive. "I cannot help it. Palamon, your cloak reveals some things in you—though you still try to hide them from us—I cannot explain. I cannot help but wonder..."

"Wonder, then. You all have wondered at me till my ears rebel to hear it spoken of again. If my old hauberk so excites all folk, perhaps I ought to bury it. Have done. But wonder not when you should cross the path of some foul viper which, with wondrous scales, can trick your eyes from seeing foul intent. I've said it oft; this mail means nothing." Palamon's lips curled as he spit out the last word. "Nothing."

"But all the same..." Ursid was interrupted again as a section of rude vine netting fell over him. He struggled frantically against its entangling folds. "By heaven, what is this?"

Palamon caught his breath and his eyes swept the branches from which the netting had dropped. There was nothing to be seen. The thick foliage concealed any possible target from his longbow, so he dropped that weapon and his hands flew to the back of his neck, releasing the clasp that secured his sword. But it was only halfway out of its hanger when he himself was struck by another section of netting, the weight of which forced him nearly to his knees. His stout blade glinted above his head as he slashed his way free.

But he had no time to free Ursid; more nets were falling. The strong netting was made from plant fibers woven together, then tied into squares like the nets used by the fishermen across the Thlassa Mey. The nets fell from the leaf draped branches as though conjured. Aelia was caught by one; her horse reared and ran. The netting about her caught on a branch and she was dragged from her mount to dangle, helpless as a fresh catch of fish.

Berengeria was borne to the ground. So was Ursid. Now only Palamon was left standing, the severed remains of two of the mysterious nets lying at his feet. Then, dropping from the branches some twenty cubits away, their antagonists appeared: these were small and apelike and the thick hair that covered all their exposed parts was green. They were green as caterpillars.

The creatures stared at him, shouting to one another. Their accent was so strange they were barely understandable but there was no mistaking their intentions. They approached cautiously, waving clubs, spears, and all kinds of rude weapons. He heard a sound behind him. More of the creatures had dropped from branches and were approaching him from that direction.

The situation was hopeless. The little green apemen attacked from everywhere with the wile and confidence that came from long experience at the hunt. One of them let fly at Palamon's head with a club and he ducked, only to feel a hairy body hurl itself against his legs. More assailants rushed him and he slashed out once with his sword, the long blade glinting fiercely. But he was unable to free his ankles; he felt himself losing his balance. The little men were all over him now. Hard, bony fingers clutched at him. One of the creatures struck his head with a stone and the blow made him groggy, even as he caught the thing in its leathery face with one elbow. A knotted club struck him, then another stone. And another. He could no longer keep track of what was happening to him or even where he was. His world was blanketed by darkness.

A great deal of time passed; at least it seemed that way. Palamon's skull was full of visions; a multitude of tiny, hairy creatures leaped and shouted and leered at him out of the darkness. His body was bounding up and down as if he were being tossed into the air in a blanket. It was an odd feeling. It was almost like being on the deck of a vessel in a storm with the mighty, black-and-white waves tossing the ship about helplessly. He was rocking back and forth, rocking, rocking.

Many things passed through his mind—the old days of training with swords and lance in the inner bailey of the Fastness of Pallas and the nights spent pondering a carved piece of horn with the word "blood" inscribed upon it; he went on quests, riding his broad courser into the northlands; he took ship to right wrongs in the pirate-infested streets of Touros; he won honor and glory.

But the visions soured. Something had happened to ruin everything, to turn the respect into loathing and the honor and glory into shame. He burned with the shame. What had happened? Where was he and what had brought this foulness into his life? He was being spat upon by his peers and he could not remember why. It was there. The memory was there, if only he could grasp it. Then he did grasp the memory; he remembered everything and the bitterness washed over him, drowning him in a caustic comber of putrid memories; it was worse by far than the blackness and confusion that had enveloped him earlier.

His eyes opened. It was still daylight. His body rang with stiffness and he was wadded up like old paper in one of the fiber nets of the apemen who had attacked earlier. He was dangling from a tree now, along with the other members of the party. That was better. At least he knew where he was.

He turned his head to look about. This was difficult; his chin was forced against his chest by the curve of the net and he winced as he twisted his neck. He could see the others, however. They had been netted and hung up the same as he had. They were all hanging from the limbs of broad trees that spread overhead like the ceiling of a great, green cathedral. This part of the forest was even thicker and older than the area where they had been captured; the trees were taller and the branches were great, knotty things that clutched vast fans of leaves the way sinuous hands would have grasped fistfuls of plumage.

Berengeria was gazing back at him, her face puffy and red. "Alas, Sir Palamon. You fought so well but now you hang on high, as do we all."

"How now, Princess? Where are we? How far have we come?"

"These creatures carried us at least a league, as hunters carry bags of fresh-caught game. I don't know where we are."

"We traveled south from where they captured us." This last voice came from Palamon's other side and it belonged to Aelia.

Palamon strained again as he rotated his painfully curved neck to look in her direction. He could also see Ursid hanging from the next tree. "Our captors, Lady. Whereto have they gone?"

"I do not know. They marched into the trees. They numbered many, swarming like green bees."

"Ursid; does he still live?"

Aelia shifted within her net, making the leaves above her rustle. She gazed at the younger knight, then twisted back until she again faced Palamon. "I think he lives. His body sways with life-supporting breath, although he makes no sound."

"Good." Palamon twisted, trying to roust the stiffness that cried out from every joint. He could not do it, so he hung quietly once more. He wondered where their captors had disappeared to.

As if to answer his unspoken question, a rustling in the brush beyond Ursid's dangling net betrayed the approach of two pairs of feet. By craning his neck about, Palamon was able to study the creatures as they approached. They were slender and wiry, like children grown from the tough bark of these trees. And although their steps were light and quick enough, they were bent as an old man would have been bent from the weight of the years upon him—or as a young man would have been bent by hanging head downward in a net. Bent as they were, it was difficult for Palamon to see their faces.

They walked toward him, glancing at Ursid and Aelia as they passed the first two nets. The two were talking to one another but it was hard to understand them. Reaching Palamon's net, one of them poked at the tall knight with a small walking staff and gazed at him silently for a moment. Palamon could see the fellow's face now; it was an interesting sight.

The skin of the face was light and leathery; it was a green face that was wrinkled as if every morning the creature had ever seen had left its own tiny fissure etched into the flesh of his cheek or brow. The eyes were dark, with a quick gleam that belied the look of age stamped across the rest of the body. Once again the creature poked at Palamon with the staff, pausing between pokes to adjust his breechclout.

"How now, old man. Am I some bag of meat, that you must tenderize me with your stick?"

The two bent creatures glanced at one another and the one with the staff jabbed upward once more. Palamon did not speak this time. Again they looked at each other before one of them spoke. "You are a mighty fighter, tall one, but we have you now."

They turned toward Aelia, the thick green hair on their arms and legs rustling as they moved, their leather breechclouts rocking as they stepped forward upon their bandy legs. They stopped and studied her, speaking in low tones. Then they walked away. At least they did not prod her with the staff.

After they had gone, Ursid stirred and looked about. "What were those things? Have any of you looked on such a people as those creatures? By the gods themselves, they're not a favored race, to judge by gait and face."

Palamon looked at Ursid and at Aelia. "'Tis well, young knight, that you are with us now. A happy crew we are and topsy-turvy we must meet our fate, though such be at the hands of this 'unfavored race,' as you may term them."

There was movement in the net on the other side of Palamon and he turned to look at Berengeria. "They fear you, Palamon," she said. "That much I know. They fear you and they don't know what to do with all of us, now that they have us here."

"Then there is hope they don't know who we are." Ursid said.

"Their words would indicate that was the case," Aelia said. "'Tis sure, if they were linked with Lothar's men, they'd know what prizes hung within their grasp."

"Yes, that is so." Ursid sounded disappointed.

Berengeria joined the conversation then; there was a desperate note of hope in her voice. "Then should we speak with them when they come back? Perhaps a bargain might be struck with them—some price or favor offered in return for our four freedoms."

"Not yet, not yet." Palamon's answer was quick. "Although it's true they may not be allied with enemies, they still are not our friends. Our silence must be kept until we know a bit more of their minds. For oft 'tis said, 'an army of regrets, by one word led.'"

No sooner did this caution leave Palamon's lips than the creatures returned, followed by two of their fellows. And there was movement in the branches above the heads of the four captives; the leaves shook and danced and the smaller limbs swayed as if an army of apes might have been passing overhead. But though eight human eyes sifted the foliage, hardly a single body was to be seen.

The four creatures stood looking up at their prizes, conversing in low tones. One of them shook his head. Another spoke back with a rising voice, gesturing with his knotty stick at Palamon. "Four are too many. The wisdom of four is greater than the wisdom of one, or even two. At least *he* should wait to go alone."

The one addressed shook his head again. "That is not in the law." The four of them moved closer to the prisoners. The one that had done the head shaking appeared to be a figure of authority, even though they were all dressed in the same type of leather garments; the others followed where he walked and attended whenever he spoke.

Indeed, so strange were the patterns and rhythms of their speech that Palamon had to concentrate to comprehend them at all. But then the leader issued an order which was easy to understand. "Come down, come down, my brothers of the trees. These tall ones are in our hands; their weapons have been made dull by our nets. It is time for their trial to begin."

He made a sweeping gesture with both hands and the thick canopy above their heads began to seethe with movement. The branches emptied. Hairy green bodies dropped from the foliage as chestnuts drop in a late autumn storm. There were dozens of the green beings; they stood looking up at the nets that hung heavy with their captives.

Had the leader spoken of a trial? While the prisoners were pondering that, another command was issued. Several of the creatures crept like spiders onto the limbs that supported the four nets. The rope connected to Palamon's net was severed and he felt himself falling, only to rebound upward on a sea of rough hands. It was an odd feeling. The handling was not unpleasant as he was borne along, passed from hands to hands toward the center of a large clearing.

He glimpsed many things—endless rows of trees and underbrush, the leafy canopy passing overhead, then a cloud-smeared sky as he was carried into the clearing itself. He could hear the pop of cordage and the rebound of branches as his companions were also cut down. Then he heard Aelia's voice. "How dare you people do this thing to us who only seek to pass these lands in peace? We have no quarrel here. Please set us free."

The procession stopped. There was silence at first, then one of the creatures spoke. "You have trespassed onto the lands of the Korred wudlings, the brotherhood of the branches." The one who said this was the same individual Palamon had identified as the leader. All movement, human and wudling, paused and all ears listened to that voice, which was harsh with age. "For days we have watched you penetrate into our hills. You have fought your own kind in our lands and you have killed our game. Now it is time for you to be dealt with."

"We meant no harm," Aelia said. "We only wish to leave."

"Down the ages since the first waves rolled across the Thlassa Mey, you tall ones have followed the wudling people. Never have you meant us harm, yet always we have died. Once we were plentiful. We spread across the land from the Outer Islands to the southern snowfields. The land was ours but we were always forced to yield to your advances. With your broad weapons you drove us back until finally, long ago, tall men took the last of the lands where we once had lived and forced us into this corner of the wilderness. Our wise ones have set these things down so that we might remember them."

Palamon tried to reply, but he was stopped by those who held him; hairy hands clamped his mouth; his hair was pulled, and he was punched and pummeled. The wudlings' leader continued. "We have learned the lessons of past ages; where a few tall ones come, many will follow. None who enter these hills may pass forth again, for they will bring others as surely as flies bring maggots. You have only one hope. You must survive your trial. I, Parso, have spoken."

"Wait. Do not paint us with the selfsame brush with which you tar our enemies." Aelia's protest was choked off.

The procession started up again. Then all at once Palamon was dumped onto the ground. He winced and his stiff muscles shrieked with the impact; still, he managed to turn his head enough to watch Ursid, Berengeria, and Aelia as they were deposited next to him. They were surrounded by their captors. Everywhere there were small, angular bodies. Unsteadily, his muscles barely obeying his will, Palamon rose from his open net. Many of the wudlings shrank back from him, while others raised clubs, spears, and slings. He looked down at the one called Parso. "Just set us free and you will not be harmed. We only wish to journey from this place."

Parso pointed a finger at Palamon. "You are a powerful warrior, tall man. No five of us can stand against you. But if you or any of your people move to escape before your time, or try to harm any hair on any one of us, you will die like a wolf in a pit." With a final wave of his arm the leader ended the conversation. Several armed wudlings surrounded the captives. Then, as if at a signal, the crowd behind them parted and they turned to see the place to which they had been brought.

They were in a clearing. At the center of the clearing, rising from the rich earth like a tower, stood a huge tree. It was different from—and far taller than—any of the other trees in this forest. It soared toward the heavens, its upper reaches obscured by its lowest branches, its full grandeur hidden from all save the birds and the sun above. But those unseen heights did not hold Palamon's attention; his eyes were drawn to the base of the great plant.

The tree did not stand with its roots buried far beneath the floor of the glade, but rather upon a huge pedestal formed by those roots. They radiated out from the bottom of the trunk, forming a large, bell-shaped chamber surrounded by sinuous stems. It was a spectacular sight—but for what purpose they had been brought here, Palamon was only beginning to understand.

The wudlings all became silent. A singsong chant drew Palamon's eyes back to the leader of these strange people; Parso had closed his eyes tightly, and his leathery fingers were extended toward the tree itself. Palamon sensed what was about to happen; his eyes traveled back to the great tree with fascinated horror. Already, the fibrous roots were beginning to pulsate with new life. They moved and undulated like wooden serpents. Then, even as he watched, they bent and stretched, and an opening large enough to admit a body appeared in the wall of roots nearest the captives.

Before he could react, Palamon found himself set upon by dozens of wudlings. He was kicked and rolled through the opening and into the space formed within the tree's roots, followed quickly by the others. Last came Aelia, shoved through the opening while still protesting to the wudling who was conducting this bizarre ceremony. Then, more suddenly than it had appeared, the opening snapped shut.

Most of the wudlings lingered for a moment to stare at the captives, and the leader approached and looked disdainfully in upon them. "This is your prison, tall ones. You will stay here until the time you come out. If you ever do." He turned to depart and the others of his kind trickled after him. After awhile the captives found themselves alone again, imprisoned within the base of a tree, of all places.

Aelia looked at Palamon, the lines in her face etched deep with concern. "They fear us and they fear you, Palamon. They seal us here because they fear us all."

Palamon smiled grimly. "And we must find a way to leave this cage." He stood, bowing his head to avoid the rooty ceiling of the chamber, rubbing his hands and arms, for they were still stiff from the time spent inside a wudling net. "How long, I wonder, shall we be mewed up?"

"Where is our trial and what will be our test?" Aelia watched Palamon as he paced across their living cell. "As you could hear, their leader, Parso, said we shall stay here until the time rolls 'round that we come out. Perhaps this is our trial, is it not?"

"But why then place us here?" Ursid asked. He had also been rubbing the stiffness from his limbs, but he could still labor to his feet only with difficulty. "We have no fight with them; there is no need for this imprisonment."

Palamon smiled as he peered at Ursid, looking at the youthful face which was crisscrossed by shadows from the roots. The older knight's finely crafted mail peeked through the rips in his mourning cloak as he spoke. "How often has one branch of humankind required a reason for some action keen, brought down upon the head of one of its supposed foemen? Have you not yourself fought gamely in some joust or heated fray against some knight you did not even know? It seems to be the common pestilence of foolish man; he fights with shadows of the things he fears while all the monsters he would best confront still leer and gibber at him, mocking him from someplace just beyond his lantern's light."

Palamon paused to peer out at the empty clearing. "One thing—no more—can we be sure of now. Though all these many captors seem quite strange, it is our consolation—danger, too—that their humanity can never be denied. They nicely qualify for it, by that condition I have just described."

Ursid was brought up short by this sudden monologue. He had no answer. But after a moment, Berengeria did speak, breaking the silence with a soft voice. "Perhaps it is an empty fear I feel, but it is still an honest fear, withal. In back of all these acts, I seem to find the cunning, waiting arm of Alyubol." She shuddered as she spoke. Aelia approached her and placed a hand gently upon her shoulder.

"Princess," Aelia said, "while we can understand your fears, our new predicament indeed does seem to have an isolated source, I think. The wudlings fear us, that much is made plain. Through all their speech that I could understand, there ran one common strain and that was this: the tall men drove them out, the tall men killed their sons, the tall men are all bad. We are no better in their childlike eyes than Lothar and his men. They hate us all."

Ursid paused as if struck by a sudden thought. "That little wudling, Parso, said this was a trial, but mayhap 'tis a test. Perhaps these wudlings, as they term themselves, intend to keep us here till we break free. Perhaps their strategy's to let us starve or perish out of thirst unless we can assert ourselves, strike out, and force this place. Perhaps the sooner we begin to dig or force our way beyond these woody walls, the sooner we'll be free and on our way."

"I think not." During the exchange of words, Palamon had been pacing about the low chamber, peering out between the roots, feeling their rough surfaces, and examining the living overhead of their cell. "I believe to force these walls would have just one result—our instant deaths."

This was a statement calculated to garrote a conversation. Ursid turned to look at Palamon, nonplussed. "What do you say?" To judge by their shocked expressions, either of the women could have made the utterance as easily.

"Have you not noticed that there is no thing, no beast or vermin, insect, rat, or roach here, sheltered with ourselves?"

"Most surely I have not," Ursid replied. "But yet that's just as well. I've no desire to share this living cell with any vermin, lonely though we be."

This time Palamon did not respond to Ursid's joke with a jest of his own. He was deadly serious. This fact unnerved the younger man as much as the older warrior's words.

"Look just between these roots before me here," the tall knight said. "Note how they stand more thickly in this place than, say, upon the side opposing this?"

"I note it."

"Your eye is good. Now look down at the middle of these roots, just where they cluster thickest. Look in there. Peer in and tell us all what you can see."

Ursid did as he had been told to. His eyes glistened as he peered between the wooden bars of the unique prison. Then he started. "Methinks I see a human skull in there."

"Indeed you do, still covered up with hair." Palamon pointed to help the younger man make out what he himself had carefully observed. "The skeleton still lies there in the shade. It's hidden by dead leaves and nitrous mold and just behind it lies another. So—two men attempted crawling from this place. But contemplate their forms. The roots all press about them on the sides and probe between the bones like tentacles. Those fellows tried escape and were impaled and pinned onto the ground by living cords that must have grown most riotously, exterminating them by horrid means." Palamon gathered his cloak around his arm, struck a heavy root, then jumped back.

Instantly their living prison writhed into frenzied action. Vile moisture boiled from pores in the wood and glided across the surface; tendrils bristled forth, piercing the space Palamon had occupied only an instant before. The tendrils lengthened and became ropes; the ropes groped relentlessly for something solid. And over all, the tree shuddered and vibrated, causing the ground itself to tremble as the plant searched for its victim.

Ursid shuddered at the sight. Berengeria sank to her knees with Aelia's arms still about her. "The very gods conspire to keep us from our goal."

Palamon watched silently as the frustrated vegetation finally abandoned its search for him and the empty tendrils dangled, still throbbing. "Not so, but we must all conspire ourselves if we're to hope we ever reach that goal."

"What can we do?"

"We wait. We watch. We've time enough for some key to be found. Perhaps your enemies may aid you yet; be sure pale Lothar seeks you still."

Berengeria's eyes fell. "I'd rather perish here than be his slave and once again be used against my will to aid his country's rape of my own land. Should he come here, these roots will have their feast."

There was no weakness in her voice; she issued the statement as a plain, although unpleasant, fact. Palamon gazed at her. How could anyone fail to admire such resolve, though he might not agree with her intent? "Fear not, brave lady. Such o'erlooking gods as do not note so firm a will as yours would seem to me to be harsh gods, indeed." As Palamon spoke, he noticed that Aelia also looked into Berengeria's eyes, her tapered hands supporting the younger woman protectively. It was a touching moment, one that even a Knight of Pallas might have yearned to be a part of—physical contact as a means to communicate affection, sympathy, and support. Palamon thought better of the notion, however, and it quickly passed.

Chapter Nine:
A Rescue

THE HOURS DRAGGED by; the afternoon passed and darkness came. Night brought the wudlings back into the clearing. Some half dozen of the green jailers bore torches to the great tree; the torchlight cast capricious shadows into the interior of the cell as the wudling chief, Parso, approached to peer between the roots, his wrinkle-tracked face distorted by the dancing light.

For several moments, Parso observed his captives. He said nothing. Then he turned away, waving his companions ahead of him as if they had been so many children. But before he had gone far, Aelia called after him. "Wait." He ignored her and she repeated herself. "Wait."

The hairy little man turned, his angular features showing what would have been annoyance on any face. "No speeches will set you free, tall woman. The trial must run its course."

"And there's no time that you might let us go?" Aelia asked.

He shrugged. The gesture was ludicrous when made

by the green, apelike body. "You will remain here. The trial will give us all the answer to that question."

"I tell you we are sought by cruel men," she said. "A tyrant, Lothar, also called the Pale, has set his forces hot upon our heels. You must release us. If his cavalry should find us here, they'll slaughter your own people as they deal with us."

His face showed no expression. "Tall men are tall men. If any others follow you, we will deal with them in our own way. You will remain here until you come out." He turned and walked away, his torch marching into the darkness.

Aelia slumped down in silence. Palamon could hear the soft sound of her breathing; he needed hear no more to understand her disappointment at the failure of her entreaties.

"Will we die here, I wonder? Comes a time when they will set us free?" Berengeria's voice was a whisper in the darkness.

"And every moment lost is Lothar's victory." Ursid's tone was quiet and Palamon noted the mutter of regret in the young knight's words. Doubtless the youth rued his rashness in aiding Berengeria, now that he was held helpless while the hounds of Lothar the Pale bayed ever more closely. He was to be pitied. Whatever he might have felt now, this young gallant, it was too late for him to undo his actions. He would be forced to live or die with the result.

"Alas, alas." These words were also spoken quietly; they were little more than a sigh from Berengeria's lips.

Conversation died away. Into the night the captives sat huddled together in the darkness at the center of the living cell, waiting, listening, listening. From the dense forest outside came no sound other than the cry of a far-off wolf and the occasional buzz of a bat in flight. Of the usual symphony of insects, toads, and other small creatures one would have expected to hear in such a place, there was no note.

The night passed dismally. The tree occasionally creaked as its upper branches were disturbed by a breeze;

a member of the party snored or sighed in his sleep. The wudlings stayed away.

At last a subtle shifting of the shadows outside the wooden cage signaled the first wakings of dawn. Palamon watched it come. Peering through the roots, he noted the approach of Parso, along with a pair of other wudlings. Their bowed legs moved them across the leafy floor of the glade with surprising quickness. Palamon shook Ursid awake while Aelia did the same for Berengeria, although more quietly.

The wudlings came to the great tree. Parso peered in between the roots and said something to Aelia, who had been the one to speak to him the night before. Aelia responded to the whispers sullenly; she had slept little during the night. Looking past the two of them, Palamon noticed that day had come to the clearing, and it was once more filling up with little green apemen. The wudlings approached from between the shadowy trunks of trees or dropped down from the leafy branches, seeming as much at ease scurrying along knobby limbs as along the flat ground.

They gathered about the great tree. Conversation buzzed through the clearing as they gathered about, peering in at the prisoners. At length Parso turned and addressed all who could hear him, speaking in measured tones with his arms upraised as though he were chanting a memorized verse. "The tall ones are alive. Their term has passed away and now they must go, according to the law and custom of our people. They have survived the night within the tree and by that they have shown us they might someday learn something of our ways. By our laws they will be freed."

The speech produced a mixed reaction. Some of the wudlings stood silently while many others grumbled or even voiced open disapproval. The protest built into a storm. "Another night must be passed," shouted one of the wudlings.

"More will come. They cannot be allowed to go," cried another. "The trial was wrongly done."

Aelia's face betrayed fear at the opposition to the leader's words. She stood to address the wudlings from within the tree. "If we have satisfied your ancient laws, then you must free us. We must be away." This was a mistake, however: the wudlings closest to the tree snarled disapproval and some picked up sticks from the forest floor, shaking them menacingly.

Ursid touched her on the arm. "Do not advise them, for it seems your pleading words incite them more."

Parso spoke again, trying to quell his angry people. They were like a green sea of hatred seething on the floor of the clearing. They glared at the captives; some made angry speeches, and a few even hurled objects at the tree. With each impact, the living prison vibrated more and the roots twitched and danced with the increasing hostility of the crowd.

"An ugly mob," Palamon said quietly. "It's easy to discern why other men have not survived their 'trials.' And till this passion fades, the closest thing to safety in my eyes is huddled in the center of this place. At all events, we must avoid the roots."

Ursid glared at the milling wudlings. "By all the gods, I wish we could do more."

"Until we can, we must preserve ourselves by what small means we have." Palamon pulled Ursid tightly against him as he stood with his head bowed in the low, dark space beneath the bole of the great tree. Aelia and Berengeria joined them. Outside, the crowd milled and bickered with all eyes riveted upon the four captives.

Then something happened. There was another commotion, this one centering at the rear of the mob on one side of the clearing. Screams attracted attention. Looking in that direction, Palamon saw an unexpected sight: arrows were singing into the glade. There was more screaming, the wudlings began to panic, a trumpet call sounded from nearby.

The erstwhile captors scattered from the clearing. Some of them scrambled away from the trumpet call, others faded into spaces between the trees themselves, many vaulted nimbly up trunks and into the leafy branches.

In half a moment, the clearing was empty, save a half

dozen dead or writhing wudling bodies and Parso himself. The wrinkled old leader stood for an instant, contemplating the prisoners with a quizzical expression; then he scurried from the area as nimbly as any of his fellows.

The trumpet sounded once more, and horses appeared between the trees. Berengeria groaned at the sight of them; they were ridden by armed men who wore the purple-and-gold capes of Lothar the Pale's cavalry.

Palamon noticed Berengeria's reaction and quickly grasped her by the arms. She fought to free herself, throwing her body this way and that, trying to jerk away from him. "Release me, Palamon. 'Tis best I die within these cursed roots."

"I know your mind but still you must keep on. No matter what may pass, you still have life and can devise a scheme for new escape. To die requires no courage in a heart; it's life's own tortures toward which we gird. Your suffering is a privilege, withal, for one can only suffer while he lives." He held her firmly until Aelia and Ursid could aid him. Then he released the struggling maiden. "My pardon, for I fear your arms are bruised."

Berengeria despaired of fighting her way free. She collapsed into Aelia's arms, sobbing bitterly. Palamon turned away, his ears afflicted by the sounds of her grief as well as Aelia's whispers as she soothed her charge. He watched the approach of the warriors instead.

There were over twenty mounted men. Some of them climbed down from their horses and went about the business of dispatching the fallen wudlings while the rest rode toward the great tree, suspiciously eyeing the occupants.

One of the horsemen dismounted and peered keenly between the roots. As a clasp for his dew-stained cape, he wore the sword-and-shield insignia, marking him as an officer in King Lothar's light cavalry. His expression was hard as chert as his gaze passed over the four of them. His eyes lingered upon Berengeria. "Good day, Princess. It is with happiness I look upon your unharmed form. Have patience, please, and soon my men will have you free from this great tree's embrace."

Berengeria had calmed herself enough to face him; she

returned his gaze with one even colder. "How much I find that I prefer the company of all these wudlings you have driven off to yours, or any minion's of Buerdaunt. My body only shall you carry back to Buerdaunt's gate. For by my soul, I'll make that journey only as a stiffened corpse."

The officer's expression did not change. "Rest easily, I have good men with me. They shall prevent unpleasant accidents." He placed a nasty accent on the last word, then allowed his gaze to pass to Aelia. "My Lady, you have caused us much concern. Intrigue no more on burden of your life, for though the good Princess is to survive her journey to Buerdaunt, no one had placed a limitation such as that on you."

At the sight of Ursid, a long breath escaped his lips. "And you, Ursid. This makes quite plain the means by which this grand escape was made. Young man, you stood in high esteem in Lothar's court but on return I wager you shall find yourself in some more fitting place: perhaps the headman's axe or molten lead or else the rack or wheel shall be your fate." Finally, his gaze rested upon Palamon. "And as for you, your place in this is small. Your execution shall be quick and just."

Palamon smiled and nodded. "My thanks to you. Such kindness lives within your noble heart my faulty tongue can scarcely give it shape."

The officer's eyes narrowed. "What's that you wear?"

"A shabby, badly torn, gray woolen cloak."

"Below the cloak, I mean, as you well know. Such chain mail ne'er is seen but on few men. One class of knight alone may don those links. This makes me think of stories I have heard; fair Pallas' Knights do not conceal themselves without due cause." He paused, assaying Palamon with glinting eyes. "I think I know you, man. If so, your execution should be welcome—kind release from your most painful shame."

He strode away. Ursid touched Palamon's shoulder. "What did he mean? Why did he speak that way?"

Palamon laughed and shrugged his shoulders. "I know him not; he does not speak of me. So many legends ring the Thlassa Mey, a man can quote one for each unknown face."

Aelia interrupted. "What shall we do? My wits are at end."

"Fear not, my Lady. One misfortune now can serve to cover up another's harm." Palamon gestured toward the living bars of their prison. "They cannot haul us back unto Buerdaunt until we're loosed from here beneath this tree."

Aelia made an impatient sound and eyed Palamon coldly. "I cannot understand you. Your best cheer seems ever close upon the heels of foulest fortune."

"So it always goes. And with good cause—no gloom can I maintain, my Lady; you have got it all."

The cavalry officer returned to the tree, accompanied by a man who carried bundles in his arms. They stopped at the margin of the roots and the officer spoke once more. "Perhaps you have not breakfasted as yet; therefore I bring you some provisions. Good wine, dried meats and fruits and hardtack biscuits, all are yours. Dine well."

"We have not supped at all since yesterday," Ursid said.

The officer turned to his subordinate. "Then draw your weapon, sirrah; hew a path through these accursed weeds. We'll soon remove these individuals and feed them all. I hope I may assume, my fair Princess, that you will promise on your honor not to flee once this is done."

"Assume as you may wish. I'll flee from you as soon as opportunity allows."

The officer bowed stiffly. "So, madam, as you please. It matters not. Some cord about your ankles will suffice as well as any vow." Again he turned to the man beside him. "Now use your sword. Hack out a path, and we will pluck them forth."

The soldier did as he had been ordered; his blade described a glinting arc and sliced into one of the great tree's roots. The plant responded violently. The sword was dragged from the soldier's fingers by tendrils that appeared from nowhere and he screamed in agony as the flesh of his arm was pierced by a living dagger of wood lancing forth from an adjoining root. The man wrenched himself free of his impalement, spun about, and sank to his knees, weeping and clutching the disabled member.

The enraged tree trembled through its entire height. Berengeria shrank into Palamon's arms and the four prisoners clung to one another in the center of the shadowy, pulsating chamber.

The officer's face lengthened and grew pale. He gazed up at the soaring heights that shook and quivered above him, the lines in his face growing dark as rain. He hardly seemed to notice his crippled man as the fellow rose and staggered toward the aid of his companions. "What sort of devil's magic have we here?"

"You have the reason we have not escaped," Aelia said. "How can you think we'd not have wriggled out unless this tree possessed some mystic power to counteract our aims? The wudlings you so rudely drove away alone possess the art to set us free."

"So that may be or so it may not be." The officer studied the tree and its roots for a moment. "But there is not an object made of wood, though diabolical, that cannot burn."

Aelia's face filled with scorn. "Consider the reception you will have at Lothar's court when you return the news your hostages were strangled by this growth. You must be foolish if you really think it will not wreak its vengeance horribly on those within its power when it feels the first caress of flames. You silly man."

For the first time, the officer lost some of his confidence. His lips formed a tight line. He stood glaring the tree, his hands upon his hips and his purple-and-gold cape spreading out behind him. "Then very well. There are more mysteries than those within this tree. King Lothar holds onto the loyalty of one you may not know, who wields mysterious powers and dark art without a parallel in all the world. This wizard's minion journeys here e'en now. I do not welcome him; I like him not. But he can master this o'erreaching plant and wring you from its clutches, by my faith."

Aelia's voice nearly failed her as she spoke. "This minion in your service, does he wear a robe of white? And does he ride a jet black mount? And doesn't he respond when called 'Navron?'"

The cavalry officer looked at her for a moment. "He wears white—but I do not know his name. The truth to tell, my Lady, he has sent us to this very place to seek you out. I do not know his information's source; he tells us where to go and what we'll find. He stated he would meet us at this place. When we have made your capture, he will come."

Ursid interrupted. "And will he come before we die of thirst? Before this tree has starved our souls from us?"

"He will arrive before the break of dawn." The officer looked the captives over one last time without further comment. Then he turned upon his heel and strode away, waving at a pair of his men. "I want you men to set a watch at once."

Aelia turned to Palamon, her eyes full of concern. "Before the break of dawn, he says. The bounds of time we have until we come again within the dark influence of our foe, foul Alyubol, are set. We must escape tonight."

Palamon nodded, sighing. "A fearful challenge, Lady, by my troth. But still, we must embrace hope till the end." Then drawing close to her, he whispered an extra word. "You must stay by this maid, our dear Princess, at any cost. I fear her loss of hope will make her rash." He looked into Aelia's eyes; they understood that fact together.

So history paused, teetering upon this point. Palamon, Ursid, Aelia, and Berengeria were trapped in the depths of a living prison that would not yield them up before the arrival of Alyubol's agent. The day wore on and they waited, parching, their insides crawling with hunger. As for the cavalrymen, they waited also. They lounged in the long, cool grass of the clearing, playing at lots or currying their horses as they watched the pair of their cohorts who in turn watched the captives.

It was now afternoon. The guard standing watch over the tree and its captives had been changed once. One of the present sentries was an ill-favored man who was called Otar.

Otar was an interesting fellow; he was older than the other men of his company and his speech was more coarse. He was not dirty as such, but an unshorn patch of beard and the untended scrapes of his harness betrayed an attention to the details of dress that was not equal to that of his fellow riders.

Otar was not of noble birth, which was unusual among the light cavalrymen of Buerdaunt. He had reached his place on his own. Through force of will, ability, determination, and willingness to climb over or dance around every obstacle, he had made the leap from common guardsman to light cavalryman. He was proud of what he had done.

In spite of this, Otar's life among the mounted soldiers of Lothar the Pale was not an easy one. He was looked down upon by his more exalted fellows. They snubbed him, they would not drink with him, they rarely even spoke to him except to carry out orders.

For this reason, Otar was a hardened, bitter man. And perhaps it was also for this reason that he had developed a streak of cruelty which betrayed itself at times when he could indulge it without risking his career.

This was one of those times. He stood his post well, watching the captives with the same endless intensity a cat displays before a mousehole. He knew them all. He knew Aelia and Berengeria by what he had heard of them and he recognized Ursid because that young man was— or had been—an officer in the light cavalry himself.

Otar knew Palamon well. He knew the tall knight from having seen him in a waterfront tavern in Buerdaunt. He also knew him from something he once had seen years ago in the city of Oron, which lay north of the Thlassa Mey. Otar seldom forgot a face; he never forgot an interesting one.

So he knew Palamon. He approached the great tree to speak with the tall warrior, who sat with bowed head. Otar dropped carelessly to his hands and knees and peered in at Palamon, then whistled a low, almost inaudible whistle. Palamon lifted his head and Otar spoke to him. "I know you, I do."

"Oh, do you?"

"I saw you in Oron once, didn't I? You were in a ceremony when I was there. When was it? I think it was about eight years ago."

The first tracings of a smile appeared at the corners of Palamon's lips. "Is that the truth?"

"It is, indeed." Otar warmed to his subject. "It was an interesting ceremony; a Knight of Pallas was being expelled from the order. Do you remember it?"

There was no answer from Palamon. There was still a slight smile on his face but it was fixed; there was no mirth in it.

"You Knights of Pallas make so many vows, no man could keep them all. I'm on your side, remember that." Otar's eyes glittered as they flicked across the forms of Aelia and Berengeria, then back to Palamon. "You vow not to drink too much. Now that's a fine vow, friend. A man can't drink too much, the way I see it; it's hard just to drink enough. You vow not to be rich, too. That's an easy one, though. It's easy not to be rich."

There was still no change in Palamon's expression.

"But the big vow is that vow of chastity, isn't it?" Otar grinned as he contemplated his prey.

Aelia interrupted. "Now hear me, sir: we've neither supped nor drunk for days. Must all this ignorant small speech be heaped upon our ears? Are things not bad enough?"

Otar spread his hands in an innocent gesture. "I'm just passing the time with this knight, Lady. Don't chastise me. By Typhon's bloody spear, I'm trying to help him pass the day along. If you don't like my words, don't listen."

Palamon spoke then, his voice low and even. "My thanks to you, sir, for your kind intent. You have no concept of the joy you bring by helping me relive those bygone days."

"I do my best, I won't deny it. But you must have been a handsome one years ago. You're tall and straight, it's no use to deny that. And you have those great, stout arms and pretty, supple thighs, too. You need a bit of a shave; the whiskers are a little thicker than they ought to be but that's understandable, given your present fix. You could be a lady killer with some cleaning up. I bet these two here have looked you over more than once, for all their noble robes."

Again Otar flicked his gaze toward the two women. Aelia glared back at him but Berengeria had turned away and only the position of her arm showed that she had pressed one hand to her face. Ursid also watched, frowning.

"So I'm on your side, and there's no denying it. There you were, a well-made fellow, all gleaming in chain mail and your great, gray cape spread across the back of your horse whenever you rode through the streets to the Fastness of Pallas. The women must have thrown themselves at you, lots of them. What a position to be in, you with normal feelings under all that shine, and those women throwing themselves at you like you were the last piece of manflesh on the Thlassa Mey. Makes those vows of chastity mighty hard to remember, doesn't it?"

"What's this you say?" Ursid's voice was filled with disbelief. Aelia silenced him with a deadly glare but the question was already out.

Otar turned and looked at Ursid, gleaming teeth punctuating his words. "Well, young sir, it was a minor transgression, and there's no use arguing. You know the feelings a man gets when he looks at a pretty girl; there's no vow in the world that can change that. So how much of a surprise could it be when this pretty young thing turned up with a little baby and no husband? By Typhon's vipers, these mistakes happen. It's one of those things, just human nature doing what it was meant to do.

"As far as I'm concerned, he did everything that was right by that young lady, and there's no arguing about that. He claimed the baby, and it made that girl a somebody in her own village instead of just a ruined woman. That's noble. Of course there was still that vow of chastity he took. There was no getting around the fact he had rumpled that a little. But, like I said, it was just one of those things, a minor transgression at the worst.

"The trouble was that the Grand Master of the Knights of Pallas didn't look at it that way, you see. There's no arguing about that; he's one man who doesn't have any sense of humor. So they paraded this poor fellow into the market square in Oron, to the front of the Temple of Pallas and they humiliated him until an average man wouldn't have been able to stand it. They ripped off his cape and they burned it; then they hauled him off his horse and they lashed the horse out of the square. They threw mud on that chain mail of his and told him he'd soiled it until a good man couldn't wear it any more. Last of all, they threw a rope around him and dragged him out through the city gate, then left him lying there in the road with all the wagons and travelers going by, staring at him." Otar shook his head. "And all because of such a little mistake, a 'half-hour indiscretion,' as we call it."

"I cannot voice my feelings. I've no words with which to thank you for your thoughtfulness in showing me the sympathy you feel." Palamon still smiled but his face looked drawn and gray, even in the shadows of the tree.

"Think nothing of it." Otar turned his head and noted the approach of the cavalry officer. "Ah, back to business, I see." He looked again at Palamon once more, tilting his head to one side. "I'll have to go back to my post now. No sense in looking too familiar with the prisoners. But I'd really like to talk more. Anytime you think you need someone to talk to, you call me over." He winked at Palamon, stood, and resumed his post. Once he turned, his face lost all expression. He was again the loyal sentry doing his duty.

Palamon sat for a long time, staring straight ahead. There was no sound at all in the root-lined chamber. Ursid sat off to one side, his face bowed between his upraised knees. Aelia and Berengeria huddled together. By turns they moved their heads to cast glances at Palamon's back, but not a word was spoken as the day crawled its endless course toward evening.

Chapter Ten:
New Allies

IT WAS EVENING. The trees in this forest stood too thickly for the sun to be seen settling against the western horizon; the light simply began to fail and the inside of the wooden cell became so dark its inmates could barely see one another's faces.

The shock caused by Otar's gossip had faded a bit. It was hard for the four fugitives to find words, though at least they were looking at one another now. But the subject of Palamon's past was still avoided.

As the shadows beneath the great tree blended into one another, Aelia knelt near Palamon's side. Her face was grave. "I'd like to have a word or two with you, Sir Knight."

"Speak, then. Some words may help to pass the time."

"I speak for both myself and my Princess. We did not know your past, though we both knew it to be mysterious. Some things about it you have kept from us, as is your right. That does not matter; it has no import. What matters now is this—you have served well. Your bravery and stout resourcefulness have helped us on our way, at least this far, at peril of your very life and limb. Whatever happens, listen to me now; you must mew up your past within this tree. When we pass from this place come morn, your past mistakes, regrets, and all things else must stay behind." She paused to study the effect of her words. Then she went on.

"You joined your fate to ours. We are as one together in this band. You joined this group; you gave your word to that. Our purpose is to see that our Princess goes free. No other fact or circumstance can matter now."

Palamon gazed back at her. To her surprise, his expression was one of light good humour; the face which had looked out toward the clearing all afternoon now bore a pleasant smile and slightly raised eyebrows. "Of course, my Lady. You should have good cheer; with such as us, escape is always near."

Even though Palamon's answer was positive, Aelia was taken aback. Was this the same knight who had lain helpless beneath the innuendoes of the cavalryman only a few hours earlier? She had watched him then, watched the life drain from his features as Otar's words had rained down upon him, piercing him like darts. She had watched his sturdy, battle-scarred limbs go slack from shame and his broad back bow under the weight of it, even as he had played the role of a man who had cared for nothing. Was he doing that now? Or was he even affected by the shame of Otar's revelation?

She shook her head inwardly; it was a puzzle. His recovery had unnerved her. Could any man be as uncaring as Palamon seemed to want her to believe he was? "I must say I am pleased to find that you are in good spirits," she said.

"There's no reason not to be. My past is all my own; you have no need to mix in it. I shall keep faith, withal, if you can still bear up beneath the shame of keeping company with such a low, whoremongering, base knave as I."

Aelia sighed. She touched him lightly on the arm, then

turned back toward Berengeria. The book that was the man inside Palamon was still closed to her.

The last glow of day quickly faded, leaving darkness broken only by a pair of campfires built by the cavalrymen. The flames leaped and crackled. By their light, the soldier's faces could be seen along with the two men who stood stiffly on watch beside the great tree and its inmates.

Inside the tree it was still quiet. Conversation had long ago given way to each captive's battle with the hunger and thirst that threatened to overpower them all. Ursid lay on the damp soil, his arms curled about his knees. Aelia and Berengeria sat together silently. Palamon watched the faces that ringed the two bounding fires at the edge of the clearing, seemingly unaffected by what was occurring within him and without.

There was a noise from one side of their rootbarred cell. It was a whisper, scarcely audible. Aelia sat up. She remained motionless for a moment, then responded, also in a whisper. The voice from outside came again.

Palamon moved closer to her. The whisper came from just a few cubits away but he could make out no shape in the gloom. "What is it?"

"It's Parso." Aelia groped for Palamon's face in the darkness, found it, and placed a finger across his lips. "Wait."

There was a quick exchange of whispers between Aelia and the wudling chieftain. Then she spoke again to her companions, her voice soft in the darkness. "He says he's come to set us free. Make not a sound."

"Though we might try, how will we pass the guards?" Although Ursid spoke in a harsh whisper, his voice was full of excitement.

"Be silent. Keep your peace; do as I say." Aelia's voice became harsh. "He says that he will open up an aisle between these moving roots. My dear Princess, you have to be the first to crawl away. Crawl straight into the trees that mark the edge of this broad clearing. Keep your body low, make not a sound, and do not stop until you feel the touch of Parso's hand."

"How do you know he does not lie to us?" Ursid asked. "How could he reach us 'tween these sentries' eyes?"

"He says no human eyes can see his kind when it is dark if they do not desire to be discerned. And to your other doubt, we have no choice. The hand of Alyubol is very near; all hope will soon be lost." Already some low sounds, the raspings of a whispered incantation, penetrated their hearing. "Go now, Princess; 'tis you who must escape. Till you are free, the rest of us are nothing."

Another faint sound came to Palamon's ears—the low, sinister rustling of the coarse roots as they drew back to form a passage. Then there was silence. "Go now," Aelia whispered.

There was a sound of nervous breathing and Palamon could sense the movement of Berengeria's body as she hitched her robe so she could crawl on her hands and knees toward the opening. He heard her gasp softly as she rubbed against the rough surface of one of the roots. Then she was gone. Fear entered his mind for a moment, fear of what fate could await her at the hands of the wudlings. Were the intentions of the apemen friendly? That seemed too good to be true after the animosity shown earlier. But would Parso have braved the swords of the cavalrymen simply for the sake of punishing his former prisoners personally? That also seemed unlikely.

Whatever awaited her, there was no hesitation on Berengeria's part. She bravely grasped the doubtful straw. Palamon was impressed: she was a woman of great courage and resolve, as was her mentor. She was fate's child; that thought kept returning to him; many were the times when he could sense its presence about her.

Aelia issued more whispered instructions. "Now we must wait a middling space of time. Then I will follow, then will come Ursid. Then lastly you, O Palamon. Now heed my words, for once again I say: keep low, be silent, crawl straight to the trees."

Palamon noted the order of her instructions. There could be no doubt she intended for them to escape in the order of their relative usefulness to her. She would follow Berengeria. He would come last. The thought brought a

thin smile to his lips; whatever Aelia might say, Otar's
story had produced a change in her estimation of him.

They waited. Palamon's eyes strayed back to the bon-
fires where the soldiers still were showing no movement.
There was no sign they had noticed the activity within
the tree. After what seemed to be a long time, Aelia's
robes rustled and she moved into the opening; then she
was also gone.

Palamon and Ursid sat together. The younger man's
breathing was soft, almost nonexistent. Palamon could
almost hear his heart pounding a cubit away. "Will we
escape, I wonder?" Ursid's voice was hardly even a whisper. "But we must. Our lives lie on the balance if we fail."

Palamon nodded, although he knew the motion could
not be seen by Ursid. "A life can be a very tiny thing, a
little flame, not very hard to snuff. Sometimes a life is
ended, though the body still may move."

There was more silence, a long, long silence. Then
Ursid spoke again, his voice even smaller than before.
"Why did you do it?"

Palamon's eyes closed. "Ah."

"If you had honor and esteem and were considered
better than most men, then how could you give those
things up for woman's arms?"

The answer was hardly more audible than the question;
it echoed from deep inside Palamon's body. "A man does
many strange things in his life. You gave up noble status
in Buerdaunt to aid the Princess Berengeria. And why
was that, I wonder?"

Now it was Ursid who was silent. It took him a long
time to reply. "I love her."

"I know you do."

"Were you in love those many years ago?"

Palamon sighed. "I hardly knew the girl. And now it's
time for you to leave."

In the darkness, Ursid groped his way to the passage
between the roots. Then he was gone. Palamon sat alone
in the gloom, occasionally glancing at the dim, dim figures
of the guards, twenty cubits away, or at the men at their
campfires. Then it was his turn. He rolled onto his belly

and crawled toward the place where the opening lay framed by the rough roots that had been his guardians for the last two days. He crawled out quickly and flattened himself in the tall, coarse grass of the clearing.

The grass had a fresh, sweet smell that filled Palamon's nostrils as he crawled to the edge of the clearing, moving himself with his knees and his elbows. It took an eternity. From the corner of one eye he could see a guard silhouetted against the fire. He felt naked and exposed but the soldier made no move.

At last, Palamon reached the trees and he crawled past the first trunk. The sounds of the encamped cavalrymen were behind him now. A hairy hand was placed upon his shoulder. Looking up, he could barely discern the angular form of the wudling who held it out, but he felt himself being grasped by the wrist and pulled to his feet. Then they ran. Palamon had to run doubled half over to maintain contact with his escort. While his back grew stiff, they ran far into the trees. They twisted and turned, and it was hard for him to keep track of the way they were going; he guessed their general direction to be southwest from the clearing where the great tree stood.

They had gone only a short way when Palamon heard a shout; the escape had been discovered. Loud curses filled the clearing behind them. The officer's voice roared out orders; torches were lighted and horses whinnied and stamped as they were hurriedly saddled. Dots of light flared up and moved about the clearing. Some of them were already moving into the trees.

There was no time for Palamon to observe more. The wudling who guided him pulled him almost off his feet as it was, forcing him to run with all the speed he could muster in his awkward position. The wudling's fleetness was amazing. Palamon could not believe the pace they set through the dark forest. He could only surrender himself to his escort's guidance as the torches and shouting were left behind.

At last, when he felt he could run no farther, the apeman stopped him. "Wait," a rough voice said.

Palamon looked about but he could not see a thing.

His companions, Aelia, Berengeria, Ursid, were neither
to be seen nor heard. But another hairy hand reached out
from somewhere above him and tugged upward. He
shrugged it off. It returned, along with many more, and
he felt fiber lines being placed about his arms and legs.
At first he resisted but he was too emptied by fatigue,
hunger, and thirst to hold out. His head rocked back and
the world swung about crazily as he felt himself being
jerked upward.

He was pulled toward the heavens at all odd angles,
sometimes with his feet above his head, sometimes with
his body level to the ground. His hands had nothing to
grasp. At last one hand made contact with something
hard. It was a platform. He was being pulled up onto a
wooden platform.

As he was roughly trundled over the edge, he reached
out and one hand made contact with something soft. It
was a woman's shoulder; the woman thrust his hand away.
"Don't." The voice belonged to Berengeria.

"I beg your pardon, Highness. I just reached to lay my
hands on any solid thing."

"Of course. Forgive me."

"Where have we arrived?"

Berengeria hesitated. "Perhaps my Lady ought to tell
you that. These wood folk will confide somewhat in her;
they have no trust for you, Ursid, or me."

"We are upon a platform residence." This voice
belonged to Aelia. "It is a simple structure, Parso's home.
Take this; you need it. It will give you strength."

He accepted the wooden bowl she pushed into his
hands. It contained a sort of thick, spicy gruel, quite
smooth and not at all unpleasant tasting, especially considering it was the first thing to pass his lips in two days.
He finished the bowl quickly, then spoke again. "Then
you have spoken with them at some length? What thing
do they intend to do with us?"

Aelia's hand took the bowl from him in the darkness,
then returned it, full once more. "I think they may intend
to set us free and even, possibly, to give us aid."

Chapter Eleven:
Inland Navigation

THE COURSE OF events over the next day and a half was both exhausting and drastically different from what it had been. The fleeing foursome rested only a short time on Parso's tree platform, then they were off with two wudling guides, scurrying through the darkness on hidden forest paths. Behind them, legions of wudlings massed to exact vengeance on the cavalrymen of Lothar the Pale.

But the wudlings' fear and hatred of Buerdaunt's soldiers was a godsend to the four fugitives; their former captors now looked upon them, especially Aelia, with new eyes. The two guides escorted them to a hilly land of lakes, streams, and marshes, which was even wilder than the forests they had just left.

They reached a village built upon pilings in one of the many small marshes; their guides told them it was the home of the Morgaine wudlings. And the Morgaine wudlings possessed boats.

With the support of the two guides, Aelia negotiated for use of a pair of the light craft; boats were of more use than horses in this stream-cut land. The talks were long, the Morgaine wudlings unsympathetic. Only Aelia's guile and skill with words and promises could have carried them off with success. But she did succeed. She admired many things, said much, promised much. The fugitives were given boats, along with goods to provision them; and a river became their highway.

But their highway led into unknown lands. The Morgaine wudlings knew only that it flowed into unexplored territory dominated by a forbidden stream called the Stilchis.

This revelation caused the four fugitives to pause. All of them had heard of the Cauldron of the Stilchis, an unknown valley untrodden by the feet of civilized men. Did they dare follow the stream to its termination? That was a hard question, but they had no choice but to ignore it and follow the stream for the time being.

So they spent the day learning to manage their tiny craft as they passed through scenes of great tranquility. The river flowed smoothly as they paddled, its progress marked only in the way it tugged at the grass roots hanging from the undercut bank or by the way the sun reflected from the smooth V's that spread from the bows of their little craft.

They camped for the night and examined the supplies given them by the wudlings. There were bronze fishhooks and line for the capture of the river's denizens, wooden containers of dried fruits and meats, rope, several small knives, a hatchet, and more. There were cooking utensils and even a quantity of strange, dark flour which, though strange looking, was tasty. But their weapons were still in the wudlings' hands. The trust of the apemen was not complete, even though they had provisioned the boats generously. This was upsetting to Palamon; the loss of his sword with its odd pommel ornament was quite disturbing to him, although he said little.

They set out early in the morning and the day was spent in the same way as the day before, paddling quietly along the stream, pulling an occasional wriggling fish from the water, stopping at dark to cook their catch. It was more like play than an escape fraught with danger.

It went thus for a large part of the next day as well. But the stream they were following gradually became swifter and rougher and the green hills rose up around it like megalithic jaws. By midafternoon, the river ran between vertical walls of dark stone: the foursome could not have landed here, even if they had wished. They did reach an open place at last; the tiny boats were hauled onto the beach and the four passengers stood for several moments to stretch stiff joints.

Aelia looked up and down the canyon before turning to the others. "I fear the dangers of this river more with each bend passed. Perhaps the time has come when we must choose between the slower, safer route—dry land— and this onrushing river's unknown path."

"Indeed," Berengeria said. "I long to know the dangers that this river holds in store. The wudlings told us that these waters flow into the Stilchis. How much do you know of such a stream?"

"I know of legends, that is all," Palamon said.

"When I was a girl," Aelia said, "old tales were some-times told about the Cauldron of the Stilchis."

Palamon nodded silently.

Aelia looked up at him. "You heard the same old tales?"

"Full many stories, down across the years."

"The tales that I remember—there are few—portray an unknown valley where no man who enters e'er can hope to leave."

Palamon looked at her and Berengeria. There were no answers to be found in his face.

"Such legends, do they hold a bit of truth?" Aelia asked.

He shrugged. "What does it matter? Our course is laid out. We have no weapons for a trek on land." His expression turned into a smile, the same smile she had seen before, making his face into a mask which she could not hope to penetrate. "Besides, my Lady, tales mean nought to us; we are the stuff ourselves from which tales come. You have escaped pale Lothar and Buerdaunt, eluded mounted cavalry and traps; a lady such as you has not the need to fret herself with cares of unknown lands. You seem to make a practice of those things that ne'er are done by other mortals. Worry not."

"You say I should not be concerned that all our fates hang on this unknown river's whim?" There was a note of irritation in Aelia's voice.

Palamon's expression did not change. "I say our thoughts mean nothing for, you see, the die is cast."

She studied him for a moment. "There's truth in what you say. But even so, if this smooth stream we follow now should change, should lead us into perils unforeseen, then we shall quit it, striking out by land."

"While minding all the while the hot pursuit by land of Lothar's minions. And of Alyubol." Palamon nodded.

"Indeed." Aelia turned away from Palamon and faced Ursid. "And you? Have you a thought, O silent knight?"

"I have no weapon other than this knife." Ursid brandished a short blade gained from the provisions. "But still, I favor land. I know that way."

But Berengeria, who had been looking about, interrupted the debate. "Look up. No matter now, the thing is gone."

"What thing?" Ursid's eyes followed Berengeria's gaze.

"Ah, yes," Palamon said. "The flash of sun from off a helm, or then perhaps it is a sword raised up on high. But listen: you can hear them as they come."

It was true. The air was fretted by the faint, faint drumming of horse's hooves. Palamon leaped to one of the boats. "Unless I miss my guess, a trail must lead down to this very beach on which we stand. We must be off. Come, help me launch away."

The others hurried to his side. The sound of the galloping horses could be heard more plainly now and it was approaching, though the thick foliage of the canyon wall still hid the men who were making it. The hulls of the boats sounded over sand and stones as they were pushed into the water. The ladies were seated in their places. Palamon and Ursid scrambled into their own seats as the craft slid into the quick current; it was a maneuver they had learned well in the last day or so.

They paddled out into the river, looking back at the thing they had escaped. Their worst fears were realized: bursting from the thick brush onto the beach came many mounted men wearing the cavalry uniforms of Buerdaunt—all of them, that is, except one. That exception wore heavy white robes, and even across the space between them, Palamon could sense the frustration in the dark eyes. It was as if the fellow could have set the hide hulls of the boats aflame with his searing orbs. Palamon recognized him. He was Navron, Alyubol's henchman.

The horsemen brought their finely trained mounts to a sliding halt on the sandy bank of the river as the two boats pulled away. Then two of them drew their bows. Arrows sliced into the water at the stern of the boat occupied by Ursid and Berengeria, and Palamon heard the white-robed Navron scold the two archers; he could not tell whether the censure was for shooting at such a valuable prize as the Princess or for missing the shot.

But at least they had escaped for the moment. Navron tried to spur his horse into the chilly waters, but the bank dropped off steeply, and he was forced to give up as the boats rounded a bend and his quarry passed out of view.

There was no time for the fugitives to rejoice in that. The river dropped into a narrow chute the way water in a ceremonial fountain drops into the fountain's sluice. The little boats were tossed about like walnut shells as they were carried along; Palamon could feel his boat's skin flex beneath him in a manner that made him uneasy.

The four novice boatmen paddled madly to keep to the least threatening parts of the channel. But though they raced through the canyon, they soon found that the threat of being overturned was not great as long as they took care with the forces that swept them dizzily along. Time was now the threat. They had to find quieter water and a place to beach the boats before nightfall.

For the moment they took courage in the fact that they had once more eluded the outstretched talons of Lothar the Pale. They had done this at a price, however; that much became plain as the walls of the canyon closed around them, nearly blocking out the passing sun. They probably had lost their last chance to choose between a land route and the clutch of this torrent that now bore them toward an unknown fate.

It was hard work, this paddling. But there were few stones to disrupt the flow of the hurtling waters, so the danger was moderate. The hours passed and still they rocked along; they could not guess the distance they had covered, but it had to have been some leagues.

At length, the river slowed; the canyon opened out at the bottom, though the walls still towered over them like great, dark borders to their world in the waning light. The day had passed and they needed to stop soon. They found this could be done, however; Ursid spotted a low beach on the inside of a bend in the river and that was where they ended their flight for the day. They landed and pulled the boats up onto dry ground.

When they had done this, Berengeria stood for a moment, one hand over her bosom and an exhausted smile lighting her face. "Now by my troth, that was a merry ride. If just one stone had blocked our course this day, we would have fed this river's fish ere now."

"Quite so but now this river's fish feed us." Ursid held up a length of cord from which dangled the day's catch. "I see some driftwood snags that shall make fire to cook a hearty meal."

And so it was done. Driftwood branches were cut with the hand axe that was part of their supplies, the fish were prepared and cooked, and the adventurers enjoyed their meal deep in the entrails of the canyon. And when the meal was eaten, they rolled their blankets out on the shore and slept the sleep of the exhausted. Here, in spite of the efforts of their foes to find them, they were alone. They had no idea what awaited them along this watery road. But for the moment at least, they slept safely in this corner of the universe, far beyond the clutches of their enemies.

The night was a peaceful one, the most peaceful they had spent for a while. As the first glow of the next day brightened the strip of sky far overhead, Palamon and Berengeria found themselves watching it while Ursid and Aelia slept. Palamon's eyes were drawn to Berengeria.

She was only a silhouette in the feeble light of the coming day; still, she was pleasant to look upon. He should not have stared at her, but he caught himself doing just that. She fascinated him. The things that lay in her past and the possibilities of her future both intrigued him in ways he himself did not fully understand.

Her gaze dropped from the pale ribbon above them. Her eyes fastened on him, and he quickly looked away. "Your pardon, my Princess," he said.

"For what?"

He paused. Perhaps she had not noticed him gazing at her in the shadows that filled the bottom of this gorge. His pause turned into a long silence.

Berengeria looked about. They would soon be able to embark, though not for a while yet. The waters of the river were still dark; the crouching stones were still hidden. " 'Twill presently be light," she said. "Then we must go."

There was a note of weary resolve in her voice, as if she would have stayed in this place longer if she could have. He did not blame her. She needed a rest: the strain of this journey was telling upon her more each day. Still, she would not relent. She was the most driven member of the party, in fact, and that was something he had to admire. He found it strange to see such an overflowing well of resolve imbedded in such luxurious beauty as hers. "Your Highness should have slept throughout the night," he said. "You should not force yourself to take the watch." Then he stood up. It was time for him to be alone.

"All backs must bear the strain till journey's end." She smiled up at him as she answered.

That smile pleased Palamon. Princess Berengeria had hardly spoken to him since those hard moments inside the great tree of the wudlings. That had troubled him. He liked her, this iron-willed Princess; were it not for her high position and the aura about her and, most of all, his past, his actions toward her might have been different from what they had been. Still, he would not dwell upon that; that way lay despair. But the smile did mean a great deal to him. "Princess, I find you are a doughty maid. Pale Lothar's hot pursuit shall not trap you." He smiled back at her for an instant, then turned to go.

She caught him by one hand; the pressure of her fingers was firm. "Thank you, Palamon." No more was said. Their eyes met for less than a moment, then he went his way while she rose to wake their companions.

When it was light enough, they started out once again. They no longer paddled; the river's swift current carried them at its own pace, flowing as quickly as a cantering horse. The sides of the canyon were forty fathoms high by now—great, brush-covered walls that loomed over their sparkling trail. Here and there, outcroppings of the jagged black stone jutted forth, hanging above them like sentinels as they drifted by. And still and always the walls loomed higher.

As the midmorning sun peeked above the rim, the sound of roaring ahead of them warned them that their watery highway was again going to make them work for their escape. They approached this new rapid carefully.

It was well that they did. They beached their small craft on a rocky patch of shore and walked downstream, threading their way between brush and boulders until they reached a point from which they could examine the new obstacle. What they saw filled them with dismay. Their way was blocked by three hundred cubits of leaping water. Stones jutted from the spume and broad waves lashed across the torrent, doubling back upon themselves.

"By Hestia's veil," Aelia said. "There is no passing this."

There was a long pause. Then Palamon spoke. "There is a way," he said. "If my eyes play me fair, I see this stony strand on which we walk extends along this bank a goodly way. The path that we must take is full of sweat, but there's no other, if we are to live. These craft that bore us down along this stream must now be borne by us."

"We'll carry them, you mean?" Aelia lifted her eyebrows.

"Indeed we must."

Aelia nodded. "It is the only way. We'll to the boats to empty them and bear them on our backs. It may require much time and several trips but we shall then be back upon our way." She turned to Palamon and smiled at him. It was not the same as the smile Berengeria had bestowed upon him earlier, however.

The portage took a long time, much longer than Palamon had expected it to. He and Ursid carried each boat in its turn while Berengeria and Aelia moved the other goods. They had to go slowly; none of them had the desire to turn an ankle or suffer some other injury with so far yet to go.

The sun continued his flight, carried ever farther aloft in his fiery chariot; the day grew warmer as the fugitives labored. Palamon grimaced as sweat trickled into his eyes. He paused long enough to wipe it away, then he and Ursid moved on. Once they were past the rapids and afloat again, all four of them relaxed from their labors, paddling only hard enough to steer their craft.

As the day wore on, they did not pause for a midday meal but ate the remainder of their fish without going ashore. It was well they did. Early in the afternoon they encountered another rapid, this one more dangerous than the other. This time they did not hesitate for discussion, for there was no question they would have to portage once more.

So it was all done again. They went through the tedious process of unloading the boats and transporting them over the rocks to a place where they dared to reembark. This series of rapids was long and treacherous, and it was late in the day before it was passed; the sun had already slipped beyond the canyon rim and the swift waters before them were often hidden by shadows. The delays were maddening. It was the fastest water that slowed them the most, surely allowing the men of Lothar the Pale to gain ground.

But rather than continue on in total darkness, they

were forced to spend the night on the sand spit they now occupied. It was not an easy choice. The clammy sand and its resident army of insects made an unfriendly river seem almost hospitable.

Chapter Twelve:
Wild Waters

THE FOUR ADVENTURERS passed an unpleasant night.
On the sandbar that was their temporary refuge, there
was no dry place; therefore, they spread their blankets
and lay down on the moist sand itself. As they had long
done, two of them slept while the other two stood watch.
But on this night, those who watched obtained nearly as
much rest as those who tried to sleep.

The damp sand was moist to the touch and there was
no escape from its clamminess. No matter how one lay,
the dank smell rose to the nostrils and the grains clung
to the skin each time the body was shifted. An acre of
robes could not have provided warmth under such conditions and the four travelers had only one blanket apiece.

At dawn they were off once more. They fished as they
floated along, hoping to catch the makings of a hot lunch,
but they had no success. That was bad. They had all
agreed on the wisdom of supplementing their rations when
possible and looked on restlessly as those supplies shrank.

As the day passed, the canyon became deeper. They

were forced to portage past one more rapid, but they made good time until afternoon. Then they entered a place where the river was compressed into a narrow channel; the current accelerated and sent them shooting along the racing flood.

There was no place for them to land, so they were forced to paddle. This they did with might and main, using all their newfound skills to keep themselves upright as they flew past the canyon walls at the pace of the swiftest stallion. It was a breathless ride.

They survived it, however, as they had survived the similar one after encountering the riders at the river's edge. But at the foot of this rapid, they were greeted by a sight vastly different from anything they had encountered before.

No longer did their river flow through a lush canyon carpeted by thick-set brush and small trees wherever a foothold could be maintained upon the granite walls. Here the banks were of stone only, and what a different sort of stone it was. It was a pale gray color and so dull on the surface that it scarcely seemed to be stone at all, but great heaps of ash or dust. Nor were these ugly walls as high as the looming palisades that had formed the channel before; they barely extended above the heads of the four travelers.

"By Hestia's veil, what manner of land is this?" Aelia said, her voice hanging in the dead air. "I see no scrap of green within the full range of my view."

No one answered. All eyes scanned the lifeless hills, what little could be seen of them from the river's breast. At last Palamon spoke. "From the low setting, we will never see the broad expanse of this mysterious land."

"That may be so," Berengeria said, "but do we have the time to look about with foemen on our trail?"

"An honest question," Palamon responded.

They paddled on for a time. There was no change in the terrain; the powdery gray hills floated by silently. There was no bird or beast to be seen within the range of their eight eyes.

The sun glided toward the western horizon, his chariot

hastening as his two steeds viewed the end of the day's journey. Now Palamon spoke again. "This day, Princess, let me make a request that we take shore while there is still some light. I fain would view the land which we must cross."

The air was full of the pause as Berengeria considered her reply. She finally consented in a soft voice. "As you may wish."

Now it was Palamon who hesitated. The consent to stop while there was still light had obviously been wrung from the maiden most grudgingly. "Then," he said, "we should beach our craft when next we spy a place with driftwood suitable for fire." By that much, at least, their time on the water would be extended.

"I think that would be wise." Aelia nodded her agreement.

The wait was a short one. There were many beaches along this desolate stretch of water where trees, carried down by floods from the river's upper course, lay piled upon the sand. They found one while the sun's golden rim still glimmered above the hills to the west.

No sooner had they beached their trusty little craft than Palamon announced he was going for a walk. "Ursid, if you will cut a portion of this wood, then I will play the truant, running off to climb yon hill to survey how this land might lie."

Ursid agreed. "In just a moment I can hew enough to last us through the night. You three go on, then I will join you."

Palamon, Aelia, and Berengeria followed the gently rising terrain up from the riverbank to a hill that stood higher than its neighbors. Like all the others in this land, it was a flat-topped, roughly carved mound. They walked quickly to the top of it. There they were greeted by a ghastly sight.

If the clinkers, ash and half-burned fuel from all the coal furnaces there had ever been or would ever be in any world were spread from horizon to horizon in one place, it would barely have matched the sight spread out before them. They stood on one of the numerous low hills that dotted the slopes of a dreary valley, many leagues across. There was nothing but desolation. The entire plain was composed of the same ashlike stuff, except for a few conical mounds that stuck up to the north, silver and black in the rays of the setting sun. Some of them smoked.

Nowhere was there any sign of life. It was a dead valley, rimmed on the near side by the jutting cliffs through which the river had swept them. The cliffs loomed imposingly, broken only by the gash cut into them by the stream itself.

A breath slipped from Aelia's throat. "The Cauldron of the Stilchis. By the gods, it does exist as legendry portrays."

"But never, in the dark recesses glimpsed within my darkest dreams, could I conceive a place of desolation such as this." Berengeria's tone was also subdued.

Palamon said nothing, nor did the two women speak again. There was nothing more to say; the appearance of this blasted land beggared any attempt at commentary. Wordlessly, the trio retraced their steps toward Ursid, who could still be heard breaking and chopping driftwood for their evening's fuel.

As they descended, Aelia found words. "Withal, there is some benefit in this; those cliffs are quite unbroken save for that deep chasm which has led us to this place. The Cauldron of the Stilchis. That same name was whispered to me when I was a girl. It lies upon the south shore of the sea, the ancient legends stated. Here it is, more awesome than those whispered women's tales could e'er have thought of being, so say I."

"Quite awesome," Palamon agreed.

"A long dead land, inhabited by none." Aelia looked at Berengeria. "There are, I understand, few ways to enter, fewer still to exit; that is what the legends say. But if that be the case, pursuit is blocked until the men of Lothar find a way to follow us. As no one will deny, no landborn creature ever enters here the way we came, save floating as a corpse."

"I still can feel the arm of Alyubol," Berengeria said. "He seems to find us any place we flee."

"His quantity cannot be ascertained, that much I must admit," Aelia said. "Yet men must eat and horses must have forage or they fall."

"And I agree," Palamon said. "What Alyubol's next move may be, we cannot know; still, our next move is easily discerned. We have no choice except the course we hold, to follow this swift stream down to the Thlassa Mey."

Aelia nodded.

"Is this the Stilchis, then?" Berengeria asked.

"Though we've no way of telling, I think not," Aelia said. "The legends all describe a mightly flood; this middling river does not seem to me to have the means of carving out this land."

While they spoke, they approached Ursid to tell him of their discovery. He was impressed, for he too had heard the stories of a land seldom entered by men. Palamon relieved him of his chores and he ran the way they had come to see for himself. He soon returned; it was nearly dark by now but he had seen enough, even in the failing light. "It is a barren land," he said as he walked toward them, shaking his head. "I wonder how a creature could exist which might be tough enough to spend its life within this land of cinders."

"True," Palamon said as he knelt to make a fire. "That question will pertain to us, as well. We must needs husband well our meager stores."

The others agreed. Then Berengeria asked if the campfire should even be lit; they had used one rarely in the past for fear of detection.

Palamon shrugged. "If danger is perceived, then this bright flame can be forgone. Still, evil Alyubol has found us thrice before in spite of all precautions tried by us. I doubt that one more fire in such a land of smoke and fire will make a difference. The point is this—our enemies have shown they have the means to track us without sight by eye. Mayhap they watch us even as we speak. But though they track us, they'll not reach us here, for horsemen ne'er could ride across that plain that we have gazed

upon today. And boatmen cannot make a better passage
than we have."

Then he smiled at Berengeria and winked. "So take
that, Lothar; Alyubol, you, too. And you, Princess, may
make whatever disrespectful, crude, and unenlightened
gesture you would like. Although they might well see,
your enemies cannot, at least for some time, do a thing."

Berengeria smiled at him. It was a pleasant expression,
this smile of hers, much like the way she had looked at
him that other morning. "Your humor buoys my heart up,
Palamon. Whatever lies behind you in the past, you've
done a noble service for my sake and that will be remembered, come what may."

"Ah, my past." Palamon's own smile changed a bit. It
hardened, became stiff, became camouflage for what lay
behind it; the other members of the party had seen this
before.

"Forgive me, for I feel I've done offence," Berengeria
said.

Palamon shook his head. "No, fear that not, Princess,
for my own past may see me where I hide, as can our
foes. But like our foemen, there is not a way that it can
reach me here within this place."

Aelia had seated herself on a driftwood log and was
watching Palamon as he spoke. He was interesting to
watch. "Are you quite sure it cannot reach you here?"
she asked.

Palamon did not answer. He merely shrugged and continued to build the fire.

They ate, washed, then retired. At dawn, they again
took to their trusty boats and resumed their journey
through the mysterious, desolate land that was called the
Cauldron of the Stilchis.

The river flowed smoothly now, having completed its
transit of the cliffs that rimmed this valley. But its course
was disconcerting. By all their calculations, there was no
doubt they would still lie many leagues south of the Thlassa
Mey. If this stream emptied into that sea, it had to turn
eventually to reach it. Yet it showed no inclination toward
doing so. Through the day it meandered to the south and

southwest, showing no respect at all for the course logic dictated.

The day was passed in steady paddling, for there were no rapids along this stretch of river. The water was flat and the current constant. For hours, the dreary banks slipped by while the four fugitives trailed their fishing lines in the water. Few fish were caught along this stretch of liquid highway, barely enough to provide them with an evening meal when they stopped for the night.

It was the same the next day. Still the river slid along, always toward the southwest; but after noon, it finally began to flow more quickly. They were descending into another canyon. They paddled carefully, trying to take advantage of the swift current without risking an upset in any of the riffles they passed through as they rushed downstream. There were no really dangerous rapids here, only bars stretching out toward the center of the stream, compressing it.

Down and down they went. The walls of this canyon exceeded in height those cliffs they had passed earlier. The river had carved its way through the coarse gray stone that had contained it up till now and their way lay between walls that were a flat, forbidding black.

Their canyon had become a narrow gorge, but on a monstrous scale. The walls towered above them for a hundred fathoms, forming a megalithic corridor where there was no place to land. Then they rounded a bend in this canyon to find that it intersected another one which was even deeper and grander.

Before they could react, they were swept into the great river that plunged through the larger chasm. The current here was swifter than in the river they had left and they had to struggle to keep from being swept onto jagged rocks. The water raged about them, geysering up as it struck huge boulders, filling the air with spray, and shooting over concealed barriers to fall back upon itself. It heaved itself up into frothy heaps all around them, filling their ears with roaring and making their little boats jump and quiver, the hide hulls flexing beneath them as the staunch craft were brutally buffeted.

Berengeria and Ursid were in the first boat; Aelia and Palamon followed in the second. There was no panic in any of them because there was no time for panic. They strained at their tasks, guiding their craft through the treacherous waters, sweat mixing with the spray and froth that drenched their bodies.

Now the end of the rapid was in sight. There was a great boulder in the middle of the channel and the water surged away from it in both directions; it was a brutal obstacle. But beyond it, quieter water could be seen. As they were swept down upon the boulder, Ursid and Berengeria tried to go to the right of it but the tricky current slapped them back. Palamon saw this and steered to the left. But it was too late for the couple in the lead boat to change course; the heaving waters carried them over the top of the boulder itself.

With a cry, Ursid and Berengeria were thrown into the air; their craft was hurled free of the water, turning over in flight before plunging into the river. All the contents of the boat rained down. Then the boat bobbed to the surface once more and could be seen half-sinking as it swept toward a driftwood covered sandbar lying downstream. Of the two passengers, nothing could be seen except foam.

With herculean effort, Palamon and Aelia guided their own craft toward the same sandbar. The task became simpler as the current slowed and they reached it at almost the same time as the empty boat.

But what of Berengeria and Ursid? Palamon leaped from his own craft and pulled it up onto the sand, all the while searching for them with his eyes. Aelia joined him, her face mummified with fear for the life of her charge.

A dark spot appeared in the foam before them. It was the head of Ursid, breaking above the waves as he swam, and his efforts were being hampered by Berengeria's dragging weight. He swam for the sandbar upon which Palamon and Aelia stood but it was easy to see that his mighty effort would be in vain; he was going to be swept past by the current.

Aelia was shouting something but Palamon could not

hear her above the roaring of the water and the ringing in his own ears. There was no time to think. He grasped a piece of driftwood, a long, crooked pole, and ran to the end of the sandbar to extend it toward the swimmers. But as the pair was swept nearer, he could not hold the pole against the current. Hurriedly, he drew it in and picked it up again for another try. They were almost past him, now.

Shouting to them, hardly hearing Aelia's cries, he held the driftwood staff out once more. The end plunged beneath the surface and he feared he had missed again. Then he felt a tug; Ursid had managed to grasp it after all.

Palamon pulled the two castaways in carefully. Then he and Aelia sent the water flying as they dashed to drag them onto dry sand, grasping Berengeria first, then Ursid, and pulling them both out of danger. Ursid was half drowned and he lay gasping, his eyes rolled back and his sides heaving like a freshly landed fish rather than a freshly saved human. But for all that, he began to recover.

As for Berengeria, she lay in Aelia's lap without moving. Aelia cradled her, rocking her back and forth, speaking to her softly. The older woman was frantic; she seemed about to lose her mind. Her eyes were glassy and her black hair had been swept into a wild fury by the ordeal. Her eyes became venomous and she glared up at Palamon. "All Knights of Pallas demonstrate the art of healing. Heal her, heal her, make her live once more."

The words stung Palamon like the gravel-laced mud hurled at him many years before. Aelia had caught him by surprise; he could not hide the pain she had inflicted. "You know that I cannot."

"Aye, that I do. Your power to restore was given up for barter of a trim-set pair of thighs. Away from me, you fragment; let me be alone with my dead child and my own grief."

But Palamon did not go away. Instead, he knelt in the sand; he touched the throat of the young woman, held the back of his rough hand beneath her nostrils. "But she still lives, though not for long unless we act at once." He took her from Aelia and stretched her nerveless form upon the sand, her body inclined down the slope of the beach with her head toward the water. Kneeling once more, he turned her face to one side, placed an arm beneath the small of her back, and lifted a bit. Water dribbled from her ashen lips.

Aelia sat watching him, her eyes glazed by shock. But when Palamon lowered his head and placed his mouth over Berengeria's, Aelia leaped upon him like a harpy. "Away, you loathsome cur. How dare you bring dishonor to her form with these caresses, all uncalled for? Take your once-befouled lips away. 'Tis most unspeakable, the thing you try to do." She clawed at his shoulders.

With one hand he shoved her backward. She stumbled and fell onto the sand but was upon him once more, with more fury than the first time. He whirled upon his knees in the sand and pulled her down with him; this time it was he who shouted. "Away yourself, mad woman. Hear me now. My patron, good, gray Pallas, has revoked my healing powers for my crime. But still I know some arts, taught long ago to me while I was just a young cadet. I simply breathe the life back into her. If I should fail, it's not for lack of care. Do not compound my crime by flaying me with words while you prevent my true attempt."

Aelia relented. The strength had gone from her; she sat silently in the sand and watched, her eyes still narrowed at the tall knight. But she did not leap upon him again. For his part, Palamon turned back to the limp body and placed his mouth over Berengeria's once more, breathing his breath into her, causing her pale cheeks to puff out with the action. Her bosom rose with the force of the breath, straining the thin robe that covered it. He repeated the act, then repeated it again. He continued for what seemed a lifetime longer than the one he had already lived; she had to be saved; otherwise, all meaning was lost and the aura of destiny about her meant nothing. Finally, his breath was met by one of her own, then another.

Her bosom rose by itself now, though it was only a shallow movement. Her eyes fluttered open; she rolled to one side and coughed. Then she attempted to rise. He restrained her, holding a broad hand across her shoulder. "Lie still, Princess, for rest is what you need."

Emotions rained from Aelia's face. Relief and joy warred with astonishment, but in a trice she was at the side of her charge: "Princess, Princess, how hard a time it was, for I had thought you lost beyond recall."

Berengeria said nothing; she was still groggy. Aelia held her dripping head in her lap, stroking the amber curls that were dark with water. Palamon stepped away. There was no longer a need for him, at least for the moment, for Aelia would care for Berengeria well enough. And Aelia's outburst had been enough to remind him of the real place he held in her thoughts, for all her outward cordiality. All the same, he was relieved that Berengeria lived. She had come to mean much to him, perhaps more than he would have admitted had she asked him his opinion of her.

He turned to Ursid, who stood and watched. Ursid shook his broad, youthful head and spat into the sand, trying to clear his throat and mouth of the water and mud he had inhaled. "By all the gods, I feared we both were lost. She struck her head as we set out for shore and I could not believe we would survive."

"To cling to your Princess was quite heroic," Palamon said. "'Twas surely done at peril of your life."

Ursid's dripping face fairly glowed. "But such a woman merits well the wager of a life."

Palamon smiled back at him. Ursid was very young and very bold. And he was, indeed, enthralled by Berengeria. It was to be wished that this youthful warrior could pass without too many scars and blows the gauntlet of slings and arrows he would face during his life's journey. The oxides of passing years, Palamon knew, could do much to dim any man's lamp.

They approached the two women together. Berengeria was still lying with her head in Aelia's lap but her eyes were clear now and her breathing was regular. She reached out and touched Palamon's ankle. "Good Palamon, I'm told you cheated fate by breathing life into my breathless body."

Palamon looked down at her and stepped back. "Princess, I only did what I was taught to aid the life to cling to your fair form. Ursid's the one who saved you, hauling you heroically across this torrent's foam. I merely watched."

Berengeria's eyes moved from Palamon to Ursid and then back again. "I am surrounded by such worthy friends, and all have done great service for my sake. You make my life seem small, the three of you. With such a band as this, we cannot fail, though Lothar, Alyubol, and all of nature's barriers block our way." Her eyes filled over as she looked up at them. It was indeed a pretty moment, set like a jewel into the stone of travail that had been theirs these past days.

But the moment had to pass. Palamon and Ursid still had to gather wood and a meal had to be prepared, for they dared go no further until Berengeria had been given a night to recover from her ordeal. But preparation of a meal was difficult now that the stores from the first boat were lost. All the flour was gone, much of the fishing equipment, some of the cooking utensils, and even Ursid's hand axe. Although they found the boat itself undamaged, those losses would hobble them as they entered the realm of the great river they had to follow.

For it was plain that the river they had left behind had in truth been but a tributary stream. Only now had they reached the mighty Stilchis itself. And after this first taste of its ways, there was no doubt that it would challenge them, extending them to the limits of their skill and endurance. The subject was not discussed through the afternoon and evening. Still, hidden in each of them was the hope that the coming contest with this powerful torrent would not become mortal combat.

Chapter Thirteen:
The Stilchis

IN THE MORNING they rose, dined on some of the food they had left, and took the time to whittle rude new paddles from driftwood. They divided their meager supplies between the two little boats. After all, the first rapid they had encountered had shown what could happen to either of the small craft at any time; they could not hazard the loss of all their provisions on the fate of one boat. Finally, they embarked.

Once afloat, they were carried by the swift waters of the great river into a strange, desolate world none of them ever could have imagined. The walls of the canyon loomed hundreds of fathoms above the foam of the torrent which had carved them. In some places, the walls were a dull brown or black; in others, they sparkled and reflected colors from black to red.

Later in the day, the boats entered a stretch of canyon where the roiling waters had exposed a towering expanse of black glass. On their right, this crystal wall soared to dizzy heights. The water was dotted with shining, jagged boulders of the stuff where it had been carved off by the river's action. On the left, there was only stone. But the sheet of jet glass formed a singular mirror, reflecting all that passed it for miles. They could see themselves as they paddled. Their actions were made grotesque by the shining undulations of the glass but no motion was lost.

Aelia found she could study herself quite closely. She could study herself and she could also study the movements of the heavy shoulders in front of her and the rippling of the muscles in the broad back, both as an image on the canyon wall and as the living, sweating man only cubits away from her. Palamon had discarded his tattered gray cloak in the heat of the day and now wore only his chain mail, its shining links forming a second skin as he labored.

Aelia regretted her outburst of the day before. There could be no doubt her words had cut Palamon to the quick. That was too bad; whatever he may have done in the past, there could also be no doubt his conduct had been honorable in the time she had known him. She regretted her harsh words and she wished she had never spoken them. Still, knowing what she did of the tall knight, she doubted that it would have been useful to bring the matter up again by apologizing. So she did not broach the subject. She paddled silently, studying his mail-bound shoulders.

It was odd that he retained this mail, rather than the gray robe and mourning cloak; Ursid had discarded the mail beneath his uniform long ago. Palamon's mail weighed less than Ursid's but, if there were an accident, it would surely make survival in the water difficult, in spite of its lightness and flexibility. It was true that a Knight of Pallas would never have thought of removing his lustrous hauberk, the badge of his order, in the presence of another human being. But this did not apply to Palamon. By his own admission, he had been expelled from that order.

Why, then, did he still retain the old custom? His armor was of no use to him at this moment; it only posed a danger. She could not resist drawing his attention to this fact. "Brave Palamon, why do you still enfold yourself with mail? It seems to be unwise. I shall avert my gaze if you desire to doff your hauberk's weight and don your cloak."

"If you would like, I shall put on my cloak."

"'Twould be far better in an accident."

"Then I will do it." He put down his paddle and she closed her eyes. When she opened them again, she was surprised to see that he had not doffed the mail at all; he had merely put the mourning cloak on over it. He looked back at her and smiled, though she could see the sweat already beginning to bead up on his face. "There. Now are you pleased?"

Aelia found his strained humor not amusing. "I had no wish to joke at such a thing. Your armor's just a hindrance to you now."

He looked straight ahead, still paddling steadily. "I wear no armor. Discipline your eyes."

His tone was flat, final. It left no doubt that he wished to discuss the matter no further and it led her mind back to the other times he had sheered away from discussion of his past as a Knight of Pallas. It certainly was a tender subject to him. That was understandable. But why, then, did he still maintain the traditions of his former order— the morning prayers, the rites of cleanliness, the wearing of the armor? Would it not have been less painful to him if he had discarded them altogether?

So Aelia pondered. Perhaps the rites were not painful after all but were comforting instead, patterns he had known all his life. Perhaps he refused to have them torn away by what had happened to him. Perhaps the rites and customs comforted him and it was only when they were questioned that they brought him pain. In that case, the sin was hers for broaching the subject. There was enough nobility in him to merit the privacy of his own past, whatever secrets the past might have contained.

Again her mind returned to the day before. She had hurt him deeply then with her reaction to his touching with his lips the tender mouth of Berengeria. To be sure, she had been half crazed with exhaustion, grief, and fear at the time, but that still had not lessened the pain her words had inflicted. Now her words had doubtless brought him pain again. And physical discomfort, too. They had caused him to don his cloak over his armor in the midday heat; there was little chance he would take the heavy garment off after the words that had passed between them.

He was such a strange, tortured man. What could she say to him? She needed to say something. "This line of talk disturbs you, Palamon. I'll not unearth the subject anymore, except to say when I spoke yesterday, I raved without my thoughts because I feared for our Princess' life. What I said then I still regret. Have peace and try to live beyond your past."

"My past life does not fret me. It is those about me who have always marked it most."

A bitter remark. Yet that was part of the fascination of Palamon; he refused to discuss his past yet he also refused to part with it. "Was she quite pretty, Palamon?" The words had leaped out by themselves. Aelia had allowed herself a lapse, her curiosity had caused her to put the lie to her thoughts and intentions of the past moments. She was not sure whether to curse herself or probe farther.

The only response from the seat in front of her was a momentary catch in the rhythm of Palamon's paddling. The silence lasted for a long, tense time. When he did speak, he spoke in clipped tones, expelling one word after another, pouring the thoughts from the crucible of his mind to be coined into phrases, and presented to her grudgingly, like a tithe. "She was as pretty as most other maids one sees a-washing clothes at some small village stream or berry picking by a road."

But Aelia had to know more. She could not resist the urge to drive in the wedge she had inserted between Palamon and his silence about his past. "Did you suspect when you crossed paths with her that you would jeopardize your rank and creed?"

There was another long silence. When he spoke again, it was with the tone of someone begging for a ghastly wound to be dressed. "My Lady, do not make me tread that path. Please let me turn aside, avert my eyes from all the shadows which are found that way."

She could not ask more; she would have had to be a

torturer to do that. His eyes stared forward; it was doubtful that he would have looked at her even if he could have. But there had been no mistaking the pain in his voice. He had told her next to nothing, yet her sympathy for him warred with her excitement; she had gained something more than information. At last she had pierced, if only for the moment, the citadel behind which Palamon lay hidden.

And she had learned a little, too. The mystery that was Palamon would be unraveled; she was now sure of that, for she was beginning to know his mind. She had seen his eyes linger on Berengeria's figure and had caught him glancing at herself as well. There was no doubt he was moved by the curve of a hip or the taper of a thigh; his instincts were those of any man.

Still, a Knight of Pallas was not allowed to indulge his instincts, though some did fail to hold their urges in check. Chastity was no easy vow to keep; as a priestess of Hestia, Aelia was aware of the difficulties. It was remarkable that more of Palamon's order had not fallen. She could not find it in her to censure him overmuch.

But how had he fallen? Always the search for the man inside Palamon returned to this question. Had Otar been right? Had Palamon's fall been simply a 'half-hour indiscretion,' a momentary breakdown? Had he and his paramour met more than once? Surely this affair could never have been worth expulsion from the order within which he had spent his entire life. Yes, she could comprehend his actions; perhaps she would have acted in the same way had she ever made the same mistake. Perhaps, had she been he, she would also have worn the old armor of the order.

So she pondered. Then she turned to another subject, guiding conversation away from Palamon's past. People who were as close together as they were forced to be in their little boats needed to talk about something, and what a person said about the weather could sometimes reveal as much as what he said about himself.

They struck more rapids, running their boats through those they dared, portaging around those that looked too rough for passage. The stores they carried with them grew lighter and required less time to carry now, but there was no solace in that; the meager provisions were all they had left until they reached the end of this great stream. And none of them knew when that would be.

Indeed, all enjoyment had gone out of their waterborne travel now. It was dull, endless labor, a race against time and against the men who pursued them. The smoothest waters forced them to paddle and delayed them maddeningly. The fastest waters were full of rapids which delayed them even more.

For days they watched their supplies dwindle as they passed through the endless corridor of this canyon. The glass cliffs were left behind. Their clothing became ragged, the gray cloak of Palamon most of all, until he discarded it. The fishing was good some days, poor others, but it never stopped the depletion of what little food they had left. When the stores were gone, fish was all they ate; on days when they caught nothing, they did not eat at all.

They were nearing the end of their tether. Tempers shortened; each person became nervous. They grew silent, seldom speaking to one another. Where they had been a cohesive, if tiny, force, they now assumed the driven look of four separate beings, each one simply trying to survive.

At this point, they encountered another rapid, one more of the series that they had battled. This one was especially difficult. Approaching it, they could see that it was very treacherous and that the sheer walls on each side prevented any attempt to portage around it.

All hearts sank. But there seemed yet a way; there was a jagged stone sticking out of the water at the head of the rapid and to this point Palamon clung, securing his craft as best he could while Aelia motioned Ursid and Berengeria to come alongside. They still possessed a quantity of rope and that was the key to Palamon's suggestion.

There were many rocks jutting from the exploding waters of this rapid. As the boat bucked beneath him, Palamon tied one end of the rope to the jagged stone which held them against the current and laid out his plan to the others. It was simple. Palamon and Aelia would take the end of the rope and proceed into the rapid while their partners paid the line out. Once they had reached the relative refuge of another boulder, they would tie to it and allow Ursid and Berengeria to set out, swinging past the first boat until they, in their turn, could tie off and the process could be repeated once more. And so it would go, the boats leapfrogging through the rapid until they could reach quiet water. It was a risky plan. But it was the one they had to use, for no one in the party could produce a better one.

Before they began, they examined the length of rope for places that might have been frayed or badly braided; their lives depended upon it now and none of them desired to be at the mercy of a weak strand. This task was quickly performed and they had to begin.

Palamon and Aelia let go and paddled heartily to guide their boat toward the next likely looking boulder. The boat bucked and bounded, its light hull twisting as the waves pummeled it. But they reached their goal safely. Then it was the turn of Berengeria and Ursid, who set out bravely into the raging torrent, passed close to the rock that sheltered Palamon and Aelia, took up the slack line, and brought their craft up against another point sixty or eighty cubits farther downstream.

The procedure was repeated once, then again. They were gaining ground against the rapid; soon they would be through it. But all was not well. As Palamon and Aelia set out for the last leg of their passage, Palamon noticed that they had brought their light craft against the last rock too sharply and the hide covering was torn. This was a catastrophe. The rip in the hull grew with every blow from the river and the water poured in, already soaking their legs. He had to shout to make himself heard above the roar of the rapid. "Our craft is lost. Do you know how to swim?"

"All those swim well, who hail from Artos' shores." There was no time to say more; the boat had already become unmanageable. It turned broadside to the current and over it went, spilling them out along with all its other contents. But there was no time to mourn its passing;

Palamon and Aelia had to swim, swim now, and swim for their lives.

Palamon was finally concerned for his chain mail. Light as it was, it would still be a liability in the water. He found it to be less so than he might have feared, however: the current swept him along so swiftly that he could not sink; he was carried with it, turned topsy-turvy, and spun like a shuttlecock, with no time to swim or think. In fact, the metal covering served him well once, as the current wrapped him around another boulder, beating the wind from his lungs and forcing him to struggle to keep from being pinned and drowned. He hoped Aelia had not met such an obstacle, but there was no chance for him to look for her.

Desperately, he worked his way toward the river bank, where the current raged less and the water was shallower. Water surged all around him. Sometimes it pushed him toward the surface, other times it sucked him toward the bottom, prying at his clenched teeth. But he was not overcome, though he began to wonder how long he could hold onto his senses.

After what seemed an eternity, he felt something new; his foot struck the bottom. Then his hand did the same. He had reached the shallow water; he would soon be safe.

The river bottom was hard stone, but it was firm footing, and he was able to scramble to his feet and wade toward shore, looking about for signs of Aelia and the other boat. In so doing, he saw that Aelia had also reached the shore, some yards downstream from him. She had survived her dunking well. She sat and watched him as he staggered toward her; they both gasped for breath and her soaked, tattered clothing clung to her like fur to a wet dog. But at least she was alert and upright.

The other boat could also be seen, Ursid and Berengeria battling their way through the last stages of the rapid. They paddled heroically while the spume churned about them. Sometimes they would disappear beneath the waves, only to reappear, rowing as hard as ever. It made a striking sight, one not to be forgotten, as they fought their way through the last leaping waves and turned their craft toward quieter water and the shoreline fifty cubits below Palamon and Aelia.

The four fugitives quickly rejoined. Each was relieved that they had survived; there was much backslapping and Aelia and Berengeria hugged one another, their drenched clothing raining water. But relief became despair as they counted their losses.

One boat was gone; Ursid said he and Berengeria had watched the sinking craft smash into a rock, then twist away and float downstream, a shattered wreck. And with it had gone half of their remaining stores, including all the fishing gear. Now there would be no more food nor decent means of getting any. Fishing line could, perhaps, have been made, but that was useless without hooks. And of the knives they had been given, only one remained.

Gloom descended upon them but Berengeria remonstrated against it. "We must continue. Always, there is hope. I'll not believe the gods will now allow us all to perish in this lonely place, not after we have battled odds so long. We shall survive. These cliffs must hold some life, though it be lizard, snake, or thing more foul. We shall survive. And I have heard you say, O Palamon, that suffering is a privilege, withal, for one may only suffer while he lives."

"Princess, I have said that," Palamon admitted.

"Then we'll continue, suffer though we may." Berengeria's lip jutted out stubbornly, and Palamon looked at her. At this, the lowest ebb of the group's misfortunes, she most showed her noble nature, her willingness to grapple with fate's adversities. She was more tenacious than ever.

So they set out again the next morning. The four of them now were crammed into the narrow confines of their remaining boat. They did not dare paddle, other than to keep the craft pointed downstream, and they could brave only the most moderate waters. This did not hinder them for the moment, however. Having vented its rage in the last rapid, the river now seemed content to carry them along smoothly, its rolling surface reflecting the narrow patch of sky and the separated canyon walls towering above them.

They floated on for the rest of the day, encountering no water more challenging than what they had already passed since the loss of their other boat. With the coming of darkness, they pulled out onto a narrow patch of shore that lay between the canyon wall and the left bank of the river. The night that they then had to pass became more of a battle than the last miles of river they had followed. They had eaten nothing since morning and that meal had been meager. Now the hunger gnawed at them, invading their fitful dreams and making even a short snatch of sleep a rare prize.

In the morning they all went hunting in the rocks, climbing about the cliff face in hopes of finding any living thing that could be turned into a meal. There was nothing. The rocks were as lifeless as they were dreary.

Since there was nothing more to be done about it, they reembarked. They floated along the smooth crest of the river, always keeping a sharp lookout for anything that could relieve their distress.

The canyon began to change as they floated onward. The walls still towered against the sky but the conformation had become more moderate; they no longer soared up from the water's edge but sloped back at an angle and were cut brutally by ravines and hollows, and the river became wider. The current flowed ever more slowly, and an occasional sandbar appeared in the midst of the broad water. They drifted through the morning, midday, and into the afternoon, watching the water lap a finger's length from the gunwale of their tiny craft. Each person was alone with his own thoughts and his gnawing hunger.

Then suddenly Ursid cried out. "Look up, up there."

Palamon followed the line of the younger man's extended arm. The cliff face on their left would soon be deserted by the setting sun and there was, indeed, something there. A building rested in a hollow, lonely and out of place amid the desolation. It looked like a temple. The lines of columns that formed the front and sides of the structure were crumbling and weathered; some had actually fallen, and there was no sign of life anywhere.

What was this place? How long had it been there, this huge and ancient pile? What would await them if they entered? The questions were meaningless; they were desperate and they had no choice but to investigate the place, if they were to have any hope of survival.

Without hesitating, they turned their boat to the shore below the mysterious structure. They pulled the craft up onto the beach and prepared to explore, Ursid hefting their remaining knife and Palamon grasping one of the paddles for use as a club, for lack of any better weapon.

The building was no longer visible; it loomed out of sight above the projecting cliffs at the water's edge. But a well-worn path led up from where they stood. None of them doubted where the path ended and they had no choice but to follow it, no matter what dangers lay in wait at the other end. Though they might discover Lothar's men, Alyubol's men, Alyubol himself, or some other grisly thing, such lurking hazards made no difference. To leave this place unexplored, to keep blindly journeying along these endless canyons, now presented as great a danger as anything that could lie before them.

Chapter Fourteen:
The Temple

THE TRAIL UP from the beach was chipped into the naked face of the cliff and appeared as ancient as the stone in which it was set. While the chisel marks at the side of the trail were still visible, the trail itself had been worn smooth; the center had been worn until it was lower than the edges by the treading of generations of feet.

It was steep and it seemed to wind forever upward. The party stopped to rest twice, for they did not wish to be caught breathless and off guard at the top. They followed its course cautiously as it wound into a vertical crevice in the cliff and then out around a prominent point; Palamon guessed that they now stood directly below the building they sought.

The trail became narrower as they climbed. They ascended to a dizzy height and they shrank against the cliff face, for the trail was only the width of a man's shoulders; a fall would have been a matter of bounding to rocks waiting beside the river a hundred fathoms below.

Then they rounded a last bend in the trail and found

themselves before the building itself. It was huge, even larger than it had looked from the water's edge. It was a temple, as they had thought it was, but it was a temple the like of which none of them had seen in their combined travels.

The towering columns of the porch stood like great, pale sentinels, and the canyon breeze wailed mournfully through the decayed remains. Who could have built the place? The architects must have belonged to a powerful order, else they could never have brought these great blocks of stone to this place and assembled them. From the point where the structure met the cliff face to the bottom step of the porch, Palamon guessed the distance to be well over a hundred cubits. It was a magnificent pile; it filled the broad shelf upon which it stood.

Ursid gazed at it a moment, wiping away the sweat that stood out on his forehead. "It is a mammoth place; what race of men could e'er have placed it here, and for what use?"

Palamon secured his grip on his club. He looked ludicrous, brandishing as a weapon the rudely carved paddle from a hide-covered boat. He rubbed his chin, his hand rasping against several days' growth of sweaty whiskers. "We cannot know till one of us goes in."

"Then I shall go," Ursid said.

"But use your powers of thought," Aelia said. "Lest you be caught by some inhuman thing. This ancient structure might hold anything—some long lost cult or beasts . . ."

"Or Alyubol," Berengeria contributed.

"Yes, even Alyubol. So use your eyes."

"Perhaps I should go in," Palamon said.

"No. I, not you." Ursid turned on the older knight, his eyes hard and defiant. "I am a warrior, too; I'm young and quick. My eyes are good as any in this group and I am fresh, untired by our ordeals. While older bones must rest and rebuild strength, I'll enter now, for I've no need to pause." Before Palamon could respond, Ursid bounded up the steps to the temple's broad porch. Once there, he shielded his body behind one of the great columns while he examined the entrance more closely. Then, stepping lightly, he moved along the porch toward the entrance itself, disappeared through the dark doorway, and was gone.

The other three waited anxiously, returning to the bend in the trail leading up to the place. There they could hide themselves behind the last outcropping of stone. They did not have to wait long. Ursid quickly reappeared, reaching the top step at the edge of the colonnade and motioning with his arm for them to come forward.

They quickly did so. Reaching him, Aelia whispered, "What lies inside this ancient structure?"

Ursid did not bother to whipser. "Faith, it is a temple as we thought. But still, it's like no temple I have ever seen. Come in, it's quite deserted. You will see my meaning."

They followed him past the colonnade, through the porch and into the dark interior of the building. "You'll need a moment for your eyes to change, adjusting for the light. It's not as dark as first it seems to be."

Ursid's words were true. The sun had not quite set and rays of light streamed through countless cracks and holes in the roof. There was a huge, dark shape before them, a statue which must have represented the deity to which the temple had been dedicated. But it was difficult to be sure who or what that deity was.

The statue was gigantic; it was the form of a naked man facing the interior of the building. It seemed to move, to challenge them, so filled with life was the stone. The long, unkempt hair and beard writhed about the face. The great, scar-traced torso was imbued with energy. In its right hand, the figure grasped by the neck a large bird of prey which it was in the act of throwing to the ground. Indeed, it was this action which gave much of the life to the carving; the battle had plainly been a hard one. The figure was scarred from head to toe. His wrists were bound in chains which he had broken; the short, twisted links swung with his endlessly preserved act of casting down the bird. And the bearded face showed terrible triumph at the victory; the stone eyes were filled with fire and the expression was one of supreme defiance.

In the left hand, the figure held an opened scroll. This was important, for it seemed to be the key to the nature of this deity. The walls of the temple's interior, unlike the tapestried walls of the temples known by the four travelers, were lined with shelves. And though the shelves were empty in places, many of them still held volumes of scroll cases. Shelves lined the side walls as well as the front wall behind the great statue; there were even orderly rows of shelves standing in the spaces between the double row of columns in the center of the chamber. The place was full of them. It was a library. But it had been built on such a scale that none of the foursome had ever seen its match.

The chamber had not been entered for a great while; dust blanketed everything. It covered the floor, the endless rows of shelves, and the statue itself. As Palamon advanced toward the nearest row, his feet left deep impressions in it.

"This floor has not been trodden for an age," Ursid said. "This dust is everywhere and undisturbed, except for footsteps left by my own passing."

Palamon saw this was so as he looked over one of the large bookshelves. Everywhere there was the dust of ages. The shelves were no longer full of scroll cases; many were empty. The books they did contain were scattered and disordered, as if they had been perused by an uncaring hand. Something else was odd; although there were no disturbances in the dust on the floor, he noted a circular spot free of dust on one of the shelves, as if one of the large scroll cases had been recently removed.

But there was no time to puzzle over this. They had to go on; their mission in this ancient building was to find food or at least the means of obtaining it. So they advanced farther into the interior of the place.

They walked past the long rows of shelves toward a great doorway barely visible at the back of the bookfilled cella. Here there was a surprise waiting for them. Instead of a small chamber that normally occupied the rear of a temple, or even a doorway to the outside, they found an antechamber leading to a large tunnel, cut back into the

cliff itself. This posed a problem for they had no light.
The cella of the temple was dark; this antechamber was
yet darker, and the passageway was only a blackness on
the far wall.

"This n'er will do," Aelia said, "We must secure a
torch."

"Of what?" It was a fair question Ursid asked.

"Whatever we can find. It must be done. To follow
this dark passage without light is grimmest folly." Aelia
was adamant.

"Yes, you spoke the truth," Palamon said. They turned
to retrace their steps. Perhaps a rude torch could be manufactured from the few wares they still had in their boat.

But as they passed once again into the great central
chamber of the temple, something was blocking their way.
It was a great, grim, hulking figure, standing a head taller
than Palamon himself—and Palamon was a tall man.

The creature was wolflike in the dimness; it was a
black, humanoid shape with a wolf's head and it carried
an axe, a broad-bladed battle axe. It held the weapon
high, ready to strike. As the four of them shrank back
into the smaller chamber, it advanced. "Who are you?
Why have you come to invade my Master's domain? Why
shouldn't I kill you?" The voice was deep and powerful,
as laden with menace as the axe itself.

Aelia was quick to speak. "We are four fugitives who
come in peace, to seek a helping hand and sustenance."

The wolf-thing paused, but the axe remained poised.
"You'll get nothing here but death.'

"What manner of creature are you?" Palamon asked.

"I am Usmu."

"Why are you here?"

"I serve my Master."

"Who is that?"

There was a moment's pause; the peppering of questions seemed to have pushed this Usmu creature off
balance. He thought for a moment. "My Master is my
Master." The axe descended a little.

Palamon looked up at him. He was an awesome figure;
the torso was wedge shaped, the shoulders were nearly

a fathom across, covered by coarse hair. Great fangs could be seen against the shadows within the wolfish maw. But the monster did not seem to be as imposing mentally as he was physically. "I tell you, then," Palamon said, "Your Master is the one we wish to see."

There was another pause. "Master told me to come here and keep away intruders. I will kill you if you try to go past me."

How sure of its mission was this Usmu creature? Did the post he kept have any real meaning to him? Palamon wondered about that and spoke accordingly. "But we are not intruders."

The axe drooped another degree and the creature put his head to one side a bit. "Why not?"

Now Aelia pitched in. "We come to see your Master. We are not some heavy-handed thieves who come at night to rob and kill."

The bulging shoulder muscles rippled as the creature lowered the weapon all the way, holding it in one great paw. "No, you are not thieves. I know what thieves are. But Master never said anything about thieves, as far as that goes. I don't trust you."

Palamon gripped his paddle-club, debating whether to try to get the axe away from the thing. A well-timed blow could still knock it from the casual grip now, for Usmu was no longer concentrating on the weapon. But that still might not be wise; the creature looked powerful enough to kill them with his bare hands. "Why does your Master not want visitors?"

"I don't know. Sometimes when I finish my other work and ask him what to do next, he tells me, 'Usmu, go and guard the library against intruders.' And then I do."

"I say again, that's one thing we are not." Aelia's manner was a study in innocence.

Before the creature could answer her, Palamon spoke again. "What must we do for you to let us by?"

"I am not supposed to do that."

"Then Usmu, gentle guardian, we'll not ask you to let us by at all."

"You won't?"

Palamon shook his head. "We'll only ask that you might take us to your Master. That is not to let us by."

It was a fine point, indeed. Still, it seemed to have good effect. Usmu was silent.

"A small request," Aelia said, catching onto the game. "We simply ask to see your Master. Tell us, what thing must we do for you to take us to him, as you should?"

Usmu seemed to be approaching despair. "I don't know. Everything has gone wrong. I was in the library watching and I saw *him* come in." He gestured with the axe toward Ursid. "Then he went back out, and you all came in, and I thought you were intruders. But you say you aren't. But I shall still kill you for my Master if you try to pass me. I never killed anyone before; I think he'd be proud of me." The building shook with the vibrations of Usmu's voice.

Palamon's mind was racing. By his own words, Usmu was still a danger to them, however weak his brain might be. "We did not try to get by you at all; in fact, we all were leaving when you came. Can you deny a word of this?"

"No."

"Then take us to your Master, as we ask," Aelia repeated. "What must we do to make you do this thing?"

Usmu stood awkwardly on one foot as he pondered all that had been said to him. Then the massive face brightened with what must, to him, have been a stroke of genius. "Sometimes I bring Master books from this library. That's what you must do. You must bring him a book."

"I'll gladly do that, Usmu," Palamon said, relieved. "One of these?" He gestured toward the shelves that surrounded them.

"Yes, yes, any one of them." There was a glint in the creature's hooded eyes, now. "It doesn't matter which one."

"This one?" Palamon reached toward one of the scroll cases. But as he did, the creature lashed out with blinding speed. The battle axe scythed through the air, breaking the case to smithereens, slicing into the stout shelf and nearly removing Palamon's hand before he could snatch it back.

Usmu shook with glee, his great lungs hurling forth peals of laughter. The laughter was childish, but there was no solace in that. It sent chills down the spines of all four of them. "A game, a game. My Master doesn't play games with me. But you will. You must take a book, but if you try, I'll cut off your hand." He was delighted with his trick. "Maybe I will get to kill you after all."

Things had taken a bad turn. Palamon backed around Usmu toward the outer end of the library, watching the wolfish head as it pivoted to follow his motion. The child-brained monster was now a picture of concentration. Palamon looked up at him. "How often will you let me play this game, to snatch a scroll at peril of my life?"

"Play, play. I like the game."

"No." Berengeria tried to push herself between the two gamesters but Ursid held her tightly. "Palamon, you cannot risk your life. The peril must be borne by all of us."

"Stay back." Palamon's words were spoken in a low, deadly tone. There was no disobeying them. "The bargain's made and it will stand." He smiled once more, that same mask of a smile that the others had seen before. "This monster is not such a worthy foe—no quicker than a lowly serpent's fang, nor stronger than a dozen or so men. The lots are drawn; I'll play this deadly game the same way we play out life's lottery. No arguing results, no second chances. Tell me, noble Usmu, may I still pick any book from all this chamber holds?"

Usmu giggled and nodded. "Any book."

The words had not even passed the hulking monster's teeth before Palamon's hand darted toward another scroll case. But once again the monster was quick beyond belief. Palamon barely snatched his fingers out of the way as the great axe again embedded itself into the shelf, carving in twain the scroll canister that had been the target. The reaction was daunting. The creature had not been ready; he had been caught off guard while still speaking, but still had been able to react with time to spare.

There was silence in the library now, broken only by

the breathing of the four humans and the huge guardian. Palamon had no more humor now, no words at all. He was deadly serious. The sweat beaded upon his arms and forehead. He flicked his fingers part way toward an open scroll and there was a crunching sound as the axe gouged into wood once more.

Breathing, breathing, the soft sound of Palamon's footsteps—there were no other sounds as he slipped along the aisle with Usmu in smiling pursuit. Palamon's eyes shifted to the floor the creature was crossing as he followed the tall knight. Usmu was leaving no tracks! There were no imprints where the clawed feet had passed.

That accounted for Ursid's mistake. No wonder there had been no tracks in the library and Ursid had thought it unoccupied. Who could have expected this? And who could be the unnamed Master who had conjured up this apparition? Surely it was an unequal contest. If Palamon was to have any hope of surviving, he needed to find some better strategem than simply trying to outgrab this thing.

On the shelf to Palamon's right, barely visible out of the corner of one eye, there was a large scroll case lying on its side on the edge of the top shelf. Palamon did not reach for it; there was no hope of succeeding that way. Instead, he feinted toward the shelf across the aisle from it and at the same time kicked the bookcase behind him as hard as he could with his heel.

There was a crash as the first case was shorn in two by the axe; at the same time, Palamon held out his right hand and allowed the toppled scroll case, the one in back of him, to drop into it. Then he danced back, holding it up before the astonished Usmu, who was still wrenching his weapon free of its target.

Usmu was a picture of rage, disappointment, and frustration. "No fair, no fair."

"The game was fair by all the rules you gave. Now take us to your Master and be quick."

"I should kill you anyway."

The foiled monster was still deadly; the edge had to be taken off his fury. Palamon had to be helped. "Methinks your Master might not be well pleased to find that you renege on your own game," Aelia said. "Our Palamon has got himself a book and it is time that he presented it."

Usmu said nothing. He stood glaring at Palamon, fairly seething. With a roar and a mighty sweep of one arm, he cast away the axe, which crashed into a column on the far side of the chamber. "No fair." Even though they were spoken in the monster's deep voice, the words had the ring of a foiled child. Then he turned and strode toward the rear of the building.

They followed him, running to keep up. At first, as they entered the passage that led from the library into the cliff, each of them feared they were to be plunged into a long, subterranean journey with a creature that could outdistance them easily in the dark—or which could turn upon them at any moment. This did not happen, however. After a moment's walk, they entered a small chamber which was well lit by torches, several of which stood in sconces carved into the stone of the walls.

"This way." Usmu barely glanced over a hairy shoulder as he turned down another corridor. Palamon still suspected the monster would have liked to kill them all, if only he could have found a way to excuse the act.

This corridor was also well lit, they walked only a short way before it opened into a large, cluttered chamber. There were long tables set up throughout the room, as if it had once been a dining hall, but it was not being used for that purpose now. Each table was covered from end to end with a jumble of scrolls, drawings, empty or partially full bowls, vials, and writing implements; there was no naming the parts of this clutter.

At the middle table sat the lord of this dominion of bric-a-brac; he was a small, whitehaired old man. He wore a formless gray robe and jotted notes onto a piece of parchment while he studied something before him on the table. He had not yet noticed his guests. He wrote silently, pausing now and then only to shift in his chair or manipulate the thing he was studying. Could this queer-looking, eccentric old creature be their nemesis, Alyubol? It seemed doubtful. He seemed too lost in his own jumbled world

even to notice his visitors, let alone steer the politics of
the feudal provinces about the Thlassa Mey.

"Well?" Aelia's voice was a soft whipser as she urged
Usmu. "Tell him we are here."

"I don't know just how to do that," the creature said.
He did not know how to whisper, either; his deep voice
filled the room.

The old man heard the disturbance and looked up. He
was a remarkable-looking fellow. His face was a mass of
wrinkles, and the age and wisdom of a generation of seers
and sages could be seen there. Some of them were so
deep there seemed to be no bottom to them at all; there
was hardly a portion of the pink, delicate skin that had
not been undulated by time. But the eyes were the face's
most striking feature. The expressive mouth, the refined
nose, the small, compact form, all were striking in their
own ways. But those eyes seemed to be filled with light,
an inner fire that consumed all before them, including the
four travelers. Palamon, mysterious, experienced Palamon, was as unnerved as the others by the sense of those
eyes shifting through his being.

All four of them were dumbstruck. Finally it was Ursid
who managed to break the silence. "What manner of man
are you?"

There was a moment's pause; then the old man
answered. "I am Reovalis, the lowly sage who lives alone.
And I know who you are."

Chapter Fifteen:
Reovalis

THE SILENCE THAT followed the statement of the sage Reovalis was long and pregnant. The four adventurers were surprised to hear this recluse tell them that he knew who they were—they who had been pursued unsuccessfully by the most powerful forces on the shores of the Thlassa Mey. They had managed to elude those forces, but this old man said he knew them. Did this alleged knowledge bode well for them, or did it bode ill? Each one remained silent, gagged by his own onrushing thoughts.

The silence was broken by Usmu. Although he had been forgotten for the moment, he had not himself forgotten his purpose in bringing the quartet here. "These human people have brought you a book, Master."

Reovalis did not answer; his eyes flicked to the hulking form of the servant, then back to his guests. But Usmu was not to be denied. He took the scroll canister from Palamon's unresisting fingers and placed it on the table before the old man. "Here it is." His voice was ludicrous, for, in spite of its heavy timbre, it sounded like a child who had been brought before a most frightful grown-up.

"I thank you," Reovalis said, without taking his eyes off his guests. He set the canister with the other items that littered the table. "You may leave us, now, Usmu. In fact, you are dismissed."

"Dismissed? Don't do that."

"Fear not. You shall be summoned in due course." Without further discussion, Reovalis made a peremptory wave with his right hand, and, before the astonished eyes of the four visitors, mighty Usmu vanished. There was no sound; all that was left was a faint whisp of smoke where the monster had stood.

A gasp escaped Berengeria's throat. Without a doubt, the four of them were in the presence of one of those unique individuals, a sorcerer. Considering this fact, the statement that he was familiar with them became less remarkable.

Astonishment begat speech. "The gods," Ursid exclaimed. "What manner of thing was that, to be with just one gesture so dismissed?"

"He is a summoned servant made of flesh. A fleshen servant, useful in his way but of no weight in matters of import. No doubt you have observed, my friends, that he is but a child. He cannot hold a place beside such notables as you—proud Berengeria, herself, the heiress of Carea's gilded throne; the Mistress Aelia, guardian royal, whose wit and fortitude have saved her charge up to this point, at least; Ursid, the young, whose great devotion to his proud Princess has led him to renounce his native land . . ."

Then his eyes fixed upon Palamon. "And lastly we have noble Palamon, by far the most interesting of all you four, who gave up everything that he held dear for one decision, made in foolish haste, concerning some young maiden he had known for—what? An hour's space or less?"

The other travelers looked at Palamon. He stood as motionless as a man encased in ice. He tried to smile his smile into the face of the sage but the attempt was a feeble one. He had turned gray. His mouth was stretched into a narrow line. "And how could you have learned these things?"

"I am Reovalis, the sage, you see. I know these things and more. Brave Palamon, your history has fascinated me these several years that I have studied you. Without your ever knowing me, by use of means you cannot understand, I've viewed your life. And I've learned much. I know of things that you do not suspect as yet, as well as others you know well."

The old man paused, studying with some satisfaction the effect of his words. There was no malice in his expression; he appeared pleased at being able to speak this way to his guests. He turned back to Palamon. "I know more than you know yourself about your past. I know your origin. I know what price incest has wrung from you, and what is more, I feel that I can say that incest's future cost could yet be dear."

"A jongleur's game, no more," Palamon muttered. But the words were forced out as if he were choking upon them.

"I know you fully, sir, as I have said. Your partners I know well, but of your life I know almost as much as of my own."

"You say you know my origin. Speak out."

"I cannot tell you everything I know." Reovalis' answer was abrupt. "To tell you things that you yourself have not yet learned could make you change your course and alter history unborn. I am a sage, you see. I learn of life, the forces that can move this world of ours. But though I spend my life in diligent research to seek out all the world's realities, I do not act. My purpose is to learn."

"You do that well; you've proven that to me. But if you do not act, then of what use are you to all these lands you study so?"

"Of what use is a rose, a summer's eve, a maiden's face, or even your own life?"

Palamon fell silent. He had no answer and it would doubtless not have mattered if he had.

Berengeria broke into the conversation. "And what of Alyubol? Do you know him?"

The old man turned to her, fingers stroking the fine, white whiskers that framed his ancient visage. He contemplated her for a moment before speaking. "I know him, yes. He hides himself from me but there are some few scraps of information I can glean."

"Then tell us of him. Tell us all you know."

Reovalis shook his head slowly as he repeated himself. "I shall not tell you all the things I know. To do so could, as I have said, affect the course of history as yet unwrit. Perhaps I have already said too much. This question gives me pause. I must consider it. How much can I inform you ere it is too much? I shall consider this and while I do, avail yourselves of all that I possess. It is not much, but it will serve your needs." He lowered he head and began writing once more.

The guests stood nonplussed. Reovalis seemed to have finished with them. But while his hospitality had been offered, he had made no move to direct them toward it. There were four corridors opening into this chamber but the only one the adventurers knew was the one leading back to the outside.

There was an uncomfortable pause. Then the sage looked up at them once more, as if puzzled that they still stood before him. His eyebrows lifted and he spread his hands. "Forgive me, please; my manner is uncouth. My work has isolated me so long that I have quite forgotten how to act before my guests." He gestured with his quill toward the opening in the wall to their right. "If you go through that door, an ample meal has been prepared for you. Considering your trip and hard conditions, I may say you'll not leave it untouched. I cannot join you now; my work will occupy me for a time."

Without another word for his guests, he again directed his eyes to the scrolls before him on the table. They concluded that they had received as much of an invitation as they ever would; besides, at the mention of food, they did not need to be urged. They crossed the cluttered chamber and entered the low hallway toward which he had pointed.

A moment's walk took them to another chamber, this

one less impressive than the last. The walls had no veneer and the chisel marks they bore attested to the fact that this chamber, like the last, had been carved into the living stone of the cliff. But that mattered little to them as they looked upon the meal laid out on the long table in the center of the room. To their famished eyes it was a divine feast; the smooth planks bore bowls of fruit and raw vegetables, flagons of wine, cakes of cheese, loaves of bread, jars of honey, and platters of roast mutton. These things lay before them like beckoning paradise.

Without hesitation, they threw themselves down upon the benches and reveled in their repast. They did not pause even for thought or consideration of the meal. Had it been poisoned? Did the spiced wine and highly peppered meat contain drugs or potions? It did not matter, they were too famished and fatigued to care.

But this was understandable; they had traveled long. Besides, they had watched the manner of their host, this mysterious sage Reovalis. His powers in unknown arts could not be denied and it seemed unlikely that he would have attempted to gain by treachery what he could have easily taken by force. So they feasted without thought. The fruits and vegetables were delicious after their days of eating fish or nothing, the mutton was hot, spicy and adequate, and the bread and honey were a flight to the alabaster regions of Paradise. It did not matter what culinary delights these four travelers had experienced in the past. This simple feast, coming as it did on the heels of their greatest deprivation, delighted their starved senses in a manner which could scarcely have been imagined.

And so they feasted, eating until they were more than full. Even Palamon, stoic, disciplined Palamon, devoured the rations before him until his midsection grew uncomfortable. Then the drowsiness came. He felt a heaviness invading his eyes and his body rebelled against his commands, crying out only for rest. He looked at Berengeria as she cast her eyes back toward him, her face reflecting his own fears. Had they, indeed, been drugged? Or was it simply a loaded belly, too much good wine, and their endless days of hardship, all working in concert? It did not matter. All Palamon desired now was rest, to close his eyes and sleep. He saw that the others were all cursed by the same need. Ursid and Aelia were slumped forward, their heads resting upon their arms, and Berengeria had actually curled up on the floor next to the bench.

There was no helping it. Palamon tried to dictate to his sagging body, to force it to rise and stand guard over his companions. But his will was breaking down; No, there was no helping it. With a yawn, he moved his wooden platter to the center of the table, pushed a bowl of glistening grapes aside, and laid his head down on the cool wood. A moment later, a soft snore escaped his lips.

Several moments passed. None of the travelers stirred. More time trickled away. After a long while, a figure entered the room; it was the lone figure of Reovalis. Without a word, he walked to the table and examined his four guests, then stood and watched them sleep, his hand resting on the back of Palamon's head. "So. Pardon me, my guests. What I have done is doubtless inhospitable in all your eyes. But I live here and am not used to all the customs of your outside world. The potion is a mild one; you'll just sleep.

"For sleep is what you need the most, I think. I am not used to guests; how could I know for sure what your reaction might become, once you have supped, regaining all your strength? Would you confront me, one old, lonely man? Your cause is just, that cannot be denied, and I may help you if your souls are true. I think they are, from what is in the Glass. Your stay will be upon my terms alone. I'm old, you see, and not conformed to guests."

He made a gesture with his left hand, a mystical, indescribable gesture. A moment passed, then another figure entered the chamber, the hulking, hairy figure of the flesh servant, Usmu, who had been dismissed into a wisp of smoke only a short time earlier. Reovalis directed the monster to the sleeping Palamon. Following the sage's pointed finger, Usmu moved to the side of the sleeping Knight of Pallas and effortlessly hoisted him up, throwing the muscular body easily over one shoulder. In Usmu's cavernous, yet childlike, eyes, there was no sign that he remembered the life-and-death contest that had taken place just a short time ago.

Chapter Sixteen:
The Glass of the Polonians

PALAMON AWAKENED. THE information his senses gave him was disconcerting. There was nothing before him but darkness, nor was there a sound to be heard; the only senses that served him were those of touch and smell. All was black. Did he lie in some tomb—or in some Tartarus? No, this was not a tomb; it was a closed chamber with the dank smell of age in it, but it was not necessarily a tomb. He concentrated, avoiding further flights of fancy. He was lying on a sleeping couch, a most luxurious one from the feel of it. He reached down and touched the linen upon which he was lying. It was fine material and it covered a couch the like of which he had not enjoyed in years. His uncertainty diminished.

So he was not in a tomb; this was no abode of the dead. Then where was he? His mind traveled back to the last events he could remember—the flight from Buerdaunt, the wudlings, the passage down the Stilchis to the ancient temple—the meal. He had been drugged. He could remember it now—the feast, the wine, the drowsiness that could not be staved off. And the sight of his fellow victims lying down before him. A potion had been in the food; he had been put to sleep and taken to this place.

With a gasp, he sat upright and swung his legs over the side of the couch, reaching for the floor with his feet. Then he paused as his head began to whirl. Either he was still drugged or he had lain here for a long time; his body hardly obeyed the command to action.

Moving more slowly, he planted his feet on the cool stones of the floor and stood. It was no easy task. Without light, without any plane of reference, standing was tricky business. But he had to explore this place. Slowly, cautiously, he examined his cell; he found a stone wash stand, a wooden chair, and a door in the blackness. He felt for a handle and found one.

Pulling the door open, he found himself standing in a low corridor where torches cast a dim glow. It was lined with other doors like the one through which he had stepped. Were his companions behind any of them? He pushed one. It gave beneath his touch, revealing a chamber exactly like the one he had just left, its darkness barely pierced by the torches' weak light.

His attention was distracted by a sound behind him, barely a sound, even. He simply sensed something. He turned and started upon seeing the massive form of Usmu towering over him—Usmu, of the great strength, quickness and stealth, and of the nonexistent mind. Before Palamon could react, the monster spoke. "You are awake. You are the last one to do that. The Master told me to bring you to him as soon as you wake because he and the others are waiting for you."

The words were spoken with little tone or inflection, as if this was a memorized speech designed to be spoken on cue. Considering what he had seen of Usmu's mental gifts, Palamon guessed this to be the case. So he was to be taken before Reovalis once more.

Palamon did not hesitate to go with Usmu. For one thing, resistance would have done no good; the flesh servant had shown himself to be more than capable of overcoming even the strongest man. Besides, he had told

Palamon that the tall knight's companions awaited. His companions had been what Palamon was seeking when Usmu had appeared; without them, his next move would be meaningless.

So Palamon walked in the direction Usmu pointed, turning into an intersecting passage. As he walked, he noticed for the first time what he was wearing. His chain mail, the hauberk he had worn for so long, was gone. In its place, he was now gowned in a soft, knee-length tunic of white cotton gathered at the waist with a cord. It was clerical garb, but the color and the design woven into it had no connection with the Knights of Pallas.

This change in dress upset Palamon more than he would ever have let his companions see, had they been there in person; it upset him far more than had the loss of his sword with its carved horn pommel. He stopped in the center of the corridor and felt at himself, pulling at his new clothing as if he might have found his armor hidden away beneath it somewhere. He stood rooted to the floor, looking up hopelessly at Usmu, who only returned the gaze with dumb impatience.

"Hurry," Usmu finally said. "I'm supposed to bring you to my Master."

Again Palamon cast his eyes along the corridor, then turned and bolted back toward the chamber he had just left. Even before huge Usmu had blocked his dash, he knew the move was useless. There were a dozen doors lining each side of the corridor he had come from, each of them identical with all the others. It would have been a tedious search at best. If his captor—for such he now considered Reovalis—desired him to, he would have the hauberk back.

He looked up at the flesh servant looming before him and managed a smile. "Forgive me, gentle monster, 'twas a lapse. I shall not break the dignity of these fair halls with any further outbursts. Have no fear, I shall not harm you. Let's march on." He winked at Usmu and again moved in the direction that was desired.

They walked back toward the dining hall, the scene of the party's late misfortune. Entering the chamber, Palamon found the great plank table once more laden with food. There sat Ursid, Aelia, and Berengeria. They turned to look at him as he entered, and so did Reovalis, who was seated at the head of the table.

"How now, brave Palamon," Reovalis said. "At last you've come. Your sleep has lasted long, far past the time your fellows slumbered."

"Yes, that is the truth." Berengeria rose, took Palamon by the arm, and brought him to a seat at the table. "'Twas almost one full day you slept. It caused concern."

"At nearly twoscore years of age, my body does not mend as well as yours. Apologies I must extend, O fair Princess."

"Infirmities of age will be your friends and boon companions, more so every year. Well could I tell you that much, even if I were no sage," Reovalis said. "But you do look well now. I hope you find yourself well satisfied with these accommodations, ancient ones though they may be. I hope the loss of certain articles does not offend you greatly." The ancient man's eyes bored into Palamon.

Palamon shrugged. "What things I may have lost mean nought to me. I had not even noticed. This fair man . . ." he turned to gesture toward Usmu but the flesh servant had gone. "Your largish servant said to me I was expected, so I came post haste. If I have lost some article, though it may be quite unimportant, I am sure it will be found and then returned to me in all good time."

"That may or may not be. If not, its value will be well made up." Reovalis turned his head, addressing all his guests now. "You see, my friends, I've not arranged my thoughts concerning what to do with all of you. I am a sage; my role is not to act. And yet, you see, I find myself provoked to aid you in your quest, which I find just. I shall decide at length. Until that time, you will be safe from your pursuers here."

He turned back to Palamon. "This much I say to you, brave Palamon: you have no future in the past. And so the articles you've lost will drag you down the more, if they're returned. If my decision is to give you aid, they all will be replaced, at least in worth. If not, then I will send you four upon your ways with all the selfsame goods that you brought here.

"My guests, as you all know, I have declined to answer inquiries about this place or who or what I am until you all were present. Now you are. And so I say to you: one question each I'll field, excluding matters deemed unsuitable by me to treat upon. So speak up now and test my knowledge. Ask me what you will."

The air about the table was filled with a babble of questions. Reovalis waited until it settled a bit, then spoke again. "One well-considered question each, no more. And young Ursid, let us begin with you."

Given the chance to speak openly and without interruption, Ursid was without words. He sat for a moment, his smooth jaw working silently. At last he did find a question. "What manner of place is this that we have found, so far away from most men's normal haunts?"

Reovalis nodded. "That question I can answer without fear about the answer's consequence. So hear. This is a great library—temple, too—a monument to learning ages old. An ancient cult, the wise Polonians, an order of great power in past times, constructed it both as a learning place and as a temple sacred to their creed. They held to sanctity of mind and thought, of learning, and of study for its own sake. Evil times then drove them out and left this place a dark, deserted ruin. But still the books are here. And thus it is a fitting place for me."

"However did you come here?" Ursid asked.

Evidently forgetting his restriction of one question per guest, Reovalis held forth happily. "This place was left deserted eons past. The wise Polonians, though they were strong, a wealthy order, quite mysterious, were driven out by stronger, evil men. And so the temple stood deserted here, abandoned and forgotten by the world. But in my studies when I was a lad, I found occasional remarks on it, well knowing what its worth would be to me. To find it was the great goal of my youth. Once I had found it, then I earnestly struck out to glean all knowledge from its shelves on items both of mystery and fact. That was my great ambition in those years that formed my middle age. I grew quite wise and strong in conjuring and all such arts. Yet still I learn. I study all the world and hope to learn without exception all items there can ever be to know. That is the goal of these, my eldest years."

"And yet such learning, never put to use, will be of little value to that world you have observed for lo these many years." There was doubt in Aelia's eyes.

"That might well be," Reovalis answered. "But how much does it matter?" He looked at her for a moment. "But you, my Aelia, what have you to ask?"

"Tell us of the forces that we flee. How close upon our trail do they now press? Do they still search for us or do they feel that we are lost, no longer worth the chase?"

Reovalis continued to study her face. "A well-framed question, gentle guardian. It is direct, concise, and covers points most valuable to you to help you frame your course. But I must ponder thoughtfully awhile. Until I choose to answer your inquiry, let us have another." He turned to Berengeria. "And you, the fair Princess, what would you ask me?"

"What of Alyubol?" Berengeria put the question as if it had been foremost in her thoughts ever since Reovalis' first offer to be quizzed. "How great is his involvement in our plight? What might we do to circumvent his wiles?"

Reovalis nodded. "Another question, probing deep and true. The answers to these queries give me pause. I must be cautious now; I shall not tell you all, for that is telling you too much." He sat motionless and silent for a bit, as if he might not even have been aware of the four pairs of eyes upon him. Finally he looked up at his guests again. "An answer of a sort I might well give; if you have eaten and are satisfied, then rise and come with me."

Without waiting for a response, Reovalis rose from his place at the head of the table and passed out of the chamber by the corridor that led back to his study. They all rose and walked after him, even Palamon, though the tall knight had hardly had a thing to eat since awakening.

Reovalis noted this. As the group passed through his cluttered study, skirting tables and articles that had rolled onto the stone floor, he spoke to the Knight of Pallas over his shoulder. "Fair Palamon, I see you follow, too. But you have eaten little for some time. Can any insignificant display that I might show you mean that much, perchance?"

Palamon was less daunted by Reovalis now than he had been at first. The sage was human, he possessed a powerful ego, and he was enjoying his audience. "You taunt me, sir. Your knowledge seems so vast that any word that you might deign to say would well be worth the loss of many meals." The answer was laced with irony; still, Reovalis acted pleased with it and walked on, a hint of a smile peeking from beneath his eiderdown beard.

They passed through the study chamber; it seemed the demonstration was not to be held there. They entered another hallway, which led downward into the bowels of the mountain. The walk was not a long one. They passed down a hundred cubits of corridor and found themselves in a small room, not much larger than the one Palamon had awakened in. It was lit by torches and the torchlight showed more in the way of furnishings than Palamon's chamber had contained; there was a small cot to sleep on, shelves bearing scrolls and papers, a large desk bearing more paper and writing utensils along with a finely crafted oil lamp, unlighted at the moment. In fact, the room was so packed with furnishings that it was impossible for all five people to cram themselves into it. Palamon, who was at the rear of the group, found himself watching through the open door.

Reovalis paused before a tapestry on the far wall of the chamber and spoke. "My guests, I show you something which no eye, save for my own, has recently observed. You stand within the quarters occupied long centuries ago by one lone man, the Grand High Priest of the Polonians. To him, in honor of his high position, was entrusted custody of this, my prize and key to all my studies. Ere we all pass in to learn and profit by its mystic teachings, I have need to warn you.

"Many, many years was I to study ere I came to learn the secrets of this instrument by which all things may be discovered and made known. Much have I learned and much have I to learn. This much I say, for it may serve you well to think on it, if you will gaze into the depths of the Polonians' far Glass.

"The Glass of the Polonians speaks out to every man in his own separate tongue. And to each man it tells a different tale, for men are varied as an ocean's waves in how they see the same occasion. So therefore, do not seek to gaze into the Glass and know all things, for your young minds do not yet hold the fruit of years of thought and study for the sake of learning all the Glass can well reveal.

"So simply seek to learn those basic things that are occurring in the present time; the future and its sights are closed to you. The secrets of the Glass may overwhelm the mind that seeks too much. A few times, even I've been nearly lost from trying to oppose my intellect with the mysterious powers of its magic."

With this speech, Reovalis pulled aside the hanging and bade his guests pass through the opening it covered. The passage was dark and the chamber it opened into was dark also. "Bear right, bear right, stay fast against the wall. The Glass is danger to a person who does not completely understand its might. Please keep your eyes closed till I give you word, for there is danger here. Place both your hands across your eyes and do not move them till I tell you to."

As they passed into the dark chamber, none of the foursome spoke; there was a quality in Reovalis' voice which stated better than words that he was in deadly earnest. As Palamon followed the others into the chamber, he kept his back pressed against the rough stone wall that curved away to the right; he held his left palm stoutly over his eyes. He could feel the eyelids flutter against the sensitive skin.

The chamber was nearly silent. Palamon could hear his own breathing as well as the exhalations of Berengeria, who was standing beside him. There was also another sound, a slight trickling or bubbling; it was difficult to tell which.

Then they heard Reovalis follow them in. The old man

cleared his throat as he passed, then the footsteps faded toward the other side of the chamber. When he spoke again, his voice came from several cubits away, directly opposite them.

"Take care, my guests, and heed each word I say. You now are in the presence of a force that issues from the voids within this world on which we run the courses of our lives. I do not understand this mighty force completely but I can survey its face and learn from it what little things I may. Heed every word. You all must certainly do as I say, exactly as I say. I cannot help you if by chance you fall." Was there a pedantic tone creeping in to the old man's voice? Palamon thought so. He suspected the lone sage was enjoying himself hugely as he played to his captive audience.

"Now which of you has questions for the Glass? You, brave Ursid. You stand so stiff and strong. Speak bravely forth; your question shall be first."

There was silence. Then Palamon heard Ursid's voice echoing from off to the right. The voice was strong, there was no lack of firmness in its timbre, yet it sounded as if there were the least bit of uneasiness on the part of the speaker, as if he were unsure of why and to whom he was speaking. "So be it. I repeat the inquiry of Lady Aelia. Do we still face hot pursuit? If so, how does it fare? Do all our foes now close upon us even as we stand?"

"Bravo, a question bravely spoken out and one that lies quite well within your own mind's bounds. Remove your hands and look down at the floor; the Glass will tell you all it wishes to."

There was a pause. There was no sound but breathing and the unidentifiable liquid sounds Palamon had been hearing. Then Reovalis spoke again. "Tell them what you see."

Ursid hesitated. When his voice did come, it was halting; it was as if the young knight were too caught up by what he was watching to fully describe it. "I see a troop of riders sitting on their steeds and looking out across some void. They stand on some high cliff for I can see a lonely mountain eagle wheel about, far in the sky above the shoulder of one rider."

"Tell what they wear," Reovalis prompted the young speaker.

"They wear the uniform of my Buerdaunt. That is, they do save one who wears white robes. They turn and look at one another, then one seems to hurl an oath; they wheel their mounts and ride along the cliff face for a way. Now, wait . . ."

"What do you see? Speak forth." Reovalis' voice was insistent, demanding.

"I see . . . I cannot tell you, things are altering. This is a different place, one that I know. It is the presence chamber in Buerdaunt, where pale King Lothar hears petitions and does his business. I can see his face." Here Ursid's voice failed him for a moment. Then he recovered and went on. "He seemed to fasten his cold, level gaze on my own eyes, but that is not the case; he watches something else with interest. I wish that I could make out more . . . and now I can. I see the scene quite well. It is, as I have said, the presentation chamber of pale Lother and upon the marble floor there has been placed a mighty cauldron. 'Round it burns a flame.

"They've placed hot, molten lead in there. It is a form of punishment I know; they mean to torture some unfortunate. And now they lead him, struggling, o'er the floor. No, there are two . . . now four. I know those men."

Again Ursid had to stop speaking for a moment as emotions warred within him. He went on, his voice was more restrained. "It is my friend, young Amos, of the guards. He stood the watch when we passed from the town and did not search our horses, for he knew me well and now, it seems, he pays the price. I know one of the other men, though not as well, an odd acquaintance only. And I know the torture, too. The men are strapped to posts set in the floor. A ladle dips the lead out of the cauldron, throwing it upon them in a spray; so many times, depending on the punishment's degree." Here Ursid stopped speaking. "I'll not go on. Please make it go away."

"You've placed your palms before your eyes once

more." Reovalis sounded grave. "I do not blame you. It's a brutal sight." He paused, giving Ursid time to gather himself. Then he spoke again. "My Lady Aelia, what inquiries do you wish to make? The Glass will now respond."

"The query that I had is answered. I do not have another."

"But are you sure."

"Indeed I am. My questions will be asked at my own time and in a manner I shall choose myself. I shall not yield my soul up to your hands for exhibition, here before my friends."

"Quite so." Reovalis' voice betrayed irritation at Aelia's reply. The sage paused a moment before he addressed Berengeria. "Now you, Princess, your question I would hear."

Berengeria did not hesitate; she spoke with the manner of one who had been waiting for the offer. "I wish to see the face of Alyubol, to know him and the land in which he dwells."

There was silence. When Reovalis finally spoke, it was in measured tones, as if he were choosing his words carefully. "You ask of Alyubol at every turn. That's quite a thorny question at the best, for I myself have difficulty when I try to see his image in the glass. He's placed a shield between himself and those who try to seek him; it requires some secret, curtained even unto me, to see him fully and, moreover, it is dangerous to try."

"Do not attempt this thing." This was Aelia's voice. "It is not wise."

"I wish to see him." Berengeria was adamant, her voice bristling with resolve.

Reovalis sighed. "Very well. I shall aid you myself, protecting you, my dear, as best I can from all the dangers found in seeking Alyubol within the Glass."

There was a moment's silence before Reovalis' voice was heard again, telling Berengeria to take her hands from her eyes. Her voice was uncertain as she began to describe what she was seeing. "I see a mass of convoluted cloud but nothing more. There's nought but swirling mist. It rushes by me; nothing can be seen . . . except, I see a wall of stone, an ancient, rotting edifice. Now more . . . it is as if I pass beyond the wall and all is dark except a candle's glow. I see a robe-draped figure at a desk; at least it seems so. There is little light. His clothing's folds all billow, billow forth. They look like ocean swells or midnight clouds, all goaded by the prod of driving winds. I cannot see his shape but only folds on folds of robing. Does he turn?" Berengeria's voice had become quite dreamy in its tone; now it died away altogether.

Palamon was about to drop his hands and reach for her when she spoke once more. "I see no more, the vision goes away."

"You took too great a risk; I ended it," Reovalis said. "I do not know the strengths of Alyubol, nor whether he can reach out from his place to grasp your mind, Princess, though it be through the Glass. His strengths are many, not all known to me. Perhaps your unschooled scrying wakens him and gives him means to do you harm. I hope that's not the case. But cover up your eyes and I will speak to noble Palamon."

"My query," Palamon said, "is the same as what I asked you in your study when we first arrived. What do you know about my birth and how I came, an orphan, to the gates of Pallas' Fastness, high upon its cliff?"

"You know enough. Young orphans, now and then, are left there. You were one."

"The elder Knights all told me I was placed before the outer gates of that great keep, a babe, a tiny, month-old babe, that I was reared on goat's milk and their charity. I know that much of my beginnings. Show me now the rest."

The impatience grew large in Reovalis' voice as he responded. "I cannot show you that. It might well change the course of history as yet untold. Your question lies too close. Another, please."

Palamon found himself growing irritated. Was it wrong for him to be curious about his origins? The only clue he had ever had to his beginnings had been the odd piece of horn with the word 'blood' carved into it, which he had

had set into his sword's pommel. Now even that was gone, as was his armor. All his ties to his beginnings were gone.

It was enough that Reovalis seemed to know the details of Palamon's birth, things that Palamon did not know about himself, yearned to learn but could not discover. That would have been enough by itself to take the edge off his wit. But there was more than that. Reovalis, though he was basking in the curiosity and attention of his guests, obviously knew much more of their past and future, as well as their present prospects, than he was willing to impart. It was as if they were standing in the presence of a selfish muse; past and future seemed to be united in the old man, in his manner, in his speech. But he acted determined to keep the bulk of this knowledge to himself. Although they had sparred verbally before this, Palamon felt far from trading riposte at this moment. He would not joust further with the old man. "I have no interest, then. What I have heard described by others is enough."

"Then ask a question to be politic."

Palamon could think of no fitting response so he said nothing.

"If you have not a question for my ears, perhaps I ought to let you see a shadow from your past, if just from courtesy." The amount of venom in the old man's voice was surprising.

"If you so wish."

"A vision, then, of that fair, winsome maid, for whom you have surrendered up your state, your knighthood in the Order. Drop your hands, reveal your eyes, and see."

Palamon felt a tightness grip his chest; it reached upward, dragging at his throat. "I'll not remove my hand for such a sight."

"No matter." Reovalis' voice was becoming louder with every word. "If you'll not move your hand, then it will be the same as if you had."

There was a flash and Palamon's eyes were bathed in a deep blue, iridescent light. He started, staring at the arm he was still holding up before his face. His hand was no longer there; the arm trailed off in wisps of blue-white vapor and the room in which he was standing was revealed.

It was a roundish cavern some ten or twelve cubits across; at the far side stood Reovalis, glowering at him, the old man's features bathed and distorted by the blue glow that filled the room.

Between them was the Glass of the Polonians but it was not a glass at all; it was a pool of blueness in the floor of the chamber, a swirling, tumbling pool, filled with every shade of that color and bathing all objects with its light. At first the pool appeared to be full of swirling, boiling, blue oil; but on examination it was not. There was nothing in it but color. The color was so intense, so deep and pure, that it seemed to have a substance of its own as it eddied endlessly about within the confines of its stone well.

Palamon's eyes and all his other senses were drawn into the swirling color; he was hypnotized by the purity of it. It was deep, midnight blue; it was light blue, almost white. It was intense, raging royal blue; it was nearly black. It was all these colors at once. Nor was it limited to the blue portion of the spectrum. Now there were other colors, too, all the colors a mind could grasp. Palamon realized that the pool had him now. His senses were possessed by it. It was as if his body had entered the pool; the colors were dancing all about him.

And there was also an image before him. It swirled, took shape, lived, breathed, could be identified. He recognized it: it was *she*. It was the maiden with whom he had created the great scandal on the north shore of the Thlassa Mey years ago. Her name was Arlaine.

He could hear a voice in the background; it was a man's voice shouting, telling him to describe all that he was seeing. But he could not. He could not respond; his mind and tongue were imprisoned by the image before him. She was so full of life, this Arlaine; she looked happy, even joyful, unlike the maiden Arlaine he had known. And there was a babe in her arms. Was that the babe?

No, it was not, for now another figure emerged from the veil of shifting colors. This one was a small boy, a child of eight. His hair was coal black, the same color as his mother's hair; his face was a replica of hers; he looked

bright, lively, normal in every way. That was the boy;
there could be no doubt. He was the proper age. Palamon
found himself wondering what the youngster's name might
have been. The lad had cost him greatly, yet Palamon did
not even know his name.

The boy surely bore the surname of his stepfather. As
the babe at her breast proved, Arlaine had taken a husband; no doubt he was a young man from some village
near her own who had given his name to both children.
She would have been a worthwhile mate; she still had her
beauty, and her attachment to a noble Knight, however
scandalous, would have given her prestige among her fellow villagers.

She moved, she spoke, although he could not hear her.
She looked at him, smiled at him. It was all too much.
The agony of the vision overwhelmed him, ground him
down, made his knees sag. And he was making sounds
with his mouth, unrecognizable animal sounds. He could
feel the tears scalding his cheeks. He was falling; he felt
himself falling downward, farther into the mass of color
that leaped and swirled about him.

There were more sounds. There was shouting, and he
felt himself being lifted by rough hands. He was groggy;
the image of Arlaine and the boy danced about him, even
after he had been removed from the omnipotent blueness
and there were no colors at all to be seen. He felt his feet
scraping over the floor and also felt the presence of bodies
about him, of hands supporting him. Straightening his
legs, he found he was able to stand.

He opened his eyes. To his amazement, he found that
his eyes had been tightly clenched all this time and his
hand was still intact, still held stiffly in front of his face.
The arm ached now, and he had to drop it to his side.
The room swam about him, but he was able to recognize
the faces of his companions and he realized he was back
in Reovalis' bedchamber. Usmu was there also. The hands
supporting Palamon belonged to the sage's flesh servant.

In a moment, the tapestry leading to the other chamber
moved to one side and Reovalis himself entered the room,
his deepset eyes dark in the flickering torchlight. He gazed

into Palamon's face for a moment before speaking. "Now can you stand, Sir Knight?"

Palamon nodded. He could find no words.

Reovalis' manner was changed from what it had been. The sage looked badly shaken; he had lost some of the brusqueness that had marked his words and actions until this time. He dismissed Usmu from the room; he did not dismiss him into vapors as he had before, but simply bade him leave. Then he spoke to the four fugitives. "My guests, I must apologize for deeds and thoughts it frightens me to call my own. You are the only folk to view my face in many, many years. Please bear with me. My way with you has lacked in courtesy."

Palamon heard Aelia's voice from behind him. "Quite so."

"Odd thoughts of guests have sometimes come to me, with pride in all the wonders I could show. The scenes I pictured in those musing thoughts were quite unrealistic and naive; you never did respond as I had thought you might. Now I am chastened in my heart to find that after all, I'm just a man. I have my vanities, a temper, too, and still am capable of being rash. Excuse me, please, forgive me, Palamon. Your friends cannot appreciate the wrong that I have done you, as can you and I. I must excuse myself and spend some time in self examination. What I find will then have great effect on how I act and how my treatment of yourselves will be in future. Now please go. I must be by myself, at least for now."

The four travelers gazed upon the old man for a moment, then turned to go. Palamon turned last, still shaken by his vision. Together they walked the long corridor toward more familiar halls. Once they were inside the cluttered study chamber, Aelia spoke. "And you, Sir Palamon, how fare you now?"

Palamon found his answer coming by itself. "I feel quite well. What harm can visions do?"

Aelia peered into his face, studying him intently. "No ill effects from what you just went through?"

"No ill effects. A vision is just air."

She studied him for another moment, then turned without expression to the other members of the party. "Then very well. Our time is ours, it seems. And for my part, if such things can be done, I'll find if Usmu's learned to draw a bath. If he does have such skills, then they shall be well utilized by me, for such a luxury is rare and much to be appreciated."

"Yes," Ursid said. "And sleep is my concern. I've had no great amount in recent weeks."

Aelia started to walk away but turned and gazed into Palamon's face once more. "Your vision has been painful, nonetheless."

"It does not matter. What I saw has passed. If knights are strong, then that's what I must be. I have not eaten for a day or more, and so I'll sample our long table's fare. Enough food, I am sure, will ease all pain. And suffering is ended with a draught—if it is deep enough—of sweet spiced wine."

Berengeria took hold of Palamon's arm. "Then I accompany you as you go dine, for you should not be left with ancient thoughts and visions as your only company. Excuse me, my dear Aelia and Ursid, for Palamon has not been shown this nest of sages and old wizards as we have, a service I shall render after food." With her fingers on his arm, she led Palamon toward the dining hall.

Still shaken by his experience, Palamon went with her, turning to nod a quick farewell to his other two companions. Aelia looked back with a face masked of all emotion. But the eyes of Ursid were burning.

Chapter Seventeen:
Princess Berengeria

IT WENT WITHOUT saying that Berengeria's words about company and showing Palamon the extent of the ancient catacomb were only an excuse and not an original one at that. Aelia was bemused by it, Ursid was offended. It lacked any sort of ingenuity. But it did serve its purpose. Palamon walked with her now, casting his eyes upon her as they returned to the dining hall. She was a beautiful maiden. But why was she doing this?

That was a question worth asking. And the answer lay deep in the mind of Berengeria herself, for she had made a long mental journey quite apart from her bodily trek through the forests of the wudlings and down the waters of the Stilchis.

From the time she had been spirited into the keep of Lothar the Pale, she had pursued one goal—her return to her homeland. For two years, that single objective had stood at the center of her existence. Still, there existed a woman within this Princess, and that woman now wished to speak with Palamon at greater length than during their previous exchanges.

She had watched him for weeks and he had filled her with questions. He was very attractive. But there was more to him than that. Her mind often strayed back to that awful moment when she had nearly been drowned. She had known at the time that death had been upon her; the instant had been a terrible one. She had awakened to find herself lying in the sand beside the Stilchis with Palamon's mouth clamped over her own, his wet lips guiding the living breath from his lungs into her body. That touch, that moment of closeness, was still with her.

But there had been more. What of the contest in the Library of the Polonians, when he had offered his own life for the lives of his companions? She had watched him then as he had backed away from Usmu's fearsome axe, seeking a way to outwit the monster. At that time also, death had hovered nearby. It had filled the room and he had faced it for all of them, smiling his grim smile. So he was very brave, this knight, and honorable. And attractive.

But what of the other side of Palamon? What about the questions that had gone unanswered? What horrors lay hidden in the dust which bore his footprints? Berengeria had stood before Reovalis and had heard the old sage speak to Palamon of incest. How had this brave, honorable knight committed incest? What could he have done? With whom could he have done it?

So her mind ran. She sat at the long dining table, pondering all these things and watching Palamon eat; the only sound was the occasional click of his knife on his wooden platter.

It was Palamon who finally broke the silence. "Princess," he said. "Although you said that you would come and keep me company while I ate breakfast, still your wordless tongue gives scant companionship."

Berengeria smiled a small, half-visible smile. "I must apologize. I could not help but wonder at the vision you just saw. Was she quite pretty, that lost love of yours?"

Palamon did not stop chewing. Would he talk about it?

Would he be that open with her? It took a long time for him to frame an answer but he did speak at last. "I never met a lady who was not all pleasing to the eye and fair to see."

"You try to fence with words and parry my hard question. But she meant a deal to you. She must have, to have brought you such great pain."

"She was an honest, honorable girl, beset by evil fortune without cause. To me, there was no more. That's all she was," Palamon said with an air of complete honesty.

"You did not love her?"

Palamon glanced across the table at her. A smile crept onto his face. "No."

"But how, then, could you enter into this illicit love, destroy your standing with the Knights of Pallas, knowing that you would become an outcast even to this time, was love not strong between the two of you?"

Palamon paused in his eating. Her note of exasperation had stopped him for a moment; he looked at her, then reached across the table to pluck a single cherry from a bowl of fruit which lay between them. He ate this viand in a series of tiny bites and placed the pit carefully on his platter. "I did it so that, as the years crept by, I could excite the curiosity of maidens fair, such comely ones as you, and thereby lure them well within my reach."

"You toy with me, brave Palamon. Do not."

"What would you have me say?" Palamon asked. "I cannot change my past; it has been formed and it is what it is. Must I explain all things unwisely done? Must I relive the pain I brought myself?"

"Of course not. You speak truth; I was unfair." Berengeria's head turned and her eyes strayed toward a corridor opening from the far end of the dining hall.

Palamon looked at her. "Unfairness cannot be a property of such a maiden fair as you are. I spoke falsely if you read my words that way."

"You toy with me once more, but let it pass."

Palamon had emptied his platter by now. He had eaten only a small meal; still, he seemed satisfied. "The food is good. Reovalis' odd arts—whatever else I think of them aside—produce a quality of table fare with which I cannot find a truthful fault." He pushed the platter away, stood, and walked across the room.

Berengeria followed him with her eyes. She could have asked him why, if the food had been good, he had not taken more. But there would have been no direct answer to that question. Not from him. But what was she to say, then? "You are upset. You need to walk a bit, at least take exercise or do some work to let your body burn your spirit's woes."

"My spirit's woes." Palamon turned to gaze down at her. "My spirit's woes? What must you think of me, O gentle maid? Am I repulsive and reptilian, and does my sordid past not make you blanch?" He turned away. "I had been happier had I remained a handyman within the Silver Knight. I was a cipher then; I had no past."

She lowered her head and gazed at the floor—but not for long. She looked up at him once more, and their eyes met. Her words were clear, direct. "Good Palamon, I'll not believe those words. Your past was with you long before we met; I see your very soul's an open wound."

He did not reply. It was plain that much of his glibness had been sheared away by the morning's events; he had little left for the present conversation. He wore the look of a man who had taken a beating from the inside out. A mocking expression began to crawl onto his lips but it was only a weak attempt. His curtain wall had been breached. His resilience had been exhausted.

"At least you do not smile and try to jest," she said, "when jesting is the last thing in your heart. Your stout facade at last has crumbled; I can see a little of the man within."

He stood beside the table and gazed at her silently. He did look weary.

Now she stood and walked toward him. He did not retreat. "Dear Palamon, remember we are friends. You have no need to guard yourself from me. My hand's extended; let us take a walk."

He sighed, drew himself up, then spoke. "A walk, you say? Yes, that would suit me well. But where, in this great, ancient catacomb, could any person find a place to walk? I doubt that we'll find sights to ease our souls by strolling down these torchlit corridors. If you will deign accept my company, we might at least return along the path that leads down to the riverbank below."

Berengeria smiled. "No, that's not necessary, Palamon. I know a place a hundred cubits off where there are flowers, orchards, gentle sights, and it would give me happiness to go and show them to you, walking by your side."

"Then lead on, gentle maiden. I would fain see sunlight for awhile."

Berengeria reached for his arm and pointed toward the doorway on the far side of the chamber. "This is the way." Together they walked into what was obviously a kitchen, from the great hearth and the cooking utensils which lined the walls. Then they passed into another room from which spiraled a great, bronze staircase. It was an object of fine workmanship. There were no torches lighting this chamber because the bright shaft of sunlight piercing down from above made torches unnecessary.

Berengeria turned to Palamon. "You see, we three have all had time to tour this lair of the Polonians' long halls. The food you ate comes not from magic's art but rather from a process more mundane."

She suddenly seemed to be bursting with a huge happiness. She laughed at the expression on his face, then led him up the ringing stairs to the world above. Silently, Palamon followed the whimsical lead of this robust maid. What was he to think, after all? He had been reared in the Fastness of Pallas, far from any female companionship. By the same token, his few years in Buerdaunt had been spent without associating with the female element save for the innkeeper's wife, who had been left as chaste and sacred as Pallas herself, as far as Palamon had been concerned. So the tall knight's only experience with a woman had been what had passed between himself and Arlaine, the raven-haired specter from his past. That had hardly been a proper apprenticeship for dealing with the young beauty who now danced up the steps ahead of him.

He followed Berengeria. For the first time since their journey had begun, she seemed to have thrown off the weight of her royal position. She was only a happy young woman a score of years in age; a full eighteen years Palamon's junior. But this was still her game to play, not his.

At the top of the sprial staircase, they emerged from a small marble enclosure to find themselves in the garden Berengeria had spoken of. It was a charming place, breathtaking in its beauty. It was a symphony of immaculately trimmed fruit trees, grape arbors, row upon row of carefully tended vegetables, and beds of cunningly cultivated flowers. But there was not a soul to be seen.

Palamon gazed across this unexpected bit of loveliness in the barren setting of the Cauldron of the Stilchis. "And Usmu tends it all."

"That is correct. At least Reovalis has told us so."

Together they strolled beside a bed of bright flowers. The setting seemed proper for her: she was in her element in the midst of these blooms and the other growing things of the garden. Her femininity was accented without loss to the great strength of will that balanced her nature. Palamon looked at her longer than he meant to.

They rested on a stone bench and Berengeria sat quietly for a moment, her eyes tracing the massive cliffs that surrounded this oasis. Then she looked back at Palamon. "Now do you know, Sir Knight, Ursid, our gallant friend, is growing a strong jealousy of you?"

Palamon was nonplussed by this information. It was not a total surprise; the young warrior had cast unfriendly glances in Palamon's direction in the last few days. Still, there was little for Ursid to be jealous of. Palamon was a Knight of Pallas, inside at least, and the possession of a woman was something to be kept beyond arm's length, whatever his past might have held. But he was still flattered to hear that the younger man considered him a fit rival. He smiled at Berengeria. "He strives for your affection, does he not? In watching hot young men from many lands, I've seen a heart in love build enemies from whole cloth, placing them at every hand. When lovestruck eyes hoard every sign away, equating every move or gesture seen as germane to the quest the heart has set, then what is just a simple, passing glance can seem to be a setback, verging on catastrophe, directed the wrong way."

The slightest twinkle brightened Berengeria's eye. "Suppose our brave Ursid has some just cause to see you as a rival, Palamon?"

"He has no cause." Palamon spat the words out, then stood, turning away from her.

"Suppose he knows the way I feel toward you?"

Palamon turned again and gazed down at her, stunned, his jaw working. "What could he know? Whatever could you feel? I am a time-scarred, scandal-tainted man and there could be no love between us two. I grant that you have been inside my thoughts, but you are the Princess of Carea and heir unto the throne of that great land. Ursid need not have jealousy of me."

She did not answer him in a direct way; her eyes swept away from his and her gaze paused on the trees that formed the orchard. "I think that jealousy has ill effects on any person who possesses it; its weight is great on any shoulders, though they may be male or female. Palamon, do you know that I, too, was riddled by this same emotion's thrusts an hour or less gone by."

Palamon had no answer; he could only stand and stare down at her.

"When old Reovalis forced you to gaze into the Glass of the Polonians and great tears rolled from your two manly eyes to look once more upon that maid you loved, a feeling gripped my heart that could not be described, except to say that it shot pain and envy through my soul until I gasped. I gaze into your eyes and tell you now that, even if I live to reach my home and gain Carea's crown, become her queen, and thus could make my fair land great once more and go down in the annals of that land as 'Berengeria, Carea's Saviour Queen,' it could not give my soul so great a joy as I would feel if only I might see that same expression on your face once more, if that one time those tears could flow for me."

Palamon could not tear his eyes from her. How could

he ever have affected this maiden in this manner? "This cannot be."

"Palamon, speak true. Is there some chance, though slender it may be, that you might someday have the love for me that you once bore for that fair maiden then? I take no count of scandals long gone by, for your past errors merit no concern. I only see before me what you are at present time, and what I see is good, fine, manly, brave, intelligent. And if you feel dishonored by the past, then cast it off and be my knight without a past." She stood as she spoke, placing her hands upon his shoulders and gazing into his eyes.

This was all too much for Palamon. This fair maiden— fair in every sense of that word—was not for him, if for no other reason than the fact that he could not see how the fates would ever allow such a match. But what could he do? The only phrase he could find was a weak one. "My ears will not accept the words you speak." Having said that, he would have turned from her but there were many forces warring within him.

Her fingers glided down the trunks of his arms until they reached the cordy joinings of his wrists. He did not move his hands; she took them in her own and lifted them, holding them against her. "I am the master here, that's obvious. Your own heart's feelings will betray and sap you, Palamon. No discipline from any school of knights can wring emotions totally from you."

He shook his head. "I've looked on you at times. That I admit. Your beauty draws my eyes, my will is weak. Still, all the passion I may feel for you must be discarded; it's a travesty on that to which I dedicate my life."

She did not bother to reply. Her hands released his, traveled back to his shoulders, and rested there lightly. He stood stiffly for a moment, his face reflecting the warfare that was taking place behind his expression. They drank in one another's gaze. Then he reached out and his arms settled about her waist.

The moment was like a night full of lightning. She came to him, pressed herself against him, and they stood clinging to one another. While time's passage was marked only by the throbbing of their two hearts, he clasped her tightly, reveling in the sensations he drew from the fullness within her robe, taking both strength and a sense of foreboding from the embrace. His mind reeled as he was washed by a flood of unfamiliar feelings. In the time that their bodies had touched, he had crossed a line between what he had been and what he was now forced to be. He was in love. He knew this, even though he had never before experienced the full depth of feeling contained within that simple term.

He was in love; he loved Berengeria and he knew it. That sudden, overpowering knowledge staggered him. Was it safe for him to feel this way? Did he dare love her? No, he did not. Their arms slipped apart as he dropped onto the stone bench, glancing away from her as she sat down next to him.

"You feel it, too," she said. "I know this, Palamon. The love that has been formed between us two is not on my part only."

"That is so."

"You share the passion that I feel for you?"

"I must own that I do. I have no heart to disavow the love I know we share." His mind raced; he was searching for words. There were so many wrong words and so few that were not the wrong ones. "But there can be no match between us two, for I am what I am and you are you."

She grasped his arms, forcing him to face her. Her hands were rough after the travail of the past weeks, but beneath the skin they still bore the quality of hands that had been formed to grasp the scepter. Now they turned him and the two unmatched lovers gazed into one another's eyes. "That cannot matter if it's not our will," she said. "You can discard your past, dear Palamon. Some way can still be found; it can be done."

He could not take his eyes off her. "It shall not be, my darling—that you are. In this brief moment, you have taught me love, a gift that brings me joy and dark despair. For all of that, we shall remain apart, for what I am and what is past are one; my past is what I am; it will not change. I also cannot be restructured at a whim. So what has passed between us, though it is a beautiful reflection of a thing that could have been, had we not been ourselves, must now be put aside. Our love is like the Gorgon; just to look on it is death." He twisted free of her embrace, stood, and strode toward the enclosure that led back into the corridors of Reovalis.

His pace quickened as he heard her call out behind him; he walked rapidly, then sprinted down the steep bronze steps. He did not hear her following him; he doubted that she was. But he did not slow down. Through the underground halls he dashed, through the dining chamber and the study, and through the shadowy library of the Polonians. On he ran. He did not stop until he had reached the banks of the Stilchis itself where it flowed quietly, far below the abandoned temple.

Chapter Eighteen:
Gifts

PALAMON LINGERED BESIDE the river for a long time. His conversation with Berengeria had complicated matters beyond measure. Before, the issue had been simple—return Carea's Princess to her native land and reclaim that land from the curse of Alyubol. But now he was faced with the dilemma posed by Berengeria herself.

The question was not, however, whether to love her. That issue had been decided for him. Palamon conceded this, smiling bitterly as he flicked a small stone into the gliding waters. The touch of her body, her voice, her face, even the feel of her breath upon the skin of his throat— there was no training so ruthless, no discipline so harsh, that they could withstand such delights. No, the decision to love her was one over which he had no control. Now the question was this: what was he to do about it?

He lingered beside the river until evening swept the sun's golden rays from the swirling surface of the water. But he had to go back to the library of the Polonians and face the others sometime. And he had to face Berengeria.

The four fugitives gathered once more about the table in the underground dining hall where Usmu had laid out for them a feast identical to the repasts they had enjoyed there before. Reovalis was not present and Aelia looked up at the flesh servant, asking whether the presence of the old sage was to be anticipated.

"The Master will not be here," Usmu said. "He has told me to say to you that he is in meditation. He did not tell me what meditation is, so I hope you know what it is," he added helpfully.

"It is a time of deep and earnest thought," Palamon said, looking up at the wolfish face and smiling. "A person meditates at diverse times; religious thought, philosophy, or what some person may have said that afternoon are all fit food for meditation." He glanced across the table at Berengeria as he spoke. She was eating her meal in tiny bites; she had not looked directly at him since sitting down.

Usmu looked at Palamon blankly. There was no hint of comprehension in his eyes. "I don't understand all that. But those were the words the Master told me to say to you." He turned and walked toward the kitchen, moving silently on his clawed feet.

The meal proceeded as it had gone before. There was talk at the table. Aelia discussed the course they would take when they had reembarked upon the river. Ursid spoke of the need for proper weapons and wondered aloud what stratagems their enemies were preparing at that very moment; Palamon and Berengeria added small bits to the conversation. But it was clear that neither of the two lovers was concentrating on the topics at hand.

That very fact irritated Palamon, made him angry with himself. Early in his career as a Knight of Pallas, it had been drummed into him that he had to master the art of centering all his senses on a single subject until that subject was consumed. But this evening, he found himself unable to do that. Over and again, his thoughts floated back to the young woman he loved and feared, separated from him by only some two or three cubits of table, although worlds may have stood between them in other ways.

He would have spoken with her again, but he dared not do it in front of the others. He hoped a chance would come after the meal, but that was not to be. After eating, Berengeria quietly excused herself and returned to her chamber. Shortly after that, Palamon retired to his own small cell; the evening and the night that followed it were long.

After what seemed an eternity, Palamon managed to fall asleep. He was awakened almost immediately by a pounding upon his chamber door.

He sat up on his couch, collected his thoughts, and went to the door, swinging the heavy wooden panel aside to reveal the towering Usmu. "What is it?" he asked the monster.

"Master says to come."

"Where is he? And what hour can it be?"

Usmu was already walking away as Palamon spoke. He looked over his shoulder to answer. "He is waiting in the dining hall. It's morning."

As Palamon watched, Usmu stopped to rap on another door several chambers away. Ursid's head appeared and Usmu repeated what he had told Palamon; soon all four of the travelers were pacing along the corridors that led to the dining hall.

Reovalis met them as they entered and dismissed the flesh servant. The old sage seemed more grim than was his wont; he bade his guests stand and returned to the table, upon which rested an oblong case and a vial of clear, golden liquid.

"My guests," he said, "the time has come when you shall be my guests no more. To tarry long with me might well advance your capture by your foes. For now, they do not know where you are hid. A day, or half a day, might change all that. Your cause is just; I'll give what aid I can."

He paused for a moment, looked at Palamon, then continued. "Before I tell you more, I must give thanks, for you have brought perspective to my eyes. An old man, living much too long alone, will form opinions of himself that are, at best, distortions of the truth. My time with you has taught me much. I might not be as wise as I had thought; my agéd eyes are not so filled with vision and my brain not quite so free from human prejudice. This shows that any man may learn—or teach.

"I said that I would choose the aid I gave and so I shall, while knowing better now that my decisions are not free from flaws. Princess, you asked me of the hidden lair of Alyubol, your father's enemy. I know him not; he hides himself from me. But of his keep, this much I still may say: look for a tow'r that cannot stand but does, a place that gives back to the roiling sea the thing that makes its waters what they are. I know not where that is but look on it and you have found the keep of Alyubol."

Berengeria nodded her head. "I thank you, sir. I'll not forget a word."

The old man turned toward the others. "I have another gift to all of you which will, I'm certain, be of later use." He turned and lifted the crystal vial from the table. "This vial contains the essence of my art and all my study for a score of years has gone into the liquid it contains." Approaching Aelia, he handed her the vial.

She rotated the little piece of crystal in her hand, marveling at the hues which bounded off the angles of the crafted glass. The liquid within changed colors with the slightest movement. "This seems a bit of mystic workmanship. But what, pray tell me, is the stuff within and what effect has it upon our quest?"

"The liquid has been formulated by myself and cunningly it was devised. When you are in dire straits, break off the seal and shake the vial one time at what most threatens you. But three times only may this vial be used, and never will its liquids take a life."

"And what does it contain, exactly?" Berengeria asked. But Reovalis smiled, shook his head, and turned toward Palamon.

"O Knight of Pallas, I feel it is you whom I have wronged the most before the Glass. Now hear me, it was done without intent. Your glistening chain mail also I removed, and promised equal value in return."

"My mail would be most adequate," answered Palamon, who towered over the aged wizard.

"I know that its return would satisfy. But still I have not altered in my first belief that you would be a better man without it. So to take its place, I offer you this sword." He turned back to the table and with some effort lifted the heavy box which had been lying there; the box was longer than the old man was tall.

He carried it to Palamon, cradling the case in his arms for the tall knight to open. "I bid you open this."

"I will, indeed." Palamon flipped the bronze catch which secured the box's ornate lid. Carefully, he swung the lid back upon its hinges, revealing an interior of soft velvet laced with intricate designs embroidered in gold thread. Upon this velvet couch reposed a great, two-handed sword, a blade the length of a man's body with its finely crafted handle and pommel a cubit beyond that. The blade itself glinted in the torchlight and Palamon's instincts as a fighter prompted him to take it up.

Lifting it slowly from its case, he held it before him in wordless wonder. It was light. Its weight was no more than what he would have expected from a much smaller weapon. He wrapped his fingers slowly around the handle, holding the sword before him in the guard position, noting the way it melted into his grasp.

The blade had a savage look to it; Palamon's experienced eye noted that there was none of the polish and gleam of a weapon made for show. It had been made for work—carnage, blood, and death; the double edges bore the minute scars of tedious, careful honing. He glided his fingertips across one edge noting the tingle produced thereby. The heavy swords Palamon had seen possessed a coarser edge than this one. There was no doubt this blade would have shaved the mustache off his face, if he had desired to use it to that purpose; the case's crafted cover bore the dust of long neglect, yet the blade itself appeared as if it had been honed within the last hour. How it ever could have been used without blunting and knicking that fine edge was a mystery to him. "A noble weapon," he said, "most impressive. But what is its history, O ancient sage?"

Reovalis smiled. There could be no mistaking his expression; he had gained satisfaction from watching Palamon's reaction to the sword. "I do not know the history of this great blade in full. I do believe, from what I have deduced, that it was forged and tempered in the fires built by the legendary smiths that lived on Muse, the southernmost of all the outer Isles. Their race has long since been disbursed by war, but in their time they crafted cunning weaponry.

"It traveled to the hands of Parthelon, surnamed the Great, who, with this mighty blade, assembled armies, swept out of the north, and conquered all the lands that lay about the Thlassa Mey. He formed an empire, named it for himself, and cast his shadow far across the world; yes, every map then drawn could only show the lands that he proclaimed as his own fief. But this Great Empire crumbled when he died and this great sword was spirited away, out of the hands of all his striving heirs, concealed with the vaults, then newly dug by this library's founders, ages past. Here has it lain, unknown to all mankind, until I found it many years ago." Reovalis spoke the last words with obvious pride. As an afterthought he added, "The name is scribed beside the pommel stone."

Palamon's eyes followed the old man's gesture. About the pommel that blossomed at the end of the long handle were letters so tiny they were hard to read. The inscription was in the ancient style and tongue of the Great Empire, which did lend credibility to Reovalis' statements. Softly, Palamon mouthed the two words thus formed: "*Spada Korrigaine.*"

While the syllables were still floating upon the air in front of him, Palamon felt his fingers cramp about the hilt of the sword; the weapon forged itself into his grasp. The sensation was indescribable, more surprising than painful. At the same time, also without conscious effort on his part, he found he had again raised the weapon to the guard position. Astounded, he looked up at the gleaming blade he held. "Magic," he heard Aelia whisper.

"It's possible," Reovalis said. "The smiths of Muse knew arts of weapons making long since lost to men."

"I spoke the name and felt it move, withal," Palamon said. "I've held fine weapons in my travelings but this stands full as far above them all as . . ." He found himself searching for a proper metaphor. "As our fair Berengeria above all other woman." He glanced up at the maiden he had just complimented, but her face remained without expression. Aelia looked uneasy and Ursid fairly bristled.

Though the remark had been intended as a jest, Palamon regretted it now. But the sword was the subject of the moment. He laid it back down in the velvet-lined case, then took the case from Reovalis and leaned it against the rough wall of the chamber. He stepped back and spoke the name once more. "*Spada Korrigaine.*" No one in the dining hall saw the weapon move. But the handle was firmly set into Palamon's hands once more and the blade was raised, ready for battle.

Reovalis studied the tall knight who in turn stared in wonder at the marvelous weapon he had inherited. "The trade, then, is a fair one, Palamon?" the ancient sage asked.

"The trade?"

"Between your past and this, your future's key."

"My mail, you mean." Palamon hesitated. "It seems a fair exchange, although if I were truthfully to speak, I fain would have things as they were before."

Reovalis nodded, although it was plain that he was disappointed with Palamon's response. "Then if you wish, your hauberk will be brought. You bargain most unwisely, Palamon."

"So be it." Palamon placed the *Spada Korrigaine* back into its case, closed and latched the cover, and offered it to the old man.

"Place it on the table there; unseal the case, ungracious Palamon."

Palamon did as he had been told. Then he turned once more to face his host. "*Spada Korrigaine,*" Reovalis said, his voice ringing through the chamber. Nothing happened. The ancient blade rested upon its velvet cushion, looking no more mobile than a common kitchen knife. "The bargain has been struck, O Pallas' Knight. Your magic blade shows no more love for me than I for it. It is the sword of noble warriors and thus is, will you, nil you, yours to keep."

Palamon gazed at him for an instant. "Be that the case, my hands will take it up." With a sigh, he removed the sword once more from its place and stood with it, resting the tip upon the floor.

"And what of us?" Ursid's voice was loud and indignant and filled the chamber. "One weapon will not serve if we should be assaulted once again by those strong foes who follow us about the Thlassa Mey."

"You'll find few weapons in these ancient halls," Reovalis said, eyeing the young knight narrowly. "All those that can be had, one hunting bow, some daggers, have been placed by Usmu down within your craft still lying beached below." He let his gaze wash over all the members of the party as he finished his statement.

"The things you need, provisions, weapons, gear, have been provided and await below. My guests, I learn from you more things than ever you begin to guess. But time flows on. You must be to your quest while I return alone unto my studies."

He studied them for another moment, then walked from the chamber; from the other corridor came Usmu, bringing a great platter laden with bread and fruits. The travelers ate this farewell breakfast with little conversation. Before they had finished, Usmu had reentered the room and was now standing silently, watching them; all eyes noted that he was once more bearing the great battle axe with which he had greeted them when they first had found the place. None of them could say for sure whether the monster had simply found the weapon where he had hurled it against the library's wall and had decided with his child's brain to carry it once more, or whether it was a hint from Reovalis. It had to be noted, however, that this weapon had been withheld from the stock Reovalis had given them.

In any event it was obvious to all that their visit to the Temple of the Polonians was at an end.

At the library's entrance, Usmu handed them a large basket of fruit, and they took their leave. Without speaking a word, he retreated into the shadows of the great Temple.

At the foot of the path, they found their tiny boat drawn up onto the beach exactly where they had left it. But now there was more. The weapons mentioned by Reovalis were lying in the little craft, along with all manner of other provisions. In fact, so well supplied were they that there were more goods than the craft could ever have been expected to handle. For this reason, a raft had been built, its crafting so meticulous that it was plain it had been designed by Reovalis himself. It rested upon the beach, tethered to the boat by a line.

Quickly, the travelers examined the raft and the store of provisions Reovalis had bestowed upon them. Then they fell to the process of rearranging the stowage of their goods, for they had become experienced watermen in these canyons; they knew the measures that had to be taken to prevent their supplies from being damaged or lost.

Partway through this reloading, as Palamon was hurriedly retying a stout cord, he heard Ursid call Berengeria's name, and out of the corner of one eye he saw the maiden rise and walk toward the sound. A moment later, Palamon's activities moved him to a different position. When he looked up again in the midst of his labors, it was to see Ursid and Berengeria talking earnestly a few paces up the beach.

The breezes swept the low tones of their conversation from Palamon's ears; the subject of their speech was something he could only guess at. But then he saw Ursid take an object from his tunic and give it to the maiden. It was a flower. Ursid had taken one of the blooms from the garden of Reovalis, had kept it in his tunic, and was presenting it to Berengeria.

Berengeria herself seemed nonplussed. Even from the place where Palamon stood, her blush was apparent. She spread her hands, seemed to force a smile, then said something which Palamon could not hear. She never once seemed to look directly into the young man's face. At last, at his urging, she took the blossom and used a loose bit of thread to tie it to the mantle of her robe, above her bosom.

Palamon grimaced. Ursid knew; as Berengeria had said, the younger knight had sensed the shift in her emotions and surely realized he was losing her. What a cruel prank fate had played upon him. Palamon could not accept the maiden's love for reasons that were numberless and partly nameless. And yet, as hard as Ursid strove for that same love, it was slipping away from him as relentlessly as smoke through the fingers of a blind man. The poor lad. Why did these things happen? Palamon went back to his labors, tugging viciously at one of the cords until it snapped.

It was late morning by the time they were finally ready to reembark onto the Stilchis. They had rearranged their bounty with care. The weapons had been divided. Ursid had been awarded the bow because he had been judged to be the best shot of the group. Each person had also taken a dagger.

Carefully Palamon and Ursid pushed the raft off the beach and into the water while the two female voyagers paid out the line. Then, as the men stepped into the boat, it, too, was launched. They seated themselves carefully and all four of them set about learning how to control the boat and the raft together.

But that was not difficult; the river had become sluggish in spite of the great volume of water it now bore. Toward evening, the cliffs fell back and the current slowed even more. Sandbars appeared everywhere. Weeds sprouted here and there and the river itself became stagnant and foul smelling; the four travelers had to paddle constantly to make any headway at all along this broad flood with its idle current.

For the rest of the afternoon, they sweated at their paddles. As the sun began to sink low ahead of them, they beached their gallant craft on one of the largest sandbars, where they would spend the night. Crossing the top of the dune, they found their labors had been rewarded. Ahead of them, beyond a sandbar-dotted estuary, lay a great body of open water. They had reached the Thlassa Mey.

Chapter Nineteen:
The Thlassa Mey

IT WAS MORNING. The sun had not yet risen, but the light of the new day streamed across the skies like a colorful cloak, gilding the tasseled clouds and marking the cliffs that fell away to the east. The waters about the sand spit were still black and shadowy, but the rising sun would soon turn them into a sea of diamond sparkles.

Berengeria was awake. At her own insistence, she had maintained the morning watch, and it was now nearly time for her to wake her companions. But one was awake already. A few moments ago she had watched as Palamon had sat up in his blanket, looked about, then stood and walked up over the sandy crest of their little island and toward the far shore, hidden from her by the dune itself.

This had not surprised Berengeria; nearly every morning since their escape from Buerdaunt, Palamon had gone off to be by himself for awhile at sunrise. It was something that was never mentioned, this habit of the tall knight's. But it was then he prayed to his patron, Pallas of the gray eyes and the wise and pure heart, Pallas, who heard each

morning at sunrise the respects of all her Knights, wherever they might have been across the lands that surrounded the Thlassa Mey. Whether she heard the prayers
of a fallen Knight was a subject open to debate; never-
theless, Palamon had not wavered in paying homage
whenever possible.

Berengeria was sure what was in Palamon's mind,
because she doubted there had been any opportunity for
him to observe the rite in the underground vaults of the
Polonians. So it was with the satisfaction of an alchemist
seeing the predicted result of an experiment that she
watched her knight top the sand dune and disappear down
the far side. She had not been in Aelia's care all these
years without learning something.

The day's first zephyr twirled her hair into ringlets as
she stood and followed him. She had forgotten the events
of the previous day, the conversation with Ursid, the
unsolicited gift of the flower. Her desire at this time was
to speak with the elusive Palamon. She spotted him easily
as she peered above the sand dune; there was no concealment on this island.

He was kneeling, facing the Thlassa Mey. The rising
breeze caused his white chiton to flap about him as he
knelt; the great sword lay in the sand before him. Berengeria easily heard his words as she approached him
from behind, even though they were spoken softly. "O
mighty Pallas, gray-eyed Maiden dear, give audience to
one who calls thy name. Thy humble servant seeks not
wealth or fame but only that his prayers thou shalt hear.
O blessed patron, grant surcease from fear and let thy
power guide my arm and aim. I am a simple warrior without claim but that thy aegis be forever near. Oh, guide
me in my quest to do thy will; bring succor to all those
who cannot speak to thee themselves. With power this
sword fill, that it might bring protection to the weak.
Through this imperfect world I seek thee still. Oh, grant
that I might find the things I seek."

Berengeria's fingertips floated to her mouth. She waited
in silence during the lone ceremony, for she was loathe
to break into the sanctity of this intense moment. And by

its design, the prayer was that; it was intense, unique, and devout, and there could have been no doubt that Palamon would have viewed any interruption as an act of brutal sacrilege.

This very fact was the crux of her difficulty. It troubled her; for all its sanctity, this moment was a symbol of Palamon's affliction with the past. He could not let go of what he once had been. And until he could find a way to do that, how much hope could there be for this new love she bore him?

Still, she waited. Palamon prayed on, unaware of her, his words sometimes swept away by the wind, sometimes carried clearly to her ears. He was concerned for the safety of his companions, he was concerned about the legal continuation of the royal line of Carea, and, notwithstanding his scandalous history and ouster from his order, he was concerned about maintaining his remaining faith and purity in the face of the world's temptations. As she listened, it occurred to her that she was, perhaps, one of those temptations.

At length he was finished. He remained kneeling for a moment, his eyes fixed upon some point beyond the horizon. Finally, with a sigh, he rose from the sand and brushed off his knees. He turned and his eyes fell upon her, widening.

She started in spite of herself. "Forgive me, Palamon, I meant no harm. Do not upbraid me for my interest; we have to speak together, you and I."

A glare flashed across his face, but it faded quickly. "Indeed, Princess, no bad thing may I say to you, who have so totally consumed my heart. In fact, I wished to speak with you and have for all the time that's passed since you inflamed my soul upon that bench within the garden of Reovalis."

"You have indeed?"

"I have. For what I said was far too short; it was not courteous. I spoke to you in haste, my mind all filled with unfamiliar thoughts and feelings." He paused. His eyes flicked away from her face. "I cannot deny I love you some. You are a most impressive woman, for your youth."

"You speak in earnest?" Berengeria's eyes were full upon Palamon's face. She was vulnerable at this moment and such a sight unsettled him.

"Yes, for once I do."

Without another word, she wrapped her arms about him, burying her head against his chest. He stood uncomfortably, one hand at his side and the other still grasping the haft of the *Spada Korrigaine*. He did adore this Berengeria. Yet he was unsure. "Ah, maiden, you do not know what you do. My loyalty was pledged long years ago unto my patron, Pallas. Earthly love, this passion for a maiden such as you, is something I have had no schooling in. Such closeness as we share this moment is a thing that must be felt to be believed." He sighed. Then he moved his free hand and pressed her to him. "The bursting of this love inflicts a wound more difficult to heal than any slash I've e'er been dealt in tournament or war."

"I'm sorry, Palamon."

"Oh, do not be. The fault lies deep in me; had I the strength..." He became silent; the only sound was his struggling breath. All at once he slipped to his knees and brought her with him. The great sword slipped from his fingers and fell, spraying the fine sand from its upset tip as he threw his arms about her. He leaned his moustached face upon the softness of her hair, feeling with his broad hands the smoothness of her back, pressing to his own chest the gentle swelling of her bosom.

She turned her head to the side and spoke. "I knew it, Palamon. Although you hide your inner self, I knew you had to love me, just as I love you."

"How did you know?"

"I knew because of times when I could see the shield about you crack. You let no person see into your heart; when watching you, that very fact's learned first. But still, sometimes, when we two were alone, I thought I saw those bastions 'round your soul give way somewhat, though 'twas the slightest bit. Yet I knew then that love was germinating in your soul, a love that was for me."

Palamon released her from his embrace, leaned back, and looked at her. "Yes, it is so."

She smiled as she looked up at him. "You see, you met your match when you met me."

"I've met my match before."

She went on, giving no notice to Palamon's dry remark. "When we reach Carea, I'll be your bride; my father will accept you, I know that. You've faced great dangers all in my behalf and more, I fancy, lie 'twixt here and home. That much alone should make you dear to him. But you are great and noble, Palamon, as shown but yesterday. Your great sword is the proof. The *Spada Korrigaine*, the Fairy Blade, the Sword of Emperors, once hammered out by mystic smiths upon an ancient isle. It is your slave, it comes upon your call. That proves you are of fine and noble heart; that's what I'll tell my father when you plead for my most willing hand."

"I'll not do that." The ache had swept down upon Palamon once more, this time more voracious and overwhelming than he would have believed possible.

"Do not be daunted, love. You'll gain my hand. As I am a Princess, that much is sure."

It was hard for Palamon to force his words out. "My dearest love—Princess—I still cannot, for all the love that I maintain for you, ask even once for your most blessed hand. And even if 'twas offered, I would have no choice, but must respectfully decline."

Berengeria looked up at him, blinking at his words. Through the haze of her own tears, she could not miss the pain, the agony that lay behind the eyes of her knight. Finally, through the fog of her own disappointment, she found her voice. "You said I was your love."

"And so you are."

"Then why should we not spend our lives enjoined, together bonded by this sacred love? What keeps us from fulfilling this desire?"

"The past," Palamon said. "The past, the past. It is my tomb. It is my prison and my torture, too; and for it, I've no chance of winning you."

"Forget the past," Berengeria said. "It's done."

"I cannot do that."

"Yes, you can. You had a woman once, long years ago.

The price for that was paid with your own shame. The very gods would say your debt's fulfilled. The vows that held you to your order then cannot still bind you now. You were released when they degraded you."

"No, I was not," Palamon said. "My vows still hold me firmly in my mind—as strongly as they did in younger times when I was still a Knight. For these eight years, I have not kept the rites, my prayers and other ways did I forsake. While in your service, though, I have returned to all my former custom; it is good. This love for you makes me a better man, but I must demonstrate it from afar, for though I'm fallen from those sacred ranks, a Knight of Pallas am I in my soul."

He paused to gaze into her face, then went on. "I say I love you; to our grief it's true. For all of that, our love must stay within our hearts. I cannot bind my body to your own though I would give my very life for that."

"You said you never loved the maid Arlaine and yet you sacrificed your covenant to satisfy the lusting of your flesh. That much I can forgive; a man may err. But now, though your old order cast you out, and old bonds hold you only in your mind, you still refuse my honorable love, although you say you love me in return." Berengeria rose to her feet, every inch a Princess, one hand sweeping away hairs that the wind had blown askew. The flower that had been tied to her robe had come loose; it fell and the wind blew it skipping across the sand. But neither of the lovers noticed that as Berengeria spoke again. "I sacrificed my dignity for you and told you out of love the way I feel. It is your right to spurn me, Palamon, but I'll not open my heart again."

Palamon continued to gaze at her. What was he to do, this miserable knight who returned her love, yet could not accept it? What was he to say? He lifted his hands in an empty gesture. "I do love you."

"But less than you still love your bygone days." With those words she left him; he watched her as she made her way over the top of the sand dune.

What other answer could he have given? A match between the two of them was out of the question. His past and his faith placed an unbridgeable gulf between them; and there was something else, too. He did not claim to understand the feeling, but above all the logical reasons that separated them, there was his unshakable sense that the forces spinning their fates would never allow their two threads to become entwined. He knew that. For all the love he bore Berengeria, he knew that single fact as well as he knew his own name. And he sensed that he would be inviting catastrophe if he ever weakened and mocked those fates. He remained where he was for a moment, then lurched to his feet, picked up his sword, and followed her back.

Aelia and Ursid were awake by now and they were watching Palamon as he approached. Ursid had noticed what Palamon and Berengeria had not—that the flower Ursid had given her was gone from her robe. The young knight's face was alive with jealousy and frustration. "How now, bold knight," he said. "Have you been guarding us against some foray from the seaward flank?"

"Ursid." The sharpness of Aelia's voice caused the young man's head to snap about.

Palamon's wit searched for a properly arid response to Ursid's anger but he was not up to the task after having spoken so openly to Berengeria. So he ignored the remark. "We may have reached the sea, but our skin boat is hardly adequate to brave these waves, though it has served us well for many days. We therefore must decide what we shall do—attempt to circumvent the sea by use of feet or seek some vessel which can transport us."

"A matter I have given thought," Aelia said. "Both paths lead into danger. If we go by land, our course is mapped out by the coastline. All our foes need do is lie in wait for us."

Palamon nodded, glad to put his seared brain to work on a practical problem; maps were more easily dealt with than maidens, it seemed.

Aelia continued. "If, on the other hand, our path should cross the sea, we are presented with the problem posed by transportation's woes. We must seek out a vessel first of all; and once we find it, how shall we be sure the captain's not allied with all our foes?" From the way she discussed the problem, she showed she had given it much thought.

"Yet," Palamon said, "if we do advance our course by land, can four unmounted persons pack supplies to transit this long-desolated shore?"

"Indeed." She bit her knuckle thoughtfully as she looked in turn upon each of her fellow fugitives, then out over the rolling combers of the Thlassa Mey.

"Then let's choose one," Ursid said. "The rest be damned." There was no mistaking the fact that the young knight was in no mood for long consideration of any question. But to some degree, he was right, and his fellows knew it; time spent idly at the mouth of the Stilchis was time given back to Lothar the Pale and his soldiers.

"The farest course," Palamon said, "would be to wade along the shoreline, towing our supplies packed on the raft. At least we would advance somewhat while looking for a fairer course."

It was agreed that this was the best plan, at least for the moment. There were a few small trading ports on the southern coast of the Thlassa Mey; perhaps upon reaching one, they could find a quicker way to travel. Perhaps, that is, if they could elude Lothar's agents long enough to do so.

But as they breakfasted a better way presented itself; a sail approached along the coast from the southwest. It was a coastal merchant, perhaps, or maybe even a corsair seeking plunder. In either event there was no doubt that the four travelers would soon be spotted for the ship was sailing only a few hundred cubits off the flat beach, taking advantage of the morning breeze.

As the ship approached, they decided it could not be a corsair; it was a tub-shaped little vessel, a merchantman. Besides, a corsair would have been more likely to stand out to sea, both to extend the amount of water across which it could have searched for game and to give itself sea room for maneuver. It was a merchant, then, headed toward Buerdaunt, probably with trade goods from Ourms or some other port.

That posed another problem; if she was bound for Buerdaunt, how could they embark upon her for Carea without exciting suspicion?

Aelia suggested a way. The vessel's captain would be bribed to take them to the island of Kolpos, which lay in the center of the Thlassa Mey, commanding sea routes to all lands. The harbor of its only large city, Touros, sheltered many vessels and all classes of seamen; surely passage out of Lothar's clutches could be purchased there.

They prepared quickly. Aelia examined her purse and found ample gold for her purposes; for the moment, she and Palamon became minor nobles from the northern city of Oron, taking Ursid back to marry their supposed daughter, Berengeria. Ursid enjoyed the role.

They hid the raft and boat, concealed their goods in bundles, then walked out onto the beach, waving their arms. They soon saw a response; a boat was lowered and rowed toward the beach to investigate. Aelia told the coxswain her tale and the ruse worked; they were taken to the mother ship.

They found her to be a typical small merchantman, the likes of which plied the waters all across the Thlassa Mey, as well as the ocean beyond the Narrow Strait. She was stout, heavy timbered, squatty; her single sail was a distorted square of filthy, patched canvas. And she stank. Like most of her sisters in the coastal trade, she was more valuable underway, however slowly, than hauled ashore in some seaport for careening. She had been at sea long enough to ferment wonderfully, and the odor that rose from her overcharged bilges prompted the new passengers to go pale. Berengeria was forced to cover her nostrils with her sleeve.

They had only an instant to marvel at the aroma before they were introduced to the vessel's master, a puffy, self-important fellow who called himself Schemeff. His thick hair was black, his mouth was broad and leering, and he moved and spoke with the air of the martinet. He eyed Berengeria approvingly as he looked the foursome over. "I'm told you claim to be marooned nobles from some northern land. Should I believe that?"

"What you believe is not of our concern," Aelia said. She was playing the role of the matriarch now, and playing it to the hilt. Palamon could see that it had been with some wisdom she had been chosen as Berengeria's guardian. "But if our speech, our bearing, and our dress mean nothing to you, by my troth, you've never seen a blooded person in your life."

Schemeff looked at Aelia narrowly, then his eyes again traveled over her companions. It was clear he did not appreciate her words. "It's all the same to me. You'll be set ashore in Buerdaunt when we arrive. Until then, you can keep your goods and yourselves upon the deck here as long as you stay out of the way of my men."

"Buerdaunt is not the place we wish to go," she said.

"Oh, no?" Schemeff's wide mouth twisted in an unpleasant grin.

"We want to sail to Touros, where we may take passage on another vessel bound with goods unto Oron, our native land."

Schemeff gazed at her in mocking disbelief. "And I have to change my course to take you to Touros?"

"Indeed, you must."

He smirked. "Not likely. You'll have to make passage from Buerdaunt." He turned away.

"And I refuse." Aelia stamped her foot.

He paused, looking back at the tall woman, impatience causing the corner of his mouth to twitch. "Madam, I don't know who you are but if you believe I'll change the course set down by the owners of this vessel, then you should be exposed upon the nearest hilltop, along with any others you can find who might be as mentally diseased as yourself." He turned on his heel and walked aft toward the sterncastle.

"And what would be required to cause that change in course?"

"It will never happen," he said over his shoulder.

"A golden price would purchase this old slime-encrusted hulk. Would you then change your course?"

He turned to look at her narrowly. "If you spoke the

truth to my coxswain, you have no gold. You said brigands siezed your ship and set you ashore."

Aelia smiled at him, a slow, enticing smile. "They took our ship but could not find the gold." While he watched with renewed interest, she pulled the blanket off the parcel she had been carrying. Removing the upper contents of the large fruit basket, she revealed a gleaming pile of gold coins.

Schemeff was impressed. He retraced his steps and stood looking down at the small fortune she was holding. She presented the gold cunningly, holding it so the sun's rays danced and sparkled off the heavy coins. Like an angler enticing a fish, she baited her prey. "Your merchant owners surely shan't object to passage paid above this vessel's worth. A good deposit I will pay you now; the rest I then can forward from Oron by messenger into the owners' hands."

The ship's master cleared his throat as if the sight of Aelia's hoard had given him a blockage. "I'm sure such a large sum won't be necessary. Some hundred and fifty talents would more than satisfy my backers and repay any losses of cargo. And I can deliver that sum myself on the return voyage."

This was the answer Aelia desired. Of course she realized the gold would never reach the ship's owners. For all his pompous words, Schemeff would pocket the money and concoct an excuse for the delay, something he could not have done if more payment had been coming to the owners directly. She had him now; the trout had taken the fly. She pressed her advantage. "How long, I ask, will be the northward run to Touros?"

"A day and a night, I should imagine." Schemeff was already gathering the proper count of gold pieces into a kerchief while Aelia watched, holding the basket forth generously.

"A place of shelter also is desired," she said. "To store our goods as well as our own selves for the duration of the voyage."

"Unfortunately that isn't possible. The hold is too dank and musty for you and there's no other place except the deck itself. But the sun has gone without garments the last few days. The weather should be fair for the short time you'll be with us."

"But you yourself have quarters, have you not?"

"Indeed."

"Then that fair sky you say will smile on us can smile on you with equal warmth and love. I've no intention that this fair young maid—here Aelia gestured toward Berengeria—should spend another night beneath the skies." She offered a few more talents to the ship's master. "Now come, sir, this should serve to heal the wounds from vacating your cabin for the night."

This time Schemeff did not even begin to argue; he gazed at the additional gold pieces with the air of a man more than pleased to add to his take. It was remarkable how his attitude toward his passengers had changed over the last few moments.

The bargain was quickly struck, accounting for three quarters of the gold pieces Aelia had begun the day with. But as soon as the agreement was reached, she ended her conversation with this most consonant captain; she wrapped the remainder of her tender, took up her bundle, and walked toward the stern of the tubby vessel. Palamon and the rest followed after her like a squadron of lighters in the wake of a great galley.

Schemeff took them to the low doorway leading to his cabin, showed them the workings of the swinging lamp and stowable bunks, then retired. When he had gone, Berengeria closed the door and threw her arms about her guardian. "Oh, Aelia, you are precious and without a scruple. You would purchase heaven's gates for mortal coin and make the mighty gods rejoice the bargain had been made, I know."

"Oh, hush, my child. Until this voyage is done, we must assume our every move is watched and every word is passed unto our foes."

"Then very well." Berengeria relinquished her embrace but there was still a smile lifting the corners of her mouth.

"Indeed, those words are true," Palamon said. "And I suggest that when we all retire, one man at least stand guard throughout the night, the same as when we camped upon the shore. In fact, we're still encamped, although it is aboard this tiny ship."

Ursid moved to the narrow window on the aft bulkhead of the cabin and threw wide the shutters. Along with light and fresh air, the opening also admitted sounds from the deck above: commands and the scampering of sailors' nimble feet as the ship was brought about and headed on a new course. She would sail due north; the voyage to Touros was beginning.

Chapter Twenty:
Schemeff's Bargain

IT WAS EVENING. The little roundship lumbered north, driven by steady breezes as she carried the fugitives toward the isle called Kolpos. Master Schemeff had been congenial to the point of nausea through the afternoon, a fact which convinced Palamon the man would cut all their throats, take their remaining gold, and cast them into the sea at the slightest opportunity. He would bear watching until landfall.

And landfall would be made before another day had passed; there was no doubt of that. The mountains that had stood as sentries over the Cauldron of the Stilchis were falling toward the horizon behind them while the blue hump that was Kolpos was rising slowly out of the seas toward which they were plowing. Even at the snail's pace of this little vessel, the land mass in front had grown greatly since it had first appeared.

So Palamon stood on the sterncastle, leaned upon the taffrail, braced himself against the roll of the ship in these friendly seas, and inhaled the breeze that was sweeping across the port quarter. This lull in the tension of their long flight was a welcome one, and he expected that Aelia, Ursid, and Berengeria were enjoying it as much as he was.

And what of Berengeria? What was he to do about her? She was not for him, that much was certain. However much he might love her, he knew her hand had to go to some young prince or duke when the time came, perhaps a Carean noble, perhaps a man from some other land. That she would bring joy to the mate her father selected for her was certain, certain, that was, if the match brought joy to her. Palamon hoped that would be the case. In any event, his own wanderings would doubtless continue. What *he* would do, this knight without a country— or even an order—was a question he did not choose to ponder on this pleasant evening.

He heard a sound behind him and turned to see Aelia climbing the ladder to the sterncastle, approaching him across the high quarterdeck. "You venture far afield, my Lady," he said. "This broad deck is warrior's province during battle, sailor's province on a day like this."

"That tiny cabin's far too close for me." Aelia stood beside him, placing her hands upon the rail a cubit from his own. Her fingers rested upon the worn wood lightly, pensively. "I thought that I would come out for some air and join you while you watched the rough waves roll."

"These waves are not as rough as you imply." He looked down at her, smiling. She was a tall woman but he still towered over her when they stood this close to one another. "So you have left the young ones down below to pass the time by what device they choose. A sea voyage, so it's said, gives dalliance full rein."

She looked up at him and spoke dryly. "If that is so, good knight, it's not Ursid who causes me alarm in that respect, but one you know full well."

"Oh, is that so?"

"It is and that is why I ventured onto deck to speak with you. Our dear Princess has, as you may already know," she paused to look at him. "I'm sure you know that she has now become infatuated with you, Palamon.

She is a willful maid and never rests till she achieves the goal toward which she strives. Your feelings toward her are something I know nothing of. However, as you surely see, a group in flight lacks opportunity for feelings 'twixt its members. Does it not?"

Palamon was expressionless. "I understand your meaning and I shall repulse her lewd advances on all fronts."

Aelia studied his features. "This is no topic for your mirth, O knight. Th'effects of her attachment unto you may well o'erturn the ship of our escape and I do not make play on words. Our Berengeria must still return to Carea or else all things are lost."

"Why yes, indeed. And yet I can recall Ursid's deep love for her was nurtured by yourself because it was the key out of Buerdaunt. Are your Princess' own amours and hates mere matters of your kingdom's policy?" Palamon turned toward her and leaned upon the taffrail with one elbow.

"She's my responsibility. Upon the time when we have reached Carea's shores, her life becomes her own once more to lead. Till then, I do all necessary things."

Palamon laughed at her, a caustic, bitter, burning laugh. There was no humor in it. Aelia shrank before such a laugh, even from this knight whose bitterness had become so familiar to her. "Ah, yes," he said, "Necessity, the mighty god in whose great name we do all manner of things—inflict harsh pain, cut life short, swallow up great multitudes of hopes. I must bow down." He did just that, kneeling before her and clenching his hands as if in worship. "Away with all volition. We shall do whatever's called for by necessity."

"Hush, Palamon. By Hestia's sheer veil, are you quite mad to rant so at one word?" She glanced nervously over her shoulder at the ship's master, who was watching them with an amused smile.

"Your pardon. I'll maintain a proper air." Palamon did not speak another word. He rose to his feet and resumed his position at the rail, his eyes fixed on the gentle swells of the Thlassa Mey. His mind was no longer aboard the roundship, however. It had been pierced by a harsh vision, an interview within a most secluded chamber in the Fastness of Pallas. Honor died at such confrontations. "Necessity," he finally said. The word was spoken softly but it was expelled like spittle.

Aelia gazed at the back of his head for a moment, speaking words that went unheeded. Then she stood away from the rail, watching him silently. She finally left.

Palamon turned his head and watched her go. She descended the ladder to the main deck and vanished as she returned to the master's cabin. He sighed. She was right, of course—her thoughts on the matter matched his exactly. The necessary thing would be done.

Palamon stood for a long time, watching out over the waves as the land mass ahead of the vessel grew. The early evening twilight slowly turned into night and the land vanished, absorbed by darkness. He looked upward and studied the stars smeared across the dome of the night sky. There were so many. In such a confusing sky, how did the star gazers chart the lives of men, he wondered.

When he finally went below, he entered the cabin to find Aelia and Berengeria already asleep in the compartment's two tiny bunks. Ursid was seated at the master's desk, watching the tall knight silently, his emotions hidden by the shadows. "I see you have the watch," Palamon said in a low whisper.

"I have the watch. The ladies have the beds. You stood on deck and they were both quite tired."

Palamon nodded and seated himself on a large sea chest that stood beneath the shuttered window at the aft end of the cabin. He was tired himself, but there could be no sleep for him; his mind was too full of thoughts for sleep to enter. He watched Ursid, who remained seated at the desk, staring into the darkness.

The chamber rolled endlessly as the vessel wallowed its way toward Touros. Then Palamon heard something. There were lively footfalls echoing through the ship and from the stern window floated sounds of the rigging being shifted. He tilted his head and listened harder.

Ursid was also listening. But from within the blind

confines of the cabin, it was difficult to tell how much of a rigging change was being made. Had the wind shifted, forcing the sailors to reset the sail carried by the vessel's single mast? Had one of Buerdaunt's war galleys appeared? It was impossible to tell.

Palamon rose and jammed his head and shoulders through the narrow window, attempting to obtain a view of the decks above. What little he did see was enough; the constellations he had gazed up at earlier had all rotated nearly one hundred eighty degrees. Schemeff was wearing ship; the vessel was reversing its course.

Palamon pulled his head back between the shutters and grasped Ursid by the shoulder. "Awake the ladies. We have been betrayed."

"Can you be sure?" Ursid looked up at the older knight, then leaped to his feet. While he roused the two women, Palamon tried to peer through the cabin door, only to find it barred from the outside. So silently had the deed been performed that neither of them ever heard a sound. So both men moved to the window again and took turns peering up. Ursid, as the younger and nimbler of the two, decided there was a good enough foothold on the molding above the shutters for him to climb up, at least enough to obtain a view of the quarterdeck.

It was quickly done. With Palamon's help, Ursid squeezed through the narrow opening and hauled himself upward until he could see. With his body hanging out over the vessel's wake, he watched Schemeff as the cunning shipmaster completed his orders for the course change. Then while Ursid secretly watched, Schemeff spoke with another man, one the young knight had not seen before. But what Ursid heard said between the two was enough to confirm his worst fears.

He wriggled back into the cabin and told the others all he had seen. Even in the cabin's murk, his face was pale as he whispered the news: "It was a captain of pale Lothar's guard that I saw Schemeff speaking with. It was a ruse, all done to get us onto this foul ship."

"And one most ably done," Berengeria whispered. She was very downcast.

Ursid went on. "They sailed that coast on watch for us for days. A score of Lothar's men were hidden in the hold and all the sailors schooled to act adverse enough to make us use some masquerade. But all the while, they were to offer passage to the place desired by us and to allow us to avail ourselves of this, the master's cabin. And the bolt was fitted to the entrance for this charge."

"A doorway fitted to be barred without." Palamon clenched his fist. "And we walked in, not noticing the trap."

"Now what are we to do? What can we do?" Aelia looked as if the situation was causing her to fall in upon herself. "Can we have come so far to be thus trapped?"

Palamon was silent for a moment; they were all silent as they stared into one another's dark faces. At last he spoke quietly, with measured resolve. "Now we must fight."

Berengeria stared at him. "You cannot fight. It's death."

"He's right," Ursid said. "It's also death for us to bide our time and wait for them to come remove us to the keep of Uncle Lothar once we've docked. For Lothar's men cannot kill us more dead than he himself will, once he has us there. And you, dear Berengeria, will be brought back in any case, no worse off than before, although perhaps more tightly mewed."

Berengeria cast her eyes onto the smooth wooden deck of the cabin. "That fate I cannot countenance, withal."

"Then all the reason more we must resist our capture." Palamon stood, his grim smile barely visible in the darkness. "And besides, some hours ago, I was most sternly lectured on the way my conduct should be shaped, not by desire but by necessity. This I shall do. If we go to our deaths, the gods will know 'twas from necessity." He fumbled beneath one of the cots and withdrew the blanket-covered bundle which contained the great sword given him by Reovalis.

He unwrapped the weapon quietly, then held it up, grasping the haft securely in his broad hands. He moved slowly toward the barred door while Ursid strung the longbow.

The overhead of the chamber was low, hampering Palamon's movement. Even so, his muscles strained as he delivered as hard a blow as he could. The blade was silent in the darkness but to Palamon's surprise, it cleaved through jam, door, and wooden crossbar with ease. The shorn barricade burst, the pieces fell with a crash to reveal a deck crowded with astonished sailors. There were others, too, men wearing uniforms of the army of Buerdaunt.

The roundship's deck instantly became a battleground. Sailors fled, crying out. But despite the fact that they had been caught off guard, the soldiers of King Lothar quickly drew their longswords and advanced upon Palamon and Ursid. Ursid had the time to fire only a single arrow before a man leaping from the sterncastle grappled with him.

While the two men struggled, Palamon advanced steadily, forcing back the men before him with his deadly *Spada Korrigaine*. The blade cleaved a path of death, laying low a pair of foeman on the first swing; their sundered trunks toppled with motions that were grotesque, sickening. There was also a groan from behind him; the voice did not belong to Ursid so he knew the young knight had slain his antagonist.

The mighty blade enabled Palamon to dominate the aft end of the deck. Rather than face him directly, the soldiers attempted to outflank him, advancing with their backs against the gunwales of the vessel. He leaped to his left, forestalling an advance from that route, then had to recover and dash just as quickly to his right. In the meantime, a half-dozen opponents piled down the ladder into the fo'c'sle and the ship's hold.

Palamon heard Aelia's cry. "Their bows. Oh, Palamon, they go to fetch their bows."

She was right. He had to reach the fo'c'sle companionway and prevent the return of the archers before he and his companions could be slaughtered like so many chickens. "Protect my back as best you can," he shouted, and pressed forward with even greater effort.

He fought his way along the starboard rail. The steersman had already fled and the steering oar waved to and fro, causing the vessel to wallow in the shallow troughs of the Thlassa Mey. This made the struggle a clumsy, haphazard business.

All the same, two more men went down before him, hardly slowing his sword in its arc as it truncated them. Their beheaded bodies were grisly trophies which rolled across the deck, making the planks slimy with blood and difficult to walk upon. But the fugitives were making progress. Now that he had vanquished his foe from the sterncastle, Ursid was using his bow to good advantage, laying low a man who was trying to advance across the deck out of the reach of Palamon's sword. The singing arrows prevented any repetition of such a tactic.

In the light that shone from the fo'c'sle hatch, Palamon could see the archers struggling to climb onto deck. But now the swordsmen were in full retreat belowdecks, blocking those who were trying to climb up. With one last, mighty swing, Palamon sent his last opponent leaping down the hatchway onto the shoulders of his fellows and the tall knight gasped from exertion as he kicked the hatch closed.

Having no more enemies before him, he turned and looked about. The upper decks of the roundship belonged to the four travelers. The only living soul still visible besides themselves was the wily Schemeff, who remained on the quarterdeck, apoplectic with astonishment.

But Palamon had a companion whose presence he had not noticed during the battle. Behind him all the while as he had wreaked his carnage with his sword had been Berengeria, her dagger drawn. The plucky maiden looked up at him as he turned. "My dear Princess," he said, "you've courage, by my troth, but of your wisdom I've few words to say."

"You said to guard your back as you advanced," she replied simply. "I broke from Aelia's clutches and obeyed, and there was little danger, for our foes all fled Ursid's quick arrows and your sword."

Palamon frowned at her. Had his foot slipped in the gory mess spilled across the deck, her situation would have become dangerous. Still, the deed was done. His frown evaporated. After all, it had been a courageous act on the part of this maiden and her presence behind him had perhaps prevented the frustrated Schemeff from slipping a dagger between his ribs while he was fighting.

Schemeff was the center of their attention now. While Palamon guarded the fo'c'sle hatch, Ursid trained his bow upon the shipmaster. "Come down, you scum, or else your blood will flow."

Schemeff quickly did as he had been ordered. Ursid searched him, removed a pair of wicked-looking knives, and prodded him toward Palamon, who was leaning on his sword now, his sides still heaving. "The situation now has been reversed," Palamon said. "Short moments past, you thought you had us snared; but we control your boat, and all your arms and men are pinned beneath these boards. Now you must tell them that this is the case. For if we must, in desperation, we'll burn this vessel to the waterline along with all our catch. Now speak your piece."

In unsteady tones, Schemeff followed Palamon's instructions. Then he turned to the tall knight. "As you seem to be the older and wiser man, I must tell you that I was forced into all this. My ship was commandeered by these soldiers. I had no choice."

Palamon gazed at Schemeff without expression. He expected he had been a most willing vassal but the point was not worth debating. "It matters little. When we go ashore on Kolpos, then your ship will be your own. But first, I think this vessel has a carpenter."

Schemeff nodded.

"Then fetch his stores, that we might seal this hatch."

Schemeff spread his hands weakly; all the fight seemed to have left him. "I can't do that. The carpenter's stores are in the fo'c'sle."

This presented a problem. How were the four fugitives to stand guard over a hold full of men and sail this cumbersome vessel all at the same time? It was a poser and Palamon said as much to Ursid. Some way of sealing the hatchway had to be found.

Now Aelia advanced. During the battle, as well as the conversation with Schemeff, she had been standing behind the ship's mast, watching, drinking in all that had passed. Palamon had forgotten her. He turned to look at her as she spoke. "Perhaps we need not sail this clumsy craft. The gift of wise Reovalis was meant to be employed in any troubled times." She held forth her hand and in it was the crystal vial. "Perhaps the time to utilize the first of its three draughts is now."

So this was why she had not joined the fighting. Her qualities as a warrior were limited by age, experience, and inclination. Still, she had stood ready with an object that might have been useful had the situation become hopeless. Would it have worked? Would the liquid in the vial have stopped the onrushing soldiers of Lothar the Pale? That was impossible to say, but she had the perfect opportunity to test its mettle now: the ship had to be sailed. Already, it was difficult to be sure how far they had strayed from their course. They could only bring the vessel about and strike north in the general direction of Kolpos; their course would have to be corrected when the island showed itself at sunrise.

Palamon looked at Aelia, then at the object cupped in her palm. "Then use the vial, for we have nothing in the world to lose."

With a deft motion, Aelia peeled the wax seal from the top of the little vial. Then, her hands moving nimbly, she shook it at the ship's mast for want of a better target.

A few drops of the glowing liquid squirted forth but they did not fall to the deck. Instead, they vaporized immediately; they formed a multicolored mist that spread about the mast, spiraling upward like millions of tiny fireflies. The droplets glowed and spiraled, spreading out as they rose until they had reached the masthead. Outward they spread, casting a strange light upon the sailcloth until the sail itself began to glow, entering the fabric the way wine soaks into a napkin. Now, instead of flapping idly in the breeze, the sail began to belly out with a life of its own.

"Ursid, take up the tiller. Let us see what happens as you steer to come about."

Ursid put down his bow and obeyed. Already the

ungainly vessel had picked up enough headway to heel over a bit as he changed her course. He brought her about until the sky's constellations had assumed their proper positions, then Palamon checked him with a word. All was lost in wonder at the magic light that filled the sail; the jealousy that Ursid had felt for Palamon was a thing forgotten for the moment. Even Schemeff seemed to be overwhelmed by the sight.

Palamon caught himself. He could not allow the beauty of Reovalis' art to distract him from watching over the soldiers who were seething only a few cubits away. While Aelia and Berengeria secured Schemeff to the rail, Palamon lowered his sword, resting the point upon the deck once more. He would have to call upon his iron will now, for he had to remain watchful through the night.

And so the time passed. Palamon stood like a statue, his concentration upon the fo'c'sle hatch never wavering; Ursid, Aelia, and Berengeria took turns at the tiller. Through the night the roundship glided forward, its single sail aglow with the ancient, mystic art of Reovalis.

At last Palamon could stand up no longer. The battle had worn him out; he needed rest. He had lost the stamina he had once possessed as a Knight of Pallas; he could not finish his vigil. He finally yielded his position to Ursid, lay down upon the deck with his sword, and slept.

Chapter Twenty-one:
The Isle of Kolpos

THE NIGHT PASSED. As dawn flooded the Thlassa Mey, Palamon's estimate of the ship's position proved correct; the events of the night had set the vessel to the east of the island of Kolpos. Still, the situation was not serious; Aelia and Berengeria, who were manning the tiller together, changed their course a bit, the magic breeze shifted accordingly, and the vessel sailed on, driven as rapidly as before.

Indeed, the clumsy roundship was making a speed her builders would have thought impossible. As they approached the southern coast of the island, it became obvious they would shortly make landfall.

There was a broad headland which needed to be cleared before the vessel could enter the long bay that formed the natural harbor for Touros, the island's largest city. But they had no intention of entering the harbor. Rather, they would run the ship aground and walk the last miles overland to Touros, for they feared it would have been difficult to enter the city anonymously on a captured roundship powered by a magical breeze. And so it was, as they neared the final headland that concealed the towers of the city, Palamon was awakened and the ship was steered toward the broad beach.

Their breeze, receptive to their every whim, gained strength as they approached the shore. It whistled through the rigging and the ship heeled as they turned. Her rail dipped dangerously close to the water. With every instant she surged nearer land until the sand loomed before them and there could be only a few heartbeats until they crashed.

At the last moment, Palamon retreated from his place by the fo'c'sle hatch and grasped the ship's rail to brace himself against the coming shock. "Protect yourselves," he cried. "Be wary of the mast."

Then the ship plowed into the sand. The planks and timbers of the vessel's hull protested such punishment with cracking and groaning, the men below shrieked, and the mast snapped as Palamon had feared it would. It wavered, there was a great popping of tackle, then it crashed down upon the fo'c'sle hatch itself. That piece of equipment was conveniently put out of commission for some time to come.

Schemeff was still tied to the base of the broken mast. Miraculously, he had not been injured. But he was pale from fright, both because of the grounding of his ship and his narrow escape from the falling timber and also because a memberless body had been jounced across the deck and now rested comfortably against his knee. But he remained as securely tied as ever.

Mindless of the attendant body, Aelia knelt at Schemeff's side and felt for his purse. "The money that we gave for passage, sir, was taken under false pretenses. So I feel a refund is in order." With these words she cut the bulging purse from his belt.

"My Lady makes a passing decent thief." Palamon watched Aelia's activities with a smile. "To strip a body," here he nodded at the grimacing, struggling Schemeff, "which appears alive, while headless corpses nuzzle at your side; methinks your worldly fortune is assured."

"I've no time for riposte, fair Palamon. But if necessity

makes me a thief, by that same token we are brigands all." She tired Schemeff's purse to her own sash and flung a few coins back into his face, causing him to wince as the heavy disks struck. "There, sirrah. Thus, I pay you for our fare."

In the meantime Palamon looked at the hatchway to assure himself that it was still held securely by the fallen mast, and Ursid and Berengeria took some fruits from the store of food they had left in the master's cabin. They grasped their weapons—Ursid had wrenched a sword from one of the corpses lying upon the deck—climbed over the rail, and dropped into the breakers below. The ship was so canted now where she lay beached that the starboard side was practically in the water. It was with ease that the four of them made their landing.

This beach was broad and sandy, ending in low, grass-covered bluffs. The foursome quickly climbed the nearest bluff. They found themselves on a grassy savanna that stretched away and upward until it ended in rocky hills, sparsely covered with scrubby trees and the olive groves of the Kolpians. They hurried toward this range of hills.

Once they had reached the trees, they looked back down upon the vessel they had just left. So far there was no sign of activity. Still, their erstwhile captors would soon batter their way back onto deck and the pursuit would begin again. But this time Lothar the Pale's soldiers would have to seek the four of them in an unfriendly land; there were no bonds between Kolpos and Buerdaunt. As for the roundship, she had been grounded so firmly that even high tide would not be likely to free her. In spite of these things, Palamon knew there would be a search; if the quarry could not be recaptured, there would be little doubt that there would soon be more bodies to torture in the presence chamber of Lothar the Pale. The pursuit would be furious, once it was resumed.

They made their way northwest toward Touros, keeping to the rocks; after going a way, they found a little stream bounding down a boulder-strewn course and they turned to follow it. The sun had barely shortened their shadows to the midday point when they encountered an ancient dame, pounding out her laundry upon a stone.

The emotions of this unschooled old woman were brutally tweaked as she looked up the hillside behind her to find herself accosted by this extraordinary group of strangers. They were carrying fierce weapons, and all of them but one were attired richly, though their garb showed hard wear. "The gods defend me," the old one cried, her hands flying to her face. "Please don't harm me. I have nothing, nothing."

"Old soul, we would not harm you for the world," Aelia said in her most soothing tone. "We ourselves escaped from evil men a little while ago at our great risk."

The aged one continued to stare up at them, her fears allayed a little. "Truly, you don't have the look of thieves. But you reek with blood, especially this fellow with his fearsome sword." Here she gestured toward Palamon.

Palamon looked down, actually gazing at himself for the first time that morning. To his surprise, he found that his arms and the cloth of his chiton had been drenched with gore, both his own and that of his foemen. He had been so intent upon his duties during the night, as well as the later details of their flight across Kolpos, that this matter had eluded him until now. He looked at his companions. All of them had been splattered with blood, though none had been drenched to the extent he had. Surely the four of them would have made a grim spectacle entering the city of Touros, decorated the way they were. "Old woman, I was painted in this way in honorable battle with those foes my Lady speaks of."

"We need your aid," Aelia said. "Do you live near this place?"

The old woman gestured along the steeply sloping streambed toward the thatched roof of a hut just visible between the trees. "I live in that house with my daughter and her husband. We live poor lives here on what we can scratch from the soil and what my son-in-law can bring home from the fishing boats. Be gentle with us; we have nothing for you to take."

"What is your name, old woman?"

"My name is Disciola, Lady."

"Good Disciola, we are in dire straits," Aelia said. "We dare not ener Touros as we are; our clothing by itself would advertise us to our enemies. We must have clothes that mark us as no more than common folk. You see, we seek return to our own land and fear we shall be waylaid undisguised."

Since it had become apparent that she was in no danger of being robbed or killed, Disciola became more friendly. "My Lady, a change of clothing can be had by yourself, the young Lady, and the young Lord. If simple clothing is all you need, my daughter's clothes, along with the clothes of my son-in-law and myself, can be made to suit you." She looked up at Palamon hopelessly. "As for you, bloody sir, I don't know what to say. There's not a piece of clothing in our poor house that will suit you, tall as you are."

"Obtain the clothing that you can from here," Palamon said to Aelia. "My simple tunic shan't stand out at all if we can clean it some."

Aelia and Berengeria both shook their heads. "That cannot be," Aelia said. "The bloody rivers that have drenched that cloth will ne'er be washed away without a stain."

Berengeria brightened. "Then, Palamon, a tunic can be made from clothing worn by Aelia and myself. We two have linen ample for the deed if your own clothing is to be replaced."

Aelia turned back to the old woman. "Tell me, good Disciola, can you sew? Stitch up a tunic for this bloody man and there's reward enough for many chores."

Disciola peered back at Aelia, gathering up the wet clothing that lay beside her at the stream's edge. "You bear the faces of honest men and women, for all your bloody conditions. The gods bid us to be generous in our use of strangers. Follow me. My daughter and I will garb you anew, and you needn't impoverish yourselves for the sake of it."

Most of the day was spent in Disciola's hut, washing away blood and dirt, caring for wounds, burying Ursid's tattered uniform, donning the new wardrobe they hoped would let them enter Touros undetected. When Aelia attempted to pay the two women in gold for their services, Disciola and her daughter were astonished at the weight of her purse. To these poor folk, the merest portion of such wealth was a greater fortune than anything they had ever laid eyes upon.

The four fugitives then set forth for Touros, their daggers concealed inside their clothing and Palamon's great blade wrapped in a blanket. It was evening by the time they saw the lights of the city twinkling below them. The shapes of the stone buildings were barely visible in the waning light, and beyond them washed the blue of the bay. There was a forest of masts in the harbor, enough to guarantee a ship to take them to any possible destination.

They found a simple inn as they followed the road into the city. There lodging was purchased for the night. Palamon, who had visited Touros before, inquired of the innkeeper where passage could be obtained to Carea.

The innkeeper shook his grizzled head and frowned. "You'll not be traveling to any western port for awhile. Buerdaunt's ships are sailing blockade a league off Cape Lookout and they've cut off all shipping in that direction. No declarations nor nothing. All traffic that way is stopped."

Palamon grimaced. Lothar the Pale had countered their every move and beaten their strategy before they had even begun to act. There could be no doubt that he fully understood his quarry.

The tall knight turned away, walking slowly back to the table where his companions were sitting with the inn's other patrons, devouring roast beef, bread, and wine. He approached Aelia and touched her on the shoulder, whispering in her ear when she turned. "I have foul news. Once we're alone, I'll speak."

Aelia nodded and the meal went on. Palamon ate little, picking at his fare until the inn's other guests rose and departed to their chambers, one by one. At last, at a word from Aelia, the foursome rose; they went to their own rooms and there Palamon repeated what the innkeeper had told him.

Ursid smacked a fist into the palm of his other hand. "Does Kolpos have no navy to protect its trade from interdict by Lothar's hand?"

"It is a simple land," Aelia said. "And commerce is its blood. For ages, navies of the lands well served by Kolpos' ships have acted to secure this island's shores."

"Indeed," Berengeria said, taking up Aelia's line of reasoning. "And who can act for open trade along the western lanes but Carea? 'Twill be a while at best, ere word is passed to Berevald, my father, and he acts."

Aelia nodded. "And even then no ships may come, for who's told Berevald that we've escaped?" Gloom settled upon the chamber. Was there no way for them to outrange the grasp of Lother the Pale?

The suggestion was made that they take ship for one of the northern ports along the Thlassa Mey—Oron, Danaar, or Gesvon—and travel overland from there. But that thought was dismissed as being too risky. If Lothar was blockading all trade with the western ports, it meant he was as aware of his quarry's options as they were, doubly so when one considered his success at countering their every move so far. It was likely that all ships were being stopped and searched, which would leave them trapped, if they were found. Their next encounter with Buerdaunt's soldiers would not be as fortunate as the last ones, considering they now had a score of war galleys to contend with.

No, there was only one proper course. They needed to find a captain capable of slipping past the blockade, no matter what the price. Such a thing surely could be done; Kolpos was an island of smugglers. The blockade would simply elevate the price of passage.

It was so decided. Palamon and Ursid would set out in the morning to seek such transportation. The two women would barricade themselves inside their own room with Ursid's bow and Palamon's sword. To separate this way was an unpleasant arrangement but it was necessary; after all, Lothar's agents would be searching for two men and

two women, primarily Berengeria herself. Two men alone
would be less conspicuous than the entire foursome would
have been. Besides that, there was no way of concealing
the great weapon, other then by keeping it hidden behind
a locked door.

Armed with the gold of Aelia's purse, the two men set
out to scour the waterfront and alleyways of Touros to
find a ship; it was a weary search and the first day was
wasted without result. Not only was that frustrating, but
each day they spent upon Kolpos strengthened the grip
of Lothar the Pale. The soldiers left caged in the hold of
Schemeff's vessel were doubtless free; they surely had
informed the proper agents, and the net could only grow
tighter.

On the second day of searching, Palamon and Ursid
gained their first real lead. It took them to a little fishing
village north of Touros, at the extreme northern end of
the bay. They were put into contact with a man called
Phatyr, to whom they spoke in a seedy tavern which reeked
with the odors of too-old fish and too-new ale.

This Phatyr was a rough-looking fellow. He entered the
place alone, said a word to the tavern keeper, and then
sauntered to the corner table where Palamon and Ursid
were sitting. He was no youth; he was about the same
age as Palamon. His face was hard, the skin tanned like
leather and creased from squinting into sunsets, shoal-
bound harbors, and the bottoms of too many tankards of
ale. The short growth of beard that masked the lower half
of his face looked as if the black whiskers might have
been more easily pounded back into the skin than shaved
off.

His foul-smelling cape, sewn from the hides of the giant
seals that swam in Kolpos' rocky waters, rubbed against
his leather jerkin as he settled onto the bench opposite
them. He studied their faces intently with the look of a
surgeon. Palamon found that to be an appropriate metaphor; the man doubtless intended to perform that craft
upon their finances before he was finished.

After a moment, Phatyr spoke. "I believe you men are
in a great deal of trouble to need my services."

"And does that matter?" Palamon asked, smiling.

"It does. Greater risks demand greater pay." The surgery was beginning already.

"Money is of no concern to us," Ursid said carelessly.

"It is to me. The waters about us are crawling with Buerdaunt's galleys. Does that have anything to do with you fellows, by the way?" Phatyr sipped his ale from its tankard, eyeing the reaction produced by his question.

"And if it does?" Palamon responded.

"The price goes up. Poor men can't afford to be in trouble in this world, gentlemen." He looked at Palamon and a smile realigned his whiskers. "You told me what I wanted to know, by the way."

"How can we know you'll not betray us, sir, and yield us up to Lothar's ships yourself?" The words burst from Ursid's lips before a stern glance from Palamon could staunch their flow.

"Because I'm a businessman, my green young friend. You can be sure I'll abide by the terms of the agreement—but the agreement will be an expensive one. I'll not take you out of the clutches of Buerdaunt's navy as a charity."

"Agreements have been reached before this time," Palamon said.

"Can you afford this one? I have seventy men to provide for in addition to all my other considerations."

Palamon spread his hands, smiling. "We have resources."

"Gold is harder than resources. Five hundred talents."

"A somewhat largish figure, by my troth," Palamon said, knowing that Aelia's purse contained perhaps half that amount. "For such a sum, a craft most suitable could well be built and outfitted and launched and we could bypass all your services."

"Then do it."

"Three hundred talents is a worthy sum."

Phatyr looked into Palamon's face. He was searching, probing for a sign of what the tall man's upper price limit was. Three hundred Carean talents was a huge sum. Even so, would the shipmaster be doing his duty by his followers if he did not attempt to get more? "You're fugitives with many galleys straining this island's traffic for your sake. My vessel is at risk. Four hundred is my bottom offer; I'd be a fool to take you up for less."

Palamon looked at Ursid and they whispered together for a moment. In reality, there was no new insight the young knight could give; the conference was for effect. "Four hundred talents, then. A princely sum. The first two hundred I will pass to you when we have gone aboard, the rest shall not be placed into your hands until our destination is gained."

There was finality in the tall knight's tone. Phatyr did not question the arrangement of payments but turned to a new point. "And what will be your destination?"

"The harbor mole of Lower Carea."

The shipmaster whistled and took another slow draught of ale. The yeasty foam left froth upon his black beard as he lowered the tankard to speak. "Then my crew and I will be earning our four hundred talents. This must be prize game, this cargo I'm going to slide between King Lothar's fingers."

"If you should feel the task's beyond your grasp, then say it now. We'll choose another route." Ursid's words drew a stern glance from Palamon, to which the younger man replied with a withering glare of his own.

Phatyr watched this bit of byplay with interest; clearly, all was not congenial between the two men. He was silent for a moment; his dark face was a thoughtful mask. "No, young fellow, you needn't fret. I'll take the charge. But remember this—everything that happens after the *Proteus* leaves her anchorage will be at my choosing and at my command. Is that understood?"

The two men across the table from him nodded.

"You'll be aboard my vessel by the time the sun rises tomorrow."

"And so we shall, if you tell where it lies," Palamon said.

Phatyr shook his head. "Nay. I'll tell no such thing. You'll meet a man of my choosing at this very table at midnight." He then described his contact and concluded his instructions. "After taking all the precautions I order, he'll bring you to the *Proteus*. We'll depart before sunrise, running east along the coast until we reach the easternmost cape of Kolpos. We'll show the proper signal pendants all that time, a single vessel making for Buerdaunt."

Palamon smiled. "Or so 'twould seem, withal."

"Or so it seems. At sunset we'll change course and proceed north through the evening and the night, past Mount Jephthys, past the Dark Capes, and into open water, navigating by the stars. We won't turn west until we reach landfall on the northern beaches of the Thlassa Mey. From there, we'll hug the coast until we reach the Narrow Strait. Fear not; this sea is large and many ships can hide upon her bosom. Have I made myself clear?"

Palamon nodded. "You have. Now estimate our time at sea."

"Using all sail and bending oars for the first part of the journey, my vessel will make that passage in . . ." Phatyr pursed his lips. "Perhaps four or five days."

"A rapid voyage, summing all accounts."

"A rapid voyage," Phatyr agreed. "Be back here at midnight."

The bargain had been made. Palamon and Ursid returned to the inn where Aelia and Berengeria had been waiting. It was a relief to both knights to find the two women still present at their arrival; there was no knowing what Lothar the Pale's agents had accomplished during the day. But all was well and the four of them made ready for their escape from the island.

They set out from their inn after sundown but they were still early when they reached the tavern. So they left. They loitered about the quays of the fishing hamlet while they waited, keeping the front of the tavern in view to prevent surprises.

At the agreed upon time they returned. Soon after that, they were met by Phatyr's emissary, an aging, one-legged fellow who was wearing a sealskin cape identical to the one worn by Phatyr. The words of recognition were exchanged and they left together. Outside, they found that he had come in a rickety, two-wheeled horsecart covered by a mildewed canvas tarpaulin and drawn by a horse that appeared to have left its good years far behind it. The messenger told them to climb in.

They obeyed, crawling one by one into the musty-smelling bed of the little cart, lying down on splintery boards and pulling the tarpaulin over themselves for concealment. They listened as the old seaman climbed up into his seat; indeed, it seemed to Palamon a wonderful feat for the fellow to do so at all, considering his missing limb. But he did succeed, with much clattering and shaking of the cart. Then they were off, their ears filled with the *clop-clop* of the horse's hooves as they were jostled over the rough stones that paved this ancient waterfront street.

It was impossible to tell how far they were traveling in the noisy old cart. Still, the journey was not at all unpleasant for Palamon; Berengeria lay next to him beneath the tarpaulin, and he could hear her steady breathing as they rattled along. It was a pleasure to be close to the maiden, however strong the forces were that separated them. He would have moved his hand across the fraction of an inch which lay between them; he would have caressed her. Still, that would not have been wise or proper. So he lay beside her in the bed of the cart, taking pleasure in their closeness.

He could have laughed at himself. He was nearing his fourth decade, yet this maiden filled him with ideas and feelings which would have been cause for amusement even in a youth. He could not help feeling a little ashamed of himself.

Then the heavy canvas moved. Berengeria turned onto her side and rested her hand upon his shoulder. He was touched, though her act made him uneasy, and he was glad she could not see his face. Still, he was pleased by the gesture. He brought his hand up and rested it upon hers. After all, what harm could there be in that?

The cart clattered endlessly, continuing on its shaky journey; after a time, it ceased jostling them over paving stones and instead rolled through the rutted irregularities of dirt byways. Once or twice, there was more jostling and a gurgling rush as they crossed water.

At length the jostling stopped entirely and was replaced by the sounds of many men working. Different voices could be heard shouting orders or speaking in lower tones, and in the distance there was the rhythmic chorus of a crew manning a windlass. The cart shook as the driver climbed to the ground. Then, with a suddenness that caught them all by surprise, the tarpaulin was hauled back. There was the sweetness of fresh air; Palamon was surprised to note the change. The air beneath the tarpaulin had become stuffy without his noticing it.

At the rear of the cart of stood Phatyr. He greeted them with raised eyebrows as his eyes roved over the two women. "You bring a prize catch with you, gentlemen. I'll be hard pressed to keep my men at their oars in the face of such beauty. Let me help these lovely ladies down."

Both Aelia and Berengeria were too busy taking stock of their surroundings to pay much heed to the shipmaster as he lifted them to the dewy ground of the anchorage. Actually, it was not an anchorage at all but rather a concealed slip. The sleek black hull of the *Proteus*, made blacker by the darkness, occupied the width of a streambed which had been dredged out to make way for her bulk. Everywhere men were busily preparing the vessel for sea by the light of lanterns that festooned the trees about and also hung from the high mast and the towering bow and stern posts of the vessel. The lantern light flickered off the undersides of thick leaves. This was a snug harbor indeed, guarded well from prying eyes by the thick foliage.

"We shall be prepared for sea well in advance of the time I gave you," Phatyr said. On his dark, beardbound face was pride in his ship and the lads who manned her. "I suggest you go aboard and wait in the deck shelter; we'll tow her into the bay when we can. The tide is already at its peak; if we can catch the full ebb, we'll be well begun."

They did as he suggested, allowing him to go with them up the bow and onto the slender deck of the vessel. How unlike Schemeff's roundship this craft was. Every line exuded speed and suppleness, from the delicate sweep of the bow and stern, to the lapstraked planking that formed the narrow hull, and to the graceful mast and the sail which was still furled.

Phatyr accompanied them to a deck shelter which was no more than a canvas structure stretched upon poles on the aft part of the deck. There, Palamon paid him the agreed upon count of gold coins. He accepted with few words. "Seats have been prepared for you within; there's also bread and wine. We'll cast off lines shortly." He touched his forehead as he smiled at Aelia and Berengeria. "Good day, Ladies."

Then he was gone, his footsteps sounding along the deck after he had left the gaily colored shelter. Without comment, Palamon, who had completed the transaction according to plan, handed Aelia's purse back to her. The advance paid to Phatyr had left the pouch almost empty.

"A goodly vessel have we chartered," Aelia said. "For my part, I now maintain high hopes that these gold pieces were well spent."

"There's hope of that," Palamon said. "For by my tarnished troth, Pale Lothar's gallies might charge dearer fare, for shorter passage, likely."

"By my faith," Berengeria said. "Nay, our most fertile hope is with this craft. I've no complaint; you both have bargained well." Here she addressed both Palamon and Ursid. There was no slight here, but Ursid's reaction to even this tiniest bit of attention paid to his imagined rival betrayed his sensitivity. But Berengeria went on without noticing. "If Phatyr's navigation matches his appearance, then I'm almost home." She turned her back upon all three of her companions, pressed aside the shelter's canvas flap, and became silent. She gazed out at the seamen who had nearly finished their preparations for departure. After a moment, she spoke once more. "It is a thing I cannot comprehend. I shall believe it when it comes to pass." Then her voice trailed off.

Chapter Twenty-two:
Wind, Waves, and Warriors

WHEN THE MOORING lines were cast off, the stream's current nudged the *Proteus* toward the bay. At the movement and shouting, the four fugitives moved to the deck and found the bulk of Phatyr's men seated at their benches: tall, bronze-backed men who held their long oars vertically, ready to unship.

The stream was little more than a canal here. Since there was no room for the vessel to be rowed, a line remained secured from her stem to the harness of a mule driven along the bank. The mule strained along its towpath, keeping the ship from turning with the sweep of the current.

It was a grand sight, that unfolded before the four travelers. The lanterns of the tree-lined shelter receded, the vessel was towed toward the bay. The mouth of the stream was cleared, the last line was thrown free, the muleteer waved a farewell, and there was the thump and rumble of many pairs of oars being run out through the gunwales. Then the *Proteus* thrust her stem forward, driven by scores of strong backs that worked forward and back, forward and back, like great, sinewy metronomes. The men repeated the movement endlessly, surging together as if driven by the same spring.

The glow of day floated over the hills to the east, but it had not yet reached the black waters over which they were gliding. Little could be seen. Phatyr and his steersman guided the ship out of her snug harbor by guile and memory. More than once Palamon heard the sound of waves breaking over rocks, but the pace never slowed, and the vessel did not so much as scrape bottom.

The lights of Touros soon slid past the port bow. As the daylight grew, a few spires and towers could be made out against the emerging hills. The tide was running; the swiftness with which the city fell astern was impressive.

As dawn arrived, the fleet vessel approached the mouth of the bay; before her lay the open waters of the Thlassa Mey. As course was shaped toward the east, the mainsail was set to catch a serviceable morning breeze; even so, a number of men were left at the oars to increase speed. And true to his words of the day before, Phatyr was flying all proper identification pendants, as if his voyage might have been the most ordinary in all the world.

Throughout the day, the passengers watched the island of Kolpos pass along their port side. Phatyr kept his distance, a space of perhaps three leagues; mountains, hills, and headlands passed in an endless parade. Toward evening the last promontory was cleared and course was set due north, with less progress being made without the wind's aid. The benches were full of rowers as the *Proteus* made her way.

As darkness cast her robes across the Thlassa Mey, a wind sprang up out of the southeast. Again the sail bellied out and the vessel leaped forward in the freshening breeze, her finely planked hull flexing with each surge as she rode the waves the way Actea, goddess of the hunt, might have ridden her palfrey.

The darkness became complete. The stars were invisible on this night; clouds blanketed the sky and the wind

increased until it approached gale force. Still, Phatyr left
the sail set and his vessel pounded her way northward.

Their shoulders wrapped in furs to protect them from
the chill, the four adventurers flanked Phatyr as he directed
the ship through the darkness. Palamon noted a great
mountain on the horizon. Its summit was crowned with
fire; the red glow outlined the steep slopes and reflected
off the lowering clouds above it. He spoke to Phatyr,
raising his voice against the gale. "You have a mighty
landmark in these seas. Is there a name for yonder glowing
peak?"

"Mount Jephthys," the shipmaster said. "It dominates
the northern reaches of Kolpos, spewing up flame and
melted stone. It can be seen for many leagues, in day or
night. The peninsula to the north is called the Dark Capes
because it's all capped over by the mountain's belchings,
even to the very shore. It's a lonely land."

"And so you see to steer your ship at night?"

"And in the daytime as well. It's said that any of Kolpos' seamen who would count themselves navigators can
fix their ship's position within a cable's length, if only
they have a clear view of that mountain."

Palamon smiled. "Can you?"

"I can. The gale has set us west of the course I wanted.
Still, we're in safe water, a half dozen leagues off the
coast. If the wind holds, the Dark Capes will be off our
beam come daybreak."

But the wind did not hold. It increased, whipping the
sea into frothy heaps that dashed over the gunwales,
drenching the crew and forcing Aelia and Berengeria back
into the canvas shelter at the ship's waist. So fierce was
the wind, however, that even that sanctuary was hardly
drier than the decks.

At last the screaming gale forced Phatyr to order the
sail furled, which in itself demanded the greatest efforts
of his crew. And still the wind increased. The oars were
manned again in order to maintain headway; bailing began
and continued throughout the night. The glowing summit
of Mount Jephthys was obscured by the spray, but it could
sometimes be glimpsed falling south only a little and

creeping ever nearer. Phatyr's look betrayed his concern about the ship's lack of progress against the towering beacon.

The night dragged on. Great combers rolled out of the darkness and the crew labored mightily at the oars to keep the *Proteus*' head into the wind. Whenever the winds relented enough to allow it, Phatyr exhorted them, bidding them to break their backs to gain as much distance north as possible.

By dawn the fiery peaks of Mount Jephthys could be seen south-southwest of the ship. The water-glazed rocks of the Dark Capes were lashed by the sea only a thousand cubits away. The storm had not abated at all; if anything, the force of the wind had increased. No one needed to tell the four passengers that the vessel was in peril of being blown aground against this coast. The shore loomed like gnashing jaws.

Braving the bucking deck, Aelia approached Phatyr as he stood flanked by Palamon and Ursid, his face turned into the wind in defiance of the gale, his black hair and beard writhing as the gusts tore at him. Aelia reached inside her robe and produced Reovalis' crystal vial, which had been used to such good advantage aboard Schemeff's roundship. "Sir Mariner, the potions in this vial, though not yet well assayed, may offer hope against the weather's threat."

Phatyr's eyes moved from the vial to Aelia's spray-drenched face. "What is it?"

"I know not what the composition is, save that its powers are prodigious."

Phatyr turned to bellow out orders, then spoke once more to Aelia. "Thank you for the offer, madam. But I put more trust in the seaworthiness of my ship and the backs of my hearty men than in any potion. If you'll look before us, we still gain against this foul sea. Gods willing, we can still labor past this coast, though I've never seen a transit of these Capes that was more plagued."

No sooner were these brave words out of Phatyr's mouth, however, than the whooping wind redoubled itself as if of its own will, to put the lie to what he had said.

Oars bowed and cracked against the increased force of the current and the hobbled vessel rolled near the black rocks of the shore as if drawn by unseen lines. Exhausted sailors slumped on their rowing benches while the wind ripped at their clothing.

The *Proteus* heaved and tossed, sometimes vaulting over a great swell, sometimes burying her stem in green water. Aelia was swept from her feet, still clasping the crystal vial. Palamon attempted to help her up and suffered the same fate; they rolled in a heap at the shipmaster's feet.

But Phatyr paid them no heed; he peered through the spray and bellowed orders, although half of his words were lost in the tumult. "I see a beach and a break in the rocks. Row, you hearty fellows. Row for your lives. Bear to port and we'll shelter in the lee of that promontory."

Scrambling to his feet, Palamon saw the place Phatyr was speaking of. The tall knight helped Aelia up and gestured toward it; it was a narrow strip of dark sand nestled between two jutting points formed by the harsh black stone of the cape. It was plain that Phatyr intended to beach his vessel in this sheltered place to save his crew from the worst of the elements.

Aelia turned her face up toward Palamon's. "Our captain does not trust this crystal vial. It's true its qualities are not all tried, and yet I fear it is our savior still."

Perhaps her words were true; their situation would be precarious even in the shelter of the tiny cove toward which the ship was laboring. "Then do as you think best," Palamon shouted back.

All at once there was an explosion; a blinding bolt of lightning struck from the black clouds, shattering the mast into a storm of splinters. Palamon felt one of the wooden missiles gouge into his cheek and he saw a flower of blood sprout on Aelia's forearm; she had also been struck. But the two of them were unhurt compared to those crewmen who lay crushed beneath the severed timber; the screams and moans of broken and dying men rose pitifully above the howling of the gale.

The vessel lurched helplessly, reeling at the mercy of

the elements. Aelia's crystal vial rolled upon the deck where she had dropped it and as she reached for it, another bolt of lightning hit the sternpost, shattering it as the mast had been shattered. Again Palamon and Aelia flinched away from flying splinters, some of which could not be avoided.

But another glance at the jagged shoreline showed that the graceful *Proteus* was not to be crushed against cruel rocks after all. The breakers slid her toward the sheltered strip of beach anyway. Clinging to lines with his splinter-pierced hands, Phatyr made his way down to the benches to encourage the men who still could to row for the tiny inlet, ignoring their broken cohorts for the moment.

And so it was done. By superhuman effort, with Ursid and Palamon aiding at the oars, the crippled ship limped toward the beach. The waves piling into the inlet lifted her up and forward, then there was a shudder as she grounded. Men were pitched off their benches by the force of the blow. Another wave cast her even farther onto the sand, and there she lay, beached as neatly as a fish hurled onto a river bank.

Only now was there time to count wounds and mend them. The dead and injured were carried off the still-rocking decks of the *Proteus* and laid down on the dark sand in her lee. Aelia and Berengeria themselves gave aid to the victims of the disaster. And there were many. Of the crew of seventy, a score had been badly injured; of those, a dozen were dead or dying. Compared to this carnage, a few wood shavings in the skin were nothing.

All the same, though Palamon belittled his wounds and those of Aelia, Berengeria insisted on bandaging them with strips of cloth torn from the mantle of her own robe. Aelia was tended first, then Phatyr. After they had been treated, Berengeria turned to bandage Palamon's hurts.

Palamon watched as she wrapped the deepest of his gashes, which stained the cloth as it was applied, the blood mixing painfully with the salt spray that had soaked the fabric. He looked at her face. She was downcast, but it was hard to read the extent of emotion that had laid hold of her in the wake of this catastrophe.

Then he saw her glance up, directing her eyes along
the beach behind him. The color drained from her features, and a gasp escaped the fullness of her lips. He
turned and looked to see what she had seen. A hundred
cubits from them came a great troop of warriors, men-
acing, white-robed men, brandishing great axes, longswords, cruelly spiked maces, and knotted war clubs.
Berengeria's stout heart seemed to fail her; she half-
swooned with a groan. "O Hestia fair and all your godly
kin, defend us from the horror that comes next."

Palamon caught her as she sagged, lifted her, carried
her back toward the wooden walls of the *Proteus*. Here
at least, there was a bulwark against the attack. But she
quickly regained control of herself and pushed out of his
grasp. She reached into her robe and pulled forth a dagger.
"We cannot flee, my love. We'll stand and fight, and if
all comes to naught, then we fall here."

"Yes, we shall fight. But not to fall—to live." Palamon
caught her up once more and heaved her over the ship's
rail. "I'll have my weapon first." He vaulted in after her,
shouting over his shoulder as he went to retrieve the mighty
sword. "But fight to live—your duty calls for your surrender rather than your valiant death. To die when there
is hope is cowardice, and life is hope, however great the
pain."

He scrambled across the shuddering deck toward the
tattered canvas shelter. Inside, all was in disarray; the
sword was not to be seen amid the tempest-stirred mess
he found. In the frustration of the moment, he cried out
the name of his weapon: "*Spada Korrigaine!*"

As it had in the halls of the library of the Polonians
when he had first uttered the title scribed upon the pommel, the sword leaped up, scattering the blankets that had
lain on top of it, welding itself into his grasp. Without
pausing to reflect upon this prodigy, Palamon turned back
toward the battle that was developing upon the beach.

And he was none too soon. Already the pale-robed
forces had fallen upon the weary mariners, beating in
helmets and hewing limbs. Caught without a proper
weapon, Ursid fought gallantly with his dagger; the sea-

men responded to the attack with their bare hands and what few weapons they could pick up. With a cry, Palamon leaped over the rail and into a knot of milling warriors. Using the advantage of surprise, he struck at the nearest of the robed figures, the deadly blade of the *Spada Korrigaine* hewing into the wool as well as the chain mail beneath.

It was a frightful struggle. All about him surged men of both sides, maddened by the lust and passion of unrestrained battle. He slashed savagely forward and soon was surrounded by disembodied arms, heads, torsos, cleaved in two, and gruesome bits and pieces of slaughtered humanity.

Palamon was a fearsome spectacle. All the deadly skills perfected in his questing years as a Knight of Pallas now combined with the might of the *Spada Korrigaine* to produce indescribable butchery. It was his fighter's craft at its most terrible. Even so, the battle was swaying against the men of the *Proteus*; there were simply too many attackers.

White robes were everywhere. Palamon saw Ursid go down, his head and shoulders flowering with blood from many wounds. And his heart sank as he saw Berengeria surrounded by pallid figures upon her wooden citadel. Her dagger flashed right and left but it was plain she would soon fall. Even as he watched, the blade was wrung from her fingers and her arms were pinioned while she writhed and shrieked.

Then a voice boomed above the noise of storm and battle. "Your Princess is taken; your fighting insures her quick death. Her blood will flow unless your weapons are lowered. Thus, yield."

As much from shock at this disembodied ultimatum as from the logic of the command itself, the defenders lowered their weapons. And as quickly as resistance stopped, the robed attackers suspended their onslaught.

There was silence; even the wind ceased its raging. There was only the clank of arms and the sobbing of Berengeria as she was hauled from the *Proteus* and hustled up the beach. She was ringed by white-robed men.

Some held her arms, some carried their deadly blades ready to pierce her hostage flesh. Palamon's breath died within him as he saw her taken away.

Again the voice boomed forth. "Now, prisoners, follow your escort. Rebellion means death. Who remains on this beach but a moment hence forfeits his life."

The pallid army marched back up the beach and the stunned crewmen of the *Proteus* followed. Palamon moved to join the procession, but Aelia stopped him. "Come help me, Palamon, for we must bear the body of Ursid. He still has breath and so cannot be given up to death."

Palamon was dazed. The events of the night and morning would have strained any mind and soul to the breaking point. Still, he mustered his will and responded to her plea. "Then take my sword, for my few wounds are slight. I then shall bear Ursid upon my back." And so it was done. Palamon handed the mighty blade to Aelia and grasped the fallen warrior, lifting him in his scarred arms. Then they followed victors and vanquished up the beach to their unknown destination.

Chapter Twenty-three:
Carea's Nemesis

AT THE UPPER end of the beach, there was a broad path, or trail rather, worn into the black stone of the cape. Berengeria was hauled up this path, her captors' weapons poised and ready to make her life the payment for further hostilities. For their part, the mariners—the few who were still upright—were too battered to resist further. They meekly accompanied the white-robed victors. Following them was Palamon, who bore with difficulty the body of Ursid, and then came Aelia, lagging behind the rest of the party.

The trail was steep but the walk was a short one; then the company reached a large, flat area surrounded by more of the escarpments of the Dark Capes. Here on this broad place, the captives were astounded to see a castle; the place had been mauled and torn by the storms of the Capes and it was of odd construction.

They passed through the worn gate and into the courtyard of this edifice. The very stone had been eaten into strange shapes by the sea spray and the rains. Upon passing the gatehouse, Palamon could see that this was not remarkable; the place had been constructed of great blocks of salt.

The company stopped in the courtyard of this strange fortress and stood silently, waiting. The surviving crewmen of the *Proteus* waited as well. The pause allowed Palamon and Aelia to pass to Berengeria's side; she stood as pale as death, still tightly guarded by a knot of the grim warriors.

"This is the end," Berengeria said quietly. "You must know where we are."

"Your duty is to live." Palamon put down the limp form of Ursid. "Yield not to black despair and never grant the easy victory."

"'Look for a tow'r that cannot stand, but does; a place that gives back to the roiling sea the thing that makes its waters what they are.'" There was no life at all in Berengeria's words; her tone was flat, her manner desolate. "So ran the words of old Reovalis; we've found the place, though it would have been better had we not."

Before Palamon could respond, a high iron portcullis rang down behind them, insuring that there was no escape from this saline citadel. He looked about. The inner walls of the bailey were lined with cells that looked out into the courtyard. Clearly there was no shortage of space for the keeping of prisoners. Before them was the keep itself, a shapeless pile constructed of the same weirdly sculpted blocks as the rest of the fortress. As he watched, a figure appeared atop the highest battlement of the keep. There was no face to be seen, only a mass of pallid robes, the same type of robes worn by the grim army that stood silently below. "Now bring all the prisoners forward, for I have desire to see them who wantonly trespass this land." The voice boomed out from the figure upon the battlement; it was the same voice which had ordered the end to the struggle upon the beach where the *Proteus* had been grounded.

One of the pale warriors answered. "We do so, O Master." The entire company surged forward several paces. All eyes within their wool hoods were fastened upon the pale specter speaking down at them; each soldier looked up with devout attention. Palamon and Aelia also stepped forward, as did Phatyr and his men.

"I see she's a beautiful maiden, as I often have heard. Do not move a limb, for I now shall come down. All remember: struggle means death." The figure vanished from the battlement without a sign, reappearing on the stones of the courtyard directly before Berengeria. The transformation was instant; it left the prisoners blinking in amazement.

"Foul Alyubol." Berengeria's whisper was filled with loathing and despair.

"Indeed I am Alyubol, master of all I desire. I laugh that you fools were so stupid you did think to flee beyond my long reach, all the while making simpler my task. And now you have brought yourselves here." He smiled at them and shook his head. "You will never pass forth."

He gloated into Berengeria's face, and she shrank from him as far as the arms restraining her would allow. His face was the quintessence of fascinating ugliness. His features were wizened, pinched, sucked in upon themselves as if each cell had dried out from mutual avarice and distrust. The complexion was waxy, the face clean-shaven. The sinuous lips curled across jagged teeth in a loathsome sneer of triumph.

The sight of such a face and expression put spurs to Palamon's tongue. "How can you heap continued punishment so gleefully upon the torments of this maiden's blameless past?"

The face turned on Palamon, the hatred in the eyes searing him. "Oh, how can I do it?" The words were mocking at first, then they rose to an enraged scream. "It's venegeance for wrongs done to me. For promises broken, for long persecution of me." He whirled back a few steps and gestured toward the ragged body of men who once had formed the crew of the *Proteus*. "First, take these dogs thither; they'll feel more secure in my cells."

Not a word was spoken by Alyubol's soldiers. Most of the white robed warriors escorted Phatyr and his men to a block of the cells that faced into the courtyard. The haggard men did not resist. If the long storm had not been enough to break their spirits, the battle and Alyubol's wraithlike appearance had certainly done so.

Carea's nemesis watched with satisfaction as the men were locked away, the ponderous iron doors clanging into place one by one. "This keep is my palace. It doubles as prison, as well. Those cells have awaited my enemies' bodies too long; for many a year have they stood. So look well on them, fools. Let your own milky bones be my gay decorations till doomsday."

"Our capture is quite purposeless to you, O Alyubol," Aelia said. "Our bodies shall consume nor less nor more of victuals and drink than bodies of the most innocuous folk. But ransom us to old King Berevald; that act would gorge your fading years with wealth."

Alyubol began to laugh; his thin lips curled back and the sound of his derision drifted out across the courtyard. "Do you think, you dried-up old woman, that riches move me? The ransom of Berevald's pride is the fortune I crave; the pride that brought hatred, made him cast me out when he found that Goswinth, his queen, would have me over him. And now I'm to give back the daughter of that senile fool?"

The wizard roared with laughter. There was neither mirth nor wit in his gaiety; he whooped at the image of his imagined love rival, Berevald, brought to despair once more by these machinations. And Alyubol believed Goswinth had loved him; Goswinth, who had never held anything but loathing for the mercurial advisor. Clearly, his mind had turned. Palamon gazed at him, grimacing at such a twisted shell of what might once have been a genius. It was the world's misfortune that ever Alyubol could have been loosed upon it.

"Oh, Palamon, how could you yield us up to the hands of this ill-favored man?" Surprised, Palamon looked down. Ursid had revived enough to speak; he had been listening to Alyubol's words and now he gazed at the Knight of Pallas. "Far better we had died than fall'n to him. Dishonor is your history, from when you once dishonored that chaste maid long years ago, until the present time when you elect to quit the fight alive. Our flight was doomed the moment we were joined by such as you, you base, ignoble man."

The wounded man's words pierced Palamon like fangs but Alyubol did not give the older knight time to reply. The wizard bent low to examine the young warrior. "And you are the noble young man who turned traitor for love and twisted the key that helped gain these two ladies escape from my friend and ally, good Lothar the Pale. Do not fret. I might send you back to the hands of your uncle and King if you have the fortune to live, which I doubt. You life ebbs away; you'll not be with us long."

He walked around the four of them, smirking as he circled them. "I know all of you; I've kept track of the lives of you all. Ursid gained your freedom, Princess, because you were his love. How little you love him; it's Palamon whom you love most." He snickered again. "But that is pure folly as well. He can never have you, your hand would be ever forbidden to him, were you free."

"That cannot be. His past transgressions are forgiven; I would take him as he stands." Berengeria glanced over her shoulder at Palamon. Her look tore at the tall knight's vitals; he could see she was disputing Alyubol with her heart only. She was fighting back from instinct. Her spirit was nearly broken, yet she still stood by the dishonored knight. His eyes almost revealed his thoughts with moisture.

For his part, Alyubol savored his victim, timing his next verbal thrust. "The love you may feel is most touching. Yes, there is no doubt. But still, it will come to no more than the song of a jay." He half giggled once more and paused to wipe spittle from his lips. "How much should I tell you? Suffice it to say this amount: this knight was left at the portal before the Fastness of Pallas by parents too poor for his keep. I've watched him and all of you; you have no secrets from me. This knight—as you call him—will not vie for your hand. He cannot. You might say he is worthless and low as the dust. Adalmo and Orras, two serfs, left this worm-blooded knave."

Alyubol watched Berengeria's reaction with glittering

eyes. She said nothing; the bowing of her head told the wizard of his victory over her. He laughed at her then, his lean sides shaking with glee.

As for Palamon, his reaction differed little from Berengeria's. His fears were confirmed. Alyubol had revealed why that aura of intervening fate had always lain across his feelings toward Berengeria; the decision over his union with her was taken from his hands forever. The lowness of his birth made him as unworthy to love her as the snail to love the gazelle.

Alyubol gazed down at Ursid once more. "Besides, this young man spoke the truth. Had this Palamon courage to go with his high reputation, you'd not have been seized." He turned to his somber minions and dismissed them with a wave of one arm. "Go now, all you shadows, and demonstrate how I have conquered."

One by one, the soldiers in this army of grim, pallid warriors began to disappear. While the four captives watched in amazement, their opponents in battle faded into nothingness; they were illusory and there was not even a wisp of smoke to prove they had ever existed. Only the half dozen who surrounded Berengeria remained.

Alyubol faced his victims, once more reveling in the way he had defeated them. "A simple illusion. Had you ever failed to believe, the foreman you faced would have faded as quickly as mist beneath the sun's brilliance. And all of the wounds of Ursid were caused by himself, from believing the blows of his foemen were real."

He stepped back a few feet. "Well enough. The frolic has ended." He turned to one of his henchmen. "Do any of these lowly worms bear arms in concealment, my servant Navron?"

Indeed, Navron stood before them now; they had not noticed the evil minion among all the other white robes. He shook his head. "The woman called Aelia still carries the tall fighter's sword. Save that, there is nothing; their weapons have all been thrown down."

"Disarm her. The sword can be broken or cast to the waves. Then throw them all into my cells." Alyubol turned away and strode toward the keep, his woolen robe swaying with his movement. Before him a tall wooden door swung silently open.

Navron walked boldly to Aelia; after all, how could she resist when keen daggers were being held to Berengeria's throat? But as he snatched the great sword from her grasp, there was a snap, a flash of light, and he screamed. He fell to his knees, wringing his seared hands and cursing the astonished woman. The sword lay upon the stones of the courtyard.

The sound caused Alyubol to wheel and face them again. For the first time, the mad wizard seemed nonplussed. "And what is this foolishness?" His voice was a roar.

"The sword is enchanted. It burned me when I took it up." Navron's lips were still twisted with the pain from his burned hands; his words passed between clenched teeth.

Alyubol's face changed. Rage replaced the mirth and mockery that had been spread across it only moments ago. And perhaps there was a flicker of fear, too. "How could they have got such a weapon? What else have they got?" The wizard extended both hands and walked toward the captives. Before each one he paused, holding both hands over each person's head in turn. Only with Aelia was there any effect. She grimaced, as if in pain, her robes moved slightly, and Reovalis' crystal vial floated up into his grasp as if upon a piece of twine.

Alyubol stepped away, looking at the crystal vial keenly, rotating it in his serpentine fingers. "It's magic—a remnant of potion, of powerful art." He wheeled upon Aelia and slapped her. "And where did you get it, you whore?"

The blow snapped Aelia's head back but she did not respond. Her face was grimly set.

With a whine of fury, Alyubol struck her again. "Tell me now or you die."

The blow sent Aelia to the paving. She rose slowly, her nose streaming blood, her mouth and chin turning into a crimson mask. With a cry, Palamon leaped at the attacker, but Alyubol was nimble for all his years. He leaped away, his face white with anger. "Oh, fool, if you move one more time, Berengeria's blood will flow from a full dozen wounds. Strike again, if you wish."

Palamon was rooted to the stone by those words. Even as he had made his impetuous move, the henchmen of Alyubol had pressed their weapons against Berengeria's throat. It was clear they were only too eager to carry out the threat. Even now, blood trickled onto her bosom from one tip which had pressed her fair skin too far.

Alyubol returned to Aelia, striking her again, shoving her farther away from her friends. "As for you, all your magic is taken, for all of its art. My minions cry out in the night for some sport; I may give you to them." He whirled and flung the crystal vial against the saline wall of the keep. It shattered and a small cloud of smoke rose from the place where it had hit. Whatever hope it might have contained now lay shattered with the fragments of glass at the base of the wall. Aelia turned away, holding her sleeve to her bloody mouth.

Alyubol reached forth again. He extended his fingers over Palamon's sword and gestured; the sword rose slowly from the paving, the way the crystal vial had risen from Aelia's robe. Flashing and hissing, it hung in the air before the wizard. He examined it closely. "My troth. 'Spada Korrigaine' reads the inscription I see. The Sword of the Conquerors, thought to be lost long ago. I thank you, Sir Palamon. Once I have altered the stamp—the temperament shown by the metal—I'll turn it to my own ends, for I doubt you're aware of the myriad tasks performed by this weapon. For now, it will stay where it hangs." He gestured once more and the sword rose to a height of several cubits above the courtyard where it remained, suspended by his mystical powers, as secure as it would have been inside any vault. Tiny flames crackled and played along the length of the blade as if the sword were protesting its imprisonment but was unable to burst the bonds which held it.

Alyubol turned from it with the air of a man who has done satisfying work. He had humbled his opponents, both individually and as a group. Still, one last thought had crept into his brain, one last idea which needed to be brought to fruition before he was finished. He stepped in front of Berengeria. His features were alight with the brilliance of his thought.

He looked deeply into her eyes. She resisted the stare but the men who were restraining her forced her to return his gaze. "And you, my fair maiden, the fact has just struck me right now that you are not far from the image of Goswinth, the love that Berevald stole from me decades ago. We shall see." He mused for a moment, then advanced upon her, his thin hands grasping her shoulders, his breath raping her nostrils as he spoke. "I'll wed you this evening. Till then you may rest with your friends."

Berengeria became pale as the baneful statement penetrated her mind. Alyubol took no heed; he had already disappeared through the door of his castle's inner sanctum. The young woman sagged and her captors had to carry her to her imprisonment.

The adjoining cells the four captives were thrown into were more like cages than anything meant for human occupation. They were cramped, dirty, and vermin-ridden. Berengeria and Aelia were placed into one while Palamon was prodded into another, bearing the limp form of Ursid. As the tall knight laid the young warrior down gently onto the basalt floor of his cell, he heard Berengeria's sobbing. He would have told her to take heart, to keep hope alive. But any words he might have found would have been so ludicrous he could never have uttered them. What real hope could there be?

In the women's cell, Aelia slumped against a rough wall, wiping her face with the mantle of her robe. Her nose and cheek were still sore from Alyubol's blows but the bleeding had at least stopped for the moment. She was half-dead from fatigue. Still, she steadfastly rose and placed her arms about the shoulders of Berengeria, who was cowering in one corner, weeping as if her heart would break. "My darling girl, would I could take your place. But still, you cannot weep while there is time to rack our brains for means of our escape."

"There's no escape. Our story closes here."

Aelia cradled Berengeria's head in her arms. They

crouched together in a corner of their bleak cell, Aelia
and her charge. For twenty years the care of this child
had been hers; it could not end here. She whispered into
Berengeria's ear, "Do not lose hope. I say we have the
means." She lifted the hem of her robe. There, upon the
inside of one finely tapered thigh, was a nasty sore, a
carbuncle which appeared agonizing.

Without another word, once Berengeria had seen the
purulent mound, Aelia moved the hem back to her ankles.
As for Berengeria, she did not understand the meaning
of the exhibit. How could hope lie in such a mass of
diseased tissue? Indeed, how had her guardian even moved
without wincing all this time. Was that the meaning in
itself? If Aelia could harbor such necrosis without complaint, could Berengeria, a Princess, yield to the weakness
of despair while she still lived? She dried her eyes upon
her own robe. She would weep no more.

Still, waiting could not be idle; something had to be
done or the ravages of despair would return. Rising, Aelia
went to the iron door of the cell. "How goes it with Ursid,
O Palamon?" She hoped her voice was only loud enough
to be heard for a short distance.

"I have no pleasant words. I've bound his wounds with
cloth torn from my tunic. Still, in all, the blood that's
drained, I fear, shall end his life."

Without replying, Aelia returned to Berengeria's side
and slumped down. She mused upon the nature of Alyubol. "His vision's not omniscient, that's a fact; he did not
know the *Spada Korrigaine*, nor how it came to Palamon's
firm grasp." She paused. "He does not know what passed
while we sojourned with old Reovalis, the goodly sage.
We know his minions' numbers are but few and one more
secret he himself revealed; by disbelief may we defeat his
host."

"We have one day," Berengeria said. "It is a sorry
plight."

Aelia brushed Berengeria's hair back with her long
fingers. "Now sleep, my good Princess, for it will come;
our opportunity for quick escape must not be missed.

We'll have one chance, so we must rest ourselves, gain strength through sweet repose's medicines."

Berengeria's exhaustion conquered her and she did drop into a fitful sleep, dozing in the arms of her guardian. For her part, Aelia pondered on, only occasionally succumbing to the seduction of fatigue, dozing only for moments when she did. She waited through the day, listening to the crackling and fuming of Palamon's great sword. It remained above the courtyard, held grudgingly by the wizardry of Alyubol.

And what of Palamon himself? What was passing through his mind while he waited out the day beside mangled Ursid? Aelia did not know, but she hoped he was also plotting escape; his aid would be priceless. She had become fond of him. She would leave the dishonored Knight of Pallas if she had to, but he possessed a stout arm and he was Berengeria's beloved. Even though he was of the lowest birth and most questionable history, the royal maiden loved him; that much had become plain. Their union would—could—never come to pass, but Berengeria would fare better for the moment with him near her. And for that reason, if for no other, Aelia wanted to have him with them when they did attempt escape.

The day passed away minute by minute, hour by hour. From the cells occupied by Phatyr and his sailors came an occasional groan, but the two cells which held the four fugitives emitted no sounds whatever. Palamon sat with Ursid, who was barely breathing. The tall knight was lost in thought, his head bowed upon his chest. And he did plot escape.

Once, he went to the door of his cell to gaze out at his mystic blade. *"Spada Korrigaine."* He spoke the phrase softly several times but the only result was an increase in the fire that played along the weapon's length. Alyubol's magic seemed unbreakable. Sighing, Palamon seated himself once more beside Ursid.

So it went. In the other cell, Aelia and Berengeria sat together, sometimes sleeping, sometimes pondering and picking one another's brains. Escape would be attempted when Alyubol came for his bride; that went without saying. The racking question was this: how were they to make the attempt and survive? One thing was certain; they had to find a way to help Palamon regain that sword which crackled overhead, held in thrall by the powers of the mad wizard. The two women even discussed this in whispers. Alyubol had chided Palamon for not knowing all the secrets of the wondrous weapon. But did Alyubol know all those secrets himself? Did he know the *Spada Korrigaine's* fealty to its new owner? In the past, Alyubol had overestimated his own powers or position, as he had when he had thought Goswinth had loved him instead of her future husband. There was hope in this.

Afternoon came; the shadows of the saline battlements lengthened. Berengeria fidgeted. She wondered when the time of her ordeal would arrive. Then doors hidden in the walls of the castle's turrets opened and white-robed figures began to file out, lining the curtain walls and the towers, each one reaching his place, then turning to face into the courtyard. Each one was carrying a longbow and a great quiver full of arrows. Berengeria's time was now.

Chapter Twenty-four:
Some Wonders

THE INMATES OF the cells watched breathlessly as the portals of Alyubol's sanctum swung open and several more of the familiar, white-robed figures emerged, walking down the twisting steps in single file. It was impossible to see their faces. But as they approached Aelia and Berengeria, it became plain that Alyubol himself was not among them. The leader of the sextet was Navron; he reached the iron door of the cell and poked through the grating with the blade of his sword, forcing the two women back into the interior.

Once they had backed away, the sword was withdrawn and they could hear the rattling of key in lock. Then the heavy door swung open. "The time has now come for the union of you and your lord." It was Navron who said this.

Berengeria drew herself up and responded with a chilling glare. "I do not choose to go."

"You haven't a choice in the matter; you'll walk or be dragged." Navron's voice was harsh as he leered back at them.

Silently the two women approached the doorway, moving together. When the escape attempt came, it would be better made if they had as free a hand as possible; Aelia, especially, did not wish to be bound or restrained. So they went quietly. But when Aelia tried to pass from the cell, she was roughly shoved back in, Berengeria was snatched out, and the door was slammed shut. Alyubol was not to be tricked; only the maiden was to be allowed into his presence at all.

Berengeria began to scream, struggle, and fight. It was a part of one plan. Alyubol had to be distracted somehow, although this task was made formidable by his absence, and since Berengeria had excited his lust, it was hoped that his henchmen would be slow to kill her.

So Berengeria bit, kicked, and clawed. Alyubol's henchmen dragged her toward the center of the courtyard, but she fought back ably, clinging to the grating in the door with her white fingers. They beat and pummeled her, trying to break her grasp. Aelia shouted and screamed also, straining to reach through the grating to aid her charge. For his part, Palamon watched silently. He studied the great, two-handed sword suspended by Alyubol's magic. Had the wizard been distracted? Would his grip weaken? It had to be tested.

The archers on the walls were already nocking arrows to their bowstrings as Palamon shouted out at the top of his lungs. *"Spada Korrigaine. Spada Korrigaine. Spada Korrigaine."* The flames that were dancing along the great blade flashed and sputtered. Would the gambit succeed? Palamon knew their lives would be the price if it did not.

The pale archers were at the ready but Palamon did not fear them; Alyubol himself had demonstrated that the legions of white-robed warriors were deadly only if they were believed to be deadly. But Navron and his henchmen were another matter; they were deadly indeed. They were unlocking the door to his cell; soon they would be upon him. *"Spada Korrigaine,"* he cried. Could Alyubol, from within his chambers, extend his power both to his illusory minions and to his grip on the great sword? Was he that superhuman in his wizardry?

But his hold on the sword was weakening. Flashing and thundering in a war of magic against magic, the weapon had, indeed, dropped a few cubits. It had also moved closer to Palamon's cell. But there was now little time; the door burst open and three of Alyubol's minions poured into the chamber. The question would be decided now if Palamon was to survive. He backed away from his attackers, calling out for the weapon once more, then he held his bare arm ready for the blow about to fall.

But the question was decided. There was an explosion above the courtyard; the castle shuddered as the *Spada Korrigaine* broke free from its magical fetters. Searing the very air through which it moved, it darted, smoking, through the doorway and into the hands of its master, even as he was forced against the back wall of the cell.

Now things were different. The pale-robed henchmen recoiled toward the door, their faces long with fear at the sight of the murderous blade. This much respite was all Palamon needed. With three strokes, his work with these men was complete; their bodies lay in sections upon the floor; their blood was pooling on the basalt.

Palamon leaped from his cell, ready to hack the rest of the villains into pieces. But one was already fleeing: Navron's robes were flapping about his legs as he raced toward the central tower. Already the air was whirring with arrows but Palamon ignored them. He felled his remaining opponents, then struck the lock that closed Aelia's cell; the blade screamed as it cleaved through the metal. The door swung back and Palamon stepped in, dragging Berengeria with him.

Aelia spoke hurriedly. "We cannot tarry here; come, let us fly."

"Indeed," Palamon gasped in reply. "But I must free the other men."

"We have no time," Aelia said. "We do not know what horrors may emerge to strike us at the whim of Alyubol."

"We still cannot forsake them. When they sailed into this net, they did it for our sakes. The arrows will not harm me; it will take a moment only to do what is right." Even as he spoke, Palamon leaped outside, slashing at

the cell doors amid a shower of arrows which rattled
against the paving like hailstones. Palamon swung down
on the hinge of each door in the row of cages; never did
he have to pause for a second blow. As Phatyr and his
men scrambled to freedom, the tall knight shouted for
them to ignore the arrows and to show their gratitude by
bearing Ursid.

Three of them did this, grasping the blood-caked form
of the young warrior and carrying him toward the gate.
They carried a number of their own wounded as well and,
with Aelia and Berengeria in the lead, they hurried toward
the closed portcullis.

Dark clouds were rolling and heaving overhead, hurtling along before a rising wind, drawing together and
lowering their bulging bellies toward the fleeing captives.
Here was a threat. Soon the lightning would come and
there would be no escape from Alyubol's rage. But there
was something else to fear as well. As Palamon pulled up
before the castle gate, he felt a blow to the calf of his
right leg. Looking down, he saw that he had been struck
by an arrow; already the blood streamed from the punc-
ture where the keen-bladed shaft had passed through.

How could this be? The arrows had to be illusions,
like the archers who fired them. But the blood was no
illusion. Even now, another man fell; he struggled weakly
to rise with a feathered shaft protruding from his side.
Had Palamon guessed wrong? Had he led all of them to
certain death? Some of the mariners cried out in panic.

But the archers *had* to be imaginary. An arrow struck
Aelia full in the back but did no harm, vanishing upon
impact. Then a thought came to Palamon: Alyubol had
outwitted them once more. His living minions had not
been at Navron's side when he had come to fetch Berengeria, but upon the walls, among the illusory archers.
The men Palamon had thought he was slaying with the
Spada Korrigaine had been the illusions. So the danger
was now quite as real as if all the arrows had been made
of yew wood and had iron heads. Upon seeing a score of
missiles flying at him, no man could ignore some and try
to elude others; the addition of the few real ones created

a deadly particle of doubt. That was all that was needed for the illusory arrows to take a greater toll with each instant.

Feverishly, Palamon and a brace of mariners heaved at the windlass which raised the iron portcullis; so mightily did the tall knight strain at the mechanism that his hands chafed; blisters rose and began to bleed. But he ignored the pain; had he not guessed wrong, the haste would have been unnecessary. The heavy grating could not be raised more than a couple of cubits; still, that was enough. The mariners poured through the opening, followed by the four fugitives.

One of the men carrying Ursid was struck by an arrow and fell; the other two dropped their burden and fled onward, racing for the trail which led back to the stranded *Proteus*. Quickly, Palamon took up the fallen youth, handing his sword once more to protesting Aelia. The *Spada Korrigaine* had done its work for now.

Palamon could not move quickly, for he was lamed by the arrow that had pierced his leg. And the trail the mariners were racing down would lead only to destruction in any event. Already, a lightning bolt struck in that direction, hitting between two men and sending them hurtling through the air.

"One moment," Aelia said, panting as she paused in her flight. With a swift motion, she set down Palamon's sword and jerked up the hem of her gown, exposing the whiteness of her thighs and the horrid carbuncle which Berengeria had noted earlier. In astonishment, Palamon stared at her as she peeled the awful thing from her leg, taking it into her hands and squeezing from it a few drops of clear, golden liquid. The product of the sore spread, floated, glimmered, formed a wall between the fleeing foursome and the archers behind them.

Arrows clattered off this gleaming shield. Even as they bounced away, Palamon noted that some fell to the ground while most of them simply vanished as they struck. Would that he had guessed the truth earlier.

In an instant, the shield expanded and curved until it took the shape of a great clamshell. Abruptly, the four fugitives were scooped up; the shell closed about them and floated away, skimming over the ground in a breathtaking race with the magic winds of Alyubol.

In the few heartbeats it had taken for this to happen, Alyubol's lightning had played over the beach where the *Proteus* lay, as well as the trail down from the saline castle. Then the wizard became aware that his real prey was escaping; the lighting bolts flashed toward the moving shell, one of them blasting a crater in the black stone over which it had hovered an instant ago.

The conveyance floated away from the *Proteus* and her beleaguered crew, traveling toward the sea on the other side of the Dark Capes. The flight dizzied the occupants; even so, the mad wizard's lightning bolts were striking close by. The shell cleared the last stones and dipped toward the heaving waves at the very instant a bolt blasted the top of it; the blinding explosion jarred and dazzled those within. But the shell held. It slid beneath the water's surface, while above it the sea was whipped into a froth by Alyubol's wrath.

But the four fugitives were safe, at least for the moment. The lightning could not penetrate beneath the surface of the sea. They were floating just above the bottom, now, marveling at the fury being released in the waters over their heads.

It was not dark within the shell; rather, their refuge was filled by a soft, golden glow. Aided by this light, Aelia rose to examine the damage done by the lightning bolt which had hit them. It was difficult to tell whether the blow had been serious or not. The damaged area was scorched across the breadth of a large shield; it was a dark, burnt yellow. But the shell was not leaking.

When Aelia sat down again, Berengeria flung her arms about the older woman, tearfully kissing her upon one perspiring cheek. "How do you do these things, my Aelia? Tell. For how long have you borne that awful sore upon your lovely thigh? What did it hold?"

"Can you not guess? I emptied out the vial, the crystal vial, before we all came to the castle of foul Alyubol. The second charge I used to form a case in which to guard the last, well out of view and well beyond detection. And Reovalis' great art must have intelligence itself; the second charge produced that pustule clinging to my flesh."

"And so we fare," Berengeria said. "Lest Alyubol's long reach can penetrate the waters of the sea, we have, perchance, outdistanced him at last."

But Aelia was watching Palamon, who had ripped a strip of cloth from his torn tunic and was binding his calf. He winced as he applied the dressing to the bloody injury. Then he knelt beside Ursid, whose shallow breathing barely lifted his blood-caked chest.

Berengeria also observed the tall knight's actions. "How goes it, Palamon?" she asked. "How fares Ursid?"

"My leg is stiff, although the wound is clean. I fare as well as one may dare expect with any wound. As for our young Ursid, he goes down fast. He dies within the hour." The face of the Knight of Pallas was grave as he spoke.

"It's curious, this mystic art which struck him down. Believing false illusion's swords were real gave them the full effect of earthly steel." Berengeria's eyes passed across Ursid's form as she spoke.

"No more was needed. Magic is strange stuff." Palamon gazed into her face. "Of course you know he loved you. All he did was from infatuation for your sake."

"I know. And now he dies. And Phatyr's crew—their transport of my person cost them dear." Berengeria's mouth formed a tight line. She turned her head away from the tall knight and gazed through the translucent shell about them, studying the shadowy depths through which they were passing.

But Aelia was studying Palamon; her eyes were probing his features. "His wounds are deep. And yet, O Pallas' Knight, the dearest, most divine ability of all your order's this: with touch of hands, a Knight of Pallas may seal up great hurts. Cannot you do this thing for poor Ursid?"

Palamon looked up at her. The old expression was upon his face again, that mask of a smile he always donned to conceal the inner workings of his mind. "A Knight of Pallas well might do such things," he said. "Yet Knight of Pallas is a sobriquet you chose for me; it's not my own device."

"Your past is fully known by all of us. It's quite well demonstrated by your deeds that all your skills are warded in you still."

"The laying on of hands is not a skill. It is a gift the gracious Pallas gives to men who keep her code and honor her. Our chastity—avoidance of foul lust, including the mere mention of such acts—is chief among the ways that we may honor her. It is the price we pay that we might have the power to restore the body's hurts." He looked down at the young warrior lying before him. There was a curl on Palamon's lip. His shield was beginning to crack. "Now fate has made Ursid the poor cosigner for my past. My nonchalance, which led to my disgrace and quick expulsion from the Knights, wrote debts for which he now must be foreclosed."

Berengeria had again turned her head and was watching the exchange. The look in Aelia's eyes was intense, piercing. "But tell me," the older woman said, "when we fled the castle made of salt, you specified that we should carry him with us. What for? You then knew everything that you know now—that he would have no chance in any case."

"It was the proper thing. We could not leave him there to face the mercies of those fiends."

"Indeed. And you must try to heal him now. Though you may fail, you must make that attempt. In your own words, it is the proper thing."

Berengeria was beginning to understand. Palamon had to try. If he failed, he would at least have made the attempt; besides, Ursid could only be better off for it. So she entered the debate. "Sir Palamon, if what you say is true, it is the only chance Ursid still has."

"It is no chance at all; it's less than none." Palamon's face was showing more pain now than he had ever expressed when the arrow had pierced his leg. "It's blasphemy so to mock Pallas' name, for one who has disgraced her order's ranks to try to use the powers forfeited." He looked at them both, one after the other. "Believe my

words—if there was but one chance in any number that
I might succeed, then I would joyfully make the attempt."

But Aelia was relentless. "Yet you must try. Though
there may be no chance, you still must try. Why bring the
lad this far to let him die without the least attempt to save
his life?"

Palamon did not reply. He gazed down at the pale face
of Ursid, who already lay as still as death. It was only
by placing a finger on the throat to feel the pulse or by
holding a sweat-soaked palm at the nostrils to sense a
feeble breath, that the last flickers of life could be perceived at all.

Aelia went on. "To let him die this way's the blasphemy. You will regret it in your agéd days."

Palamon stared at the fallen warrior. There was little
time to spare. The blood Ursid had lost was taking its
toll; Palamon had to act now or not act at all. The only
sound within the crystal shell was breathing—Palamon's
breathing, Aelia's breathing, Berengeria's breathing. Sec-
onds passed, marked by nothing more.

With a deep sigh, Palamon at last clasped his hands
above Ursid. He was in thought for a moment, then he
began. "O mighty Pallas, I have not the right to ask this
blessing; still I must implore. Please hear me out while I
say this much more: I beg consideration for this knight,
so mangled in an honorable fight. He soon shall disembark
from his life's shore without thy aid. His wounds are
grievous sore. I now pray in his name and not from spite."
Fascinated, Aelia and Berengeria watched while Palamon
prayed. They both noted his fingers; he had clenched them
so tightly that his knuckles had become as white as ivory.
"I humbly beg thee, grant Ursid this boon: close up his
many cuts from swordblades thin. Heal up his flesh, bind
up his bloody wounds, bless with your breath the breath
that he draws in. Give back his life or else it passes soon.
Let him not die in payment of my sin."

The sweat was beaded across Palamon's forehead as
he prayed; it stood out in great drops that were trickling
from his face, making dark splotches upon his tunic. His
hair grew dark with moisture as if he had just been bap-

tized. The prayer was finished; he leaned forward and placed his broad hands upon Ursid's chest, then upon the young knight's forehead, then back upon his chest.

There was no doubting the sincerity of Palamon's efforts; his eyes were clenched shut and he was trembling with the strain of what he was doing. It was as if he were trying to will the life energy from his own body into the prostrate form of the young warrior. He maintained this attitude for a long time; the chamber was filled with the tension of it. Then he was exhausted. He fell away from Ursid's body, gasping, his chest heaving, his breath coming in great, rasping draughts.

The two women looked down at Ursid. There was no change. He was as pale and motionless as before, his breath was scarcely to be noticed, and the end of his life could be only moments away. But there had been a change in the atmosphere of the shell itself; the air was warmer than it had been and there was the least hint of fragrance, a faint perfume that teased their nostrils.

And then there came a change in the young knight's appearance as well. It was hardly to be noticed at first. But it was there. The features were still waxy but a glow seemed to be working its way from within, a life that had not been there before. Ursid's chest moved slightly; he stirred, shifted, rolled onto his side. That was all. There was no more change in his condition than that. He adjusted himself a bit, then a soft snore escaped his lips. He was sleeping now; the struggle for life was no longer straining his features.

Aghast, Berengeria glanced at both her companions, then back at Ursid. "He lives, he lives! His life has been restored." Aelia also stared at the young warrior, openmouthed in astonishment.

As for Palamon, the performer of this miracle appeared to be more astonished than either Aelia or Berengeria. He stared glassily at sleeping Ursid as if the young knight had turned into a chimera, a phoenix, or some other prodigy. Berengeria watched the tall knight as he reacted. Surely, he was about to break into a joyful smile. But this did not happen.

Instead, the tall knight sagged, sliding down into a heap. His face dissolved into a mass of lines, and then the tears came. He wept. He wept like a maiden. Other than by turning his face away from them, he made no attempt to hide the overflow of his feelings. It was as if he had neither the strength nor the will left to regain his self-control. His shoulders quaked and the closeness of the shell was filled with the sound of his sobbing. The salty tears flooded down his cheeks, mingling with his sweat, dripping off his chin. For a long while he remained that way, giving vent to overwhelming emotion. When he was spent from the release, he lay at the feet of the youth he had saved, panting, his eyes shut.

Berengeria was taken aback, almost frightened. This was not the reaction she would have expected from this laconic knight, even had he failed. She looked at Aelia, who was studying Palamon the way an alchemist would have gazed at a beaker. "My Lady," Berengeria said. "This reaction does not seem to fit the man who is my Palamon. I must surmise it is his great relief to find his goddess still must hold him dear."

Aelia shook her head. "It's more than that. I understand his creed, the canons of great Pallas' Knights. A man once stained with sin can never hope to wield the healing power of her hand. I urged him to the task for his own sake, that he would be divided from his past. That past is not the thing it seems to be."

As she spoke Aelia continued to watch Palamon, her mind turning. He was a book which, though intriguing in its parts, had remained largely closed, even to her observation. But he had revealed himself a bit in these last moments. "I now begin to know his mind."

Berengeria looked at her. "What have you found?"

Aelia's eyes did not move from Palamon's face as she spoke. "As I have said, the Knight of Pallas who neglects to keep his order's dearest law—that maiden's bed is sacred and forbid—has not a fallen nestling's gleam of hope of ever wielding power by her hand. The very mention of that moral breach will place his grace in mortal jeopardy." She was choosing her words carefully now. "But Palamon, we've seen, retains that grace."

Her eyes became more gentle as she spoke to Palamon, smiling with admiration into the tall knight's sagging face. "So tell us, Palamon, how did you come to keep the powers of your deity? I think that I have guessed but say it out. What secret have you left untold to us? Fear not to tell us, for we are your friends."

Palamon did not reply for a long time. Berengeria began wondering whether he was asleep, dreaming, because he lay so quietly against the side of the crystal shell. But at last he did react; his eyes opened and his lips moved as if he would have brought words from a great depth. But he remained silent. Perhaps he was not going to say anything after all.

Aelia prodded him once more. "Arlaine, was that her name?"

His face became a mask of painful memory. "Indeed it was. A count that dwelt some leagues off to the east of far Oron had caused much wrath among his serfs because the tithes he set were somewhat strict. Revolt was in the air. There I was sent to mediate the strife before great bloodshed spread across that land. The task was difficult, but it was done by wit, by force, and by the Knights' prestige.

"And when I then set out for my own home, gray Pallas' Fastness on its windswept cliff, I chanced to tarry at a hostelry in Fabas village, not far to the east. 'Twas there at next day's sunrise that I met the maid Arlaine.

"As I was riding from the village inn, I saw her come a-running to my horse to grasp my stirrup as I hauled the reins. 'What can it be, fair maiden,' I then asked, 'that makes your face so pale and full of woe?'

"'O, Knight,' she said, 'I am a lowly maid but still I must cry out to you for aid. If Knights of Pallas do not limit deeds to service of the landed, my own need cries out as loudly for your strong support as any plight of wealthy nobleman. You are my only source of hope; there are no others I can turn to.'

"'Then climb up behind me,' I replied, 'and you may tell your story as I take you home.'

"'Nay, nay,' she cried. 'I cannot tell my tale at home. But on the road out of this town, there is a vale where we may go to talk.'

"And so she rode behind me on my steed until we reached the place that she described. There, while I listened, she described to me a life so full of anguish and mischance it made me hide my face to hear her speak."

Palamon paused for a moment. He was like a balladeer who had overrun his train of thought and needed to collect himself once more before he could finish his tale. Finally, he resumed the story. "Her father was the drunkard of the town and had no sense of right or decency. Long years ago, her mother turned and fled away and left this maid to suffer what might fall to her from chance's hands and his hands, too. Enraged this drunkard was when in his cups; full lusty, like an animal. He forced this child to yield her body up to him and lovers were they, though there was no love. In such a way, the short years of her life had been turned into death within a life. He seldom let her stray from house's door and though she was a fair young maid, withal, no suitors came for fear of their young lives.

"And now into her life, unhappy though it was, came something that must surely dash whatever muffled hope she might have cherished still. She was with child. Her tears came when she spoke to me of this most frightful, sordid tale.

"So there it was, and nothing I could do. This was no foe that I could meet with arms. To see her face, I knew her tale was true and yet no quick solution could I give. She might be rescued from her father. Still, her child, once it was born, would have been slain, and she herself faced lifelong banishment. For such is e'er the fate of those whom incest marks in tiny villages across our world."

Palamon shook his head. "By all my vows, this was the very sort of awful plight that I had been reared up to reconcile. What could I do? I could not take her to my order's home; no women ever pass those hallowed gates.

I could not leave her with her name befouled by deeds that had been done against her will, at cost of many tears.

"There was no answer that I could divine but one. 'Young maid,' I said, 'we'll take to horse again. A league or so from here, I've often passed a chapel made of stone, set in the trees. It is a temple dedicated to Actea, the hunter goddess who oft is called upon by women-folk when they are caught in childbirth's painful throes. There I shall leave you. Go in through the gate and tell those whom you meet you are with child. But do not blame your father. Mention me. And give them my description; when it comes upon me, I will not deny the charge."

Berengeria's mouth fell open and she gasped to hear the revelation. But Aelia only nodded. "But did you know the hard result that had to fall upon you once this all was done?"

Palamon nodded, a grim smile crawling across his lips. "Indeed, I knew it when she came to me. I knew full well the risks. But still, I could not turn away from her. She did deserve to have her baby saved. To me it would be scandalous and foul but still, within her village, it would make her shine. To bear a bastard child of any Knight would give her status. She would be sought out by any tradesman's family of the town. The two conditions made were that she stay within that temple till the child was born and that she never more would even look upon her father and his wicked ways."

"And did that come to pass?"

"Her luck from there ran well. The child was born, a healthy baby boy, unmarked by his sore lineage. She went into a nearby village, where she met a lad she came to marry. So it ends."

"But not for you." Fascination was etched into Aelia's face.

Palamon shrugged. Perhaps it had been an unwise deed, this bit of charity performed upon the spur of the moment, years ago, for a maiden he had not even known. It had cost him dearly. The scars of it were scribbled across his actions toward his companions over many weeks. Still, what he had done was what he had done.

But his deity had not deserted him. Through all the shame and bitterness of all the years, the wandering and the lapses in observing the rites of his order, at least that last great humiliation had not come, even though he had never known that until now. And so he sat slumped against the side of the crystal shell, great tides of emotion washing across his face, rudely concealed. And the two women looked upon him silently. There was little for either of them to say.

Chapter Twenty-five:
A Kiss Beneath the Sea

TIME HAD PASSED. Silence reigned within the transparent shell as it had for several hours. Ursid, Aelia, and Berengeria were all sleeping; Palamon was sitting on the transport's rounded bottom, alone with his thoughts. Occasionally he looked out at the dark waters of the Thlassa Mey. Every so often, shoals of fish would swim up for a peek at this unusual invader of their realm, falling behind after a moment. Once or twice, he had spotted larger denizens of this dark world.

There was no knowing the course their transport was following, nor the speed at which it traveled. When they had escaped Alyubol's castle, the shell had been traveling west; if it still did so and if it was making any speed at all, they should soon reach Carean waters. But there was no knowing for sure. The crystal shell was a dazzling manifestation of the powers of Reovalis; even Alyubol himself would have been forced to admit that. It had saved them from the mad wizard's clutches and was transporting them unseen and unopposed through the waters of the

Thlassa Mey—but no provision had been made for the material needs of its human cargo. As he sat, Palamon had to fight to quell the hunger and thirst that were surging up within him.

He gazed at Aelia and Berengeria. Surely these ravages were affecting them as much as they were him; for this reason he was glad the two women were asleep. He wished he could share that condition. But his thoughts turned and turned again, swirling through his mind like fish swimming in a tank.

His patron, the Maiden Pallas, had not forsaken him; that much was certain. That knowledge removed a crushing weight from his shoulders; the future was now something he could approach squarely for the first time in years. But what was that future to bring? How was he to approach it? Should their flight end in success, his services to Berengeria would insure his future materially. There was no doubt he would be provided for. But the great question remained unanswered—what was he to do with himself?

For all his longing, he could not ever return to the Fastness of Pallas. The expulsion of a member was a trauma rarely undergone by that order and it was never revoked. He could doubtless obtain a commission in the legions of Carea. Still, he was not interested in a military life; he had had enough fighting.

Then there was Berengeria; what was he to do about her? He had grown to love her. He longed for her, body and soul, spirit and mind, even as they were traveling in this crystal shell beneath the sea. That was strange in itself. His self control, drilled into him from his earliest moment as a child within the Fastness of Pallas, was of no use to him in this regard. The lustrous maiden had captured him. But that was wrong. Whenever he was near her, whenever he wanted most to touch her, he could sense that old, unseen barrier the fates had placed between them. Even now, as he looked down at her sleeping, there seemed to be an endless, bottomless gulf dividing them.

It would be hard to give her up, but that was the sacrifice he was ultimately going to have to make. The very

love they bore one another made him responsible for her
future. She would have to marry and she would have to
produce heirs to Carea's throne. Some noble youth, someone deemed worthy by her father, would receive her hand.

Palamon's thoughts were interrupted. Berengeria stirred
and awakened, her blue eyes fluttering open and darting
about the little chamber to settle upon him. She smiled
at him, sleep still softening her features. "I see you are
awake. Have I slept long?"

He smiled back. He was very fond of her. "One cannot
tell, for here there is no time."

She looked through the crystal walls of their magical
craft, her hair falling across one shoulder as she turned
her head to study the watery world through which they
were passing. "It's like a dream, this passage undersea;
the rate at which we move, the places reached, are all
unknown to us." She looked up at him again. "From all
the pangs of hunger that devour my poor insides, my guess
is that a two weeks' span, at least, has passed since last
we dined. Do you agree?"

Palamon shrugged. "As you have said yourself, it's
hard to tell. Methinks a day or more now separates us
from the seaswept rocks of Alyubol, the Dark Capes, and
his keep of hard salt blocks."

"A day or two? No more? It seems like more." She
tilted her head as she studied Palamon. "But tell me,
gentle Knight, I long to know: what thoughts stirred in
your mind as I awoke?"

Palamon looked almost as if he were about to laugh.
"I think of you. These times, whenever I may pause, I
find my thoughts run down to you like rivers flowing to
the salty sea. It is a pleasant subject, by my troth."

Berengeria seemed pleased by this speech. "And just
of me? Have you no other thoughts to pass the time?"

"Just one or two, perhaps." That was all Palamon had
to say upon that subject. Still, it was several words more
than he would have uttered a few months earlier; Berengeria was surprised to hear him speak this openly about
his feelings, and in such an easy tone.

"Can you guess what's the subject on my mind?" she asked.

He shook his head.

"I dream of food. Of fish or fowl or good roast beef. I have not eaten, lo, these many hours; I could devour the mighty earth itself."

Palamon's look hardened a bit. He shook his head again. "Beware, fair maiden, guard your thoughts. You must not think of sustenance nor drink until they are at hand. You suffer more when you allow your mind to wield the whip."

The words were sterner in tone than Palamon had meant them to be. Berengeria looked at him, her mouth wrinkling. "Of what else can I think?"

He shrugged. "Of anything."

"You say you think on me to pass the time?"

He smiled.

Berengeria did not smile. "Then should I think upon the man who could possess a high Princess' hand, but who refuses it although he must admit she fills his heart?"

There was a long pause. Palamon's smile went away; he gazed down at the sleeping forms of Ursid and Aelia, then back at Berengeria. "Indeed, indeed, the words you speak are true; we both repose in one another's hearts. And would that I could take another course. But union for us two can never be, for reasons we both know. My vows still hold. My past keeps us apart and over all, the specter hangs of my ignoble birth." He did not mention his less rational fears.

"Such reasons are just wind that fouls the mind. If you are not a nobleman by birth, your soul's been much ennobled by your life. If your great sword can recognize that fact, then Berevald, my father, also shall. Were we to strive together, we would leap such barricades like vaulting unicorns." She sighed. "For all of that, I must regret my words. I swore unto myself some time ago that I would never broach the subject more. It's not intentional, this act, these words of mine." She gazed at Palamon, her eyes open and earnest, her mouth drawn into a line. "If there were any way to cause your heart to change, I fain would have it so. Still, I have spoken twice and taken courtship in my hands, a thing that I was never taught to do. I'll speak no more of this; 'tis yours to lead."

She curled forward, drew up her legs, wrapped her hands about her knees, and rested her head on her fingers. What she had said was true; she had thrown herself before Palamon and he had not taken her up. It was a great insult. Had she not loved him at all, still it would have been an insult to the pride of any Princess to have been spurned by a man in whom she might have shown an interest. How much more so when she had bared her soul to him and they both realized their feelings were mutual?

So his mind began laboring all over again. Perhaps she was right; perhaps there was no obstacle in the way of their love that might not be overcome. Certainly she had the will to conquer much. He gazed at her a long time. She was an image of youthful loveliness as she sat before him, an image carved in flesh. Should he at least attempt to possess her—and to be possessed by her—when he had already suffered the consequences of such an act without ever having committed it? And even if the attempt could lead to some unforseen catastrophe, was their great love not worth that chance?

But what of his patron, the holy Maiden, Pallas? She had never forsaken him, even through the nadir of his degradation. When he had called her name for Ursid's sake, her aid had been freely given. Would it be blasphemy for him to join in union with this Berengeria now? He gazed at the rounded symmetry of that young lady's form and features. What was he to do?

He slid across the floor of the crystal shell until he was sitting beside her; she looked up as his arm circled her shoulder. But something more happened; the forces moving him to touch her were more powerful than he could have imagined. His longing for her would not be denied. Their lips met. They locked together, their arms twined about one another in a clinging embrace.

The kiss lasted a long time; when it was over, Palamon was without breath—but the kiss made him speak anyway. "If there is any way that I may press a suit to gain your hand, it shall be done. For I do love you, Berengeria."

There was no response, at least not a verbal one. Berengeria touched a finger to his lips to silence him. Then they kissed once more, the way lovers kiss when they are far from the nearest eyes. They kissed, although nothing but sleep separated them from their two companions in this tiny craft that was taking them through the waters, toward some unknown shore of the Thlassa Mey.

Still, no kiss could last forever. At last their arms slipped apart and they sat with Berengeria's head resting upon Palamon's shoulder. His world had shifted again upon its axis; they now belonged to one another. Still, he needed to pray to his patron, for her disapproval would stop this love. But now that he had made his decision, he was ready to contest with any forces men might array against him.

They sat together for a long time, each lost in private thoughts. Then Aelia awoke. Her eyebrows arched a bit as she looked at them but there was no greater reaction. To Berengeria's statement that she and Palamon would marry after all, Aelia only said, "If that is what my Mistress wishes most, then may it come to pass with blessings." She glanced at Palamon, then looked about the crystal shell.

Then she gasped. Her companions followed her gaze to see what she could see. The top of Reovalis' magical shell was still discolored where it had been struck by the lightning bolt sent by Alyubol. Thus far, this had mattered little. But now they could see that the discolored area was cracking. The wizard's searing bolts had done their work at last; the soft glow within the chamber showed a gossamer network of hairline fractures spreading through the yellowed crystal. There was no way of knowing how long the weakened spot would hold out the sea.

Releasing Berengeria's shoulder, Palamon stood to examine the damage. As he peered at the cracks more closely, he could see there were even more than he had at first noticed. Even as he watched, a new one traced its way only a finger's length from his nose.

He looked out at the fathoms of sea water pressing

down upon the shell; the surface of the sea was only a glimmer where the sun danced off the waves far above. He glanced once more at Berengeria and Aelia, who had both become pale. They all knew their craft would not protect them for long.

Aelia spoke. "I cannot help but wonder whether this most noble illustration of the arts of wise Reovalis will now respond to our predicament. If it does not, if its one aim is to attain the shore, four cold, drowned bodies may be all that land."

"But still, as both you guardians have taught, there never should be total loss of hope." Berengeria looked up at Palamon. "We are not trapped. My love, your noble sword can hew us from this shell before we drown."

Palamon was doubtful. "Perhaps. But still, it's not yet time for that. That act will be reserved, a last resort, for this hard crystal may be proof against an ancient sword as well as lightning bolts."

"Indeed," Aelia said. "And magic blades on magic shields make conflict leagues beyond all earthly blows. The forces thus released could do far more than carve a hole. They might well strike us down and bring our deaths more quickly than these seas."

And so they waited, reserving the powers of Palamon's blade until the last desperate moment. There was no doubt that the wait would be a short one; the cracking proceeded apace. Still, the shell did not alter its course by a degree or a fathom; it proceeded as it had done. Gone now were the pangs of hunger and the ravages of thirst that had plagued its occupants; their thirst could soon be slaked forever.

Palamon, Berengeria, and Aelia knelt once more. All six eyes were fixed upon the yellowed area, an area the size of a man's back, which was now crisscrossed by a lacy maze of tiny fractures. For what seemed like hours they waited, silently watching. Then the first failure came. A piece the size of a man's thumb fell with a ringing sound, like a goblet struck by a spoon. And the waters followed after.

The stream squirted in, striking Ursid upon the chest.

He was disoriented at finding himself so doused and started upward. Palamon took him quickly about the shoulders and raised him to a sitting position as he stared about wildly. "By all the gods," the young knight said. "What manner place is this?"

"A place in which we all may well be bathed in such a way that we'll ne'er bathe again." Even as Palamon spoke, another section of crystal fell away, allowing the stream gushing in to become the size of a man's wrist. At such a rate, water would soon overcome them.

But the crystal shell was responding. As soon as the collapse had begun, all forward motion had ceased, forcing the passengers to brace themselves to keep from being thrown down. Palamon had been jostled while supporting Ursid, in fact. But in spite of nearly being upset, he was relieved when he looked up to see the shimmering patterns of the sea's surface becoming brighter. Reovalis had foreseen all possibilities. The crystal shell's magical properties had deserted it and it was bobbing, corklike, to the surface. Still, it would have to bob to the surface quickly; even as Palamon looked up, another piece rattled down and the flood increased. The water was up to their knees and they were forced to stand; Palamon helped hold Ursid as they rose.

More pieces fell away and the flood became a torrent. But the wave dimpled surface was very near; Palamon could see the pattern of each wave as it passed above him. Then their disabled craft broke the surface with an awkward rocking motion and the hole which had before let in lethal waters, now served as gateway to the sweetness of cool morning air. They were safe for the moment, even though the crystal shell lay low in the waves and the water inside it lapped at their waists.

Palamon attempted to lift himself up, to raise himself with his hands so he could poke his head through the hole; perhaps he would be able to make out their position. But as he tried, the craft rocked crazily, then rolled over, tumbling its occupants into the frothing brine that swirled about them. Palamon's eyes smarted from the salt water and he could see his companions cough and gag as they righted themselves.

"We all must be the most sublime of sights," he said. "I erred. I never should have changed our balance point and rolled us over like a small child's toy."

Since the hole was at the bottom now, more water could not force its way in. The level stabilized. But a new problem arose—the air inside the shell quickly became extremely close. It seemed that the mystical quality which had allowed them to breath before had vanished along with all the shell's other supernatural properties. So it had to be turned over again, to allow air to enter once more.

The complications of navigating such a craft were many. They righted themselves, then time was spent bailing water, keeping the crippled shell in proper trim, coping with wounded Ursid, and combating gnawing hunger. And they waited and hoped. Waiting and hoping were the hardest tasks, because the travelers had no idea how long it would take the random breezes to blow them to some shore. They did not even know where they were. But by learning to position the hole in the side of their craft, they could at least keep a watch on the surrounding seas. When no ships appeared through the afternoon, it became ever more difficult to keep hope alive.

Chapter Twenty-six:
The Carean Flag

TOWARD EVENING, BERENGERIA saw something. For some time she had been peering out the opening in the side of their strange vessel, searching the horizon as best she could. Now excitement lit her eyes. "A ship. I see a ship. It's now quite close."

Palamon and Aelia looked at her eagerly. "What country's ship?" Aelia asked. "What flag flies from its head?"

Berengeria peered out intently but shook her head in frustration. "I cannot tell what flag. The bright sun sets into the seas behind her, blinding me."

Because the material of the shell distorted all images from the outside, Palamon hungered to look through the hole himself. But he refrained. The balance of the shell was delicate; he knew that any sudden shift could roll them all off their feet. So he contented himself with cautious glances over Berengeria's shoulder. These revealed nothing but glimpses of sea and sky. Then he did see it; it was very close indeed. It was a war galley and it was approaching them majestically; the water was frothing from the long ram and the three banks of oars rose and fell with a steady rhythm.

Even as Palamon glimpsed this magnificent sight, Berengeria released what could only be described as a scream of delight. "A friendly flag. It is Carea's flag. I see the colors hanging from the mast." Wheeling, she clutched at Palamon's tunic, her face glazed with joy. "Our journeys now will reach their proper end. Our long travails are past."

The crystal shell rolled crazily with the sudden motion of the bodies within, and its occupants lost sight of the great galley while all four of them struggled to regain their balance. Still, such a sight was worth the frantic tumbling about. All they had hoped for had come to pass. Their struggle was over.

When they regained sight of the ship, it towered over them. Its long rail was crowded with red-caped Carean archers and smoke was rising from onager stations at either end of the main deck. Clearly, the Careans viewed the crystal shell with suspicion. A knot of men could be seen at the ship's waist, the dying sun glinting off the officers' insignia on their breasts. Even as the four travelers watched, one of the officers challenged them. "I see your face. Identify yourselves and what your purpose is; lest you comply, we shall not hesitate to call you foes."

Palamon shouted out an answer. "We bear the good Princess unto her father and her rightful home."

His words had the expected result. There was a great commotion aboard the galley and the officers debated furiously. Then they hailed the shell again. "Brave words. But any thief could say as much."

"We bear the proof," Aelia said, "if you will let us show you. Hurry; neither food nor slaking draughts have passed our lips for long, uncounted days."

"And we've a wounded man aboard." This came from Palamon's lips.

A cargo net was thrown over the rail, secured, and several stout sailors climbed down it. The shouting of men at a windlass could be heard as the vessel's great wooden boom was unshipped and swung over the side.

An officer hailed them once more. "Now do not move; we're bringing you aboard. Our archers' strings are taut; one moment's lapse and arrow shafts will fill your gleaming craft."

The warning was heeded. As a second net was lowered and secured about the crystal shell, its occupants remained as still as possible. Even so, the ecstatic gleam on Berengeria's face was a celebration in itself. Her teeth shone in a desperate, almost hysterical, smile; tears glistened upon her cheeks; her eyes also glistened as she looked from Palamon to Aelia and then back again. The fittings on the boom groaned and the crystal chamber swung free of the sea's grip. Joy had seized the faces of all the travelers except Ursid; he had lapsed back into unconsiousness and Palamon had to hold him to keep his head out of the water swirling at their feet.

They had to steady themselves for the space of half a moment as they swung through the air. Then there was a jolt; they had reached the galley's deck. The officer who had been hailing them, a young man with dark hair, peered in at them. "Pass out your wounded man; we'll take him first."

"He lies as still as death," Berengeria said. "Still, out he comes."

The three of them took hold of Ursid and gently passed his head and shoulders through the opening; this was difficult because of the way the crystal shell lay upon the deck. He was received by a cluster of hands.

"Now crawl out singly. What I said before still holds. Do not attempt the least false move."

Aelia was helped out first, followed by Berengeria and then Palamon. They climbed down to the deck and found themselves standing before a half dozen stern-faced officers. The sight of the two women had tempered the suspicion in those hard eyes, however, and had replaced it with a look of expectation. One of the men approached Berengeria. "Are you the lost Princess who left our shores so many years ago?"

Aelia stepped between them. "She is. And I am Aelia, priestess to the court, her guardian for many years. I was appointed to this weighty post by good King Berevald himself. I still display the seal he gave me then." She showed them her ring of office as well as the tiny silver replica of a slave's collar she had always worn on a chain about her neck. These were both symbols of office worn by all Careans who directly served the King and they could not be disputed; the officers exchanged glances and then bowed low before the two women.

The effect was dramatic. Like an explosion, word flashed through the ship that Berengeria was on board and the archers lining the deck broke into loud huzzahs, as did the seamen, both above and below decks. Even the rowers deep within the bowels of the vessel could be heard, for their release was now likely—a gesture of thanks to the exalted gods for such a lucky event.

The galley's stout commander presented himself formally and told them Ursid was being taken below to the ship's surgeon. Then he invited them to partake of the food and drink which they had craved for so long.

"But what of our position on this sea?" Aelia asked as they walked aft. "What brought this vessel to our rescue?"

The Commander looked at her, then a smile crossed his ruddy, wrinkled face. "Such an object as that craft of yours could hardly be ignored by all the lookouts kept throughout our fleet. It gleamed with all the sun's bright, shining light, much as a beacon fire seen late at night."

Indeed, such a statement should not have surprised the travelers; after all, the galley had approached from the setting sun. Their crystal craft would have flashed with the brilliance of those waning rays. It could never have been ignored. But what of Carea's fleet? This was only a single vessel. They looked over the ship's rail and saw what the Commander had spoken of, for the galley's deck rode higher than a crystal shell. The horizon was lined with the black dots of warships, silhouetted against the glow of the departed sun.

"What brings Carea's mighty fleet to sail?" Berengeria asked.

"The navy of Buerdaunt blockades the Isle of Kolpos. Many weeks have passed and still no word has reached the King to indicate his daughter lives. For these two reasons, nearing black despair for what he saw as proof that she was lost, he ordered out our fleet to meet their own."

Aelia nodded and smiled. "Then you may set your course for Carea and dock a hero, for we are the cause why Lothar's ships have bottled up that isle."

Now it was the Commander who smiled. "And so we shall. It is no common thing—a battle won without a single blow."

They prepared to dine upon the finest fare the galley's stores could offer while a beat was struck and the rowers brought her back into line with her sister ships. First, however, they partook of the lime-flavored contents of the ship's water cask; thirst was the greater of the two demons that had plagued them through the last few days.

Later, after he had eaten and quaffed his fill, Palamon returned to the deck to oversee the removal of the items left inside the crystal shell. First among those was the *Spada Korrigaine*, which brought many a nod and low whistle from watching hands as it was removed and taken below to the quarters commandeered for the tall knight.

Then Palamon journeyed belowdecks to the ship's surgeon to inquire after Ursid's health. He found the young knight lashed into a hammock in the narrow compartment, weak but comfortable. Medication had been applied and the worst wounds had been sewn shut; the young man was still pale as paper but the danger was past. And his delirium, which had plagued him earlier in the day, was past as well. He greeted Palamon, weakly lifting one hand as the tall knight entered the chamber. "I knew that you would come, O Palamon. My mind is full of buzzing and the lights are dancing in my skull from lack of blood. But still I knew that you would come to see me here."

Palamon smiled down at him and placed a hand upon Ursid's shoulder. "How fare you, lad?"

"They say my life is saved. And I am told 'twas you who did the deed at cost of much travail of heart and soul. I must give thanks to you."

Palamon shook his head. "My duty lay in trying with

all heart to do that deed. And yet it took persuasion at great length to force me so to try. Do not thank me, 'twas Lady Aelia's words that swayed me to the task."

"It still was noble. When they'd taken us into the baleful, salten keep of Alyubol, I called you things that were, at best, unkind. I now have learned that it was wrong of me to say such things in haste. 'Twould ease my mind if e'er you could excuse my cutting words."

"I would if there were need."

Ursid lay silently for a moment. His eyes slid shut as if he were fighting off a great weariness. When he opened them again, it was with effort that he spoke. "And Berengeria has gained her goal?"

"Indeed she has. This ship is homeward bound; it takes us all to fair Carea's shores."

"Carea's shores," Ursid repeated. "I've never seen that land. Is it as lovely as she says it is?"

Palamon said, "She's never been there. She has had to judge her homeland's beauty through her heart's own eyes. All homes are beautiful when seen that way." He paused. "Carea does not have the wooded hills or lushness of your native land, Buerdaunt. The hills are rocky, olive groves abound, and herds of sheep bedot the rugged land."

"And I have lost her."

Those words, spoken suddenly with a note of despair, brought Palamon up short. The younger man did not have to explain the statement, spoken out of the blue, for Palamon to understand the meaning. After all, if Palamon's own future was uncertain, how much more so was Ursid's? The young knight had betrayed his own land for Berengeria's love. And now that love would never be his.

Ursid spoke again, old memories returning to life through the movement of his lips. "When I first beheld fair Berengeria, 'twas in a tower of Pomfract Castle. I could see her oft a-gazing down at all the sun-baked roofs across our fair Buerdaunt. Her eyes seemed far away. As you have said, she gazed at Carea, beheld it with the eye that's in her heart. How beautiful she was." He shook his head.

"She hovered far above the other maidens of Buerdaunt, like orioles above the lesser fowl. I asked to be among the guards who stood the watch upon her person. Since I was related to the King, the post was mine. I cannot tell you of the thousand ways my heart flew to her grasp. On her behalf I would have hacked pale Lothar's neck in two."

He rolled his eyes toward Palamon. "My Lady Aelia tells me there is love between yourself and my Princess most dear. She says that marriage is your likely end."

Palamon shrugged and looked away. Marriage with Berengeria was indeed on his mind; it was something he desired throughout his being. It was the course he would take if all obstacles could be overcome, even though he was not certain it was the proper course. "That act is now our goal."

"Oh, brutal wound. My heart is slain within me. I am like a man who climbs a mountain made of sand." Ursid's eyes shut and Palamon could see one hand clench. "O Palamon, you are an honest man and yet your truth is agony to me."

Palamon could feel the muscles of his face tightening as he was filled up by the guilt for Ursid's suffering. Ursid had forsaken country and kin for Berengeria; he had sustained ghastly wounds, both to his body and to his soul. Palamon's heart went out to him, yet love was a chariot in which only two could ride.

For his part, Ursid lay silently for an instant; then his features became animated. "She does not love me after all my deeds and treason I committed for her sake."

Palamon interrupted. "A heart cannot select the one it loves. There is no thought in love; it is a force which drags a woman down the path it chooses."

"That does not matter, for I have a plan. Although you're dear, more dear unto her heart than I am, there is still a strategy by which I might possess her—tournament. A man who can excel upon the field can gain a woman's hand, if not her love. O Palamon, that fact still gives me hope."

Palamon simply let the younger man speak. There was no sense interrupting him.

"Although your skill at arms may well outweigh my own, still I will challenge you when first the opportunity presents itself. If I could win her hand, then it might pass that I could strive to gain her deeper love."

Ursid's emotions were placing a greater strain upon his weakened body than it could sustain for long. His face was becoming flushed; the sweat was pouring from him. What could Palamon say? His own culpability in this affair prevented him from criticizing the younger man. "Methinks I'd do the same if I were you."

Ursid's strength was visibly deserting him. His movements slowed, the gleam in his eyes faded, and he relaxed a bit. When he spoke again, it was in a thoughtful tone. "It's sad that love has come between us two; I know that there are many things which I could learn from you in different times."

Palamon forced another smile. "Such things may happen still. One never knows."

"I hope so. Still, whatever comes, must come."

There was little more to be said. Ursid was exhausted. Palamon took his leave and mounted the ladder that led to the main deck, his emotions heated to a rolling boil. He would have to fight Ursid for the hand of Berengeria; there was no chance the young knight would relent. One look into those eyes showed that. By all reason, such a fact should have filled Palamon with regret: fighting for the hand of a woman was farther from the ways he had known all his life than love from death.

One thing was certain—he had to speak with Berengeria. He walked toward the officers' quarters. He found her on the aft deck, standing with Aelia and the Commander, watching the waves slide by as the galley's long oars rose and fell like great, wooden wings.

All three heads turned as he approached. This was not the time. He could not say the right words to Berengeria then, not with the other two looking on. He was not sure he could say them once they were alone. In any event, he would wait.

Night came. The opportunity did not come with it. Finally, after the evening meal, Palamon went with the two women to the Commander's cabin, which had been surrendered to the ship's royal passenger. The three of them spoke for a while. But the topics they discussed wandered far from what was on Palamon's mind, so he finally whispered into Berengeria's ear, "We must have words alone. I bear some news."

Berengeria nodded and turned to Aelia. "My Lady, would you pardon us awhile? My Palamon and I must step outside and speak a moment. We will not be long."

Aelia's mouth tightened into a straight line. "Your Highness must remember her life's duty."

"And so I do. But still we must depart." As she spoke, Berengeria gazed steadily into the older woman's eyes.

"Our conversation shall be most discreet," Palamon said. "My hands shall not stray forth. This fair Princess shall not be ravished while homeward bound." His expression was blank; even the smile he had worn so many times was not present.

Aelia looked from Berengeria to Palamon, then back again. "Do not converse where strangers may appear. The privacy of this small chamber shall be yours, for it is I who shall go forth." Quickly and without further words, she left the two of them alone. Palamon did not speak as he watched her go.

"She disapproves of us, as you can see," Berengeria said. "Still, she will stand beside us, even though my course is not the one she would have mapped."

Palamon took her hand. He held it before his face for a moment, studying the soft ridges and valleys of her knuckles. He had always been able to sense a fateful air about this Princess; that fate now enveloped him and Ursid, as well as her. Was that good, or bad? There could be no doubt it was bad for Ursid. "If you should choose to steer another track, I'll understand. This one is hazardous and will demand determination ere we reach our goal."

Her free hand traveled to his shoulder. "I shall not flinch if you stand by my side."

They kissed. Their lips clung together for a long time. Such a kiss was a newfound delicacy to Palamon—spiced wine to a hermit. It made thoughts of fate and guilt seem trivial things, indeed; it was a wonder and was surely reward enough for any sacrifice. But when the kiss was over and they sat down together, Palamon still turned to the subject he had come to discuss. "I spoke with young Ursid."

"And fares he well?"

"He's past all danger."

"That is good to hear." Berengeria looked at Palamon, smiling. "My love, is this the way you woo your bride? By bringing news of one who fain would be your rival?"

"Ursid will challenge me when we reach shore. A trial by combat is his hard intent, the victor to receive your nuptial hand."

She blinked as this news struck her. "A hurdle to be crossed, Ursid's intent. But we can move to circumvent his aim. When I have told my father of your deeds and how you saved Ursid's own fleeing life, you will not need to battle him to marry me." She looked up at him, her face set.

Palamon took little comfort from her touch. He sighed, cleared his throat, and looked toward the far side of the chamber. "My aim is to accept his challenge."

"No. You need not do this thing to win my love."

"I must."

"You don't know what you do." She used her hands to turn his face toward hers. "You have my love; do not court injury at fate's mere whim by battling Ursid. He might gain victory by some odd blow and take my hand from you by foul mischance."

"My skill is greater. I can conquer him."

She wrung her hands. "You're obstinate. You don't hear what I say. Although your skill in battle may outweigh his own the way the bull outweighs the gnat, still we may be undone. In tournament, the specter of ill fortune could rise up and cast you to defeat, e'en though your prowess rivaled with the gods."

"That's so. But still Ursid deserves his right."

Berengeria stood, then walked away a few steps and looked back at Palamon, her eyes blazing. "Ursid is brave and good, a worthy knight, and I admit I like him well enough. But still, my love is given unto you. I have the right to choose the man I wed. Must that right be usurped because your pride demands that you accept all challenges? Must I be fought for like a piece of meat that's cast between two hounds? Have I no choice? And if you lose this duel, must I accept the consequence and marry young Ursid? Though I am a Princess, my female role now makes of me a prize, a trophy, and no more. I'll not accept that. I will not."

Shaken by her words, Palamon gazed upward at those flashing eyes. She was right; of course she was right. But still, Ursid had sacrificed a great deal for Berengeria's sake; he had rights too. And besides that, Palamon had his own reasons for accepting the younger knight's challenge. How could he make her understand?

He stood up, the corners of his mouth no steadier than the knees of a new foal. Silently, he wrapped his arms about her. He knew she could feel the pressure of his broad hands upon her back, because she closed her eyes and returned the embrace. Finally, he spoke. "I love you so. I cannot say how much. But still I must take up the gauntlet thrown."

Her hands clenched. "Why?" Her body strained against his embrace as she expelled the word.

It took him a long time to reply; he gazed about the chamber, his lips worked silently, he placed his hands upon his hips. But he had to speak—he could not evade the moment forever. At last he did. "My line of thought should be made known to you. You are my love and you shall know my mind." But instead of going on, he crossed the cabin's deck, examined the woodwork, then turned to look at her once more. There could be no doubt he was choosing his words carefully.

"Although you are my love, my loyalty has long been pledged unto the virgin Maiden, holy Pallas, whom I've often wronged through my shortsightedness and my neglect. I shall not wrong her more. You are my love. But still, to take you to the marriage bed, forsaking this great vow that I have made, could wrong myself and you, as well as her." He paused, then went on. "Ursid gives me the means to know her will, for he can never master me upon the field of honor—not without the aid of fortune's hand. If I can conquer, we may be assured divine approval shines upon our love. If not..." He paused again. "If not, it's best we know, ere we transgress."

She looked up at him. Her anger had spent itself, her eyes were filled with moisture and it took her a moment to speak. "Very well. This thing may come to pass. But if I can prevent it, then I must."

He would not press this matter any further; he did not choose to argue with this maid. They talked awhile longer, of other things, small things. Afterward, when Palamon returned to the deck, he saw Aelia standing against the windward rail. Her face was drawn as she gazed out over the moonglazed waters of the Thlassa Mey. For an instant he was tempted to walk across the deck and speak with her. She looked quite lonely. But he did not. He walked forward, toward the bow.

Chapter Twenty-seven:
The Homecoming

WHEN THE MOUNTAINS of Berengeria's homeland stood blue on the horizon the next morning, messenger pigeons were brought on deck. The birds cooed innocently within their crates while tiny ivory capsules were strapped onto their legs. They would carry the tidings of Berengeria's rescue. Once released, they rose from the deck together, circled the ship a single time, then winged their ways toward those blue mountains.

By the time the fleet cast lines out to the great harbor mole of Lower Carea, it was evening. Still, there was no doubt that the message had been received. A great throng had gathered along the stone seawall; the cheering could be heard even though the sound had to travel hundreds of cubits.

Chariots approached along the cobbled surface of the mole and the travelers climbed into them. Even Ursid, pale and weak as he was, took part in this triumphant march up the mole, through the streets of Lower Carea, and along winding roads to Upper Carea. They rode past

tilled hillsides and olive groves, and every cubit along the
road was occupied by an exultant citizen.

The ride was a long one; dusk turned to darkness and
the procession became a torchlight parade. It wound like
a flaming river along streets and over hills, until the outer
gates of the King's stronghold, Castle Conforth, were
reached. There the heroes left their chariots. They were
escorted past the outer wall and walked the hundred cubits to the steps of the royal inner sanctum.

Palamon was walking alongside Berengeria. He could
hear her breathing quicken with each step. At the head
of the nobles clustered at the top of the steps leading to
the keep stood an imposing old man, King Berevald. He
was tall, as tall as Palamon; his long beard and the hair
beneath his crown were white and they gleamed in the
torchlight. Beside him stood Goswinth, the Queen. She
was the reflection of her daughter, Berengeria; Palamon
loved her before the first greeting.

What was there that could be said of this reunion?
There were tears and embraces. Lower lips quivered as
emotions were held in check or sobs floated through the
air as those emotions burst free. There was a kind of rich,
quiet joy everywhere.

The returned adventurers were too exhausted for a
great banquet. Ursid, in fact, was nearly fainting. He was
taken to a chamber while Palamon and Aelia accompanied
the royal family to a sitting room where they talked for
a long time.

Berengeria was seated between the royal couple and
their eyes were often upon her. There was much touching
of hands. The praise flowed freely toward Palamon and
Aelia and also Ursid, even though he was not present.
Still, one topic lay at the center of Berengeria's part of
the conversation. She smoothly introduced Palamon to
her parents and told them of her desire to marry; it was
a fair gambit. The King and Queen were so overfilled with
joy that they were easy game for her proposals.

The King examined Palamon closely and was impressed
by what he saw and heard. Palamon's actions during the
long journey to Carea spoke for themselves; despite his

fall from the Knights of Pallas, his past was without blot, as had been proven by the events within Reovalis' crystal shell. The mighty *Spada Korrigaine* was shown to the King and he looked upon it with wonder. Berengeria was quick to point out the value to the legions of Carea of any man who could wield such a weapon, for war between Carea and Buerdaunt was another topic of discussion. Upon the return of Berengeria, Berevald had closed the Narrow Strait to all ships bearing the flag of that land; it was unlikely that Lothar the Pale would fail to take up the gauntlet.

Against such a background, Berengeria skillfully secured the old King's blessing for her marriage to Pala-mon. The question of the tall knight's low birth never even arose.

So the consent of King Berenald and Queen Goswinth was received within hours of the arrival at Lower Carea. Still, the news had to be given to the court. This was done the following morning. The audience chamber was packed with courtiers, nobles, and officers; many craned their necks or cupped their ears as King Berevald made the happy announcement.

Ursid was also present. His pale features grew ghastly as the King spoke, then he turned to the monarch. "And I must exercise the right, my Lord, to challenge Palamon for that fair hand. In combat I will face him. When one falls, the victor shall wed Berengeria. This is my right; as I am a knight, my services to her have justified this chal-lenge for her hand."

There was sudden and uneasy silence. In the rear of the chamber, someone coughed; there were a few whis-pers. Drained by his speech, Ursid sagged to the tiles. And there was no one in the room to aid him. At last, Palamon stepped to his side to help him up and support him with one arm.

Berengeria folded her hands before her bosom as she looked from Palamon to Ursid, then back again. "My love, my feelings have not changed. There is no need for you to give an answer to the challenge of this man. To spurn

his words as if they ne'er were said is no disgrace, for I
have made my choice."

Palamon looked into her eyes as he helped Ursid into
a chair that had hastily been brought. "Perhaps it's so,
what you have said. But yet, it is an honorable claim.
Ursid has labored for your sake as long, as hard, and with
as much great pain as I. I cannot turn his challenge down,
for it would mark me as a low, base knight, were I to do
that after what he's suffered."

Berengeria turned to her father, imploring him with her
eyes and with her tongue. "My Father, though Ursid is
very brave, he's not my love. You must deny his challenge. Palamon has labored long and earnestly for me.
More battle now should not be forced on him."

King Berevald looked upon his daughter with his great,
gray eyes. The decision was hard, for he plainly adored
this long lost maiden and would have liked to maintain
her love. Still, he decided quickly. "The challenge has
been laid down and received. My daughter, I would not
refuse your plea, except this combat seems, from all things
said, agreeable to both these noble knights. And yet, for
I am loathe to see you frown, I shall place these restric-
tions on their fight—I shall declare a tournament be held
with near an hundred knights upon each side, one side to
be commanded by Ursid, the other by this noble Palamon.

"I further will declare now, to save blood and also to
prevent the loss of life, that square-capped lances be the
weapons used, as well as longswords, maces, and the axe.
No sharp-tipped arrows will compete that day, no stabbing
swords with biting blades, no knives, no poleaxe. And I
furthermore decree that two great stakes be set into the
field. If any knight be brought unto the stake, though he's
not yielded, there he must abide.

"And when one chieftain thus is overcome, or when,
the gods forbid, one has been slain, the tourneying shall
end. The victor shall, upon my word of honor, have the
hand of Princess Berengeria."

And so the decision was made over the wishes of the
maiden who was its object. Such was the custom of the
lands about the Thlassa Mey. The details were quickly

arranged; the great tournament would be held in late summer. The intent of the King was that this tournament be bloodless, or as nearly so as could be arranged in those hard times. The arrangements satisfied both Palamon and Ursid, even if they did not satisfy Berengeria. The space of two months which separated them from the date of the great confrontation would allow time for Ursid's wounds to heal, and Palamon could once again take up the training with arms he had forsaken for the last eight years.

So the call went out. Knights from all about the Thlassa Mey were invited to the great festival; from Ourms and Oron and all the other cities except Buerdaunt they came. They came from the Outer Islands as well, from Quarval and from Muse.

For his part, Palamon prepared for the tournament with fierce intensity. He no longer needed to ponder the rightness of his actions. If his love for Berengeria did not offend the divine Maiden, he would triumph over Ursid. If it did, he would know by the result of the combat. While Ursid went into isolated preparation for the event, Palamon trained himself at the military barracks in Upper Carea, a stone's throw from the palace, where he had been given quarters. He spent many evenings walking in the gardens with Berengeria or in conversation with the royal family.

Had it not been for Berengeria's opposition to the coming struggle and his regrets about that, his joy would have been complete. As it was, he found himself beset by nagging doubts. Even now, was he doing the right thing? Had fate selected him to become a part of Berengeria's future or had it not? But in spite of his doubts, he found his love for the robust young woman had matured into a feeling of depth. His days were as happy now as they had ever been since his expulsion from the Knights of Pallas; he devoted himself to singleminded preparation for the coming conflict.

The weeks before the tournament quickly passed away. Knights of renown arrived from all parts of the known world, to be joined by the finest gallants from Carean nobility. The seaports along the coast were busy and the hostelries of Upper Carea filled up like granaries.

On the morning of the great day, the sun rose hot and overbearing, driving the dew from the lawns in steaming clouds. All across the great city of Upper Carea there was the hubbub of armor being polished, of coursers and palfreys being saddled, of breast plates and heartspoons being laced into place, and of weapons being strapped onto waists. The streets were full of gaily dressed ladies and lords, as well as warriors riding tall upon their steeds, bearing the flags and colors of many lands.

The great throng all tended in the same direction, toward the broad meadows north of Castle Conforth, where the tournament was to be held. Wooden platforms had been erected there for the seating of the lords and ladies of the court; tables were sagging with refreshments and the steamy air hung heavy with anticipation of the drama to be played out.

It was midmorning when Palamon arrived at the meadow, the polished plates of his armor heavy upon his back. He carried a great mace and wore the colors of no land. With regret, he had decided to forego the colors of the Knights of Pallas; it would have been an abomination to have worn them while fighting for the hand of a woman.

When he arrived, he found the place filled with knights practicing for the fray, even though the tournament was not to begin until midday. He walked about, leading his courser by the reins and greeting those knights who had been assigned by lot to take his part in the mock battle. His eyes searched the banner-draped platforms which lined the broad field, hoping to pick out Berengeria's face and figure. But she had not yet appeared.

The day grew steadily warmer. The seats upon the platforms were taken by a kaleidoscope of nobility, and the field was ringed with spectators of every rank and class. Ursid appeared on the far side of the field, his face and posture painting a portrait of grim determination. He was no longer a pale youth who bled from a dozen wounds. The slashes had healed, although his body and face bore many scars. His features were dark and intense.

Then Palamon watched as the royal train appeared upon the platform reserved for King Berevald and his attendants. The highest nobles of the land were there, as were the King and Queen, tall and stately in their robes. They had changed over the last weeks; their daughter's rescue had lifted years from both of them, straightened their backs, and ignited their souls. It had made Palamon feel good to see it.

Then Berengeria climbed the steps to the platform, her features a mask of concern. Seated upon his steed, Palamon gazed at her distant features until he saw her look back. Even across the space which separated them, he saw her brighten a bit. But his excitement only increased.

In spite of everything, Palamon's mind and body were ready for the event, finely tuned for the coming moment, ringing with the tension that mounted as he and Ursid rode to the King's platform to receive their final instructions. Berevald's speech was short. He charged the two knights to remember the rules of honor and chivalry, to do honor to themselves and those they represented, and to make this day memorable for its glory rather than its tragedy. Then he bade them return to their respective places and await his signal.

As they wheeled their horses, Palamon heard Berengeria's voice. "Dear Palamon, and also you, Ursid, since I am made the object of this fray, I shall present a gift to each of you, as called for by tradition. I present you both with scarves which bear my family's crest. You both now fight for me; I bless you both."

Palamon understood the speech, the gift, and Berengeria's reasons for giving both. Her heart was not in these proceedings; she was reluctantly playing the rôle assigned to her, playing it like the noble young woman she was. She had been reared as a Princess; she would fulfill that obligation, whatever the personal price. He had no doubt of that.

His eyes fell. He regretted his part in her discomfort. Still he was proud of her. Bearing up well beneath the strain of her office, she asked the two knights to hold their helmets forth and then she tied a scarf to the beaver—

the visor—of each one, off to the side where it would not block the vision.

But for Palamon she did a trifle more. It was not a great thing; she simply let her palm rest upon his iron-bound shoulder for an instant and looked at him with an expression that seemed to say "take care." That was all she did. But when Palamon's glance next found Ursid's face, the scarred features reflected bitterness, hatred, and despair. Palamon sighed. It seemed there was no way for him to be fair to himself without being unfair to others. And the look in the young man's eyes foretold a bitter battle.

Both men put on their helmets. The weather was hot; Palamon's helmet rested heavily upon his shoulders and the sun was already turning it into a cauldron which brought the sweat popping from his brows. His horse was dancing with excitement as he turned and rode to his own side of the field.

The tension had reached the point that even the leaves on the trees seemed aflutter with it; every face Palamon saw was grim within its great helmet, and some were pale, the skin stretched tightly across the bones. The issue soon had to be decided. The crowd became quiet; silence reigned from one end of the meadow to the other as King Berevald extended his arm, his fingers clutching the corner of a white handkerchief. The handkerchief fell; the tournament had begun.

Palamon flicked his spurs into the flanks of his horse and the animal surged beneath him as its great hind legs drove it toward the opposing line. His fellow knights were all doing the same. The air was filled with the thundering of hooves, flying clods, and the cheers of the throng as the two companies hurtled against one another. Ursid was Palamon's opposite number in the other line of knights, and it was against that young man that Palamon aimed his attack. He couched his heavy lance securely and pointed the tip at Ursid's breastplate. Once unhorsed, the young knight could be pounced upon and led to one of the tall stakes at either side of the field, to meet defeat according to Berevald's instructions.

But Ursid's intent was deadly. Palamon saw the youthful warrior couch his own lance, the ironbound tip directed at the beaver of Palamon's helmet. The young man was showing no quarter; his tactic meant that he would accept a fatal result if it came. Palamon lowered his head to one side to dodge the blow. The lance missed. But in avoiding it Palamon allowed the tip of his own lance to stray from its target. Ursid caught it with his shield and the shaft shattered against the hard surface, sending splinters far into the air above their heads.

All across the field, this drama was being repeated with variations. Lances shivered against stout shields and riders were thrown from horses. There were screams as breastplates were pierced and the bright blood flowed; keen-edged swords were drawn, along with maces and battle axes, their deadly arcs ending in dented or cleaved armor or broken bones.

Palamon could not seek Ursid out again. He was set upon by knights of the opposing company and forced to defend himself. With his shield he parried one opponent's blow while freeing his heavy mace from its hanger upon his belt. Then he struck back, smiting the man high on the sword arm, bringing forth a cry and causing the knight to drop the weapon.

At the same time, he was himself struck. A heavy blow between the shoulders threw his head back and an explosion of dancing lights flared inside his brain. He was helpless for that instant but the following blow never fell. His assailant had been knocked from the saddle by yet another knight of Palamon's company.

And so the contest raged. Men were brought down and set upon by their opponents, then dragged to the stake while still struggling valiantly. There, judges recorded their names upon parchments and they were eliminated from the afternoon's combat. Soon, both sides of the field were lined with disgruntled warriors; some were unharmed, many bled or nursed broken or sprained members.

But in the center of the field the fighting continued. Palamon remained on his horse, flailing with his mace. Several times he had sent foemen reeling from their mounts, but there were always more to take the place of those who had fallen. The time galloped by. As he fought, fatigue ate at the muscles of his right arm until he transferred the mace to his other hand and fought on, in itself a prodigious feat. The sun pounded down upon his armor and made it into his personal inferno. The sweat erupted from his head, throat, and back, torrents sucked forth by that blazing sun; his armor chafed and rubbed against the wet places.

Then he saw a knot of unhorsed knights milling about, engaged in a mêlée that swirled to and fro between the stamping steeds. At the center of the fray, the crested helmet of Ursid could be seen. He had been unhorsed. But he was still fighting valiantly, his sword holding off a trio of opponents.

Dodging a blow from another would-be challenger, Palamon dismounted from his horse. The time had come. The matter would be decided here. Grasping the handle of his mace in one hand, securing his shield on his other arm, he strode toward Ursid. The other knights gave way before him and lowered their weapons, acknowledging his right to meet the young knight alone. Facing one another, the two men squared off in the center of a circle of knights, fierce men who watched the way a herd of mountain bighorns might have watched a battle between two great rams.

The two men circled one another. Then, with the crash of weapons, the duel began. The day's fighting had taken its toll upon Palamon; he was not as young as he once had been, and the fierceness of the battle had weakened him more than it would have ten years earlier. Still, he knew he had enough strength and skill left to make him more than a match for the smaller Ursid. He circled his younger opponent, beating down frenzied sword thrusts the way a man would have batted at a flight of hummingbirds.

Not for an instant did Palamon doubt the outcome, and the issue did indeed move toward a quick conclusion. Ursid impatiently swung a mighty blow with his sword; it would have cleaved Palamon's armor, had it landed.

But it did not land. Palamon's return blow struck Ursid upon the wrist and the young knight's weapon flashed to the ground.

Palamon was prepared to deliver the blow which would have ended the struggle; his muscles tensed to send his mace in an arc which would have ended at the point where Ursid's helmet joined his armor plate. But the tall knight hesitated for an instant, swaying off balance as he glimpsed Ursid's eyes, visible beyond the grating of the young knight's visor.

There was something close to insanity in those eyes. Even the visors of two helmets could not hide the rage, the despair, the desperation, and the hatred. So Palamon hesitated a half-instant in striking his opponent. That margin made the blow miss.

Ursid ducked beneath Palamon's swing, grasped his fallen weapon, rolled clumsily away, and clambered to his feet before Palamon could regain his advantage. Then he rushed the tall knight savagely, delivering a ferocious blow which cleaved the head of Palamon's mace from the handle, sending the fluted iron ball rolling away into the grass.

Another blow sliced deeply into Palamon's shield; still another left it a flopping ruin, Palamon was no longer fighting for Berengeria now, nor for honor, nor to entertain the spectators. He was fighting for his life. Ursid advanced against him, strength doubled and redoubled by fury, delivering more blows than Palamon could ever hope to block.

One blow cut through the remains of Palamon's shield and the tall knight felt the hot blood searing his arm. Another dented the plate at his waist but did not break through; still another sliced into the shoulder above his sword arm. And beyond that, the fatigue of his years was steadily turning his limbs into stone.

Now it was Palamon who faced defeat—and against this enraged foe, defeat would mean death. If Palamon's defense, which was steadily weakening, were to lapse, a half dozen fatal blows would fall before the two men could be pulled apart.

Protecting his neck with his arms, Palamon lowered

his head and charged Ursid, driving his helmet into the
younger knight's belly, denting the plate and nearly knocking himself out with the blow. Together, the two men rolled
in the grass. Palamon was sick and giddy as he strove to
pin his opponent's sword arm. Finding himself on top, he
brought the ironbound haft of his mace down against the
side of Ursid's helmet. Once, then again and again he
struck desperately, until Ursid no longer struggled, and
he had survived by knocking the younger man senseless.
He lay atop Ursid's motionless form for a moment, then
tried to lift himself enough to crawl away. But he made
it only a few cubits before he collapsed into the grass.

He had not lost his consciousness, but he could not
stand nor even sit. The clouds and sky circled above him,
and he could feel the blood slosh about as he shifted within
his armor. Then he was surrounded. Many hands were
lifting his head, raising him into a sitting position, fumbling
for buckles and straps, and removing the blood-soaked
plates which had saved his life. Hands slid under his arms
and his helmet was pulled off; he was surprised at the
air's chilliness, now that his brains were no longer being
baked within that protective shell.

And then Berengeria was there. Concern had blotted
out her anger and opposition to the tournament. Weeping,
ignoring the blood that smeared her robes, she smothered
him with kisses, even while physicians bandaged his
wounds. He smiled and clasped her wrist, too weary to
rise. Then a litter was brought and he was placed upon
it and taken to the platform where the King and Queen
were still seated.

There, Berengeria stood by as the physicians helped
Palamon rise from the litter and kneel before the King.
A wreath was placed about his temples, to the cheering
of the throng. Then he was once more upon the litter,
gazing up at Berengeria, whose tears were falling warmly
upon his throat. For this moment, he was even more
overwhelmed by her than he had been by Ursid's furious
onslaught moments ago. He smiled and lifted a sweat-
soaked, bloodstained hand to caress her cheek. Her face
drew nearer, and they kissed. It was a tender kiss, accom-

panied by sounds of approval and good-natured applause from the nobles sharing the royal platform.

Then Palamon spoke. "Have joy, my dear Princess. It's not the time for tears or sobbing. All has been attained that we have striven for through these long months." And it was so. Palamon's heart was bursting with relief. He had won this maiden's hand beneath the gaze of Pallas. He could enter into this marriage with no blot upon his happiness or hers.

Or could he? What had been the source of that furious burst of energy Ursid had displayed as he had regained his weapon and shredded Palamon's defenses with his renewed attack? Where had been Pallas' approval as the young man's blade had sent the tall knight's blood flowing? Palamon still did not know the will of his patron. He might never know her will.

He sat up and looked about, still clasping Berengeria's hand. "Where's Ursid?"

"He's being tended to across the way," Berengeria said. "His wounds are not severe."

"Still, I must go to him." Palamon rose to his feet unsteadily and took steps toward the end of the platform. Instantly, Berengeria and the attendants were at his side, steadying him, keeping him from falling. "You need not do that," Berengeria said. "I will go to him and pay him the respects his deeds deserve."

Palamon shook his head. "No, it's my duty; I shall go to him." With his arms about the shoulders of a pair of stout young men, he made his way down off the platform across the meadow, to a place where fallen knights were being tended. Berengeria went after this hobbling trio, her hand lingering upon Palamon's shoulder.

There were several knights lying upon the grass before them, the unfortunate by-products of a successful tournament. One lay near death, his breastbone pierced by a lance. There were several fractures and a multitude of bruises and contusions, which would probably not even be treated.

But Palamon's attention was turned toward Ursid. The young knight sat upon the grass beside the others, the

armor stripped off his upper body and his helmet resting
in his lap. The left side of his face was swollen and puffy
where Palamon had hammered him; the swollen tissues
were already beginning to turn purple. A pair of teeth lay
in a clay bowl beside him and his left eye was bloodshot.
By the next day, Palamon knew, he would look ghastly.

Still, he seemed alert. He glanced up at Palamon and
his attendants, at Berengeria, then turned his head away,
his expression becoming more desolate than ever. "Con-
gratulations," he said, bitterly.

"Yes, that is my due," Palamon replied, trying to smile,
releasing his hold upon the shoulders of those who supported him, and kneeling at the young man's side. "I managed to defeat a man whose sword dealt out more wounds
than any foeman I have faced for many years across the
Thlassa Mey."

"That may well be. But still, the victory's yours."
Ursid's tone tore at Palamon's heart.

"Is there a deed which I may do for you?"

Ursid looked up at him for an instant. "There's one.
You may relinquish all your right to Berengeria, for whom
we fought. All other things are chaff; I do not want them."

"Ah, lad, if I could do it, I would make her twins, for
you deserve her just as much as I."

Ursid looked at him earnestly for a moment. The bitterness and pain faded from the youthful features but a
look of great desperation was still there. "One thing I ask
in all sincerety. Should anything occur to separate your
heart from this Princess we both pursue—if such a thing
occurred—then would you speak to her and to her father
for my sake?" Ursid's fingers clutched at Palamon's shoulders as he uttered this plea.

What could Palamon say? No such thing could happen
in the short time which separated them from their wedding
day. Still, the request contained such a note of hopeless-
ness that it demanded an answer. What could it hurt for
him to make this meaningless concession, if only to give
this frustrated lover some peace of mind? He glanced over
his shoulder at Berengeria, then turned his head and nodded.

Ursid closed his eyes and sighed. "Then I may cling to hope."

Palamon patted the younger knight upon the shoulder and rose to turn away. All this had made him dizzy; now he sagged, reaching out for support, clutching Berengeria's shoulder as the others caught him. He allowed himself to be helped once more onto the litter, which fortuitously had been brought, then he relaxed and shut his eyes, holding Berengeria's hand as he was carried away. The worst was over. Gods willing, they would be wed within the month.

Chapter Twenty-eight:
An Artifact

THE DAYS PASSED away, the wedding date was debated within the royal family, and Palamon's wounds mended. He was able to rise and walk about the morning after the tournament, although the King's physician forbade it; by the day following that, he was able to assume a schedule which included a long walk with Berengeria outside the castle walls. They talked, they dreamed, they kissed more than once.

But Palamon retained doubts. With every motion, stiffness and the aching beneath his bandages reminded him of just how close Ursid had come to attaining complete victory. Had his patron, Pallas, saved him from the younger knight? Or had she aligned with the forces which had spurred Ursid's ferocious onslaught? Had Palamon won his slender victory without divine assistance? Did the holy Maiden look down disapprovingly upon the coming nuptials? Most important of all, had he made the proper decision while clinging to Berengeria's soft body inside that mystical crystal shell all those weeks ago? He still could not be sure.

On the third evening after the tournament, Palamon was dining in his apartment high in one of Castle Conforth's towers when a courier arrived with word that his presence was desired in the King's chambers.

"I certainly shall come," he said, wiping his lips with a napkin, "but to what end?"

The courier winked and smiled. "To help His Majesty decide the date."

No more explanation was needed. Palamon rose and allowed the courier to open the door leading from the chamber. He did not hurry along the corridor which led to the King's chambers; the physician had warned him against that. But his mind raced ahead of him.

When he arrived, the King and Queen, Berengeria, and Aelia were already waiting for him, seated upon campaign chairs or reclining upon couches before a fire which had been built to ward off the evening chill. Berevald stood when Palamon entered, embraced the tall knight, and examined his left forearm. "I see you still wear bandages. Perhaps that soon shall be the vogue among the young men of my court."

"Perhaps. But if I were to take them off, unwrapping all this gauze and linen, it's my fear my shielding arm would fall to pieces, for our young Ursid has hacked it up most fearfully, despite my efforts to dissuade him from the task." Palamon smiled, although he was still uncomfortable about the subject of Ursid.

The King beamed. "It gives our people entertainment, Sir. They love you now as much as they love me; I tell you it brings warmness to my heart to see the way the populace has looked upon you, taking you into their hearts. I sometimes think they'd have you for their king." He laughed at his own remark. "But now enough of that. I do believe you know the reason I have called you here."

"Indeed, I do."

"Then let us set a date. For my part, I would have it instantly, but there, of course, are thoughts of policy which must affect our actions. Wedding banns must be affixed to walls throughout our realm. I calculate three days to do that deed and two more days for folk to travel here.

The greatest lords of this and other realms are here already or the traveling would take far longer. Can you wait until the sixth dawn sends its light across this land before you claim your bride?"

Palamon smiled once more but the smile covered a raft of conflicting emotions. "All days are long when I must wait for her."

The King laughed and clapped his hands. Berengeria rose to move to Palamon's side, her face flushed. But at that moment, the happy scene was interrupted. A knock resounded against the great hardwood door to the chamber, causing all the room's occupants to turn toward the sound. An attendant stepped to the door and pulled it open, revealing a trio of stern-faced soldiers.

The King's features grew dark. "How dare you interrupt us at this time, when we consult with all our family?"

The soldier who stood farthest forward, an officer, knelt. "My Lord and Leige, this very afternoon, before the Hestian temple in the town, we found a fellow sulking on the porch in such a way we knew he meant no good."

"Indeed? Are all such matters brought to me?"

"They're not, my Lord, but this was different. When he observed us soldiers watching him, he tried to flee into an alleyway. We then pursued him and ran him down like dogs, but when we grasped him, he began to laugh and called us fools to think we could prevent the deed that he was sent here to perform."

Silently, the King motioned for the officer and the soldiers to enter the chamber.

The officer rose and did so, followed by the other two. Then he continued his account. "'What deed is that?' I asked him. Once again he laughed at me and then he said, 'Just this: the ruination of your dear Princess.'"

Gasps rose from several throats. "Describe this man," Aelia said. "Did he wear long white robes?"

The officer looked at Aelia in surprise. "Indeed he did. He wore such clothing and was very pale. A little thin moustache was all the color on his face.

Palamon, who was still standing beside Berengeria, felt the young woman's body go tense. Her voice was hardly even a whisper as she spoke. "Navron, the henchman of foul Alyubol."

At the mention of those names, the King's face became very grave. He looked at his daughter, then back at the officer. "What action did you take?"

"We cast him down into the donjon of this citadel."

"That's good. I want him under lock and key and watched without a respite. You've done well."

The officer noded, then fumbled at his belt and brought forth a small object, as big around as a large coin and half-cubit in length. "We searched him and discovered this."

"What is it?" The King took the object from the officer's hand and stared at it a moment. Then his face became a mass of lines, half-hidden by his white beard. He dismissed the soldiers with a wave of one hand, waited until the door had closed behind them, then turned toward Queen Goswinth and uttered a strange cry, a sound that was half-bestial. Then he clutched the object to his breast. "The fiends. Those cunning, less-than-human friends. Foul Alyubol has sent this thing to us at this, the moment of our reborn joy, to crush us once again with memories."

"What is it?" Berengeria asked, while her concern seeped out through her features.

The King did not answer with words; he handed the object to the Queen, whose face had already become drawn. As she touched it, a tremor ran through her body, causing her robes to move. For a moment tears flowed onto her cheeks and her shoulders shook with her ill-concealed sobbing. Then she composed herself, quickly wiped her face, and turned to Berengeria. "It is just an old baton, a badge of rank our officers once bore."

As Berengeria stared at her mother questioningly, the King began to speak. "There's not been such an item in this land since Beredoric, our own firstborn son, was stolen from us. He once played with one. You know how young ones are; they cast away some charming toy to play with useless trash. So was it with our Beredoric. His first toy was this baton, just small enough to fit his tiny hand. He clung to it."

He became silent and sat with his lower lip clamped between his teeth. The Queen continued the account he had begun, handing the baton to Berengeria. "When we knew our poor son was gone forever and would not return, your father gave the order for batons like this one in our armies to be brought together in one place and then destroyed, for it brought horrid pain to look on one. Without exception, that act was performed. Foul Alyubol has kept this one baton for eight and thirty years, until this time, in order to distress us once again." She sighed. "Prince Beredoric loved it like a pet. He'd shake it back and forth, then let it drop and laugh when it was given back to him. Almighty gods." Overcome by emotion, the old woman turned away.

"It's broken," Berengeria said, turning it about. "And there's writing on one side. Here's what is printed: 'He who serves his King becomes a noble whate'er be his...'" She stopped, puzzled. "Rank? Position, status? That word's broken off."

Palamon had been casually watching Berengeria read the inscription. Now he stared at her. He looked more closely at the object held by his bride-to-be. "Blood? Is that the word? Do you recall the words inscribed there? 'He who serves his King becomes a noble, whate'er be his blood?'" He took the object as Berengeria handed it to him, but hardly had the strength to hold it.

"Indeed, that's what it said." The King looked up at Palamon with questioning eyes. "How did you know? A flood of years has washed across this land since last I heard that phrase exclaimed aloud. How did you know?"

"That word's the very first I ever learned to read when just a child." Palamon attempted to force a smile onto his features, realizing the resulting expression probably looked ghastly. Sweat was oozing from his forehead, and his knees were practically shaking; the strength had gone from him the way water goes from a shattered urn. More than anything else, he wanted to leave, to run away, to escape the stares of the people within this chamber. But he was not sure he could even walk without his legs failing him.

The pieces of the puzzle were all falling into place. All

through his childhood he had pondered his lone possession, a broken piece of horn as big around as a large coin,
just long enough for the word "blood" to be inscribed
upon it. He had even had it attached to the pommel of
his sword to tie him to an unknown past. He understood
everything now—the inscription, the baton, and Reovalis' veiled references.

Most of all, he understood the misgivings he had always
felt. Fate had tied him to Berengeria indeed, but in a way
he never could have imagined. It was all so clear now.
He had been right and wrong, all at the same time. Fate
had bound them together and a catastrophe had awaited
them. Now that catastrophe had arrived. He understood
all these things, and he was the only one who did.

He walked away from the others. What was he to do?
What could he tell them? How would he deal with their
stares once they knew? He paced the length of the chamber, then turned about, looking back at them. The wounds
inflicted by Ursid had become no more than scratches
compared to this unseen lesion inflicted by his own folly.
He looked at them all, but stared longest at Berengeria.
How could he tell her? What would she say?

At last, he found the strength to speak and addressed
his words to the King. "My Lord, I beg indulgence from
you all. May I speak now with Berengeria?"

"How urgent can it be?" the King said.

"It's very grave."

The King looked down at the floor for an instant. "I
know your meaning, sir. It is your wish to leave the two
of us, my wife and me, alone with all our memories. I
can appreciate a gesture such as that. We two shall now
retire. Do as you wish for what remains of this long evening. In the morning we'll rejoin and then continue with
the wedding's plans." He rose and accepted the Queen's
hand. When they had left the chamber, Aelia also excused
herself, promising to return if summoned.

Now Palamon and Berengeria were alone. She turned
to him, her face full of mixed expressions. "My love, I
relish opportunities like this one, when we two are all
alone. But tell me, why have you become so pale?"

"I didn't know that I'd become all pale," Palamon said, swallowing. "No, that is not the truth. I am awhirl with eddies of emotion brought about by looking at that broken old baton." He gestured with his eyes toward the baton which now lay upon a little brass table at the center of the chamber, as if carelessly discarded. It had not been discarded carelessly, though; Palamon knew that. Even in his agitated state, he had noticed that the Queen had taken it back from Berengeria, had glanced at it, turned her head away, and put it down. Then she had exited the room. She had not been willing to have it thrown out, but neither had she been able to gaze upon it any longer. So many hard emotions, all brought about by a baton made of carved horn.

What was he to tell Berengeria? He did not know; he did not even know how he would begin. At last he was able to find some words, although he doubted that they were the best ones available. "Do you recall the sword I carried when we first escaped the walls of old Buerdaunt?"

"I hardly looked at it, except to note it as a weapon one might see displayed by noble warriors."

"You did not see the pommel, then?"

"I never looked at it."

Palamon sighed, then sat down. His legs would not bear his weight any more. He missed every drop of the blood Ursid had spilled. "The pommel bore naught save a piece of horn that I had kept with me since first I'd come to Pallas' Fastness. Where I came by it I do not know. But when I was a child, it was the lone possession I e'er held. It was a broken bit. 'Twas round and red; the color was near worn away by time and handling. 'Twas a large coin's width across—and on it there was scribed a single word." Palamon's voice died away as he looked at Berengeria. She was eighteen years his junior, yet her face seemed to be aging before his eyes.

"Go on," she said in a strange voice.

"I had it cast into the handle of my sword to tie me to my unknown past. That single word I pondered o'er was..."

"Blood." Berengeria interrupted him, her face sagging, a strange light in her eyes. "And that is how you knew the ending to the motto. You're my brother, Palamon."

Palamon nodded silently, choking on the emotion that was welling up inside him. He closed his eyes; he could no longer look at this woman who, a few moments before, had been his future bride. The sword was gone now—all physical proof was gone. But there were too many other proofs for him to ignore them all.

Berengeria turned away, a half-stunned expression across her features, and began pacing the room. "And all this time our love was just the sin of incest. What I feel for you right now is such a sin men shrink before the name. Men writhe for all eternity within the stinking caves of Tartarus for less."

Palamon rose behind her and tried to place his hands on her shoulders, but she twisted away and he let them fall to his sides. "For all of that," he said, "we did not do the deed."

"I did it in my heart." Berengeria walked to the fireplace and struck the marble mantlepiece with one hand. "I wanted you. I spoke to you before you spoke to me and cast aside my modesty for you, pursued you till I broke all barriers." She turned and looked up at him, tears bursting forth. "I want you even now, in spite of all. I love you in a way no sister should." She buried her face in her hands and sobbed.

He stepped toward her once more and they embraced, though even that embrace filled Palamon with a sense of sinfulness. It was not the embrace of a brother for a sister; it was the throbbing embrace of two lovers united by shame and misery. For a moment, Palamon was lost in that embrace. He had no tears to match Berengeria's tears, he had no sobs, no weeping. His soul was filled with desperation. They would run away together, they would find a place, a tiny village in some unknown land. They would live together in some hut. They would leave Carea and Buerdaunt and Pallas and the Dark Capes all behind. They would live not for eternity but for the here and now and for one another only.

Their arms slipped apart and Berengeria turned away once more, laughing recklessly. "I really should be glad. My parents have another child they thought was lost to them. The eldest heir is back to claim his rights; one more defeat is handed Alyubol." She paused, her lips trembling. "Just think what horror would have taken place if foul Navron had not been apprehended. Had our wedding come to pass, we'd have been lost."

Palamon had no more words. Grief and confusion were eating up all the words he could conceive; he could only stand and watch as Berengeria made her way drunkenly along the oak-paneled wall, weeping and laughing in alternate spasms. At last, her emotions spent, she sank into a chair and sat silently for a long time. Then summoning some unseen strength, she looked about, leaned to one side to remove a silk napkin from a table, and dabbed at her face. "Enough of this. We cannot curse the fates, however their betrayals make us bleed. We must go on; life's duties beckon us."

Palamon looked down at her, his heart breaking. Indeed, this all had been a prank by the Fates. Berengeria's reaction, the manner in which she was summoning up all her resources, was the embodiment of courage. How he loved her for that. But she was his sister and their love could never be anything more than the love of a brother for a sister, even though his heart ached for her and his body sang for her touch. He knelt suddenly before her and placed his head in her lap. He had so many tears for her and for himself but they would not come. He knelt there for a long time, silently resting his head on her knees.

But at last he had to stand once more. They had to come to terms. He raised his head and they looked at one another across the new gulf which had opened up between them. "And we must tell your parents," he said.

"Even so. Our parents, Beredoric."

"What of you? You still have got a suitor in Ursid."

Berengeria began what sounded like a little laugh, then broke it off with a sigh and a shrug of her shoulders. "Ah, yes, I have a suitor in Ursid. Who knows? Perhaps I'll wed him. If I do, it shall be my decision and not his."

She rose, then spoke matter-of-factly. "Now we must go and tell the King and Queen they have another child returned to them."

"I cannot do that yet. Let us stay here."

"It must be done. Imagine how their joy will fill the corridors. They've gained the son, the Beredoric who was lost to them."

"Indeed, there shall be joy. But still, I'd like to wait with you a little while. I've been a son for less time than I need to ready me to cross the unknown bridge. I'll stumble if I move too fast." He paused for a moment. "And once we walk out of this room and spread the news, we then shall just be siblings. Our poor souls may not again allow themselves to join as one in spirit. Then I'll be alone once more."

Berengeria placed a hand upon his shoulder. "No, you'll not be alone. You have a family now, and all our love—our family's love—is armor 'gainst the world."

"Perhaps." But Palamon was not convinced. He already could sense Berengeria moving away from him. "But still I feel I am adrift. Yes, even as we speak, we float apart; that refuge and that haven I have sought goes glimmering and fades beyond the waves." He stood and walked toward the door. "When I return, it shall be soon enough."

He left the chamber. How could he face his parents now, when only moments ago they had been the parents of his bride-to-be? He would grow to love his parents; he knew that. He loved them already. But Berengeria had shared his soul. Indeed, he was alone once more, and so was she.

He strode along the corridor, leaped down the steps which led to the base of the tower, and walked out into the castle's inner bailey, staggering, his body protesting the mistreatment. Almost without realizing it, he was walking toward the stables. He reached the great wooden sheds and made his way to the stall where his own courser was kept, breathing heavily as he pulled the animal into the open and began saddling it. Grooms appeared from all directions to help him. At last he stood back and watched as they unquestioningly prepared his mount.

Then, without putting on a cloak against the chilly night air, he trotted out into the courtyard, through Castle Conforth's gate, and onto the road which led toward Lower Carea.

Into the night he rode, the lights of the castle receding behind him. He looked up at the stars, the heavenly vault held up by the forces which guided the lives of men. How could they have played this prank upon him and upon Berengeria? He turned his voice to the heavens, a voice that was little more than a croak. "Ye mighty gods! In all your endless worlds, is there no scrap of mercy to be found?"

Chapter Twenty-nine:
Sir Palamon

ON THE WESTERN shore of the Thlassa Mey, dark cliffs loomed over the breakers, throwing back the spume as the relentless waves dashed themselves against the hard rocks below. At the point where these cliffs reached their greatest height, a road led along the rim, offering travelers a heart-stopping view. In this place a man could stand upon the cliff's edge and feel as if he were at the end of the world; he could feel the buffeting of the sea winds, listen to the dismal roaring of the elements, and watch the breakers a thousand cubits below as they stretched in endless rows across the sea.

This is the place Palamon had reached by morning. He lingered now upon that road, his gaze sweeping between the olive groves a league off to the northwest, and the surging sea below, highlighted by the rays of the day which had just begun. Behind him, the black cliffs stretched away and away toward the Narrow Strait, dropping off gradually until they plunged into the sea—into the white-capped channel which led to Lower Carea.

To that point Palamon would travel. He had spent the night riding his courser aimlessly; now he would ride down to the ferry which plied the Strait and begin his journey back to the Fastness of Pallas. Against the pleading of any logic, he would do this. He wanted to go back; in the depths of his soul, he knew that the great, gray castle with its high walls and turrets, its streaming banners, and its great, vaulted gates, would lie at the end of any journey.

He was chilled by the morning breeze. At this time, the abbots, clerics, and postulants who resided within the Fastness, along with the Knights who were not riding out upon this day, would be gathering in the high chapel for their early devotions. Palamon had taken part in these same services many times in the distant past. He smiled wanly at the thought. Would that he had never left those high, secure walls.

But here he was. He had paused in his journey to feel the wind tugging at his hair and to listen to the moaning of the elements below. Why had he come to this particular place, and why would he ride on? Surely there was more for him back in Carea. There, he was the heir to the throne. He was Beredoric, the eldest prince. There was honor awaiting him there, with the love of his family.

But pain also waited for him in that place. How could he face Berengeria? What would he say to her? How could he answer for what he had done to her?

On the other hand, what lay ahead of him if he did not go back? He could go to the Fastness of Pallas—for what? To petition for readmittance? He would have gladly done that, but the laws and obligations of the order were rigid. A stone could swim before a degraded Knight could even be allowed across the drawbridge, let alone be restored to his former place of honor. And there was the matter of Arlaine to consider. To claim that he had never broken his vows and compromised that maiden would be to reject the sacrifice he had originally made for her. No, the fact of her father's incest with her could never be made known.

And for that reason, there was no place for Palamon within those distant towers.

Turning in his saddle, he stared again at the waves crashing against the black rocks far below. The answer held by those glistening boulders was, perhaps, the easiest. One leap, a vault from these towering cliffs, and all questions would be answered forever.

Still, that would be a craven act, more dishonorable even than the dishonor of breaking his vows and humiliating his sister. To surrender in the face of life's pummeling—that was the ultimate cowardice. Grimacing, he looked away from the beckoning rocks below.

"Palamon." It was a female voice, one the like of which he had never heard before. It was a crisp, clear voice, a whisper that still floated plainly to his ears. "Palamon."

He looked about. There behind him, standing upon the verge of the cliff, was a maiden of unearthly beauty. Her hair was a light, light blond color where it flowed out from beneath her shawl, the grayest of ash blondes. Her body was enveloped by soft robes, leaving only her hands and face exposed to his eyes. Still, the style was such that her form was accented as well as concealed. Her face was a maiden's face; her manner befitted some world-wise matron. She smiled up at him as he stared back at her. "Come here, brave Palamon."

Amazed, he swung from his saddle and approached her. And then he looked into her eyes, those dark, bottomless, bewitching eyes. They were not human eyes. They were gray, though not the gray of the stones of the Fastness of Pallas nor the gray which graced the banners and tapestries of that structure. Her eyes were the endless gray of the sounding sea, the gray of voids between worlds. He gazed into those eyes and he saw the emptiness of eternity. And he knew who she was. Staggered, he knelt upon the rocks before her, bowing his head. "Oh holy Maiden, tell me what you will."

"The years pass by. You have both risen high and fallen low since first your infant form lay wailing at my door."

"The path is long and difficult to follow as it winds."

"Some men stray off, some who are dear to me. Still,

you have followed well, although the path is often hidden, difficult to trace."

"Indeed," Palamon said. "And there are thorns. They gouge the flesh as men seek out the way. Cannot you gods, as you observe this world, take pity's part, prune back those nettles where they press in close?"

"Do you propose to criticize the gods?"

Palamon was silent. How could he frame a response? He stammered but he could not speak; then words blurted from his mouth, words he could hold back no longer. "Oh Maiden, how the thorns of life gouge deep. Why is it you do not relieve the pain; they penetrate into men's very souls." It was impossible for him to maintain himself as he spoke; he leaned forward and wrapped his arms about Pallas' knees in helpless entreaty. Again the tears rushed to his eyes but he did not allow them to flow. He held them back. He would not shame himself before this divine Maiden. Then, in spite of all he could do, they came.

He felt the palm of the Maiden laid softly upon his hair. Something changed. His grief did not go away but he felt flowing into him the strength to withstand it awhile longer; the pain of the wounds he had sustained subsided. Her voice became tender. "We gods observe the suffering of men. We act in our own ways. Do you know how we act to heal the hurts of mortals?"

Palamon shook his head.

"We cure the world by giving it such men as kneel before me here upon this cliff."

"Can you still say that, after what I did, the grief I brought poor Berengeria?"

"Ah, Berengeria." The voice seemed far away. "She is like you. The house of Berevald is Fortune's toy; you all are playthings of your destinies. Your Berengeria will suffer some, but she shall do great things in her own time. She does not have your soul, my Palamon, but you have not her will to overcome. Her tale will not be finished for some time."

Then Pallas placed her smooth hand beneath his chin and lifted his head until their eyes met. "But now I deal

with you, and not with her. Arise, Sir Palamon, for that's
your name. Yet stay a moment; it is not my wish to send
you off without some small reward. First, noble Palamon
must take a wife. His services to me deserve that much.
This act will not betray his vows to me for my wish now
is that he get a son. My knight he is indeed, though not
in name.

"A wife. Oh, Maiden, there is none for me. My love
for Princess Berengeria was doomed by fate, forestalled
by my own birth."

Pallas laughed. The bell-like peals of her mirth floated
upon the air until the atmosphere seemed filled with
ringing music. "Not Berengeria—another one who suits
you more, although you know it not. She loves you
deeply, though she keeps that hid. Her mind is quick,
her character is strong, she is a match for you in every
way—though you, unworldly man, have marked it not."

Palamon nodded weakly. "Where shall I find this
maid?"

"She shall be found. And you will know her when it
comes to pass. Before I go, accept another gift. Although
you cannot ever in your life take up the colors of my
noble Knights, you still have earned such armor as they
wear. Accept this mail and wear it; shed your guilt."

Then she was gone. Pallas had disappeared; it was as
if she had never stood. Blinking in astonishment, Palamon
observed a hauberk of chain mail neatly folded on the
stone where her feet had rested. It was like the lustrous,
greenish-gold mail worn by the Knights of Pallas, but the
luster was far deeper than the finish of the armor he had
possessed before; it was the glow of a sunset sky over
tossing fields. This chain mail seemed alive, crafted in the
forges of the heavens. A breath escaped his lips as he
touched it. Was this his bribe? Was this to buy back his
faith after the blows fate had dealt him? Then what was
Berengeria's payment?

But those questions were without meaning. He had
spoken with the Maiden. The cares laid upon his shoulders
had become bearable burdens. And if Berengeria's inner

strength was not enough to see her through life's gauntlet, he would help her, too.

Taking the bundle up, Palamon mounted his steed and rode forth. But this time he turned his face back toward Upper Carea and Castle Conforth. It was there he would seek his future, for it was there he had begun his past.

He had gone only a short way when he spied a solitary figure riding up the sloping road toward him. As they approached one another, he was able to make out the features. It was a woman, not a man. The slender form belonged to none other than Aelia, the astute guardian who had watched over Palamon's own Berengeria for so many years. Her duty discharged, she seemed to be seeking him out in this lonely place. Was she the one, then? Was she the bride selected by the Maiden?

He hailed her as they approached one another. "My Lady, what can bring you to these cliffs?"

"My Lord, we could not find you on the road which leads down into Lower Carea. I thought perhaps you might have ridden here to watch the winds arrive from foreign lands."

He looked at her keenly. She was looking back at him, the wind tossing her short, dark hair, twisting it into patterns about her face. What was she thinking? After a pause, she spoke again. "You must go back with me; I know your tale. Your father should be told of your return. Ride with me now; your future's waiting there."

He watched her all the while she was speaking. Was she the one? He had always had high regard for her. Still, it was hard to accustom himself to the notion of her as a mate. Perhaps he had not watched her closely enough in the weeks they had traveled together. "Indeed, the words you speak are true. In fact, this same conclusion is made clear to me. Together, we shall hurry home."

Home. That was a word he had not used for many years. Whether it was by his own will or not, that word now meant rockbound Carea. It would be painful to return; he would have to reach to the bottom of his soul to become a Prince of Carea. But it had to be done. Berengeria could have done it.

Aelia turned her horse and they went together. They rode along the sloping cliffs, then turned and rode away from the sea wind that buffeted the western shore of the Thlassa Mey.

About the Author

DENNIS MCCARTY was born on June 17, 1950, in Grand Junction, a small town in western Colorado. His family traveled a great deal because of his father's work. By the time he had graduated from high school, Dennis had attended eight different public schools, most of them before he was twelve.

He graduated in English from the University of Utah and served four years in the United States Coast Guard. Over the years, his hobbies have included fishing, hunting, photography, and automobile racing.

His greatest love has always been reading and writing fiction, however. He made his first attempt at a novel of science fiction when he was seven. He began writing seriously at the age of twenty, although *Flight to Thlassa Mey* is his first published novel.

Dennis and his wife, Kathy, were married in 1972. They have two daughters and reside in Naples, Utah.

By the year 2000, 2 out of 3 Americans could be illiterate.

It's true.

Today, 75 million adults...about one American in three, can't read adequately. And by the year 2000, U.S. News & World Report envisions an America with a literacy rate of only 30%.

Before that America comes to be, you can stop it...by joining the fight against illiteracy today.

Call the Coalition for Literacy at toll-free **1-800-228-8813** and volunteer.

Volunteer Against Illiteracy. The only degree you need is a degree of caring.

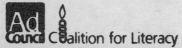

Ad Council · Coalition for Literacy

LV-2